THE SON OF NEPTUNE

Books by Rick Riordan

Percy Jackson and the Olympians, Book One:
The Lightning Thief

Percy Jackson and the Olympians, Book Two:
The Sea of Monsters

Percy Jackson and the Olympians, Book Three:
The Titan's Curse

Percy Jackson and the Olympians, Book Four:
The Battle of the Labyrinth

Percy Jackson and the Olympians, Book Five:
The Last Olympian

The Kane Chronicles, Book One:
The Red Pyramid

The Kane Chronicles, Book Two:
The Throne of Fire

The Kane Chronicles, Book Three:
The Serpent's Shadow

The Heroes of Olympus, Book One:
The Lost Hero

The Heroes of Olympus, Book Two:
The Son of Neptune

The Heroes of Olympus, Book Three:
The Mark of Athena

THE HEROES OF OLYMPUS

THE SON OF NEPTUNE

RICK RIORDAN

DISNEY · HYPERION BOOKS
NEW YORK

Text copyright © 2011 by Rick Riordan

All rights reserved. Published by Disney • Hyperion Books, an imprint
of Disney Book Group. No part of this book may be reproduced or
transmitted in any form or by any means, electronic or mechanical,
including photocopying, recording, or by any information storage and
retrieval system, without written permission from the publisher.
For information address Disney • Hyperion Books,
114 Fifth Avenue, New York, New York 10011-5690.

First Disney • Hyperion US paperback edition, 2013
Printed in the United States of America
10 9 8 7 6 5 4 3 2 1
J689-1817-1-13105
Map illustration art on pp. viii–ix by Kayley Le Faiver

Library of Congress control number for hardcover edition: 2011017658
ISBN 978-1-4231-4199-0

Visit www.disneyhyperionbooks.com

SUSTAINABLE
FORESTRY
INITIATIVE
Certified Chain of Custody
Promoting Sustainable Forestry
www.sfiprogram.org
SFI-01054
The SFI label applies to the text stock

To Becky, who shares my sanctuary in New Rome.
Even Hera could never make me forget you.

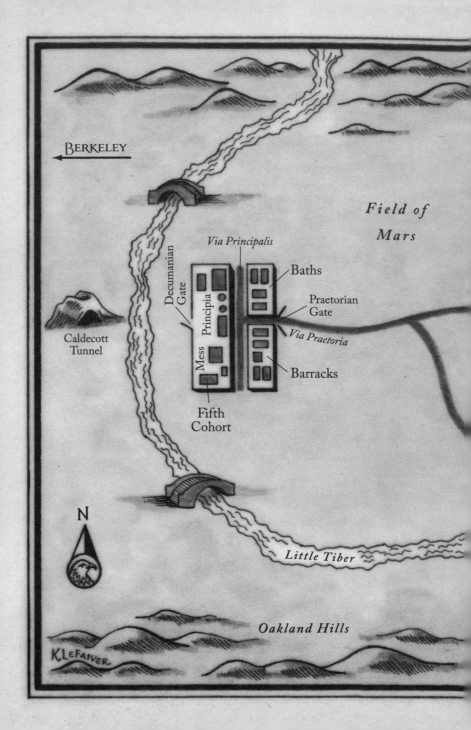

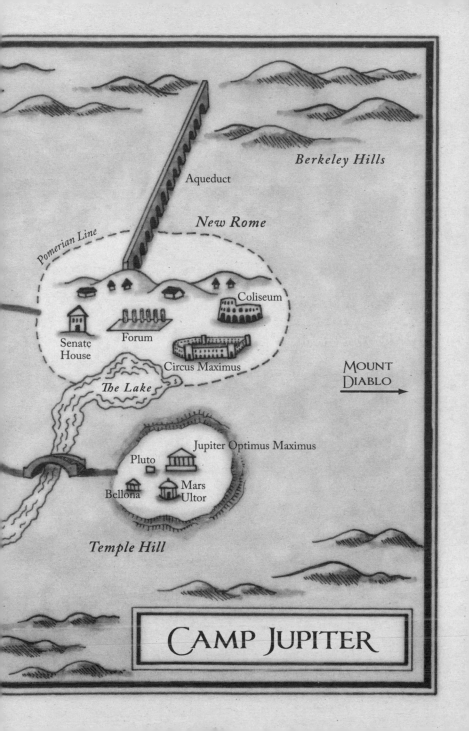

THE SON OF NEPTUNE

I

PERCY

THE SNAKE-HAIRED LADIES WERE starting to annoy Percy.

They should have died three days ago when he dropped a crate of bowling balls on them at the Napa Bargain Mart. They should have died two days ago when he ran over them with a police car in Martinez. They *definitely* should have died this morning when he cut off their heads in Tilden Park.

No matter how many times Percy killed them and watched them crumble to powder, they just kept re-forming like large evil dust bunnies. He couldn't even seem to outrun them.

He reached the top of the hill and caught his breath. How long since he'd last killed them? Maybe two hours. They never seemed to stay dead longer than that.

The past few days, he'd hardly slept. He'd eaten whatever he could scrounge—vending machine gummi bears, stale bagels, even a Jack in the Crack burrito, which was a new personal low. His clothes were torn, burned, and splattered with monster slime.

He'd only survived this long because the two snake-haired ladies—*gorgons*, they called themselves—couldn't seem to kill him either. Their claws didn't cut his skin. Their teeth broke whenever they tried to bite him. But Percy couldn't keep going much longer. Soon he'd collapse from exhaustion, and then —as hard as he was to kill, he was pretty sure the gorgons would find a way.

Where to run?

He scanned his surroundings. Under different circumstances, he might've enjoyed the view. To his left, golden hills rolled inland, dotted with lakes, woods, and a few herds of cows. To his right, the flatlands of Berkeley and Oakland marched west—a vast checkerboard of neighborhoods, with several million people who probably did not want their morning interrupted by two monsters and a filthy demigod.

Farther west, San Francisco Bay glittered under a silvery haze. Past that, a wall of fog had swallowed most of San Francisco, leaving just the tops of skyscrapers and the towers of the Golden Gate Bridge.

A vague sadness weighed on Percy's chest. Something told him he'd been to San Francisco before. The city had some connection to Annabeth—the only person he could remember from his past. His memory of her was frustratingly dim. The wolf had promised he would see her again and regain his memory—*if* he succeeded in his journey.

Should he try to cross the bay?

It was tempting. He could feel the power of the ocean just over the horizon. Water always revived him. Salt water was the best. He'd discovered that two days ago when he had strangled a sea monster in the Carquinez Strait. If he could reach the bay, he might be able to make a last stand. Maybe he could even drown the gorgons. But the shore was at least two miles away. He'd have to cross an entire city.

He hesitated for another reason. The she-wolf Lupa had taught him to sharpen his senses—to trust the instincts that had been guiding him south. His homing radar was tingling like crazy now. The end of his journey was close—almost right under his feet. But how could that be? There was nothing on the hilltop.

The wind changed. Percy caught the sour scent of reptile. A hundred yards down the slope, something rustled through the woods—snapping branches, crunching leaves, hissing.

Gorgons.

For the millionth time, Percy wished their noses weren't so good. They had always said they could *smell* him because he was a demigod—the half-blood son of some old Roman god. Percy had tried rolling in mud, splashing through creeks, even keeping air-freshener sticks in his pockets so he'd have that new car smell; but apparently demigod stink was hard to mask.

He scrambled to the west side of the summit. It was too steep to descend. The slope plummeted eighty feet, straight to the roof of an apartment complex built into the hillside. Fifty feet below that, a highway emerged from the hill's base and wound its way toward Berkeley.

Great. No other way off the hill. He'd managed to get himself cornered.

He stared at the stream of cars flowing west toward San Francisco and wished he were in one of them. Then he realized

the highway must cut through the hill. There must be a tunnel
... right under his feet.

His internal radar went nuts. He *was* in the right place,
just too high up. He had to check out that tunnel. He needed
a way down to the highway—fast.

He slung off his backpack. He'd managed to grab a lot of
supplies at the Napa Bargain Mart: a portable GPS, duct tape,
lighter, superglue, water bottle, camping roll, a Comfy Panda
Pillow Pet (as seen on TV), and a Swiss army knife—pretty
much every tool a modern demigod could want. But he had
nothing that would serve as a parachute or a sled.

That left him two options: jump eighty feet to his death,
or stand and fight. Both options sounded pretty bad.

He cursed and pulled his pen from his pocket.

The pen didn't look like much, just a regular cheap ballpoint, but when Percy uncapped it, it grew into a glowing
bronze sword. The blade balanced perfectly. The leather grip
fit his hand like it had been custom designed for him. Etched
along the guard was an Ancient Greek word Percy somehow
understood: *Anaklusmos*—Riptide.

He'd woken up with this sword his first night at the Wolf
House—two months ago? More? He'd lost track. He'd found
himself in the courtyard of a burned-out mansion in the middle of the woods, wearing shorts, an orange T-shirt, and a
leather necklace with a bunch of strange clay beads. Riptide
had been in his hand, but Percy had had no idea how he'd
gotten there, and only the vaguest idea who he was. He'd
been barefoot, freezing, and confused. And then the wolves
came....

Right next to him, a familiar voice jolted him back to the present: "There you are!"

Percy stumbled away from the gorgon, almost falling off the edge of the hill.

It was the smiley one—Beano.

Okay, her name wasn't really Beano. As near as Percy could figure, he was dyslexic, because words got twisted around when he tried to read. The first time he'd seen the gorgon, posing as a Bargain Mart greeter with a big green button that read: *Welcome! My name is* STHENO, he'd thought it said BEANO.

She was still wearing her green Bargain Mart employee vest over a flower-print dress. If you looked just at her body, you might think she was somebody's dumpy old grandmother —until you looked down and realized she had rooster feet. Or you looked up and saw bronze boar tusks sticking out of the corners of her mouth. Her eyes glowed red, and her hair was a writhing nest of bright green snakes.

The most horrible thing about her? She was still holding her big silver platter of free samples: Crispy Cheese 'n' Wieners. Her platter was dented from all the times Percy had killed her, but those little samples looked perfectly fine. Stheno just kept toting them across California so she could offer Percy a snack before she killed him. Percy didn't know why she kept doing that, but if he ever needed a suit of armor, he was going to make it out of Crispy Cheese 'n' Wieners. They were indestructible.

"Try one?" Stheno offered.

Percy fended her off with his sword. "Where's your sister?"

"Oh, put the sword away," Stheno chided. "You know by now that even Celestial bronze can't kill us for long. Have a Cheese 'n' Wiener! They're on sale this week, and I'd hate to kill you on an empty stomach."

"Stheno!" The second gorgon appeared on Percy's right so fast, he didn't have time to react. Fortunately she was too busy glaring at her sister to pay him much attention. "I told you to sneak up on him and kill him!"

Stheno's smile wavered. "But, Euryale..." She said the name so it rhymed with *Muriel*. "Can't I give him a sample first?"

"No, you imbecile!" Euryale turned toward Percy and bared her fangs.

Except for her hair, which was a nest of coral snakes instead of green vipers, she looked exactly like her sister. Her Bargain Mart vest, her flowery dress, even her tusks were decorated with 50% OFF stickers. Her name badge read: *Hello! My name is DIE, DEMIGOD SCUM!*

"You've led us on quite a chase, Percy Jackson," Euryale said. "But now you're trapped, and we'll have our revenge!"

"The Cheese 'n' Wieners are only $2.99," Stheno added helpfully. "Grocery department, aisle three."

Euryale snarled. "Stheno, the Bargain Mart was a *front*! You're going native! Now, put down that ridiculous tray and help me kill this demigod. Or have you forgotten that he's the one who vaporized Medusa?"

Percy stepped back. Six more inches, and he'd be tumbling through thin air. "Look, ladies, we've been over this. I don't even *remember* killing Medusa. I don't remember anything! Can't we just call a truce and talk about your weekly specials?"

Stheno gave her sister a pouty look, which was hard to do with giant bronze tusks. "Can we?"

"No!" Euryale's red eyes bored into Percy. "I don't care what you remember, son of the sea god. I can smell Medusa's blood on you. It's faint, yes, several years old, but *you* were the last one to defeat her. She *still* has not returned from Tartarus. It's your fault!"

Percy didn't really get that. The whole "dying then returning from Tartarus" concept gave him a headache. Of course, so did the idea that a ballpoint pen could turn into a sword, or that monsters could disguise themselves with something called the Mist, or that Percy was the son of a barnacle-encrusted god from five thousand years ago. But he *did* believe it. Even though his memory was erased, he knew he was a demigod the same way he knew his name was Percy Jackson. From his very first conversation with Lupa the wolf, he'd accepted that this crazy messed-up world of gods and monsters was his reality. Which pretty much sucked.

"How about we call it a draw?" he said. "I can't kill you. You can't kill me. If you're Medusa's sisters—like *the* Medusa who turned people to stone—shouldn't I be petrified by now?"

"Heroes!" Euryale said with disgust. "They always bring that up, just like our mother! 'Why can't you turn people to stone? Your *sister* can turn people to stone.' Well, I'm sorry to disappoint you, boy! That was Medusa's curse alone. *She* was the most hideous one in the family. She got all the luck!"

Stheno looked hurt. "Mother said *I* was the most hideous."

"Quiet!" Euryale snapped. "As for you, Percy Jackson, it's

true you bear the mark of Achilles. That makes you a little tougher to kill. But don't worry. We'll find a way."

"The mark of what?"

"Achilles," Stheno said cheerfully. "Oh, he was *gorgeous*! Dipped in the River Styx as a child, you know, so he was invulnerable except for a tiny spot on his ankle. That's what happened to you, dear. Someone must've dumped you in the Styx and made your skin like iron. But not to worry. Heroes like you always have a weak spot. We just have to find it, and then we can kill you. Won't that be lovely? Have a Cheese 'n' Wiener!"

Percy tried to think. He didn't remember any dip in the Styx. Then again, he didn't remember much of anything. His skin didn't feel like iron, but it would explain how he'd held out so long against the gorgons.

Maybe if he just fell down the mountain...would he survive? He didn't want to risk it—not without something to slow the fall, or a sled, or...

He looked at Stheno's large silver platter of free samples. Hmm...

"Reconsidering?" Stheno asked. "Very wise, dear. I added some gorgon's blood to these, so your death will be quick and painless."

Percy's throat constricted. "You added your blood to the Cheese 'n' Wieners?"

"Just a little." Stheno smiled. "A tiny nick on my arm, but you're sweet to be concerned. Blood from our right side can cure anything, you know, but blood from our left side is deadly—"

"You dimwit!" Euryale screeched. "You're not supposed to tell him that! He won't eat the wieners if you tell him they're poisoned!"

Stheno looked stunned. "He won't? But I said it would be quick and painless."

"Never mind!" Euryale's fingernails grew into claws. "We'll kill him the hard way—just keep slashing until we find the weak spot. Once we defeat Percy Jackson, we'll be more famous than Medusa! Our patron will reward us greatly!"

Percy gripped his sword. He'd have to time his move perfectly—a few seconds of confusion, grab the platter with his left hand . . .

Keep them talking, he thought.

"Before you slash me to bits," he said, "who's this patron you mentioned?"

Euryale sneered. "The goddess Gaea, of course! The one who brought us back from oblivion! You won't live long enough to meet her, but your friends below will soon face her wrath. Even now, her armies are marching south. At the Feast of Fortune, she'll awaken, and the demigods will be cut down like—like—"

"Like our low prices at Bargain Mart!" Stheno suggested.

"Gah!" Euryale stormed toward her sister. Percy took the opening. He grabbed Stheno's platter, scattering poisoned Cheese 'n' Wieners, and slashed Riptide across Euryale's waist, cutting her in half.

He raised the platter, and Stheno found herself facing her own greasy reflection.

"Medusa!" she screamed.

Her sister Euryale had crumbled to dust, but she was already starting to re-form, like a snowman un-melting.

"Stheno, you fool!" she gurgled as her half-made face rose from the mound of dust. "That's just your own reflection! Get him!"

Percy slammed the metal tray on top of Stheno's head, and she passed out cold.

He put the platter behind his butt, said a silent prayer to whatever Roman god oversaw stupid sledding tricks, and jumped off the side of the hill.

PERCY

THE THING ABOUT PLUMMETING DOWNHILL at fifty miles an hour on a snack platter—if you realize it's a bad idea when you're halfway down, it's too late.

Percy narrowly missed a tree, glanced off a boulder, and spun a three-sixty as he shot toward the highway. The stupid snack tray did not have power steering.

He heard the gorgon sisters screaming and caught a glimpse of Euryale's coral-snake hair at the top of the hill, but he didn't have time to worry about it. The roof of the apartment building loomed below him like the prow of a battleship. Head-on collision in ten, nine, eight...

He managed to swivel sideways to avoid breaking his legs on impact. The snack platter skittered across the roof and sailed through the air. The platter went one way. Percy went the other.

As he fell toward the highway, a horrible scenario flashed through his mind: his body smashing against an SUV's windshield, some annoyed commuter trying to push him off with the wipers. *Stupid sixteen-year-old kid falling from the sky! I'm late!*

Miraculously, a gust of wind blew him to one side—just enough to miss the highway and crash into a clump of bushes. It wasn't a soft landing, but it was better than asphalt.

Percy groaned. He wanted to lie there and pass out, but he had to keep moving.

He struggled to his feet. His hands were scratched up, but no bones seemed to be broken. He still had his backpack. Somewhere on the sled ride he'd lost his sword, but Percy knew it would eventually reappear in his pocket in pen form. That was part of its magic.

He glanced up the hill. The gorgons were hard to miss, with their colorful snake hair and their bright green Bargain Mart vests. They were picking their way down the slope, going slower than Percy but with a lot more control. Those chicken feet must've been good for climbing. Percy figured he had maybe five minutes before they reached him.

Next to him, a tall chain-link fence separated the highway from a neighborhood of winding streets, cozy houses, and tall eucalyptus trees. The fence was probably there to keep people from getting onto the highway and doing stupid things—like sledding into the fast lane on snack trays—but the chain-link was full of big holes. Percy could easily slip through into the neighborhood. Maybe he could find a car and drive west to the ocean. He didn't like stealing cars, but over the past few weeks, in life-and-death situations, he'd "borrowed" several, including a police cruiser. He'd meant to return them, but they never seemed to last very long.

He glanced east. Just as he'd figured, a hundred yards uphill the highway cut through the base of the cliff. Two tunnel entrances, one for each direction of traffic, stared down at him like eye sockets of a giant skull. In the middle, where the nose would have been, a cement wall jutted from the hillside, with a metal door like the entrance to a bunker.

It might have been a maintenance tunnel. That's probably what mortals thought, if they noticed the door at all. But they couldn't see through the Mist. Percy knew the door was more than that.

Two kids in armor flanked the entrance. They wore a bizarre mix of plumed Roman helmets, breastplates, scabbards, blue jeans, purple T-shirts, and white athletic shoes. The guard on the right looked like a girl, though it was hard to tell for sure with all the armor. The one on the left was a stocky guy with a bow and quiver on his back. Both kids held long wooden staffs with iron spear tips, like old-fashioned harpoons.

Percy's internal radar was pinging like crazy. After so many horrible days, he'd finally reached his goal. His instincts told him that if he could make it inside that door, he might find safety for the first time since the wolves had sent him south.

So why did he feel such dread?

Farther up the hill, the gorgons were scrambling over the roof of the apartment complex. Three minutes away—maybe less.

Part of him wanted to run to the door in the hill. He'd

have to cross to the median of the highway, but then it would be a short sprint. He could make it before the gorgons reached him.

Part of him wanted to head west to the ocean. That's where he'd be safest. That's where his power would be greatest. Those Roman guards at the door made him uneasy. Something inside him said: *This isn't my territory. This is dangerous.*

"You're right, of course," said a voice next to him.

Percy jumped. At first he thought Beano had managed to sneak up on him again, but the old lady sitting in the bushes was even more repulsive than a gorgon. She looked like a hippie who'd been kicked to the side of the road maybe forty years ago, where she'd been collecting trash and rags ever since. She wore a dress made of tie-dyed cloth, ripped-up quilts, and plastic grocery bags. Her frizzy mop of hair was gray-brown, like root-beer foam, tied back with a peace-sign headband. Warts and moles covered her face. When she smiled, she showed exactly three teeth.

"It isn't a maintenance tunnel," she confided. "It's the entrance to camp."

A jolt went up Percy's spine. *Camp.* Yes, that's where he was from. A camp. Maybe this was his home. Maybe Annabeth was close by.

But something felt wrong.

The gorgons were still on the roof of the apartment building. Then Stheno shrieked in delight and pointed in Percy's direction.

The old hippie lady raised her eyebrows. "Not much time, child. You need to make your choice."

"Who are you?" Percy asked, though he wasn't sure he wanted to know. The last thing he needed was another harmless mortal who turned out to be a monster.

"Oh, you can call me June." The old lady's eyes sparkled as if she'd made an excellent joke. "It *is* June, isn't it? They named the month after me!"

"Okay...Look, I should go. Two gorgons are coming. I don't want them to hurt you."

June clasped her hands over her heart. "How sweet! But that's part of your choice!"

"My choice..." Percy glanced nervously toward the hill. The gorgons had taken off their green vests. Wings sprouted from their backs—small bat wings, which glinted like brass.

Since when did they have *wings*? Maybe they were ornamental. Maybe they were too small to get a gorgon into the air. Then the two sisters leaped off the apartment building and soared toward him.

Great. Just great.

"Yes, a choice," June said, as if she were in no hurry. "You could leave me here at the mercy of the gorgons and go to the ocean. You'd make it there safely, I guarantee. The gorgons will be quite happy to attack me and let you go. In the sea, no monster would bother you. You could begin a new life, live to a ripe old age, and escape a great deal of pain and misery that is in your future."

Percy was pretty sure he wasn't going to like the second option. "Or?"

"Or you could do a good deed for an old lady," she said. "Carry me to the camp with you."

"Carry you?" Percy hoped she was kidding. Then June hiked up her skirts and showed him her swollen purple feet.

"I can't get there by myself," she said. "Carry me to camp —across the highway, through the tunnel, across the river."

Percy didn't know what river she meant, but it didn't sound easy. June looked pretty heavy.

The gorgons were only fifty yards away now—leisurely gliding toward him as if they knew the hunt was almost over.

Percy looked at the old lady. "And I'd carry you to this camp because—?"

"Because it's a kindness!" she said. "And if you don't, the gods will die, the world we know will perish, and everyone from your old life will be destroyed. Of course, you wouldn't remember them, so I suppose it won't matter. You'd be safe at the bottom of the sea...."

Percy swallowed. The gorgons shrieked with laughter as they soared in for the kill.

"If I go to the camp," he said, "will I get my memory back?"

"Eventually," June said. "But be warned, you will sacrifice much! You'll lose the mark of Achilles. You'll feel pain, misery, and loss beyond anything you've ever known. But you might have a chance to save your old friends and family, to reclaim your old life."

The gorgons were circling right overhead. They were probably studying the old woman, trying to figure out who the new player was before they struck.

"What about those guards at the door?" Percy asked.

June smiled. "Oh, they'll let you in, dear. You can trust

those two. So, what do you say? Will you help a defenseless old woman?"

Percy doubted June was defenseless. At worst, this was a trap. At best, it was some kind of test.

Percy hated tests. Since he'd lost his memory, his whole life was one big fill-in-the-blank. He was _____, from _____. He felt like _____, and if the monsters caught him, he'd be _____.

Then he thought about Annabeth, the only part of his old life he was sure about. He *had* to find her.

"I'll carry you." He scooped up the old woman.

She was lighter than he expected. Percy tried to ignore her sour breath and her calloused hands clinging to his neck. He made it across the first lane of traffic. A driver honked. Another yelled something that was lost in the wind. Most just swerved and looked irritated, as if they had to deal with a lot of ratty teenagers carrying old hippie women across the freeway here in Berkeley.

A shadow fell over him. Stheno called down gleefully, "Clever boy! Found a goddess to carry, did you?"

A goddess?

June cackled with delight, muttering, "Whoops!" as a car almost killed them.

Somewhere off to his left, Euryale screamed, "Get them! Two prizes are better than one!"

Percy bolted across the remaining lanes. Somehow he made it to the median alive. He saw the gorgons swooping down, cars swerving as the monsters passed overhead. He wondered what the mortals saw through the Mist—giant pelicans? Off-course hang gliders? The wolf Lupa had told him that mortal minds could believe just about anything—except the truth.

Percy ran for the door in the hillside. June got heavier with every step. Percy's heart pounded. His ribs ached.

One of the guards yelled. The guy with the bow nocked an arrow. Percy shouted, "Wait!"

But the boy wasn't aiming at him. The arrow flew over Percy's head. A gorgon wailed in pain. The second guard readied her spear, gesturing frantically at Percy to hurry.

Fifty feet from the door. Thirty feet.

"Gotcha!" shrieked Euryale. Percy turned as an arrow thudded into her forehead. Euryale tumbled into the fast lane. A truck slammed into her and carried her backward a hundred yards, but she just climbed over the cab, pulled the arrow out of her head, and launched back into the air.

Percy reached the door. "Thanks," he told the guards. "Good shot."

"That should've killed her!" the archer protested.

"Welcome to my world," Percy muttered.

"Frank," the girl said. "Get them inside, quick! Those are gorgons."

"Gorgons?" The archer's voice squeaked. It was hard to tell much about him under the helmet, but he looked stout like a wrestler, maybe fourteen or fifteen. "Will the door hold them?"

In Percy's arms, June cackled. "No, no it won't. Onward, Percy Jackson! Through the tunnel, over the river!"

"Percy Jackson?" The female guard was darker-skinned,

with curly hair sticking out the sides of her helmet. She looked younger than Frank—maybe thirteen. Her sword scabbard came down almost to her ankle. Still, she sounded like she was the one in charge. "Okay, you're obviously a demigod. But who's the—?" She glanced at June. "Never mind. Just get inside. I'll hold them off."

"Hazel," the boy said. "Don't be crazy."

"Go!" she demanded.

Frank cursed in another language—was that Latin?—and opened the door. "Come on!"

Percy followed, staggering under the weight of the old lady, who was *definitely* getting heavier. He didn't know how that girl Hazel would hold off the gorgons by herself, but he was too tired to argue.

The tunnel cut through solid rock, about the width and height of a school hallway. At first, it looked like a typical maintenance tunnel, with electric cables, warning signs, and fuse boxes on the walls, lightbulbs in wire cages along the ceiling. As they ran deeper into the hillside, the cement floor changed to tiled mosaic. The lights changed to reed torches, which burned but didn't smoke. A few hundred yards ahead, Percy saw a square of daylight.

The old lady was heavier now than a pile of sandbags. Percy's arms shook from the strain. June mumbled a song in Latin, like a lullaby, which didn't help Percy concentrate.

Behind them, the gorgons' voices echoed in the tunnel. Hazel shouted. Percy was tempted to dump June and run back to help, but then the entire tunnel shook with the rumble of falling stone. There was a squawking sound, just like the gorgons had made when Percy had dropped a crate of bowling balls on them in Napa. He glanced back. The west end of the tunnel was now filled with dust.

"Shouldn't we check on Hazel?" he asked.

"She'll be okay—I hope," Frank said. "She's good underground. Just keep moving! We're almost there."

"Almost where?"

June chuckled. "All roads lead there, child. You should know that."

"Detention?" Percy asked.

"Rome, child," the old woman said. "Rome."

Percy wasn't sure he'd heard her right. True, his memory was gone. His brain hadn't felt right since he had woken up at the Wolf House. But he was pretty sure Rome wasn't in California.

They kept running. The glow at the end of the tunnel grew brighter, and finally they burst into sunlight.

Percy froze. Spread out at his feet was a bowl-shaped valley several miles wide. The basin floor was rumpled with smaller hills, golden plains, and stretches of forest. A small clear river cut a winding course from a lake in the center and around the perimeter, like a capital G.

The geography could've been anywhere in northern California—live oaks and eucalyptus trees, gold hills and blue skies. That big inland mountain—what was it called, Mount Diablo?—rose in the distance, right where it should be.

But Percy felt like he'd stepped into a secret world. In the center of the valley, nestled by the lake, was a small city of white marble buildings with red-tiled roofs. Some had domes and columned porticoes, like national monuments. Others looked like palaces, with golden doors and large gardens. He could see an open plaza with freestanding columns, fountains, and statues. A five-story-tall Roman coliseum gleamed in the sun, next to a long oval arena like a racetrack.

Across the lake to the south, another hill was dotted with even more impressive buildings—temples, Percy guessed. Several stone bridges crossed the river as it wound through the valley, and in the north, a long line of brickwork arches stretched from the hills into the town. Percy thought it looked like an elevated train track. Then he realized it must be an aqueduct.

The strangest part of the valley was right below him. About two hundred yards away, just across the river, was some sort of military encampment. It was about a quarter mile square, with earthen ramparts on all four sides, the tops lined with sharpened spikes. Outside the walls ran a dry moat, also studded with spikes. Wooden watchtowers rose at each corner, manned by sentries with oversized, mounted crossbows. Purple banners hung from the towers. A wide gateway opened on the far side of camp, leading toward the city. A narrower gate stood closed on the riverbank side. Inside, the fortress bustled with activity: dozens of kids going to and from barracks, carrying weapons, polishing armor. Percy heard the clank of hammers at a forge and smelled meat cooking over a fire.

Something about this place felt very familiar, yet not quite right.

"Camp Jupiter," Frank said. "We'll be safe once—"

Footsteps echoed in the tunnel behind them. Hazel burst into the light. She was covered with stone dust and breathing hard. She'd lost her helmet, so her curly brown hair fell around her shoulders. Her armor had long slash marks in front from the claws of a gorgon. One of the monsters had tagged her with a 50% OFF sticker.

"I slowed them down," she said. "But they'll be here any second."

Frank cursed. "We have to get across the river."

June squeezed Percy's neck tighter. "Oh, yes, please. I can't get my dress wet."

Percy bit his tongue. If this lady was a goddess, she must've been the goddess of smelly, heavy, useless hippies. But he'd come this far. He'd better keep lugging her along.

It's a kindness, she'd said. *And if you don't, the gods will die, the world we know will perish, and everyone from your old life will be destroyed.*

If this was a test, he couldn't afford to get an F.

He stumbled a few times as they ran for the river. Frank and Hazel kept him on his feet.

They reached the riverbank, and Percy stopped to catch his breath. The current was fast, but the river didn't look deep. Only a stone's throw across stood the gates of the fort.

"Go, Hazel." Frank nocked two arrows at once. "Escort Percy so the sentries don't shoot him. It's my turn to hold off the baddies."

Hazel nodded and waded into the stream.

Percy started to follow, but something made him hesitate. Usually he loved the water, but this river seemed ... powerful, and not necessarily friendly.

"The Little Tiber," said June sympathetically. "It flows with the power of the original Tiber, river of the empire. This is your last chance to back out, child. The mark of Achilles is a Greek blessing. You can't retain it if you cross into Roman territory. The Tiber will wash it away."

Percy was too exhausted to understand all that, but he got the main point. "If I cross, I won't have iron skin anymore?"

June smiled. "So what will it be? Safety, or a future of pain and possibility?"

Behind him, the gorgons screeched as they flew from the tunnel. Frank let his arrows fly.

From the middle of the river, Hazel yelled, "Percy, come on!"

Up on the watchtowers, horns blew. The sentries shouted and swiveled their crossbows toward the gorgons.

Annabeth, Percy thought. He forged into the river. It was icy cold, much swifter than he'd imagined, but that didn't bother him. New strength surged through his limbs. His senses tingled like he'd been injected with caffeine. He reached the other side and put the old woman down as the camp's gates opened. Dozens of kids in armor poured out.

Hazel turned with a relieved smile. Then she looked over Percy's shoulder, and her expression changed to horror. "Frank!"

Frank was halfway across the river when the gorgons

caught him. They swooped out of the sky and grabbed him by either arm. He screamed in pain as their claws dug into his skin.

The sentries yelled, but Percy knew they couldn't get a clear shot. They'd end up killing Frank. The other kids drew swords and got ready to charge into the water, but they'd be too late.

There was only one way.

Percy thrust out his hands. An intense tugging sensation filled his gut, and the Tiber obeyed his will. The river surged. Whirlpools formed on either side of Frank. Giant watery hands erupted from the stream, copying Percy's movements. The giant hands grabbed the gorgons, who dropped Frank in surprise. Then the hands lifted the squawking monsters in a liquid vise grip.

Percy heard the other kids yelping and backing away, but he stayed focused on his task. He made a smashing gesture with his fists, and the giant hands plunged the gorgons into the Tiber. The monsters hit bottom and broke into dust. Glittering clouds of gorgon essence struggled to re-form, but the river pulled them apart like a blender. Soon every trace of the gorgons was swept downstream. The whirlpools vanished, and the current returned to normal.

Percy stood on the riverbank. His clothes and his skin steamed as if the Tiber's waters had given him an acid bath. He felt exposed, raw...vulnerable.

In the middle of the Tiber, Frank stumbled around, looking stunned but perfectly fine. Hazel waded out and helped him ashore. Only then did Percy realize how quiet the other kids had become.

Everyone was staring at him. Only the old lady June looked unfazed.

"Well, that was a lovely trip," she said. "Thank you, Percy Jackson, for bringing me to Camp Jupiter."

One of the girls made a choking sound. "Percy...Jackson?"

She sounded as if she recognized his name. Percy focused on her, hoping to see a familiar face.

She was obviously a leader. She wore a regal purple cloak over her armor. Her chest was decorated with medals. She must have been about Percy's age, with dark, piercing eyes and long black hair. Percy didn't recognize her, but the girl stared at him as if she'd seen him in her nightmares.

June laughed with delight. "Oh, yes. You'll have such fun together!"

Then, just because the day hadn't been weird enough already, the old lady began to glow and change form. She grew until she was a shining, seven-foot-tall goddess in a blue dress, with a cloak that looked like goat's skin over her shoulders. Her face was stern and stately. In her hand was a staff topped with a lotus flower.

If it was possible for the campers to look more stunned, they did. The girl with the purple cloak knelt. The others followed her lead. One kid got down so hastily he almost impaled himself on his sword.

Hazel was the first to speak. "Juno."

She and Frank also fell to their knees, leaving Percy the

only one standing. He knew he should probably kneel too, but after carrying the old lady so far, he didn't feel like showing her that much respect.

"Juno, huh?" he said. "If I passed your test, can I have my memory and my life back?"

The goddess smiled. "In time, Percy Jackson, if you succeed here at camp. You've done well today, which is a good start. Perhaps there's hope for you yet."

She turned to the other kids. "Romans, I present to you the son of Neptune. For months he has been slumbering, but now he is awake. His fate is in your hands. The Feast of Fortune comes quickly, and Death must be unleashed if you are to stand any hope in the battle. Do not fail me!"

Juno shimmered and disappeared. Percy looked at Hazel and Frank for some kind of explanation, but they seemed just as confused as he was. Frank was holding something Percy hadn't noticed before—two small clay flasks with cork stoppers, like potions, one in each hand. Percy had no idea where they'd come from, but he saw Frank slip them into his pockets. Frank gave him a look like: *We'll talk about it later.*

The girl in the purple cloak stepped forward. She examined Percy warily, and Percy couldn't shake the feeling that she wanted to run him through with her dagger.

"So," she said coldly, "a son of Neptune, who comes to us with the blessing of Juno."

"Look," he said, "my memory's a little fuzzy. Um, it's *gone,* actually. Do I know you?"

The girl hesitated. "I am Reyna, praetor of the Twelfth Legion. And . . . no, I don't know you."

That last part was a lie. Percy could tell from her eyes. But he also understood that if he argued with her about it here, in front of her soldiers, she wouldn't appreciate it.

"Hazel," said Reyna, "bring him inside. I want to question him at the *principia*. Then we'll send him to Octavian. We must consult the auguries before we decide what to do with him."

"What do you mean," Percy asked, "'decide what to do with' me?"

Reyna's hand tightened on her dagger. Obviously she was not used to having her orders questioned. "Before we accept anyone into camp, we must interrogate them and read the auguries. Juno said your fate is in our hands. We have to know whether the goddess has brought us as a new recruit...."

Reyna studied Percy as if she found that doubtful.

"Or," she said more hopefully, "if she's brought us an enemy to kill."

III

PERCY

PERCY WASN'T SCARED OF GHOSTS, which was lucky. Half the people in camp were dead.

Shimmering purple warriors stood outside the armory, polishing ethereal swords. Others hung out in front of the barracks. A ghostly boy chased a ghostly dog down the street. And at the stables, a big glowing red dude with the head of a wolf guarded a herd of... Were those unicorns?

None of the campers paid the ghosts much attention, but as Percy's entourage walked by, with Reyna in the lead and Frank and Hazel on either side, all the spirits stopped what they were doing and stared at Percy. A few looked angry. The little boy ghost shrieked something like "Greggus!" and turned invisible.

Percy wished he could turn invisible too. After weeks on his own, all this attention made him uneasy. He stayed between Hazel and Frank and tried to look inconspicuous.

"Am I seeing things?" he asked. "Or are those—"

"Ghosts?" Hazel turned. She had startling eyes, like fourteen-karat gold. "They're Lares. House gods."

"House gods," Percy said. "Like . . . smaller than real gods, but larger than apartment gods?"

"They're ancestral spirits," Frank explained. He'd removed his helmet, revealing a babyish face that didn't go with his military haircut or his big burly frame. He looked like a toddler who'd taken steroids and joined the Marines.

"The Lares are kind of like mascots," he continued. "Mostly they're harmless, but I've never seen them so agitated."

"They're staring at me," Percy said. "That ghost kid called me Greggus. My name isn't Greg."

"*Graecus,*" Hazel said. "Once you've been here awhile, you'll start understanding Latin. Demigods have a natural sense for it. *Graecus* means Greek."

"Is that bad?" Percy asked.

Frank cleared his throat. "Maybe not. You've got that type of complexion, the dark hair and all. Maybe they think you're actually Greek. Is your family from there?"

"Don't know. Like I said, my memory is gone."

"Or maybe . . ." Frank hesitated.

"What?" Percy asked.

"Probably nothing," Frank said. "Romans and Greeks have an old rivalry. Sometimes Romans use *graecus* as an insult for someone who's an outsider—an enemy. I wouldn't worry about it."

He sounded pretty worried.

They stopped at the center of camp, where two wide stone-paved roads met at a T.

A street sign labeled the road to the main gates as VIA PRAETORIA. The other road, cutting across the middle of camp, was labeled VIA PRINCIPALIS. Under those markers were hand-painted signs like BERKELEY 5 MILES; NEW ROME 1 MILE; OLD ROME 7280 MILES; HADES 2310 MILES (pointing straight down); RENO 208 MILES, and CERTAIN DEATH: YOU ARE HERE!

For certain death, the place looked pretty clean and orderly. The buildings were freshly whitewashed, laid out in neat grids like the camp had been designed by a fussy math teacher. The barracks had shady porches, where campers lounged in hammocks or played cards and drank sodas. Each dorm had a different collection of banners out front displaying Roman numerals and various animals—eagle, bear, wolf, horse, and something that looked like a hamster.

Along the Via Praetoria, rows of shops advertised food, armor, weapons, coffee, gladiator equipment, and toga rentals. A chariot dealership had a big advertisement out front: CAESAR XLS W/ANTILOCK BRAKES, NO DENARII DOWN!

At one corner of the crossroads stood the most impressive building—a two-story wedge of white marble with a columned portico like an old-fashioned bank. Roman guards stood out front. Over the doorway hung a big purple banner with the gold letters SPQR embroidered inside a laurel wreath.

"Your headquarters?" Percy asked.

Reyna faced him, her eyes still cold and hostile. "It's called the *principia*."

She scanned the mob of curious campers who had followed them from the river. "Everyone back to your duties. I'll give you an update at evening muster. Remember, we have war games after dinner."

The thought of dinner made Percy's stomach rumble. The scent of barbecue from the dining hall made his mouth water. The bakery down the street smelled pretty wonderful too, but he doubted Reyna would let him get an order to go.

The crowd dispersed reluctantly. Some muttered comments about Percy's chances.

"He's dead," said one.

"Would be *those* two who found him," said another.

"Yeah," muttered another. "Let him join the Fifth Cohort. Greeks and geeks."

Several kids laughed at that, but Reyna scowled at them, and they cleared off.

"Hazel," Reyna said. "Come with us. I want your report on what happened at the gates."

"Me too?" Frank said. "Percy saved my life. We've got to let him—"

Reyna gave Frank such a harsh look, he stepped back.

"I'd remind you, Frank Zhang," she said, "you are on *probatio* yourself. You've caused enough trouble this week."

Frank's ears turned red. He fiddled with a little tablet on a cord around his neck. Percy hadn't paid much attention to it, but it looked like a name tag made out of lead.

"Go to the armory," Reyna told him. "Check our inventory. I'll call you if I need you."

"But—" Frank caught himself. "Yes, Reyna."

He hurried off.

Reyna waved Hazel and Percy toward the headquarters. "Now, Percy Jackson, let's see if we can improve your memory."

The *principia* was even more impressive inside.

On the ceiling glittered a mosaic of Romulus and Remus under their adopted mama she-wolf (Lupa had told Percy that story a million times). The floor was polished marble. The walls were draped in velvet, so Percy felt like he was inside the world's most expensive camping tent. Along the back wall stood a display of banners and wooden poles studded with bronze medals—military symbols, Percy guessed. In the center was one empty display stand, as if the main banner had been taken down for cleaning or something.

In the back corner, a stairwell led down. It was blocked by a row of iron bars like a prison door. Percy wondered what was down there—monsters? Treasure? Amnesiac demigods who had gotten on Reyna's bad side?

In the center of the room, a long wooden table was cluttered with scrolls, notebooks, tablet computers, daggers, and a large bowl filled with jelly beans, which seemed kind of out of place. Two life-sized statues of greyhounds—one silver, one gold—flanked the table.

Reyna walked behind the table and sat in one of two high-backed chairs. Percy wished he could sit in the other, but Hazel remained standing. Percy got the feeling he was supposed to also.

"So..." he started to say.

The dog statues bared their teeth and growled.

Percy froze. Normally he liked dogs, but these glared at him with ruby eyes. Their fangs looked sharp as razors.

"Easy, guys," Reyna told the greyhounds.

They stopped growling, but kept eyeing Percy as though they were imagining him in a doggie bag.

"They won't attack," Reyna said, "unless you try to steal something, or unless I tell them to. That's Argentum and Aurum."

"Silver and Gold," Percy said. The Latin meanings popped into his head like Hazel had said they would. He almost asked which dog was which. Then he realized that that was a stupid question.

Reyna set her dagger on the table. Percy had the vague feeling he'd seen her before. Her hair was black and glossy as volcanic rock, woven in a single braid down her back. She had the poise of a sword fighter—relaxed yet vigilant, as if ready to spring into action at any moment. The worry lines around her eyes made her look older than she probably was.

"We *have* met," he decided. "I don't remember when. Please, if you can tell me anything—"

"First things first," Reyna said. "I want to hear your story. What *do* you remember? How did you get here? And don't lie. My dogs don't like liars."

Argentum and Aurum snarled to emphasize the point.

Percy told his story—how he'd woken up at the ruined mansion in the woods of Sonoma. He described his time with Lupa and her pack, learning their language of gestures and expressions, learning to survive and fight.

Lupa had taught him about demigods, monsters, and gods. She'd explained that she was one of the guardian spirits of Ancient Rome. Demigods like Percy were still responsible for carrying on Roman traditions in modern times—fighting monsters, serving the gods, protecting mortals, and upholding the memory of the empire. She'd spent weeks training him, until he was as strong and tough and vicious as a wolf. When she was satisfied with his skills, she'd sent him south, telling him that if he survived the journey, he might find a new home and regain his memory.

None of it seemed to surprise Reyna. In fact, she seemed to find it pretty ordinary—except for one thing.

"No memory at all?" she asked. "You *still* remember nothing?"

"Fuzzy bits and pieces." Percy glanced at the greyhounds. He didn't want to mention Annabeth. It seemed too private, and he was still confused about where to find her. He was sure they'd met at a camp—but this one didn't feel like the right place.

Also, he was reluctant to share his one clear memory: Annabeth's face, her blond hair and gray eyes, the way she laughed, threw her arms around him, and gave him a kiss whenever he did something stupid.

She must have kissed me a lot, Percy thought.

He feared that if he spoke about that memory to anyone, it would evaporate like a dream. He couldn't risk that.

Reyna spun her dagger. "Most of what you're describing is normal for demigods. At a certain age, one way or another, we find our way to the Wolf House. We're tested and trained.

If Lupa thinks we're worthy, she sends us south to join the legion. But I've never heard of someone losing his memory. How did you find Camp Jupiter?"

Percy told her about the last three days—the gorgons who wouldn't die, the old lady who turned out to be a goddess, and finally meeting Hazel and Frank at the tunnel in the hill.

Hazel took the story from there. She described Percy as brave and heroic, which made him uncomfortable. All he'd done was carry a hippie bag lady.

Reyna studied him. "You're old for a recruit. You're what, sixteen?"

"I think so," Percy said.

"If you spent that many years on your own, without training or help, you should be dead. A son of Neptune? You'd have a powerful aura that would attract all kinds of monsters."

"Yeah," Percy said. "I've been told that I smell."

Reyna almost cracked a smile, which gave Percy hope. Maybe she was human after all.

"You must've been somewhere before the Wolf House," she said.

Percy shrugged. Juno had said something about him slumbering, and he *did* have a vague feeling that he'd been asleep—maybe for a long time. But that didn't make sense.

Reyna sighed. "Well, the dogs haven't eaten you, so I suppose you're telling the truth."

"Great," Percy said. "Next time, can I take a polygraph?"

Reyna stood. She paced in front of the banners. Her metal dogs watched her go back and forth.

"Even if I accept that you're not an enemy," she said, "you're not a typical recruit. The Queen of Olympus simply doesn't appear at camp, announcing a new demigod. The last time a major god visited us in person like that..." She shook her head. "I've only heard legends about such things. And a son of Neptune...that's not a good omen. Especially now."

"What's wrong with Neptune?" Percy asked. "And what do you mean, 'especially now'?"

Hazel shot him a warning look.

Reyna kept pacing. "You've fought Medusa's sisters, who haven't been seen in thousands of years. You've agitated our Lares, who are calling you a *graecus*. And you wear strange symbols—that shirt, the beads on your necklace. What do they mean?"

Percy looked down at his tattered orange T-shirt. It might have had words on it at one point, but they were too faded to read. He should have thrown the shirt away weeks ago. It was worn to shreds, but he couldn't bear to get rid of it. He just kept washing it in streams and water fountains as best he could and putting it back on.

As for the necklace, the four clay beads were each decorated with a different symbol. One showed a trident. Another displayed a miniature Golden Fleece. The third was etched with the design of a maze, and the last had an image of a building —maybe the Empire State Building?—with names Percy didn't recognize engraved around it. The beads felt important, like pictures from a family album, but he couldn't remember what they meant.

"I don't know," he said.

"And your sword?" Reyna asked.

Percy checked his pocket. The pen had reappeared as it always did. He pulled it out, but then realized he'd never shown Reyna the sword. Hazel and Frank hadn't seen it either. How had Reyna known about it?

Too late to pretend it didn't exist.... He uncapped the pen. Riptide sprang to full form. Hazel gasped. The greyhounds barked apprehensively.

"What is that?" Hazel asked. "I've never seen a sword like that."

"I have," Reyna said darkly. "It's very old—a Greek design. We used to have a few in the armory before..." She stopped herself. "The metal is called Celestial bronze. It's deadly to monsters, like Imperial gold, but even rarer."

"Imperial gold?" Percy asked.

Reyna unsheathed her dagger. Sure enough, the blade was gold. "The metal was consecrated in ancient times, at the Pantheon in Rome. Its existence was a closely guarded secret of the emperors—a way for their champions to slay monsters that threatened the empire. We used to have more weapons like this, but now...well, we scrape by. I use this dagger. Hazel has a *spatha*, a cavalry sword. Most legionnaires use a shorter sword called a *gladius*. But that weapon of yours is not Roman at all. It's another sign you're not a typical demigod. And your arm..."

"What about it?" Percy asked.

Reyna held up her own forearm. Percy hadn't noticed before, but she had a tattoo on the inside: the letters SPQR, a crossed sword and torch, and under that, four parallel lines like score marks.

Percy glanced at Hazel.

"We all have them," she confirmed, holding up her arm. "All full members of the legion do."

Hazel's tattoo also had the letters SPQR, but she only had one score mark, and her emblem was different: a black glyph like a cross with curved arms and a head:

♇

Percy looked at his own arms. A few scrapes, some mud, and a fleck of Crispy Cheese 'n' Wiener, but no tattoos.

"So you've never been a member of the legion," Reyna said. "These marks can't be removed. I thought perhaps..." She shook her head, as if dismissing an idea.

Hazel leaned forward. "If he's survived as a loner all this time, maybe he's seen Jason." She turned to Percy. "Have you ever met a demigod like us before? A guy in a purple shirt, with marks on his arm—"

"Hazel." Reyna's voice tightened. "Percy's got enough to worry about."

Percy touched the point of his sword, and Riptide shrank back into a pen. "I haven't seen anyone like you guys before. Who's Jason?"

Reyna gave Hazel an irritated look. "He is...he *was* my colleague." She waved her hand at the second empty chair. "The legion normally has two elected praetors. Jason Grace, son of Jupiter, was our other praetor until he disappeared last October."

Percy tried to calculate. He hadn't paid much attention to the calendar out in the wilderness, but Juno had mentioned that it was now June. "You mean he's been gone eight months, and you haven't replaced him?"

"He might not be dead," Hazel said. "We haven't given up."

Reyna grimaced. Percy got the feeling this guy Jason might've been more to her than just a colleague.

"Elections only happen in two ways," Reyna said. "Either the legion raises someone on a shield after a major success on the battlefield—and we haven't had any major battles—or we hold a ballot on the evening of June 24, at the Feast of Fortuna. That's in five days."

Percy frowned. "You have a feast for *tuna*?"

"*Fortuna*," Hazel corrected. "She's the goddess of luck. Whatever happens on her feast day can affect the entire rest of the year. She can grant the camp good luck... or *really* bad luck."

Reyna and Hazel both glanced at the empty display stand, as if thinking about what was missing.

A chill went down Percy's back. "The Feast of Fortune... The gorgons mentioned that. So did Juno. They said the camp was going to be attacked on that day, something about a big bad goddess named Gaea, and an army, and Death being unleashed. You're telling me that day is this *week*?"

Reyna's fingers tightened around the hilt of her dagger. "You will say nothing about that outside this room," she ordered. "I will not have you spreading more panic in the camp."

"So it's true," Percy said. "Do you know what's going to happen? Can we stop it?"

Percy had just met these people. He wasn't sure he even liked Reyna. But he wanted to help. They were demigods, the same as him. They had the same enemies. Besides, Percy remembered what Juno had told him: it wasn't just this camp at risk. His old life, the gods, and the entire world might be destroyed. Whatever was coming down, it was huge.

"We've talked enough for now," Reyna said. "Hazel, take him to Temple Hill. Find Octavian. On the way you can answer Percy's questions. Tell him about the legion."

"Yes, Reyna."

Percy still had so many questions, his brain felt like it would melt. But Reyna made it clear the audience was over. She sheathed her dagger. The metal dogs stood and growled, inching toward Percy.

"Good luck with the augury, Percy Jackson," she said. "If Octavian lets you live, perhaps we can compare notes . . . about your past."

IV

PERCY

ON THE WAY OUT OF CAMP, Hazel bought him an espresso drink and a cherry muffin from Bombilo the two-headed coffee merchant.

Percy inhaled the muffin. The coffee was great. Now, Percy thought, if he could just get a shower, a change of clothes, and some sleep, he'd be golden. Maybe even Imperial golden.

He watched a bunch of kids in swimsuits and towels head into a building that had steam coming out of a row of chimneys. Laughter and watery sounds echoed from inside, like it was an indoor pool—Percy's kind of place.

"Bath house," Hazel said. "We'll get you in there before dinner, hopefully. You haven't lived until you've had a Roman bath."

Percy sighed with anticipation.

As they approached the front gate, the barracks got bigger and nicer. Even the ghosts looked better—with fancier armor and shinier auras. Percy tried to decipher the banners and symbols hanging in front of the buildings.

"You guys are divided into different cabins?" he asked.

"Sort of." Hazel ducked as a kid riding a giant eagle swooped overhead. "We have five cohorts of about forty kids each. Each cohort is divided into barracks of ten—like roommates, kind of."

Percy had never been great at math, but he tried to multiply. "You're telling me there's two hundred kids at camp?"

"Roughly."

"And *all* of them are children of the gods? The gods have been busy."

Hazel laughed. "Not all of them are children of *major* gods. There are hundreds of minor Roman gods. Plus, a lot of the campers are legacies—second or third generation. Maybe their parents were demigods. Or their grandparents."

Percy blinked. "Children of demigods?"

"Why? Does that surprise you?"

Percy wasn't sure. The last few weeks he'd been so worried about surviving day to day. The idea of living long enough to be an adult and have kids of his own—that seemed like an impossible dream.

"These Legos—"

"Legacies," Hazel corrected.

"They have powers like a demigod?"

"Sometimes. Sometimes not. But they can be trained. All the best Roman generals and emperors—you know, they all claimed to be descended from gods. Most of the time, they were telling the truth. The camp augur we're going to meet,

Octavian, he's a legacy, descendant of Apollo. He's got the gift of prophecy, supposedly."

"Supposedly?"

Hazel made a sour face. "You'll see."

That didn't make Percy feel so great, if this dude Octavian had Percy's fate in his hands.

"So the divisions," he asked, "the cohorts, whatever—you're divided according to who your godly parent is?"

Hazel stared at him. "What a horrible idea! No, the officers decide where to assign recruits. If we were divided according to god, the cohorts would be all uneven. I'd be alone."

Percy felt a twinge of sadness, like he'd been in that situation. "Why? What's your ancestry?"

Before she could answer, someone behind them yelled, "Wait!"

A ghost ran toward them—an old man with a medicine-ball belly and toga so long he kept tripping on it. He caught up to them and gasped for air, his purple aura flickering around him.

"This is him?" the ghost panted. "A new recruit for the Fifth, perhaps?"

"Vitellius," Hazel said, "we're sort of in a hurry."

The ghost scowled at Percy and walked around him, inspecting him like a used car. "I don't know," he grumbled. "We need only the best for the cohort. Does he have all his teeth? Can he fight? Does he clean stables?"

"Yes, yes, and no," Percy said. "Who are you?"

"Percy, this is Vitellius." Hazel's expression said: *Just humor him.* "He's one of our Lares; takes an interest in new recruits."

On a nearby porch, other ghosts snickered as Vitellius paced back and forth, tripping over his toga and hiking up his sword belt.

"Yes," Vitellius said, "back in Caesar's day—that's *Julius* Caesar, mind you—the Fifth Cohort was something! Twelfth Legion Fulminata, pride of Rome! But these days? Disgraceful what we've come to. Look at Hazel here, using a *spatha*. Ridiculous weapon for a Roman legionnaire—that's for cavalry! And you, boy—you smell like a Greek sewer. Haven't you had a bath?"

"I've been a little busy fighting gorgons," Percy said.

"Vitellius," Hazel interrupted, "we've got to get Percy's augury before he can join. Why don't you check on Frank? He's in the armory doing inventory. You *know* how much he values your help."

The ghost's furry purple eyebrows shot up. "Mars Almighty! They let the *probatio* check the armor? We'll be ruined!"

He stumbled off down the street, stopping every few feet to pick up his sword or rearrange his toga.

"O-h-h-kay," Percy said.

"Sorry," Hazel said. "He's eccentric, but he's one of the oldest Lares. Been around since the legion was founded."

"He called the legion . . . *Fulminata?*" Percy said.

"'Armed with Lightning,'" Hazel translated. "That's our motto. The Twelfth Legion was around for the entire Roman Empire. When Rome fell, a lot of legions just disappeared. We went underground, acting on secret orders from Jupiter himself: stay alive, recruit demigods and their children, keep Rome going. We've been doing that ever since, moving around to wherever Roman influence was strongest. The last few centuries, we've been in America."

As bizarre as that sounded, Percy had no trouble believing it. In fact, it sounded familiar, like something he'd always known.

"And you're in the Fifth Cohort," he guessed, "which maybe isn't the most popular?"

Hazel scowled. "Yeah. I joined up last September."

"So . . . just a few weeks before that guy Jason disappeared."

Percy knew he'd hit a sore spot. Hazel looked down. She was silent long enough to count every paving stone.

"Come on," she said at last. "I'll show you my favorite view."

They stopped outside the main gates. The fort was situated on the highest point in the valley, so they could see pretty much everything.

The road led down to the river and divided. One path led south across a bridge, up to the hill with all the temples. The other road led north into the city, a miniature version of Ancient Rome. Unlike the military camp, the city looked chaotic and colorful, with buildings crowded together at haphazard angles. Even from this far away, Percy could see people gathered in the plaza, shoppers milling around an open-air market, parents with kids playing in the parks.

"You've got families here?" he asked.

"In the city, absolutely," Hazel said. "When you're accepted into the legion, you do ten years of service. After that, you can muster out whenever you want. Most demigods go into the mortal world. But for some—well, it's pretty dangerous out there. This valley is a sanctuary. You can go to college in the city, get married, have kids, retire when you get old. It's the only safe place on earth for people like us. So yeah, a lot of veterans make their homes there, under the protection of the legion."

Adult demigods. Demigods who could live without fear, get married, raise a family. Percy couldn't quite wrap his mind around that. It seemed too good to be true. "But if this valley is attacked?"

Hazel pursed her lips. "We have defenses. The borders are magical. But our strength isn't what it used to be. Lately, the monster attacks have been increasing. What you said about the gorgons not dying...we've noticed that too, with other monsters."

"Do you know what's causing it?"

Hazel looked away. Percy could tell that she was holding something back—something she wasn't supposed to say.

"It's—it's complicated," she said. "My brother says Death isn't—"

She was interrupted by an elephant.

Someone behind them shouted, "Make way!"

Hazel dragged Percy out of the road as a demigod rode past on a full-grown pachyderm covered in black Kevlar armor. The word ELEPHANT was printed on the side of his armor, which seemed a little obvious to Percy.

The elephant thundered down the road and turned north, heading toward a big open field where some fortifications were under construction.

Percy spit dust out of his mouth. "What the—?"

"Elephant," Hazel explained.

"Yeah, I read the sign. Why do you have an elephant in a bulletproof vest?"

"War games tonight," Hazel said. "That's Hannibal. If we didn't include him, he'd get upset."

"We can't have that."

Hazel laughed. It was hard to believe she'd looked so moody a moment ago. Percy wondered what she'd been about to say. She had a brother. Yet she had claimed she'd be alone if the camp sorted her by her godly parent.

Percy couldn't figure her out. She seemed nice and easygoing, mature for somebody who couldn't have been more than thirteen. But she also seemed to be hiding a deep sadness, like she felt guilty about something.

Hazel pointed south across the river. Dark clouds were gathering over Temple Hill. Red flashes of lightning washed the monuments in blood-colored light.

"Octavian is busy," Hazel said. "We'd better get over there."

On the way, they passed some goat-legged guys hanging out on the side of the road.

"Hazel!" one of them cried.

He trotted over with a big grin on his face. He wore a faded Hawaiian shirt and nothing for pants except thick brown goat fur. His massive Afro jiggled. His eyes were hidden behind little round rainbow-tinted glasses. He held a cardboard sign that read: WILL WORK SING TALK GO AWAY FOR DENARII.

"Hi, Don," Hazel said. "Sorry, we don't have time—"

"Oh, that's cool! That's cool!" Don trotted along with them. "Hey, this guy's new!" He grinned at Percy. "Do you have three denarii for the bus? Because I left my wallet at home, and I've got to get to work, and—"

"Don," Hazel chided. "Fauns don't have wallets. Or jobs. Or homes. And we don't have buses."

"Right," he said cheerfully, "but do you have denarii?"

"Your name is Don the Faun?" Percy asked.

"Yeah. So?"

"Nothing." Percy tried to keep a straight face. "Why don't fauns have jobs? Shouldn't they work for the camp?"

Don bleated. "Fauns! Work for the camp! Hilarious!"

"Fauns are, um, free spirits," Hazel explained. "They hang out here because, well, it's a safe place to hang out and beg. We tolerate them, but—"

"Oh, Hazel is awesome," Don said. "She's so nice! All the other campers are like, 'Go away, Don.' But she's like, 'Please go away, Don.' I love her!"

The faun seemed harmless, but Percy still found him unsettling. He couldn't shake the feeling that fauns should be more than just homeless guys begging for denarii.

Don looked at the ground in front of them and gasped. "Score!"

He reached for something, but Hazel screamed, "Don, no!"

She pushed him out of the way and snatched up a small shiny object. Percy caught a glimpse of it before Hazel slipped it into her pocket. He could have sworn it was a diamond.

"Come on, Hazel," Don complained. "I could've bought a year's worth of doughnuts with that!"

"Don, please," Hazel said. "Go away."

She sounded shaken, like she'd just saved Don from a charging bulletproof elephant.

The faun sighed. "Aw, I can't stay mad at you. But I swear, it's like you're good luck. Every time you walk by—"

"Good-bye, Don," Hazel said quickly. "Let's go, Percy."

She started jogging. Percy had to sprint to catch up.

"What was that about?" Percy asked. "That diamond in the road—"

"Please," she said. "Don't ask."

They walked in uneasy silence the rest of the way to Temple Hill. A crooked stone path led past a crazy assortment of tiny altars and massive domed vaults. Statues of gods seemed to follow Percy with their eyes.

Hazel pointed out the Temple of Bellona. "Goddess of war," she said. "That's Reyna's mom." Then they passed a massive red crypt decorated with human skulls on iron spikes.

"Please tell me we're not going in there," Percy said.

Hazel shook her head. "That's the Temple of Mars Ultor."

"Mars... Ares, the war god?"

"That's his Greek name," Hazel said. "But, yeah, same guy. Ultor means 'the Avenger.' He's the second-most important god of Rome."

Percy wasn't thrilled to hear that. For some reason, just looking at the ugly red building made him feel angry.

He pointed toward the summit. Clouds swirled over the largest temple, a round pavilion with a ring of white columns supporting a domed roof. "I'm guessing that's Zeus—uh, I mean, Jupiter's? That's where we're heading?"

"Yeah." Hazel sounded edgy. "Octavian reads auguries there—the Temple of Jupiter Optimus Maximus."

Percy had to think about it, but the Latin words clicked into English. "Jupiter . . . the best and the greatest?"

"Right."

"What's Neptune's title?" Percy asked. "The coolest and most awesome?"

"Um, not quite." Hazel gestured to a small blue building the size of a toolshed. A cobweb-covered trident was nailed above the door.

Percy peeked inside. On a small altar sat a bowl with three dried-up, moldy apples.

His heart sank. "Popular place."

"I'm sorry, Percy," Hazel said. "It's just . . . Romans were always scared of the sea. They only used ships if they *had* to. Even in modern times, having a child of Neptune around has always been a bad omen. The last time one joined the legion . . . well, it was 1906, when Camp Jupiter was located across the bay in San Francisco. There was this huge earthquake—"

"You're telling me a child of Neptune caused that?"

"So they say." Hazel looked apologetic. "Anyway . . . Romans fear Neptune, but they don't love him much."

Percy stared at the cobwebs on the trident.

Great, he thought. Even if he joined the camp, he would never be loved. His best hope was to be scary to his new camp mates. Maybe if he did really well, they'd give him some moldy apples.

Still . . . standing at Neptune's altar, he felt something stirring inside him, like waves rippling through his veins.

He reached in his backpack and dug out the last bit of food from his trip—a stale bagel. It wasn't much, but he set it on the altar.

"Hey...uh, Dad." He felt pretty stupid talking to a bowl of fruit. "If you can hear me, help me out, okay? Give me my memory back. Tell me—tell me what to do."

His voice cracked. He hadn't meant to get emotional, but he was exhausted and scared, and he'd been lost for so long, he would've given anything for some guidance. He wanted to know something about his life for sure, without grabbing for missing memories.

Hazel put her hand on his shoulder. "It'll be okay. You're here now. You're one of us."

He felt awkward, depending on an eighth-grade girl he barely knew for comfort, but he was glad she was there.

Above them, thunder rumbled. Red lightning lit up the hill.

"Octavian's almost done," Hazel said. "Let's go."

Compared to Neptune's toolshed, Jupiter's temple was definitely optimus and maximus.

The marble floor was etched with fancy mosaics and Latin inscriptions. Sixty feet above, the domed ceiling sparkled gold. The whole temple was open to the wind.

In the center stood a marble altar, where a kid in a toga was doing some sort of ritual in front of a massive golden statue of the big dude himself: Jupiter the sky god, dressed in a silk XXXL purple toga, holding a lightning bolt.

"It doesn't look like that," Percy muttered.

"What?" Hazel asked.

"The master bolt," Percy said.

"What are you *talking* about?"

"I—" Percy frowned. For a second, he'd thought he remembered something. Now it was gone. "Nothing, I guess."

The kid at the altar raised his hands. More red lightning flashed in the sky, shaking the temple. Then he put his hands down, and the rumbling stopped. The clouds turned from gray to white and broke apart.

A pretty impressive trick, considering the kid didn't look like much. He was tall and skinny, with straw-colored hair, oversized jeans, a baggy T-shirt, and a drooping toga. He looked like a scarecrow wearing a bedsheet.

"What's he doing?" Percy murmured.

The guy in the toga turned. He had a crooked smile and a slightly crazy look in his eyes, like he'd just been playing an intense video game. In one hand he held a knife. In the other hand was something like a dead animal. That didn't make him look any less crazy.

"Percy," Hazel said, "this is Octavian."

"The *graecus*!" Octavian announced. "How interesting."

"Uh, hi," Percy said. "Are you killing small animals?"

Octavian looked at the fuzzy thing in his hand and laughed. "No, no. Once upon a time, yes. We used to read the will of the gods by examining animal guts—chickens, goats, that sort of thing. Nowadays, we use these."

He tossed the fuzzy thing to Percy. It was a disemboweled teddy bear. Then Percy noticed that there was a whole pile of mutilated stuffed animals at the foot of Jupiter's statue.

"Seriously?" Percy asked.

Octavian stepped off the dais. He was probably about eighteen, but so skinny and sickly pale, he could've passed for younger. At first he looked harmless, but as he got closer, Percy wasn't so sure. Octavian's eyes glittered with harsh curiosity, like he might gut Percy just as easily as a teddy bear if he thought he could learn something from it.

Octavian narrowed his eyes. "You seem nervous."

"You remind me of someone," Percy said. "I can't remember who."

"Possibly my namesake, Octavian—Augustus Caesar. Everyone says I bear a remarkable resemblance."

Percy didn't think that was it, but he couldn't pin down the memory. "Why did you call me 'the Greek'?"

"I saw it in the auguries." Octavian waved his knife at the pile of stuffing on the altar. "The message said: *The Greek has arrived.* Or possibly: *The goose has cried.* I'm thinking the first interpretation is correct. You seek to join the legion?"

Hazel spoke for him. She told Octavian everything that had happened since they met at the tunnel—the gorgons, the fight at the river, the appearance of Juno, their conversation with Reyna.

When she mentioned Juno, Octavian looked surprised.

"Juno," he mused. "We call her Juno Moneta. Juno the Warner. She appears in times of crisis, to counsel Rome about great threats."

He glanced at Percy, as if to say: *like mysterious Greeks, for instance.*

"I hear the Feast of Fortuna is this week," Percy said. "The gorgons warned there'd be an invasion on that day. Did you see that in your stuffing?"

"Sadly, no." Octavian sighed. "The will of the gods is hard to discern. And these days, my vision is even darker."

"Don't you have…I don't know," Percy said, "an oracle or something?"

"An oracle!" Octavian smiled. "What a cute idea. No, I'm afraid we're fresh out of oracles. Now, if we'd gone questing for the Sibylline books, like I recommended—"

"The Siba-what?" Percy asked.

"Books of prophecy," Hazel said, "which Octavian is *obsessed* with. Romans used to consult them when disasters happened. Most people believe they burned up when Rome fell."

"*Some* people believe that," Octavian corrected. "Unfortunately our present leadership won't authorize a quest to look for them—"

"Because Reyna isn't stupid," Hazel said.

"—so we have only a few remaining scraps from the books," Octavian continued. "A few mysterious predictions, like these."

He nodded to the inscriptions on the marble floor. Percy stared at the lines of words, not really expecting to understand them. He almost choked.

"That one." He pointed, translating as he read aloud: "*Seven half-bloods shall answer the call. To storm or fire the world must fall—*"

"Yes, yes." Octavian finished it without looking: "*An oath to keep with a final breath, and foes bear arms to the Doors of Death.*"

"I—I know that one." Percy thought thunder was shaking the temple again. Then he realized his whole body was trembling. "That's *important*."

Octavian arched an eyebrow. "Of course it's important. We call it the Prophecy of Seven, but it's several thousand years old. We don't know what it means. Every time someone tries to interpret it . . . Well, Hazel can tell you. Bad things happen."

Hazel glared at him. "Just read the augury for Percy. Can he join the legion or not?"

Percy could almost see Octavian's mind working, calculating whether or not Percy would be useful. He held out his hand for Percy's backpack. "That's a beautiful specimen. May I?"

Percy didn't understand what he meant, but Octavian snatched the Bargain Mart panda pillow that was sticking out of the top of his pack. It was just a silly stuffed toy, but Percy had carried it a long way. He was kind of fond of it. Octavian turned toward the altar and raised his knife.

"Hey!" Percy protested.

Octavian slashed open the panda's belly and poured its stuffing over the altar. He tossed the panda carcass aside, muttered a few words over the fluff, and turned with a big smile on his face.

"Good news!" he said. "Percy may join the legion. We'll assign him a cohort at evening muster. Tell Reyna that I approve."

Hazel's shoulders relaxed. "Uh . . . great. Come on, Percy."

"Oh, and Hazel," Octavian said. "I'm happy to welcome

Percy into the legion. But when the election for praetor comes up, I hope you'll remember—"

"Jason *isn't* dead," Hazel snapped. "You're the augur. You're supposed to be looking for him!"

"Oh, I am!" Octavian pointed at the pile of gutted stuffed animals. "I consult the gods every day! Alas, after eight months, I've found nothing. Of course, I'm still looking. But if Jason doesn't return by the Feast of Fortuna, we must act. We can't have a power vacuum any longer. I hope you'll support me for praetor. It would mean so much to me."

Hazel clenched her fists. "Me. Support. You?"

Octavian took off his toga, setting it and his knife on the altar. Percy noticed seven lines on Octavian's arm—seven years of camp, Percy guessed. Octavian's mark was a harp, the symbol of Apollo.

"After all," Octavian told Hazel, "I might be able to help you. It would be a shame if those awful rumors about you kept circulating . . . or, gods forbid, if they turned out to be true."

Percy slipped his hand into his pocket and grabbed his pen. This guy was blackmailing Hazel. That was obvious. One sign from Hazel, and Percy was ready to bust out Riptide and see how Octavian liked being at the other end of a blade.

Hazel took a deep breath. Her knuckles were white. "I'll think about it."

"Excellent," Octavian said. "By the way, your brother is here."

Hazel stiffened. "My brother? Why?"

Octavian shrugged. "Why does your brother do *anything*? He's waiting for you at your father's shrine. Just . . . ah, don't invite him to stay too long. He has a disturbing effect on the others. Now, if you'll excuse me, I have to keep searching for our poor lost friend, Jason. Nice to meet you, Percy."

Hazel stormed out of the pavilion, and Percy followed. He was sure he'd never been so glad to leave a temple in his life.

As Hazel marched down the hill, she cursed in Latin. Percy didn't understand all of it, but he got *son of a gorgon*, *power-hungry snake*, and a few choice suggestions about where Octavian could stick his knife.

"I *hate* that guy," she muttered in English. "If I had my way—"

"He won't really get elected praetor, will he?" Percy asked.

"I wish I could be certain. Octavian has a lot of friends, most of them *bought*. The rest of the campers are afraid of him."

"Afraid of that skinny little guy?"

"Don't underestimate him. Reyna's not so bad by herself, but if Octavian shares her power . . ." Hazel shuddered. "Let's go see my brother. He'll want to meet you."

Percy didn't argue. He wanted to meet this mysterious brother, maybe learn something about Hazel's background —who her dad was, what secret she was hiding. Percy couldn't believe she'd done anything to be guilty about. She seemed too nice. But Octavian had acted like he had some first-class dirt on her.

Hazel led Percy to a black crypt built into the side of the hill. Standing in front was a teenage boy in black jeans and an aviator jacket.

"Hey," Hazel called. "I've brought a friend."

The boy turned. Percy had another one of those weird flashes: like this was somebody he should know. The kid was almost as pale as Octavian, but with dark eyes and messy black hair. He didn't look anything like Hazel. He wore a silver skull ring, a chain for a belt, and a black T-shirt with skull designs. At his side hung a pure-black sword.

For a microsecond when he saw Percy, the boy seemed shocked—panicked even, like he'd been caught in a searchlight.

"This is Percy Jackson," Hazel said. "He's a good guy. Percy, this is my brother, the son of Pluto."

The boy regained his composure and held out his hand. "Pleased to meet you," he said. "I'm Nico di Angelo."

V

HAZEL

HAZEL FELT LIKE SHE'D JUST INTRODUCED two nuclear bombs. Now she was waiting to see which one exploded first.

Until that morning, her brother Nico had been the most powerful demigod she knew. The others at Camp Jupiter saw him as a traveling oddball, about as harmless as the fauns. Hazel knew better. She hadn't grown up with Nico, hadn't even known him very long. But she knew Nico was more dangerous than Reyna, or Octavian, or maybe even Jason.

Then she'd met Percy.

At first, when she saw him stumbling up the highway with the old lady in his arms, Hazel had thought he might be a god in disguise. Even though he was beat up, dirty, and stooped with exhaustion, he'd had an aura of power. He had the good looks of a Roman god, with sea-green eyes and windblown black hair.

She'd ordered Frank not to fire on him. She thought the gods might be testing them. She'd heard myths like that: a kid with an old lady begs for shelter, and when the rude mortals refuse—*boom*, they get turned into banana slugs.

Then Percy had controlled the river and destroyed the gorgons. He'd turned a pen into a bronze sword. He'd stirred up the whole camp with talk about the *graecus*.

A son of the sea god...

Long ago, Hazel had been told that a descendant of Neptune would save her. But could Percy really take away her curse? It seemed too much to hope for.

Percy and Nico shook hands. They studied each other warily, and Hazel fought the urge to run. If these two busted out the magic swords, things could get ugly.

Nico didn't appear scary. He was skinny and sloppy in his rumpled black clothes. His hair, as always, looked like he'd just rolled out of bed.

Hazel remembered when she'd met him. The first time she'd seen him draw that black sword of his, she'd almost laughed. The way he called it "Stygian iron," all serious-like— he'd looked ridiculous. This scrawny white boy was no fighter. She certainly hadn't believed they were related.

She had changed her mind about that quick enough.

Percy scowled. "I—I know you."

Nico raised his eyebrows. "Do you?" He looked at Hazel for explanation.

Hazel hesitated. Something about her brother's reaction wasn't right. He was trying hard to act casual, but when he had first seen Percy, Hazel had noticed his momentary look of panic. Nico already knew Percy. She was sure of it. Why was he pretending otherwise?

Hazel forced herself to speak. "Um...Percy's lost his memory." She told her brother what had happened since Percy had arrived at the gates.

"So, Nico..." she continued carefully, "I thought...you know, you travel all over. Maybe you've met demigods like Percy before, or..."

Nico's expression turned as dark as Tartarus. Hazel didn't understand why, but she got the message: *Drop it.*

"This story about Gaea's army," Nico said. "You warned Reyna?"

Percy nodded. "Who is Gaea, anyway?"

Hazel's mouth went dry. Just hearing that name...It was all she could do to keep her knees from buckling. She remembered a woman's soft sleepy voice, a glowing cave, and feeling her lungs fill with black oil.

"She's the earth goddess." Nico glanced at the ground as if it might be listening. "The oldest goddess of all. She's in a deep sleep most of the time, but she hates the gods and their children."

"Mother Earth...is evil?" Percy asked.

"Very," Nico said gravely. "She convinced her son, the Titan Kronos—um, I mean, Saturn—to kill his dad, Uranus, and take over the world. The Titans ruled for a long time. Then the Titans' children, the Olympian gods, overthrew them."

"That story seems familiar," Percy sounded surprised, like an old memory had partially surfaced. "But I don't think I ever heard the part about Gaea."

Nico shrugged. "She got mad when the gods took over. She took a new husband—Tartarus, the spirit of the abyss—and gave birth to a race of giants. They tried to destroy Mount Olympus, but the gods finally beat them. At least... the first time."

"The first time?" Percy repeated.

Nico glanced at Hazel. He probably wasn't meaning to make her feel guilty, but she couldn't help it. If Percy knew the truth about her, and the horrible things she'd done...

"Last summer," Nico continued, "Saturn tried to make a comeback. There was a second Titan war. The Romans at Camp Jupiter stormed his headquarters on Mount Othrys, across the bay, and destroyed his throne. Saturn disappeared—" He hesitated, watching Percy's face. Hazel got the feeling her brother was nervous that more of Percy's memory might come back.

"Um, anyway," Nico continued, "Saturn probably faded back to the abyss. We all thought the war was over. Now it looks like the Titans' defeat stirred up Gaea. She's starting to wake. I've heard reports of giants being reborn. If they mean to challenge the gods again, they'll probably start by destroying the demigods...."

"You've told Reyna this?" Percy asked.

"Of course." Nico's jaw tensed. "The Romans don't trust me. That's why I was hoping she'd listen to you. Children of Pluto... well, no offense, but they think we're even worse than children of Neptune. We're bad luck."

"They let Hazel stay here," Percy noted.

"That's different," Nico said.

"Why?"

"Percy," Hazel cut in, "look, the giants aren't the worst problem. Even... even *Gaea* isn't the worst problem. The thing you noticed about the gorgons, how they wouldn't die, *that's* our biggest worry." She looked at Nico. She was getting dangerously close to her own secret now, but for some reason Hazel trusted Percy. Maybe because he was also an outsider, maybe because he'd saved Frank at the river. He deserved to know what they were facing.

"Nico and I," she said carefully, "we think that what's happening is... Death isn't—"

Before she could finish, a shout came from down the hill.

Frank jogged toward them, wearing his jeans, purple camp shirt, and denim jacket. His hands were covered with grease from cleaning weapons.

As it did every time she saw Frank, Hazel's heart performed a little skip-beat tap-dance—which *really* irritated her. Sure, he was a good friend—one of the only people at camp who didn't treat her as if she had a contagious disease. But she didn't like him in *that* way.

He was three years older than she was, and he wasn't exactly Prince Charming, with that strange combination of baby face and bulky wrestler's body. He looked like a cuddly koala bear with muscles. The fact that everyone always tried to pair them up—*the two biggest losers at camp! You guys are perfect for each other*—just made Hazel more determined not to like him.

But her heart wasn't with the program. It went nuts whenever Frank was around. She hadn't felt like that since ... well, since Sammy.

Stop it, she thought. You're here for one reason—and it isn't to get a new boyfriend.

Besides, Frank didn't know her secret. If he knew, he wouldn't be so nice to her.

He reached the shrine. "Hey, Nico..."

"Frank." Nico smiled. He seemed to find Frank amusing, maybe because Frank was the only one at camp who wasn't uneasy around the children of Pluto.

"Reyna sent me to get Percy," Frank said. "Did Octavian accept you?"

"Yeah," Percy said. "He slaughtered my panda."

"He...Oh. The augury? Yeah, teddy bears must have nightmares about that guy. But you're in! We need to get you cleaned up before evening muster."

Hazel realized the sun was getting low over the hills. How had the day gone so fast? "You're right," she said. "We'd better—"

"Frank," Nico interrupted, "why don't you take Percy down? Hazel and I will be along soon."

Uh-oh, Hazel thought. She tried not to look anxious.

"That's—that's a good idea," she managed. "Go ahead, guys. We'll catch up."

Percy looked at Nico one more time, as though he was still trying to place a memory. "I'd like to talk with you some more. I can't shake the feeling—"

"Sure," Nico agreed. "Later. I'll be staying overnight."

"You will?" Hazel blurted. The campers were going to love that—the son of Neptune and the son of Pluto arriving on the same day. Now all they needed was some black cats and broken mirrors.

"Go on, Percy," Nico said. "Settle in." He turned to Hazel,

and she got the sense that the worst part of her day was yet to come. "My sister and I need to talk."

"You know him, don't you," Hazel said.

They sat on the roof of Pluto's shrine, which was covered with bones and diamonds. As far as Hazel knew, the bones had always been there. The diamonds were her fault. If she sat anywhere too long, or just got anxious, they started popping up all around her like mushrooms after a rain. Several million dollars' worth of stones glittered on the roof, but fortunately the other campers wouldn't touch them. They knew better than to steal from temples—especially Pluto's—and the fauns never came up here.

Hazel shuddered, remembering her close call with Don that afternoon. If she hadn't moved quickly and snatched that diamond off the road . . . She didn't want to think about it. She didn't need another death on her conscience.

Nico swung his feet like a little kid. His Stygian iron sword lay by his side, next to Hazel's *spatha*. He gazed across the valley, where construction crews were working in the Field of Mars, building fortifications for tonight's games.

"Percy Jackson." He said the name like an incantation. "Hazel, I have to be careful what I say. Important things are at work here. Some secrets need to stay secret. You of all people—you should understand that."

Hazel's cheeks felt hot. "But he's not like . . . like me?"

"No," Nico said. "I'm sorry I can't tell you more. I can't interfere. Percy has to find his own way at this camp."

"Is he dangerous?" she asked.

Nico managed a dry smile. "Very. To his enemies. But he's not a threat to Camp Jupiter. You can trust him."

"Like I trust you," Hazel said bitterly.

Nico twisted his skull ring. Around him, bones began to quiver as if they were trying to form a new skeleton. Whenever he got moody, Nico had that effect on the dead, kind of like Hazel's curse. Between them, they represented Pluto's two spheres of control: death and riches. Sometimes Hazel thought Nico had gotten the better end of the deal.

"Look, I know this is hard," Nico said. "But you have a second chance. You can make things right."

"Nothing about this is right," Hazel said. "If they find out the truth about me—"

"They won't," Nico promised. "They'll call a quest soon. They have to. You'll make me proud. Trust me, Bi—"

He caught himself, but Hazel knew what he'd almost called her: *Bianca*. Nico's *real* sister—the one he'd grown up with. Nico might care about Hazel, but she'd never be Bianca. Hazel was the simply the next best thing Nico could manage —a consolation prize from the Underworld.

"I'm sorry," he said.

Hazel's mouth tasted like metal, as if gold nuggets were popping up under her tongue. "Then it's true about Death? Is Alcyoneus to blame?"

"I think so," Nico said. "It's getting bad in the Underworld. Dad's going crazy trying to keep things under control. From what Percy said about the gorgons, things are getting worse up here, too. But look, that's why you're here. All that stuff in your past—you can make something *good* come out of it. You belong at Camp Jupiter."

That sounded so ridiculous, Hazel almost laughed. She didn't belong in this place. She didn't even belong in this century.

She should have known better than to focus on the past, but she remembered the day when her old life had been shattered. The blackout hit her so suddenly, she didn't even have time to say, *Uh-oh*. She shifted back in time. Not a dream or a vision. The memory washed over her with such perfect clarity, she felt she was actually there.

Her most recent birthday. She'd just turned thirteen. But not *last* December—December 17, 1941, the last day she had lived in New Orleans.

VI

HAZEL

HAZEL WAS WALKING HOME ALONE from the riding stables. Despite the cold evening, she was buzzing with warmth. Sammy had just kissed her on the cheek.

The day had been full of ups and downs. Kids at school had teased her about her mother, calling her a witch and a lot of other names. That had been going on for a long time, of course, but it was getting worse. Rumors were spreading about Hazel's curse. The school was called St. Agnes Academy for Colored Children and Indians, a name that hadn't changed in a hundred years. Just like its name, the place masked a whole lot of cruelty under a thin veneer of kindness.

Hazel didn't understand how other black kids could be so mean. They should've known better, since they themselves had to put up with name-calling all the time. But they yelled at her and stole her lunch, always asking for those famous jewels: "Where's those cursed diamonds, girl? Gimme some or I'll hurt you!" They pushed her away at the water fountain, and threw rocks at her if she tried to approach them on the playground.

Despite how horrible they were, Hazel never gave them diamonds or gold. She didn't hate anyone *that* much. Besides, she had one friend—Sammy—and that was enough.

Sammy liked to joke that he was the perfect St. Agnes student. He was Mexican American, so he considered himself colored *and* Indian. "They should give me a *double* scholarship," he said.

He wasn't big or strong, but he had a crazy smile and he made Hazel laugh.

That afternoon he'd taken her to the stables where he worked as a groom. It was a "whites only" riding club, of course, but it was closed on weekdays, and with the war on, there was talk that the club might have to shut down completely until the Japanese were whipped and the soldiers came back home. Sammy could usually sneak Hazel in to help take care of the horses. Once in a while they'd go riding.

Hazel loved horses. They seemed to be the only living things that weren't scared of her. People hated her. Cats hissed. Dogs growled. Even the stupid hamster in Miss Finley's classroom squeaked in terror when she gave it a carrot. But horses didn't mind. When she was in the saddle, she could ride so fast that there was no chance of gemstones cropping up in her wake. She almost felt free of her curse.

That afternoon, she'd taken out a tan roan stallion with a gorgeous black mane. She galloped into the fields so swiftly, she left Sammy behind. By the time he caught up, he and his horse were both winded.

"What are you running from?" He laughed. "I'm not *that* ugly, am I?"

It was too cold for a picnic, but they had one anyway, sitting under a magnolia tree with the horses tethered to a split-rail fence. Sammy had brought her a cupcake with a birthday candle, which had gotten smashed on the ride but was still the sweetest thing Hazel had ever seen. They broke it in half and shared it.

Sammy talked about the war. He wished he were old enough to go. He asked Hazel if she would write him letters if he were a soldier going overseas.

"'Course, dummy," she said.

He grinned. Then, as if moved by a sudden impulse, he lurched forward and kissed her on the cheek. "Happy birthday, Hazel."

It wasn't much. Just one kiss, and not even on the lips. But Hazel felt like she was floating. She hardly remembered the ride back to the stables, or telling Sammy good-bye. He said, "See you tomorrow," like he always did. But she would never see him again.

By the time she got back to the French Quarter, it was getting dark. As she approached home, her warm feeling faded, replaced by dread.

Hazel and her mother—Queen Marie, she liked to be called—lived in an old apartment above a jazz club. Despite the beginning of the war, there was a festive mood in the air. New recruits would roam the streets, laughing and talking about fighting the Japanese. They'd get tattoos in the parlors or propose to their sweethearts right on the sidewalk. Some would go upstairs to Hazel's mother to have their fortunes read or to buy charms from Marie Levesque, the famous *gris-gris* queen.

"Did you hear?" one would say. "Two bits for this good-luck charm. I took it to a guy I know, and he says it's a real silver nugget. Worth twenty dollars! That voodoo woman is crazy!"

For a while, that kind of talk brought Queen Marie a lot of business. Hazel's curse had started out slowly. At first it seemed like a blessing. The precious stones and gold only appeared once in a while, never in huge quantities. Queen Marie paid her bills. They ate steak for dinner once a week. Hazel even got a new dress. But then stories started spreading. The locals began to realize how many horrible things happened to people who bought those good-luck charms or got paid with Queen Marie's treasure. Charlie Gasceaux lost his arm in a harvester while wearing a gold bracelet. Mr. Henry at the general store dropped dead from a heart attack after Queen Marie settled her tab with a ruby.

Folks started whispering about Hazel—how she could find cursed jewels just by walking down the street. These days only out-of-towners came to visit her mother, and not so many of them, either. Hazel's mom had become short-tempered. She gave Hazel resentful looks.

Hazel climbed the stairs as quietly as she could, in case her mother had a customer. In the club downstairs, the band was tuning their instruments. The bakery next door had started making beignets for tomorrow morning, filling the stairwell with the smell of melting butter.

When she got to the top, Hazel thought she heard two voices inside the apartment. But when she peeked into the parlor, her mother was sitting alone at the séance table, her eyes closed, as if in a trance.

Hazel had seen her that way many times, pretending to talk to spirits for her clients—but not ever when she was by herself. Queen Marie had always told Hazel her *gris-gris* was "bunk and hokum." She didn't really believe in charms or fortune telling or ghosts. She was just a performer, like a singer or an actress, doing a show for money.

But Hazel knew her mother *did* believe in some magic. Hazel's curse wasn't hokum. Queen Marie just didn't want to think it was her fault—that somehow she had made Hazel the way she was.

"It was your blasted father," Queen Marie would grumble in her darker moods. "Coming here in his fancy silver-and-black suit. The one time I *actually* summon a spirit, and what do I get? Fulfills my wish and ruins my life. I should've been a *real* queen. It's *his* fault you turned out this way."

She would never explain what she meant, and Hazel had learned not to ask about her father. It just made her mother angrier.

As Hazel watched, Queen Marie muttered something to herself. Her face was calm and relaxed. Hazel was struck by how beautiful she looked, without her scowl and the creases in her brow. She had a lush mane of gold-brown hair like Hazel's, and the same dark complexion, brown as a roasted coffee bean. She wasn't wearing the fancy saffron robes or gold bangles she wore to impress clients—just a simple white dress. Still, she had a regal air, sitting straight and dignified in her gilded chair as if she really were a queen.

"You'll be safe there," she murmured. "Far from the gods."

Hazel stifled a scream. The voice coming from her mother's mouth wasn't *hers*. It sounded like an older woman's. The tone was soft and soothing, but also commanding—like a hypnotist giving orders.

Queen Marie tensed. She grimaced in her trance, then spoke in her normal voice: "It's too far. Too cold. Too dangerous. He told me not to."

The other voice responded: "What has he ever done for you? He gave you a poisoned child! But we can use her gift for good. We can strike back at the gods. You will be under my protection in the north, far from the gods' domain. I'll make my son your protector. You'll live like a queen at last."

Queen Marie winced. "But what about Hazel..."

Then her face contorted in a sneer. Both voices spoke in unison, as if they'd found something to agree on: "A poisoned child."

Hazel fled down the stairs, her pulse racing.

At the bottom, she ran into a man in a dark suit. He gripped her shoulders with strong, cold fingers.

"Easy, child," the man said.

Hazel noticed the silver skull ring on his finger, then the strange fabric of his suit. In the shadows, the solid black wool seemed to shift and boil, forming images of faces in agony, as if lost souls were trying to escape from the folds of his clothes.

His tie was black with platinum stripes. His shirt was tombstone gray. His face—Hazel's heart nearly leaped out of her throat. His skin was so white it looked almost blue, like cold milk. He had a flap of greasy black hair. His smile was kind enough, but his eyes were fiery and angry, full of mad power. Hazel had seen that look in the newsreels at the movie theater. This man looked like that awful Adolf Hitler. He had no mustache, but otherwise he could've been Hitler's twin—or his father.

Hazel tried to pull away. Even when the man let go, she couldn't seem to move. His eyes froze her in place.

"Hazel Levesque," he said in a melancholy voice. "You've grown."

Hazel started to tremble. At the base of the stairs, the cement stoop cracked under the man's feet. A glittering stone popped up from the concrete like the earth had spit out a watermelon seed. The man looked at it, unsurprised. He bent down.

"Don't!" Hazel cried. "It's cursed!"

He picked up the stone—a perfectly formed emerald. "Yes, it is. But not to me. So beautiful...worth more than this building, I imagine." He slipped the emerald in his pocket. "I'm sorry for your fate, child. I imagine you hate me."

Hazel didn't understand. The man sounded sad, as if he were personally responsible for her life. Then the truth hit her: a spirit in silver and black, who'd fulfilled her mother's wishes and ruined her life.

Her eyes widened. "You? You're my..."

He cupped his hand under her chin. "I am Pluto. Life is never easy for my children, but you have a special burden. Now that you're thirteen, we must make provisions—"

She pushed his hand away.

"You *did* this to me?" she demanded. "You cursed me and my mother? You left us alone?"

Her eyes stung with tears. This rich white man in a fine suit was her *father*? Now that she was thirteen, he showed up for the first time and said he was sorry?

"You're evil!" she shouted. "You ruined our lives!"

Pluto's eyes narrowed. "What has your mother told you, Hazel? Has she never explained her wish? Or told you why you were born under a curse?"

Hazel was too angry to speak, but Pluto seemed to read the answers in her face.

"No..." He sighed. "I suppose she wouldn't. Much easier to blame me."

"What do you mean?"

Pluto sighed. "Poor child. You were born too soon. I cannot see your future clearly, but someday you will find your place. A descendant of Neptune will wash away your curse and give you peace. I fear, though, that is not for many years...."

Hazel didn't follow any of that. Before she could respond, Pluto held out his hand. A sketchpad and a box of colored pencils appeared in his palm.

"I understand you enjoy art and horseback riding," he said. "These are for your art. As for the horse..." His eyes gleamed. "That, you'll have to manage yourself. Now I must speak with your mother. Happy birthday, Hazel."

He turned and headed up the stairs—just like that, as if he'd checked Hazel off his "to do" list and had already forgotten her. *Happy birthday. Go draw a picture. See you in another thirteen years.*

She was so stunned, so angry, so upside-down confused that she just stood paralyzed at the base of the steps. She wanted to throw down the colored pencils and stomp on them. She wanted to charge after Pluto and kick him. She wanted to run away, find Sammy, steal a horse, leave town and never come back. But she didn't do any of those things.

Above her, the apartment door opened, and Pluto stepped inside.

Hazel was still shivering from his cold touch, but she crept up the stairs to see what he would do. What would he say to Queen Marie? Who would speak back—Hazel's mother, or that awful voice?

When she reached the doorway, Hazel heard arguing. She peeked in. Her mother seemed back to normal—screaming and angry, throwing things around the parlor while Pluto tried to reason with her.

"Marie, it's insanity," he said. "You'll be far beyond my power to protect you."

"Protect me?" Queen Marie yelled. "When have you *ever* protected me?"

Pluto's dark suit shimmered, as if the souls trapped in the fabric were getting agitated.

"You have no idea," he said. "I've kept you alive, you and the child. My enemies are everywhere among gods and men. Now with the war on, it will only get worse. You *must* stay where I can—"

"The police think I'm a murderer!" Queen Marie shouted. "My clients want to hang me as a witch! And Hazel—her curse is getting worse. Your *protection* is killing us."

Pluto spread his hands in a pleading gesture. "Marie, please—"

"No!" Queen Marie turned to the closet, pulled out a leather valise, and threw it on the table. "We're leaving," she announced. "You can keep your protection. We're going north."

"Marie, it's a trap," Pluto warned. "Whoever's whispering in your ear, whoever's turning you against me—"

"*You* turned me against you!" She picked up a porcelain vase and threw it at him. It shattered on the floor, and precious stones spilled everywhere—emeralds, rubies, diamonds. Hazel's entire collection.

"You won't survive," Pluto said. "If you go north, you'll both die. I can foresee that clearly."

"Get out!" she said.

Hazel wished Pluto would stay and argue. Whatever her mother was talking about, Hazel didn't like it. But her father slashed his hand across the air and dissolved into shadows... like he really *was* a spirit.

Queen Marie closed her eyes. She took a deep breath. Hazel was afraid the strange voice might possess her again. But when she spoke, she was her regular self.

"Hazel," she snapped, "come out from behind that door."

Trembling, Hazel obeyed. She clutched the sketchpad and colored pencils to her chest.

Her mother studied her like she was a bitter disappointment. *A poisoned child*, the voices had said.

"Pack a bag," she ordered. "We're moving."

"Wh-where?" Hazel asked.

"Alaska," Queen Marie answered. "You're going to make yourself useful. We're going to start a new life."

The way her mother said that, it sounded as if they were going to create a "new life" for someone else—or some*thing* else.

"What did Pluto mean?" Hazel asked. "Is he really my father? He said you made a wish—"

"Go to your room!" her mother shouted. "Pack!"

Hazel fled, and suddenly she was ripped out of the past.

Nico was shaking her shoulders. "You did it again."

Hazel blinked. They were still sitting on the roof of Pluto's shrine. The sun was lower in the sky. More diamonds had surfaced around her, and her eyes stung from crying.

"S-sorry," she murmured.

"Don't be," Nico said. "Where were you?"

"My mother's apartment. The day we moved."

Nico nodded. He understood her history better than most people could. He was also a kid from the 1940s. He'd been born only a few years after Hazel, and had been locked away in a magic hotel for decades. But Hazel's past was much worse than Nico's. She'd caused so much damage and misery....

"You have to work on controlling those memories," Nico warned. "If a flashback like that happens when you're in combat—"

"I know," she said. "I'm trying."

Nico squeezed her hand. "It's okay. I think it's a side effect from ... you know, your time in the Underworld. Hopefully it'll get easier."

Hazel wasn't so sure. After eight months, the blackouts seemed to be getting worse, as if her soul were attempting to live in two different time periods at once. No one had ever come back from the dead before—at least, not the way *she* had. Nico was trying to reassure her, but neither of them knew what would happen.

"I can't go north again," Hazel said. "Nico, if I have to go back to where it happened—"

"You'll be fine," he promised. "You'll have friends this time. Percy Jackson—he's got a role to play in this. You can sense that, can't you? He's a good person to have at your side."

Hazel remembered what Pluto told her long ago: *A descendant of Neptune will wash away your curse and give you peace.*

Was Percy the one? Maybe, but Hazel sensed it wouldn't be so easy. She wasn't sure even Percy could survive what was waiting in the north.

"Where did he come from?" she asked. "Why do the ghosts call him the Greek?"

Before Nico could respond, horns blew across the river. The legionnaires were gathering for evening muster.

"We'd better get down there," Nico said. "I have a feeling tonight's war games are going to be interesting."

VII

HAZEL

On the way back, Hazel tripped over a gold bar.

She should have known not to run so fast, but she was afraid of being late for muster. The Fifth Cohort had the nicest centurions in camp. Still, even *they* would have to punish her if she was tardy. Roman punishments were harsh: scrubbing the streets with a toothbrush, cleaning the bull pens at the coliseum, getting sewn inside a sack full of angry weasels and dumped into the Little Tiber—the options were not great.

The gold bar popped out of the ground just in time for her foot to hit it. Nico tried to catch her, but she took a spill and scraped her hands.

"You okay?" Nico knelt next to her and reached for the bar of gold.

"Don't!" Hazel warned.

Nico froze. "Right. Sorry. It's just...jeez. That thing is *huge*." He pulled a flask of nectar from his aviator jacket and poured a little on Hazel's hands. Immediately the cuts started to heal. "Can you stand?"

He helped her up. They both stared at the gold. It was the size of a bread loaf, stamped with a serial number and the words U.S. TREASURY.

Nico shook his head. "How in Tartarus—?"

"I don't know," Hazel said miserably. "It could've been buried there by robbers or dropped off a wagon a hundred years ago. Maybe it migrated from the nearest bank vault. Whatever's in the ground, anywhere close to me—it just pops up. And the more valuable it is—"

"The more dangerous it is." Nico frowned. "Should we cover it up? If the fauns find it..."

Hazel imagined a mushroom cloud billowing up from the road, char-broiled fauns tossed in every direction. It was too horrible to consider. "It *should* sink back underground after I leave, eventually, but just to be sure..."

She'd been practicing this trick, but never with something so heavy and dense. She pointed at the gold bar and tried to concentrate.

The gold levitated. She channeled her anger, which wasn't hard—she hated that gold, she hated her curse, she hated thinking about her past and all the ways she'd failed. Her fingers tingled. The gold bar glowed with heat.

Nico gulped. "Um, Hazel, are you sure...?"

She made a fist. The gold bent like putty. Hazel forced it to twist into a giant, lumpy ring. Then she flicked her hand toward the ground. Her million-dollar doughnut slammed into the earth. It sank so deep, nothing was left but a scar of fresh dirt.

Nico's eyes widened. "That was ... terrifying."

Hazel didn't think it was so impressive compared to the powers of a guy who could reanimate skeletons and bring people back from the dead, but it felt good to surprise *him* for a change.

Inside the camp, horns blew again. The cohorts would be starting roll call, and Hazel had no desire to be sewn into a sack of weasels.

"Hurry!" she told Nico, and they ran for the gates.

The first time Hazel had seen the legion assemble, she'd been so intimidated, she'd almost slunk back to the barracks to hide. Even after being at camp for nine months, she still found it an impressive sight.

The first four cohorts, each forty kids strong, stood in rows in front of their barracks on either side of the Via Praetoria. The Fifth Cohort assembled at the very end, in front of the *principia*, since their barracks were tucked in the back corner of camp next to the stables and the latrines. Hazel had to run right down the middle of the legion to reach her place.

The campers were dressed for war. Their polished chain mail and greaves gleamed over purple T-shirts and jeans. Sword-and-skull designs decorated their helmets. Even their leather combat boots looked ferocious with their iron cleats, great for marching through mud or stomping on faces.

In front of the legionnaires, like a line of giant dominoes, stood their red and gold shields, each the size of a refrigerator door. Every legionnaire carried a harpoonlike spear called a *pilum*, a *gladius*, a dagger, and about a hundred pounds of other equipment. If you were out of shape when you came to the legion, you didn't stay that way for long. Just walking around in your armor was a full-body workout.

Hazel and Nico jogged down the street as everyone was coming to attention, so their entrance was *really* obvious. Their footsteps echoed on the stones. Hazel tried to avoid eye contact, but she caught Octavian at the head of the First Cohort smirking at her, looking smug in his plumed centurion's helmet with a dozen medals pinned on his chest.

Hazel was still seething from his blackmail threats earlier. Stupid augur and his gift of prophecy—of all the people at camp to discover her secrets, why did it have to be *him*? She was sure he would have told on her weeks ago, except that he knew her secrets were worth more to him as leverage. She wished she'd kept that bar of gold so she could hit him in the face with it.

She ran past Reyna, who was cantering back and forth on her pegasus Scipio—nicknamed Skippy because he was the color of peanut butter. The metal dogs Aurum and Argentum trotted at her side. Her purple officer's cape billowed behind her.

"Hazel Levesque," she called, "so glad you could join us."

Hazel knew better than to respond. She was missing most of her equipment, but she hurried to her place in line next to Frank and stood at attention. Their lead centurion, a big seventeen-year-old guy named Dakota, was just calling her name—the last one on the roll.

"Present!" she squeaked.

Thank the gods. Technically, she wasn't late.

Nico joined Percy Jackson, who was standing off to one side with a couple of guards. Percy's hair was wet from the baths. He'd put on fresh clothes, but he still looked uncomfortable. Hazel couldn't blame him. He was about to be introduced to two hundred heavily armed kids.

The Lares were the last ones to fall in. Their purple forms flickered as they jockeyed for places. They had an annoying habit of standing halfway inside living people, so that the ranks looked like a blurry photograph, but finally the centurions got them sorted out.

Octavian shouted, "Colors!"

The standard-bearers stepped forward. They wore lion-skin capes and held poles decorated with each cohort's emblems. The last to present his standard was Jacob, the legion's eagle bearer. He held a long pole with absolutely nothing on top. The job was supposed to be a big honor, but Jacob obviously hated it. Even though Reyna insisted on following tradition, every time the eagleless pole was raised, Hazel could feel embarrassment rippling through the legion.

Reyna brought her pegasus to a halt.

"Romans!" she announced. "You've probably heard about the incursion today. Two gorgons were swept into the river by this newcomer, Percy Jackson. Juno herself guided him here, and proclaimed him a son of Neptune."

The kids in the back rows craned their necks to see Percy. He raised his hand and said, "Hi."

"He seeks to join the legion," Reyna continued. "What do the auguries say?"

"I have read the entrails!" Octavian announced, as if he'd killed a lion with his bare hands rather than ripping up a stuffed panda pillow. "The auguries are favorable. He is qualified to serve!"

The campers gave a shout: *"Ave!" Hail!*

Frank was a little late with his *"ave,"* so it came out as a high-pitched echo. The other legionnaires snickered.

Reyna motioned the senior officers forward—one from each cohort. Octavian, as the most senior centurion, turned to Percy.

"Recruit," he asked, "do you have credentials? Letters of reference?"

Hazel remembered this from her own arrival. A lot of kids brought letters from older demigods in the outside world, adults who were veterans of the camp. Some recruits had rich and famous sponsors. Some were third- or fourth-generation campers. A good letter could get you a position in the better cohorts, sometimes even special jobs like legion messenger, which made you exempt from the grunt work like digging ditches or conjugating Latin verbs.

Percy shifted. "Letters? Um, no."

Octavian wrinkled his nose.

Unfair! Hazel wanted to shout. Percy had carried a goddess into camp. What better recommendation could you want?

But Octavian's family had been sending kids to camp for over a century. He loved reminding recruits that they were less important than he was.

"No letters," Octavian said regretfully. "Will any legionnaires stand for him?"

"I will!" Frank stepped forward. "He saved my life!"

Immediately there were shouts of protest from the other cohorts. Reyna raised her hand for quiet and glared at Frank.

"Frank Zhang," she said, "for the second time today, I remind you that you are on *probatio*. Your godly parent has not even claimed you yet. You're not eligible to stand for another camper until you've earned your first stripe."

Frank looked like he might die of embarrassment.

Hazel couldn't leave him hanging. She stepped out of line and said, "What Frank means is that Percy saved *both* our lives. I am a full member of the legion. I will stand for Percy Jackson."

Frank glanced at her gratefully, but the other campers started to mutter. Hazel was barely eligible. She'd only gotten her stripe a few weeks ago, and the "act of valor" that earned it for her had been mostly an accident. Besides, she was a daughter of Pluto, and a member of the disgraced Fifth Cohort. She wasn't doing Percy much of a favor by giving him her support.

Reyna wrinkled her nose, but she turned to Octavian. The augur smiled and shrugged, like the idea amused him.

Why not? Hazel thought. Putting Percy in the Fifth would make him less of a threat, and Octavian liked to keep all his enemies in one place.

"Very well," Reyna announced. "Hazel Levesque, you may stand for the recruit. Does your cohort accept him?"

The other cohorts started coughing, trying not to laugh. Hazel knew what they were thinking: *Another loser for the Fifth.*

Frank pounded his shield against the ground. The other members of the Fifth followed his lead, though they didn't seem very excited. Their centurions, Dakota and Gwen, exchanged pained looks, like: *Here we go again.*

"My cohort has spoken," Dakota said. "We accept the recruit."

Reyna looked at Percy with pity. "Congratulations, Percy Jackson. You stand on *probatio*. You will be given a tablet with your name and cohort. In one year's time, or as soon as you complete an act of valor, you will become a full member of the Twelfth Legion Fulminata. Serve Rome, obey the rules of the legion, and defend the camp with honor. *Senatus Populusque Romanus!*"

The rest of the legion echoed the cheer.

Reyna wheeled her pegasus away from Percy, like she was glad to be done with him. Skippy spread his beautiful wings. Hazel couldn't help feeling a pang of envy. She'd give anything for a horse like that, but it would never happen. Horses were for officers only, or barbarian cavalry, not for Roman legionnaires.

"Centurions," Reyna said, "you and your troops have one hour for dinner. Then we will meet on the Field of Mars. The First and Second Cohorts will defend. The Third, Fourth, and Fifth will attack. Good fortune!"

A bigger cheer went up—for the war games and for dinner. The cohorts broke ranks and ran for the mess hall.

Hazel waved at Percy, who made his way through the crowd with Nico at his side. To Hazel's surprise, Nico was beaming at her.

"Good job, Sis," he said. "That took guts, standing for him."

He had never called her *Sis* before. She wondered if that was what he had called Bianca.

One of the guards had given Percy his *probatio* nameplate. Percy strung it on his leather necklace with the strange beads.

"Thanks, Hazel," he said. "Um, what exactly does it mean —your standing for me?"

"I guarantee your good behavior," Hazel explained. "I teach you the rules, answer your questions, make sure you don't disgrace the legion."

"And . . . if I do something wrong?"

"Then I get killed along with you," Hazel said. "Hungry? Let's eat."

VIII

HAZEL

AT LEAST THE CAMP FOOD WAS GOOD. Invisible wind spirits —*aurae*—waited on the campers and seemed to know exactly what everyone wanted. They blew plates and cups around so quickly, the mess hall looked like a delicious hurricane. If you got up too fast, you were likely to get beaned by beans or potted by a pot roast.

Hazel got shrimp gumbo—her favorite comfort food. It made her think about being a little girl in New Orleans, before her curse set in and her mom got so bitter. Percy got a cheeseburger and a strange-looking soda that was bright blue. Hazel didn't understand that, but Percy tried it and grinned.

"This makes me happy," he said. "I don't know why... but it does."

Just for a moment, one of the *aurae* became visible—an elfin girl in a white silk dress. She giggled as she topped off Percy's glass, then disappeared in a gust.

The mess hall seemed especially noisy tonight. Laughter

echoed off the walls. War banners rustled from cedar ceiling beams as *aurae* blew back and forth, keeping everyone's plates full. The campers dined Roman style, sitting on couches around low tables. Kids were constantly getting up and trading places, spreading rumors about who liked whom and all the other gossip.

As usual, the Fifth Cohort took the place of *least* honor. Their tables were at the back of the dining hall next to the kitchen. Hazel's table was always the least crowded. Tonight it was she and Frank, as usual, with Percy and Nico and their centurion Dakota, who sat there, Hazel figured, because he felt obligated to welcome the new recruit.

Dakota reclined glumly on his couch, mixing sugar into his drink and chugging it. He was a beefy guy with curly black hair and eyes that didn't quite line up straight, so Hazel felt like the world was leaning whenever she looked at him. It wasn't a good sign that he was drinking so much so early in the night.

"So." He burped, waving his goblet. "Welcome to the Percy, party." He frowned. "Party, Percy. Whatever."

"Um, thanks," Percy said, but his attention was focused on Nico. "I was wondering if we could talk, you know...about where I might have seen you before."

"Sure," Nico said a little too quickly. "The thing is, I spend most of my time in the Underworld. So unless I met you there somehow—"

Dakota belched. "Ambassador from Pluto, they call him. Reyna's never sure what to do with this guy when he visits.

You should have seen her face when he showed up with Hazel, asking Reyna to take her in. Um, no offense."

"None taken." Nico seemed relieved to change the topic. "Dakota was really helpful, standing for Hazel."

Dakota blushed. "Yeah, well... She seemed like a good kid. Turned out I was right. Last month, when she saved me from, uh, you know."

"Oh, man!" Frank looked up from his fish and chips. "Percy, you should have seen her! That's how Hazel got her stripe. The unicorns decided to stampede—"

"It was nothing," Hazel said.

"Nothing?" Frank protested. "Dakota would've gotten trampled! You stood right in front of them, shooed them away, saved his hide. I've never seen anything like it."

Hazel bit her lip. She didn't like to talk about it, and she felt uncomfortable, the way Frank made her sound like a hero. In truth, she'd been mostly afraid that the unicorns would hurt themselves in their panic. Their horns were precious metal—silver and gold—so she'd managed to turn them aside simply by concentrating, steering the animals by their horns and guiding them back to the stables. It had gotten her a full place in the legion, but it had also started rumors about her strange powers—rumors that reminded her of the bad old days.

Percy studied her. Those sea green eyes made her unsettled.

"Did you and Nico grow up together?" he asked.

"No," Nico answered for her. "I found out that Hazel was my sister only recently. She's from New Orleans."

That was true, of course, but not the whole truth. Nico let people think he'd stumbled upon her in modern New Orleans and brought her to camp. It was easier than telling the real story.

Hazel had tried to pass herself off as a modern kid. It wasn't easy. Thankfully, demigods didn't use a lot of technology at camp. Their powers tended to make electronic gadgets go haywire. But the first time she went on furlough to Berkeley, she had nearly had a stroke. Televisions, computers, iPods, the Internet...It made her glad to get back to the world of ghosts, unicorns, and gods. That seemed *much* less of a fantasy than the twenty-first century.

Nico was still talking about the children of Pluto. "There aren't many of us," he said, "so we have to stick together. When I found Hazel—"

"You have other sisters?" Percy asked, almost as if he knew the answer. Hazel wondered again when he and Nico had met, and what her brother was hiding.

"One," Nico admitted. "But she died. I saw her spirit a few times in the Underworld, except that the last time I went down there..."

To bring her back, Hazel thought, though Nico didn't say that.

"She was gone." Nico's voice turned hoarse. "She used to be in Elysium—like, the Underworld paradise—but she chose to be reborn into a new life. Now I'll never see her again. I was just lucky to find Hazel...in New Orleans, I mean."

Dakota grunted. "Unless you believe the rumors. Not saying that I do."

"Rumors?" Percy asked.

From across the room, Don the faun yelled, "Hazel!"

Hazel had never been so glad to see the faun. He wasn't allowed in camp, but of course he always managed to get in. He was working his way toward their table, grinning at everybody, sneaking food off plates, and pointing at campers: "Hey! Call me!" A flying pizza smacked him in the head, and he disappeared behind a couch. Then he popped up, still grinning, and made his way over.

"My favorite girl!" He smelled like a wet goat wrapped in old cheese. He leaned over their couches and checked out their food. "Say, new kid, you going to eat that?"

Percy frowned. "Aren't fauns vegetarian?"

"Not the cheeseburger, man! The plate!" He sniffed Percy's hair. "Hey... what's that smell?"

"Don!" Hazel said. "Don't be rude."

"No, man, I just—"

Their house god Vitellius shimmered into existence, standing half embedded in Frank's couch. "Fauns in the dining hall! What are we coming to? Centurion Dakota, do your duty!"

"I am," Dakota grumbled into his goblet. "I'm having dinner!"

Don was still sniffing around Percy. "Man, you've got an empathy link with a faun!"

Percy leaned away from him. "A what?"

"An empathy link! It's real faint, like somebody's suppressed it, but—"

"I know what!" Nico stood suddenly. "Hazel, how about

we give you and Frank time to get Percy oriented? Dakota and I can visit the praetor's table. Don and Vitellius, you come too. We can discuss strategies for the war games."

"Strategies for losing?" Dakota muttered.

"Death Boy is right!" Vitellius said. "This legion fights worse than we did in Judea, and that was the *first* time we lost our eagle. Why, if *I* were in charge—"

"Could I just eat the silverware first?" Don asked.

"Let's go!" Nico stood and grabbed Don and Vitellius by the ears.

Nobody but Nico could actually touch the Lares. Vitellius spluttered with outrage as he was dragged off to the praetor's table.

"Ow!" Don protested. "Man, watch the 'fro!"

"Come on, Dakota!" Nico called over his shoulder.

The centurion got up reluctantly. He wiped his mouth—uselessly, since it was permanently stained red. "Back soon." He shook all over, like a dog trying to get dry. Then he staggered away, his goblet sloshing.

"What was that about?" Percy asked. "And what's wrong with Dakota?"

Frank sighed. "He's okay. He's a son of Bacchus, the wine god. He's got a drinking problem."

Percy's eyes widened. "You let him drink *wine*?"

"Gods, no!" Hazel said. "That would be a disaster. He's addicted to red Kool-Aid. Drinks it with three times the normal sugar, and he's already ADHD—you know, attention deficit/hyperactive. One of these days, his head is going to explode."

Percy looked over at the praetor's table. Most of the senior officers were in deep conversation with Reyna. Nico and his two captives, Don and Vitellius, stood on the periphery. Dakota was running back and forth along a line of stacked shields, banging his goblet on them like they were a xylophone.

"ADHD," Percy said. "You don't say."

Hazel tried not to laugh. "Well... most demigods are. Or dyslexic. Just being a demigod means that our brains are wired differently. Like you—you said you had trouble reading."

"Are you guys that way too?" Percy asked.

"I don't know," Hazel admitted. "Maybe. Back in my day, they just called kids like us 'lazy.'"

Percy frowned. "Back in *your* day?"

Hazel cursed herself.

Luckily for her, Frank spoke up: "I wish I was ADHD or dyslexic. All I got is lactose intolerance."

Percy grinned. "Seriously?"

Frank might've been the silliest demigod ever, but Hazel thought he was cute when he pouted. His shoulders slumped. "And I love ice cream, too...."

Percy laughed. Hazel couldn't help joining in. It was good to sit at dinner and actually feel like she was among friends.

"Okay, so tell me," Percy said, "why is it bad to be in the Fifth Cohort? You guys are great."

The compliment made Hazel's toes tingle. "It's... complicated. Aside from being Pluto's kid, I want to ride horses."

"That's why you use a cavalry sword?"

She nodded. "It's stupid, I guess. Wishful thinking. There's only one pegasus at camp—Reyna's. The unicorns are just kept for medicine, because the shavings off their horns cure poison and stuff. Anyway, Roman fighting is always done on foot. Cavalry...they kind of look down on that. So they look down on me."

"Their loss," Percy said. "What about you, Frank?"

"Archery," he muttered. "They don't like that either, unless you're a child of Apollo. Then you've got an excuse. I hope my dad *is* Apollo, but I don't know. I can't do poetry very well. And I'm not sure I want to be related to Octavian."

"Can't blame you," Percy said. "But you're excellent with the bow—the way you pegged those gorgons? Forget what other people think."

Frank's face turned as red as Dakota's Kool-Aid. "Wish I could. They all think I should be a sword fighter because I'm big and bulky." He looked down at his body, like he couldn't quite believe it was his. "They say I'm too stocky for an archer. Maybe if my dad would ever claim me..."

They ate in silence for a few minutes. A dad who wouldn't claim you...Hazel knew that feeling. She sensed Percy could relate, too.

"You asked about the Fifth," she said at last. "Why it's the worst cohort. That actually started way before us."

She pointed to the back wall, where the legion's standards were on display. "See the empty pole in the middle?"

"The eagle," Percy said.

Hazel was stunned. "How'd you know?"

Percy shrugged. "Vitellius was talking about how the legion lost its eagle a long time ago—the *first* time, he said. He acted like it was a huge disgrace. I'm guessing that's what's missing. And from the way you and Reyna were talking earlier, I'm guessing your eagle got lost a second time, more recently, and it had something to do with the Fifth Cohort."

Hazel made a mental note not to underestimate Percy again. When he'd first arrived, she'd thought he was a little goofy from the questions he'd asked—about the Feast of Tuna and all—but clearly he was smarter than he let on.

"You're right," she said. "That's exactly what happened."

"So what *is* this eagle, anyway? Why is it a big deal?"

Frank looked around to make sure no one was eavesdropping. "It's the symbol of the whole camp—a big eagle made of gold. It's supposed to protect us in battle and make our enemies afraid. Each legion's eagle gave it all sorts of power, and ours came from Jupiter himself. Supposedly Julius Caesar nicknamed our legion 'Fulminata'—armed with lightning —because of what the eagle could do."

"I don't like lightning," Percy said.

"Yeah, well," Hazel said, "it didn't make us invincible. The Twelfth lost its eagle the first time way back in ancient days, during the Jewish Rebellion."

"I think I saw a movie like that," Percy said.

Hazel shrugged. "Could be. There have been lots of books and movies about legions losing their eagles. Unfortunately it happened quite a few times. The eagle was so important... well, archaeologists have *never* recovered a single eagle from ancient Rome. Each legion guarded theirs to the last man, because it was charged with power from the gods. They'd rather hide it or melt it down than surrender it to an enemy.

The Twelfth was lucky the first time. We got our eagle back. But the second time . . ."

"You guys were there?" Percy asked.

They both shook their heads.

"I'm almost as new as you." Frank tapped his *probatio* plate. "Just got here last month. But everyone's heard the story. It's bad luck to even talk about this. There was this huge expedition to Alaska back in the eighties. . . ."

"That prophecy you noticed in the temple," Hazel continued, "the one about the seven demigods and the Doors of Death? Our senior praetor at the time was Michael Varus, from the Fifth Cohort. Back then the Fifth was the best in camp. He thought it would bring glory to the legion if he could figure out the prophecy and make it come true—save the world from storm and fire and all that. He talked to the augur, and the augur said the answer was in Alaska. But he warned Michael it wasn't time yet. The prophecy wasn't for him."

"But he went anyway," Percy guessed. "What happened?"

Frank lowered his voice. "Long, gruesome story. Almost the entire Fifth Cohort was wiped out. Most of legion's Imperial gold weapons were lost, along with the eagle. The survivors went crazy or refused to talk about what had attacked them."

I know, Hazel thought solemnly. But she kept silent.

"Since the eagle was lost," Frank continued, "the camp has been getting weaker. Quests are more dangerous. Monsters attack the borders more often. Morale is lower. The last month or so, things have been getting much worse, much faster."

"And the Fifth Cohort took the blame," Percy guessed. "So now everyone thinks we're cursed."

Hazel realized her gumbo was cold. She sipped a spoonful, but the comfort food didn't taste very comforting. "We've been the outcasts of the legion since . . . well, since the Alaska disaster. Our reputation got better when Jason became praetor—"

"The kid who's missing?" Percy asked.

"Yeah," Frank said. "I never met him. Before my time. But I hear he was a good leader. He practically grew up in the Fifth Cohort. He didn't care what people thought about us. He started to rebuild our reputation. Then he disappeared."

"Which put us back at square one," Hazel said bitterly. "Made us look cursed all over again. I'm sorry, Percy. Now you know what you've gotten yourself into."

Percy sipped his blue soda and gazed thoughtfully across the dining hall. "I don't even know where I come from . . . but I've got a feeling this isn't the first time I've been an underdog." He focused on Hazel and managed a smile. "Besides, joining the legion is better than being chased through the wilderness by monsters. I've got myself some new friends. Maybe together we can turn things around for the Fifth Cohort, huh?"

A horn blew at the end of the hall. The officers at the praetor's table got to their feet—even Dakota, his mouth vampire-red from Kool-Aid.

"The games begin!" Reyna announced. The campers cheered and rushed to collect their equipment from the stacks along the walls.

"So we're the attacking team?" Percy asked over the noise. "Is that good?"

Hazel shrugged. "Good news: we get the elephant. Bad news—"

"Let me guess," said Percy. "The Fifth Cohort always loses."

Frank slapped Percy on the shoulder. "I love this guy. Come on, new friend. Let's go chalk up my thirteenth defeat in a row!"

IX

FRANK

As HE MARCHED TO THE WAR GAMES, Frank replayed the day in his mind. He couldn't believe how close he'd come to death.

That morning on sentry duty, before Percy showed up, Frank had almost told Hazel his secret. The two of them had been standing for hours in the chilly fog, watching the commuter traffic on Highway 24. Hazel had been complaining about the cold.

"I'd give anything to be warm," she said, her teeth chattering. "I wish we had a fire."

Even with her armor on, she looked great. Frank liked the way her cinnamon-toast–colored hair curled around the edges of her helmet, and the way her chin dimpled when she frowned. She was tiny compared to Frank, which made him feel like a big clumsy ox. He wanted to put his arms around her to warm her up, but he'd never do that. She'd probably hit him, and he'd lose the only friend he had at camp.

I could make a really impressive fire, he thought. Of course, it would only burn for a few minutes, and then I'd die. . . .

It was scary that he even considered it. Hazel had that effect on him. Whenever she wanted something, he had the irrational urge to provide it. He wanted to be the old-fashioned knight riding to her rescue, which was stupid, as she was way more capable at *everything* than he was.

He imagined what his grandmother would say: *Frank Zhang riding to the rescue? Ha! He'd fall off his horse and break his neck.*

Hard to believe it had been only six weeks since he'd left his grandmother's house—six weeks since his mom's funeral.

Everything had happened since then: wolves arriving at his grandmother's door, the journey to Camp Jupiter, the weeks he'd spent in the Fifth Cohort trying not to be a complete failure. Through it all, he'd kept the half-burned piece of firewood wrapped in a cloth in his coat pocket.

Keep it close, his grandmother had warned. *As long as it is safe, you are safe.*

The problem was that it burned so easily. He remembered the trip south from Vancouver. When the temperature dropped below freezing near Mount Hood, Frank had brought out the piece of tinder and held it in his hands, imagining how nice it would be to have some fire. Immediately, the charred end blazed with a searing yellow flame. It lit up the night and warmed Frank to the bone, but he could feel his life slipping away, as if *he* were being consumed rather than the wood. He'd thrust the flame into a snowbank. For a horrible moment it kept burning. When it finally went out,

Frank got his panic under control. He wrapped the piece of wood and put it back in his coat pocket, determined not to bring it out again. But he couldn't forget it.

It was as though someone had said, "Whatever you do, don't think about that stick bursting into flame!"

So of course, that's all he thought about.

On sentry duty with Hazel, he would try to take his mind off it. He loved spending time with her. He asked her about growing up in New Orleans, but she got edgy at his questions, so they made small talk instead. Just for fun, they tried to speak French to each other. Hazel had some Creole blood on her mother's side. Frank had taken French in school. Neither of them was very fluent, and Louisiana French was so different from Canadian French it was almost impossible to converse. When Frank asked Hazel how her beef was feeling today, and she replied that his shoe was green, they decided to give up.

Then Percy Jackson had arrived.

Sure, Frank had seen kids fight monsters before. He'd fought plenty of them himself on his journey from Vancouver. But he'd never seen gorgons. He'd never seen a goddess in person. And the way Percy had controlled the Little Tiber —wow. Frank wished he had powers like that.

He could still feel the gorgons' claws pressing into his arms and smell their snaky breath—like dead mice and poison. If not for Percy, those grotesque hags would have carried him away. He'd be a pile of bones in the back of a Bargain Mart by now.

After the incident at the river, Reyna had sent Frank to the armory, which had given him way too much time to think.

While he polished swords, he remembered Juno, warning them to unleash Death.

Unfortunately Frank had a pretty good idea of what the goddess meant. He had tried to hide his shock when Juno had appeared, but she looked exactly like his grandmother had described—right down to the goatskin cape.

She chose your path years ago, Grandmother had told him. *And it will not be easy.*

Frank glanced at his bow in the corner of the armory. He'd feel better if Apollo would claim him as a son. Frank had been *sure* his godly parent would speak up on his sixteenth birthday, which had passed two weeks ago.

Sixteen was an important milestone for Romans. It had been Frank's first birthday at camp. But nothing had happened. Now Frank hoped he would be claimed on the Feast of Fortuna, though from what Juno had said, they'd be in a battle for their lives on that day.

His father *had* to be Apollo. Archery was the only thing Frank was good at. Years ago, his mother had told him that their family name, *Zhang,* meant "master of bows" in Chinese. That must have been a hint about his dad.

Frank put down his polishing rags. He looked at the ceiling. "Please, Apollo, if you're my dad, tell me. I want to be an archer like you."

"No, you don't," a voice grumbled.

Frank jumped out of his seat. Vitellius, the Fifth Cohort's Lar, was shimmering behind him. His full name was Gaius Vitellius Reticulus, but the other cohorts called him Vitellius the Ridiculous.

"Hazel Levesque sent me to check on you," Vitellius said, hiking up his sword belt. "Good thing, too. Look at the state of this armor!"

Vitellius wasn't one to talk. His toga was baggy, his tunic barely fit over his belly, and his scabbard fell off his belt every three seconds, but Frank didn't bother pointing that out.

"As for archers," the ghost said, "they're wimps! Back in my day, archery was a job for barbarians. A good Roman should be in the fray, gutting his enemy with spear and sword like a civilized man! That's how we did it in the Punic Wars. Roman up, boy!"

Frank sighed. "I thought you were in Caesar's army."

"I was!"

"Vitellius, Caesar was hundreds of years after the Punic Wars. You couldn't have been alive that long."

"Questioning my honor?" Vitellius looked so mad, his purple aura glowed. He drew his ghostly *gladius* and yelled, "Take that!"

He ran the sword, which was about as deadly as a laser pointer, through Frank's chest a few times.

"Ouch," Frank said, just to be nice.

Vitellius looked satisfied and put his sword away. "Perhaps you'll think twice about doubting your elders next time! Now . . . it was your sixteenth birthday recently, wasn't it?"

Frank nodded. He wasn't sure how Vitellius knew this, since Frank hadn't told anyone except Hazel, but ghosts had ways of finding out secrets. Eavesdropping while invisible was probably one of them.

"So that's why you're such a grumpy gladiator," the Lar

said. "Understandable. The sixteenth birthday is your day of manhood! Your godly parent should have claimed you, no doubt about it, even if with only a small omen. Perhaps he thought you were younger. You look younger, you know, with that pudgy baby face."

"Thanks for reminding me," Frank muttered.

"Yes, I remember my sixteenth," Vitellius said happily. "Wonderful omen! A chicken in my underpants."

"Excuse me?"

Vitellius puffed up with pride. "That's right! I was at the river changing my clothes for my Liberalia. Rite of passage into manhood, you know. We did things properly back then. I'd taken off my childhood toga and was washing up to don the adult one. Suddenly, a pure-white chicken ran out of nowhere, dove into my loincloth, and ran off with it. I wasn't wearing it at the time."

"That's good," Frank said. "And can I just say: Too much information?"

"Mm." Vitellius wasn't listening. "That was the sign I was descended from Aesculapius, the god of medicine. I took my cognomen, my third name, Reticulus, because it meant *undergarment*, to remind me of the blessed day when a chicken stole my loincloth."

"So . . . your name means Mr. Underwear?"

"Praise the gods! I became a surgeon in the legion, and the rest is history." He spread his arms generously. "Don't give up, boy. Maybe your father is running late. Most omens are not as dramatic as a chicken, of course. I knew a fellow once who got a dung beetle—"

"Thanks, Vitellius," Frank said. "But I have to finish polishing this armor—"

"And the gorgon's blood?"

Frank froze. He hadn't told anyone about that. As far as he knew, only Percy had seen him pocket the vials at the river, and they hadn't had a chance to talk about it.

"Come now," Vitellius chided. "I'm a healer. I know the legends about gorgon's blood. Show me the vials."

Reluctantly, Frank brought out the two ceramic flasks he'd retrieved from the Little Tiber. Spoils of war were often left behind when a monster dissolved—sometimes a tooth, or a weapon, or even the monster's entire head. Frank had known what the two vials were immediately. By tradition they belonged to Percy, who had killed the gorgons, but Frank couldn't help thinking, What if I could use them?

"Yes." Vitellius studied the vials approvingly. "Blood taken from the right side of a gorgon's body can cure any disease, even bring the dead back to life. The goddess Minerva once gave a vial of it to my divine ancestor, Aesculapius. But blood taken from the left side of a gorgon—instantly fatal. So, which is which?"

Frank looked down at the vials. "I don't know. They're identical."

"Ha! But you're hoping the right vial could solve your problem with the burned stick, eh? Maybe break your curse?"

Frank was so stunned, he couldn't talk.

"Oh, don't worry, boy." The ghost chuckled. "I won't tell anyone. I'm a Lar, a protector of the cohort! I wouldn't do anything to endanger you."

"You stabbed me through the chest with your sword."

"Trust me, boy! I have sympathy for you, carrying the curse of that Argonaut."

"The . . . what?"

Vitellius waved away the question. "Don't be modest. You've got ancient roots. Greek as well as Roman. It's no wonder Juno—" He tilted his head, as if listening to a voice from above. His face went slack. His entire aura flickered green. "But I've said enough! At any rate, I'll let you work out who gets the gorgon's blood. I suppose that newcomer Percy could use it too, with his memory problem."

Frank wondered what Vitellius had been about to say and what had made him so scared, but he got the feeling that for once Vitellius was going to keep his mouth shut.

He looked down at the two vials. He hadn't even thought of Percy's needing them. He felt guilty that he'd been intending to use the blood for himself. "Yeah. Of course. He should have it."

"Ah, but if you want my advice . . ." Vitellius looked up nervously again. "You should both wait on that gorgon blood. If my sources are right, you're going to need it on your quest."

"Quest?"

The doors of the armory flew open.

Reyna stormed in with her metal greyhounds. Vitellius vanished. He might have liked chickens, but he did not like the praetor's dogs.

"Frank." Reyna looked troubled. "That's enough with the armor. Go find Hazel. Get Percy Jackson down here. He's been up there too long. I don't want Octavian..." She hesitated. "Just get Percy down here."

So Frank had run all the way to Temple Hill.

Walking back, Percy had asked tons of questions about Hazel's brother, Nico, but Frank didn't know that much.

"He's okay," Frank said. "He's not like Hazel—"

"How do you mean?" Percy asked.

"Oh, um..." Frank coughed. He'd meant that Hazel was better looking and nicer, but he decided not to say that. "Nico is kind of mysterious. He makes everybody else nervous, being the son of Pluto, and all."

"But not you?"

Frank shrugged. "Pluto's cool. It's not his fault he runs the Underworld. He just got bad luck when the gods were dividing up the world, you know? Jupiter got the sky, Neptune got the sea, and Pluto got the shaft."

"Death doesn't scare you?"

Frank almost wanted to laugh. *Not at all! Got a match?*

Instead he said, "Back in the old times, like the Greek times, when Pluto was called Hades, he was more of a death god. When he became Roman, he got more...I don't know, respectable. He became the god of wealth, too. Everything under the earth belongs to him. So I don't think of him as being real scary."

Percy scratched his head. "How does a god *become* Roman? If he's Greek, wouldn't he stay Greek?"

Frank walked a few steps, thinking about that. Vitellius

would've given Percy an hour-long lecture on the subject, probably with a PowerPoint presentation, but Frank took his best shot. "The way Romans saw it, they adopted the Greek stuff and perfected it."

Percy made a sour face. "Perfected it? Like there was something wrong with it?"

Frank remembered what Vitellius had said: *You've got ancient roots. Greek as well as Roman.* His grandmother had said something similar.

"I don't know," he admitted. "Rome was more successful than Greece. They made this huge empire. The gods became a bigger deal in Roman times—more powerful and widely known. That's why they're still around today. So many civilizations base themselves on Rome. The gods changed to Roman because that's where the center of power was. Jupiter was...well, more responsible as a Roman god than he had been when he was Zeus. Mars became a lot more important and disciplined."

"And Juno became a hippie bag lady," Percy noted. "So you're saying the old Greek gods—they just changed permanently to Roman? There's nothing left of the Greek?"

"Uh..." Frank looked around to make sure there were no campers or Lares nearby, but the main gates were still a hundred yards away. "That's a sensitive topic. Some people say Greek influence is still around, like it's still a part of the gods' personalities. I've heard stories of demigods occasionally leaving Camp Jupiter. They reject Roman training and try to follow the older Greek style—like being solo heroes instead of working as a team the way the legion does. And back in the ancient days, when Rome fell, the eastern half of the empire survived—the Greek half."

Percy stared at him. "I didn't know that."

"It was called Byzantium." Frank liked saying that word. It sounded cool. "The eastern empire lasted another thousand years, but it was always more Greek than Roman. For those of us who follow the Roman way, it's kind of a sore subject. That's why, whatever country we settle in, Camp Jupiter is always in the west—the *Roman* part of the territory. The east is considered bad luck."

"Huh." Percy frowned.

Frank couldn't blame him for feeling confused. The Greek/Roman stuff gave him a headache, too.

They reached the gates.

"I'll take you to the baths to get you cleaned up," Frank said. "But first ... about those vials I found at the river."

"Gorgon's blood," Percy said. "One vial heals. One is deadly poison."

Frank's eyes widened. "You *know* about that? Listen, I wasn't going to keep them. I just—"

"I know why you did it, Frank."

"You do?"

"Yeah." Percy smiled. "If I'd come into camp carrying a vial of poison, that would've looked bad. You were trying to protect me."

"Oh ... right." Frank wiped the sweat off his palms. "But if we could figure out which vial was which, it might heal your memory."

Percy's smile faded. He gazed across the hills. "Maybe ... I guess. But you should hang on to those vials for now. There's a battle coming. We may need them to save lives."

Frank stared at him, a little bit in awe. Percy had a chance to get his memory back, and he was willing to wait in case someone else needed the vial more? Romans were supposed to be unselfish and help their comrades, but Frank wasn't sure anyone else at camp would have made that choice.

"So you don't remember anything?" Frank asked. "Family, friends?"

Percy fingered the clay beads around his neck. "Only glimpses. Murky stuff. A girlfriend...I thought she'd be at camp." He looked at Frank carefully, as if making a decision. "Her name was Annabeth. You don't know her, do you?"

Frank shook his head. "I know everybody at camp, but no Annabeth. What about your family? Is your mom mortal?"

"I guess so...she's probably worried out of her mind. Does your mom get to see you much?"

Frank stopped at the bathhouse entrance. He grabbed some towels from the supply shed. "She died."

Percy knit his brow. "How?"

Usually Frank would lie. He'd say *an accident* and shut off the conversation. Otherwise his emotions got out of control. He couldn't cry at Camp Jupiter. He couldn't show weakness. But with Percy, Frank found it easier to talk.

"She died in the war," he said. "Afghanistan."

"She was in the military?"

"Canadian. Yeah."

"Canada? I didn't know—"

"Most Americans don't." Frank sighed. "But yeah, Canada

has troops there. My mom was a captain. She was one of the first women to die in combat. She saved some soldiers who were pinned down by enemy fire. She . . . she didn't make it. The funeral was right before I came down here."

Percy nodded. He didn't ask for more details, which Frank appreciated. He didn't say he was sorry, or make any of the well-meaning comments Frank always hated: *Oh, you poor guy. That must be so hard on you. You have my deepest condolences.*

It was like Percy had faced death before, like he knew about grief. What mattered was listening. You didn't need to say you were sorry. The only thing that helped was moving on—moving forward.

"How about you show me the baths now?" Percy suggested. "I'm filthy."

Frank managed a smile. "Yeah. You kind of are."

As they walked into the steam room, Frank thought of his grandmother, his mom, and his cursed childhood, thanks to Juno and her piece of firewood. He almost wished he could forget his past, the way Percy had.

X

FRANK

FRANK DIDN'T REMEMBER MUCH ABOUT the funeral itself. But he remembered the hours leading up to it—his grandmother coming out into the backyard to find him shooting arrows at her porcelain collection.

His grandmother's house was a rambling gray stone mansion on twelve acres in North Vancouver. Her backyard ran straight into Lynn Canyon Park.

The morning was cold and drizzly, but Frank didn't feel the chill. He wore a black wool suit and a black overcoat that had once belonged to his grandfather. Frank had been startled and upset to find that they fit him fine. The clothes smelled like wet mothballs and jasmine. The fabric was itchy but warm. With his bow and quiver, he probably looked like a very dangerous butler.

He'd loaded some of his grandmother's porcelain in a wagon and toted it into the yard, where he set up targets on old fenceposts at the edge of the property. He'd been shooting so long, his fingers were starting to lose their feeling. With every arrow, he imagined he was striking down his problems.

Snipers in Afghanistan. *Smash*. A teapot exploded with an arrow through the middle.

The sacrifice medal, a silver disk on a red-and-black ribbon, given for death in the line of duty, presented to Frank as if it were something important, something that made everything all right. *Thwack*. A teacup spun into the woods.

The officer who came to tell him: "Your mother is a hero. Captain Emily Zhang died trying to save her comrades." *Crack*. A blue-and-white plate split into pieces.

His grandmother's chastisement: *Men do not cry. Especially Zhang men. You will endure, Fai.*

No one called him Fai except his grandmother.

What sort of name is Frank? she would scold. *That is not a Chinese name.*

I'm not Chinese, Frank thought, but he didn't dare say that. His mother had told him years ago: *There is no arguing with Grandmother. It'll only make you suffer worse.* She'd been right. And now Frank had no one except his grandmother.

Thud. A fourth arrow hit the fencepost and stuck there, quivering.

"Fai," said his grandmother.

Frank turned.

She was clutching a shoebox-sized mahogany chest that Frank had never seen before. With her high-collared black dress and severe bun of gray hair, she looked like a schoolteacher from the 1800s.

She surveyed the carnage: her porcelain in the wagon, the

shards of her favorite tea sets scattered over the lawn, Frank's arrows sticking out of the ground, the trees, the fenceposts, and one in the head of a smiling garden gnome.

Frank thought she would yell, or hit him with the box. He'd never done anything this bad before. He'd never felt so angry.

Grandmother's face was full of bitterness and disapproval. She looked nothing like Frank's mom. He wondered how his mother had turned out to be so nice—always laughing, always gentle. Frank couldn't imagine his mom growing up with Grandmother any more than he could imagine her on the battlefield—though the two situations probably weren't that different.

He waited for Grandmother to explode. Maybe he'd be grounded and wouldn't have to go to the funeral. He wanted to hurt her for being so mean all the time, for letting his mother go off to war, for scolding him to get over it. All she cared about was her stupid collection.

"Stop this ridiculous behavior," Grandmother said. She didn't sound very irritated. "It is beneath you."

To Frank's astonishment, she kicked aside one of her favorite teacups.

"The car will be here soon," she said. "We must talk."

Frank was dumbfounded. He looked more closely at the mahogany box. For a horrible moment, he wondered if it contained his mother's ashes, but that was impossible. Grandmother had told him there would be a military burial. Then why did Grandmother hold the box so gingerly, as if its contents grieved her?

"Come inside," she said. Without waiting to see if he would follow, she turned and marched toward the house.

In the parlor, Frank sat on a velvet sofa, surrounded by vintage family photos, porcelain vases that had been too large for his wagon, and red Chinese calligraphy banners. Frank didn't know what the calligraphy said. He'd never had much interest in learning. He didn't know most of the people in the photographs, either.

Whenever Grandmother started lecturing him about his ancestors—how they'd come over from China and prospered in the import/export business, eventually becoming one of the wealthiest Chinese families in Vancouver—well, it was boring. Frank was fourth-generation Canadian. He didn't care about China and all these musty antiques. The only Chinese characters he could recognize were his family name: Zhang. *Master of bows.* That was cool.

Grandmother sat next to him, her posture stiff, her hands folded over the box.

"Your mother wanted you to have this," she said with reluctance. "She kept it since you were a baby. When she went away to the war, she entrusted it to me. But now she is gone. And soon you will be going, too."

Frank's stomach fluttered. "Going? Where?"

"I am old," Grandmother said, as if that were a surprising announcement. "I have my own appointment with Death soon enough. I cannot teach you the skills you will need, and I cannot keep this burden. If something were to happen to it, I would never forgive myself. You would die."

Frank wasn't sure he'd heard her right. It sounded like she

had said his life depended on that box. He wondered why he'd never seen it before. She must have kept it locked in the attic —the one room Frank was forbidden to explore. She'd always said she kept her most valuable treasures up there.

She handed the box to him. He opened the lid with trembling fingers. Inside, cushioned in velvet lining, was a terrifying, life-altering, incredibly important . . . piece of wood.

It looked like driftwood—hard and smooth, sculpted into a wavy shape. It was about the size of a TV remote control. The tip was charred. Frank touched the burned end. It still felt warm. The ashes left a black smudge on his finger.

"It's a stick," he said. He couldn't figure out why Grandmother was acting so tense and serious about it.

Her eyes glittered. "Fai, do you know of prophecies? Do you know of the gods?"

The questions made him uncomfortable. He thought about Grandmother's silly gold statues of Chinese immortals, her superstitions about putting furniture in certain places and avoiding unlucky numbers. Prophecies made him think of fortune cookies, which weren't even Chinese—not really— but the bullies at school teased him about stupid stuff like that: *Confucius say . . .* all that garbage. Frank had never even been to China. He wanted nothing to do with it. But of course, Grandmother didn't want to hear that.

"A little, Grandmother," he said. "Not much."

"Most would have scoffed at your mother's tale," she said, "But I did not. I know of prophecies and gods. Greek, Roman, Chinese—they intertwine in our family. I did not question what she told me about your father."

"Wait... what?"

"Your father was a god," she said plainly.

If Grandmother had had a sense of humor, Frank would have thought she was kidding. But Grandmother never teased. Was she going senile?

"Stop gaping at me!" she snapped. "My mind is not addled. Haven't you ever wondered why your father never came back?"

"He was..." Frank faltered. Losing his mother was painful enough. He didn't want to think about his father, too. "He was in the army, like Mom. He went missing in action. In Iraq."

"Bah. He was a god. He fell in love with your mother because she was a natural warrior. She was like me—strong, brave, good, beautiful."

Strong and brave, Frank could believe. Picturing Grandmother as good or beautiful was more difficult.

He still suspected she might be losing her marbles, but he asked, "What kind of god?"

"Roman," she said. "Beyond that, I don't know. Your mother wouldn't say, or perhaps she didn't know herself. It is no surprise a god would fall in love with her, given our family. He must have known she was of ancient blood."

"Wait... we're Chinese. Why would Roman gods want to date Chinese Canadians?"

Grandmother's nostrils flared. "If you bothered to learn the family history, Fai, you might know this. China and Rome are not so different, nor as separate as you might believe. Our family is from Gansu Province, a town once called Li-Jien. And before that... as I said, ancient blood. The blood of princes and heroes."

Frank just stared at her.

She sighed in exasperation. "My words are wasted on this young ox! You will learn the truth when you go to camp. Perhaps your father will claim you. But for now, I must explain the firewood."

She pointed at the big stone fireplace. "Shortly after you were born, a visitor appeared at our hearth. Your mother and I sat here on the couch, just where you and I are sitting. You were a tiny thing, swaddled in a blue blanket, and she cradled you in her arms."

It sounded like a sweet memory, but Grandmother told it in a bitter tone, as if she knew, even then, that Frank would turn into a big lumbering oaf.

"A woman appeared at the fire," she continued. "She was a white woman—a *gwai poh*—dressed in blue silk, with a strange cloak like the skin of a goat."

"A goat," Frank said numbly.

Grandmother scowled. "Yes, clean your ears, Fai Zhang! I'm too old to tell every story twice! The woman with the goatskin was a goddess. I can always tell these things. She smiled at the baby—at you—and she told your mother, in perfect Mandarin, no less: 'He will close the circle. He will return your family to its roots and bring you great honor.'"

Grandmother snorted. "I do not argue with goddesses, but perhaps this one did not see the future clearly. Whatever the case, she said, 'He will go to camp and restore your reputation there. He will free Thanatos from his icy chains—'"

"Wait, who?"

"Thanatos," Grandmother said impatiently. "The Greek

name for Death. Now may I continue without interruptions? The goddess said, 'The blood of Pylos is strong in this child from his mother's side. He will have the Zhang family gift, but he will also have the powers of his father.'"

Suddenly Frank's family history didn't seem so boring. He desperately wanted to ask what it all meant—powers, gifts, blood of Pylos. What was this camp, and who was his father? But he didn't want to interrupt Grandmother again. He wanted her to keep talking.

"No power comes without a price, Fai," she said. "Before the goddess disappeared, she pointed at the fire and said, 'He will be the strongest of your clan, and the greatest. But the Fates have decreed he will also be the most vulnerable. His life will burn bright and short. As soon as that piece of tinder is consumed—that stick at the edge of the fire—your son is destined to die.'"

Frank could hardly breathe. He looked at the box in his lap, and the smudge of ash on his finger. The story sounded ridiculous, but suddenly the piece of driftwood seemed more sinister, colder and heavier. "This . . . this—"

"Yes, my thick-headed ox," Grandmother said. "That is the very stick. The goddess disappeared, and I snatched the wood from the fire immediately. We have kept it ever since."

"If it burns up, I die?"

"It is not so strange," Grandmother said. "Roman, Chinese —the destinies of men can often be predicted, and sometimes guarded against, at least for a time. The firewood is in your possession now. Keep it close. As long as it is safe, you are safe."

Frank shook his head. He wanted to protest that this was just a stupid legend. Maybe Grandmother was trying to scare him as some sort of revenge for breaking her porcelain.

But her eyes were defiant. She seemed to be challenging Frank: *If you do not believe it, burn it.*

Frank closed the box. "If it's so dangerous, why not seal the wood in something that won't burn, like plastic or steel? Why not put it in a safe deposit box?"

"What would happen," Grandmother wondered, "if we coated the stick in another substance. Would you, too, suffocate? I do not know. Your mother would not take the risk. She couldn't bear to part with it, for fear something would go wrong. Banks can be robbed. Buildings can burn down. Strange things conspire when one tries to cheat fate. Your mother thought the stick was only safe in her possession, until she went to war. Then she gave it to me."

Grandmother exhaled sourly. "Emily was foolish, going to war, though I suppose I always knew it was her destiny. She hoped to meet your father again."

"She thought . . . she thought he'd be in Afghanistan?"

Grandmother spread her hands, as if this was beyond her understanding. "She went. She died bravely. She thought the family gift would protect her. No doubt that's how she saved those soldiers. But the gift has never kept our family safe. It did not help my father, or *his* father. It did not help me. And now you have become a man. You must follow the path."

"But . . . what path? What's our gift—archery?"

"You and your archery! Foolish boy. Soon you will find out. Tonight, after the funeral, you must go south. Your mother said if she did not come back from combat, Lupa would send messengers. They will escort you to a place where the children of the gods can be trained for their destiny."

Frank felt as if he were being shot with arrows, his heart splitting into porcelain shards. He didn't understand most of what Grandmother said, but one thing was clear: she was kicking him out.

"You'd just let me go?" he asked. "Your last family?"

Grandmother's mouth quivered. Her eyes looked moist. Frank was shocked to realize she was near tears. She'd lost her husband years ago, then her daughter, and now she was about to send away her only grandson. But she rose from the couch and stood tall, her posture as stiff and correct as ever.

"When you arrive at camp," she instructed, "you must speak to the praetor in private. Tell her your great-grandfather was Shen Lun. It has been many years since the San Francisco incident. Hopefully they will not kill you for what he did, but you might want to beg forgiveness for his actions."

"This is sounding better and better," Frank mumbled.

"The goddess said you would bring our family full circle." Grandmother's voice had no trace of sympathy. "She chose your path years ago, and it will not be easy. But now it is time for the funeral. We have obligations. Come. The car will be waiting."

The ceremony was a blur: solemn faces, the patter of rain on the graveside awning, the crack of rifles from the honor guard, the casket sinking into the earth.

That night, the wolves came. They howled on the front porch. Frank came out to meet them. He took his travel pack, his warmest clothes, his bow and his quiver. His mother's sacrifice medal was tucked in his pack. The charred stick was wrapped carefully in three layers of cloth in his coat pocket, next to his heart.

His journey south began—to the Wolf House in Sonoma, and eventually to Camp Jupiter, where he spoke to Reyna privately as Grandmother had instructed. He begged forgiveness for the great-grandfather he knew nothing about. Reyna let him join the legion. She never did tell him what his great-grandfather had done, but she obviously knew. Frank could tell it was bad.

"I judge people by their own merits," Reyna had told him. "But do not mention the name Shen Lun to anyone else. It must remain our secret, or you'll be treated badly."

Unfortunately, Frank didn't have many merits. His first month at camp was spent knocking over rows of weapons, breaking chariots, and tripping entire cohorts as they marched. His favorite job was caring for Hannibal the elephant, but he'd managed to mess that up, too—giving Hannibal indigestion by feeding him peanuts. Who knew elephants could be peanut-intolerant? Frank figured Reyna was regretting her decision to let him join.

Every day, he woke up wondering if the stick would somehow catch fire and burn, and he would cease to exist.

All of this ran through Frank's head as he walked with Hazel and Percy to the war games. He thought about the stick wrapped inside his coat pocket, and what it meant that Juno had appeared at camp. Was he about to die? He hoped not. He hadn't brought his family any honor yet—that was for sure. Maybe Apollo would claim him today and explain his powers and gifts.

Once they got out of camp, the Fifth Cohort formed two lines behind their centurions, Dakota and Gwen. They marched north, skirting the edge of the city, and headed to the Field of Mars—the largest, flattest part of the valley. The grass was cropped short by all the unicorns, bulls, and homeless fauns that grazed here. The earth was pitted with explosion craters and scarred with trenches from past games. At the north end of the field stood their target. The engineers had built a stone fortress with an iron portcullis, guard towers, scorpion ballistae, water cannons, and no doubt many other nasty surprises for the defenders to use.

"They did a good job today," Hazel noted. "That's bad for us."

"Wait," Percy said. "You're telling me that fortress was built *today*?"

Hazel grinned. "Legionnaires are trained to build. If we had to, we could break down the entire camp and rebuild it somewhere else. Take maybe three or four days, but we could do it."

"Let's not," Percy said. "So you attack a different fort every night?"

"Not every night," Frank said. "We have different training exercises. Sometimes deathball—um, which is like paintball, except with . . . you know, poison and acid and fire balls. Sometimes we do chariots and gladiator competitions, sometimes war games."

Hazel pointed at the fort. "Somewhere inside, the First and Second Cohorts are keeping their banners. Our job is to get inside and capture them without getting slaughtered. We do that, we win."

Percy's eyes lit up. "Like capture-the-flag. I think I like capture-the-flag."

Frank laughed. "Yeah, well . . . it's harder than it sounds. We have to get past those scorpions and water cannons on the walls, fight through the inside of the fortress, find the banners, and defeat the guards, all while protecting our own banners and troops from capture. And *our* cohort is in competition with the other two attacking cohorts. We sort of work together, but not really. The cohort that captures the banners gets all the glory."

Percy stumbled, trying to keep time with the left-right marching rhythm. Frank sympathized. He'd spent his first two weeks falling down.

"So why are we practicing this, anyway?" Percy asked. "Do you guys spend a lot of time laying siege to fortified cities?"

"Teamwork," Hazel said. "Quick thinking. Tactics. Battle skills. You'd be surprised what you can learn in the war games."

"Like who will stab you in the back," Frank said.

"Especially that," Hazel agreed.

They marched to the center of the Field of Mars and formed ranks. The Third and Fourth Cohorts assembled as far as possible from the Fifth. The centurions for the attacking side gathered for a conference. In the sky above them, Reyna circled on her pegasus, Scipio, ready to play referee.

Half a dozen giant eagles flew in formation behind her—prepared for ambulance airlift duty if necessary. The only person not participating in the game was Nico di Angelo, "Pluto's ambassador," who had climbed an observation tower about a hundred yards from the fort and would be watching with binoculars.

Frank propped his *pilum* against his shield and checked Percy's armor. Every strap was correct. Every piece of armor was properly adjusted.

"You did it right," he said in amazement. "Percy, you must've done war games before."

"I don't know. Maybe."

The only thing that wasn't regulation was Percy's glowing bronze sword—not Imperial gold, and not a *gladius*. The blade was leaf-shaped, and the writing on the hilt was Greek. Looking at it made Frank uneasy.

Percy frowned. "We *can* use real weapons, right?"

"Yeah," Frank agreed. "For sure. I've just never seen a sword like that."

"What if I hurt somebody?"

"We heal them," Frank said. "Or try to. The legion medics are pretty good with ambrosia and nectar, and unicorn draught."

"No one dies," Hazel said. "Well, not usually. And if they do —"

Frank imitated the voice of Vitellius: "They're wimps! Back in my day, we died all the time, and we liked it!"

Hazel laughed. "Just stay with us, Percy. Chances are we'll get the worst duty and get eliminated early. They'll throw us at the walls first to soften up the defenses. Then the Third and Fourth Cohorts will march in and get the honors, *if* they can even breach the fort."

Horns blew. Dakota and Gwen walked back from the officers' conference, looking grim.

"All right, here's the plan!" Dakota took a quick swig of Kool-Aid from his travel flask. "They're throwing us at the walls first to soften up the defenses."

The whole cohort groaned.

"I know, I know," Gwen said. "But maybe this time we'll have some luck!"

Leave it to Gwen to be the optimist. Everybody liked her because she took care of her people and tried to keep their spirits up. She could even control Dakota during his hyperactive bug-juice fits. Still, the campers grumbled and complained. Nobody believed in luck for the Fifth.

"First line with Dakota," Gwen said. "Lock shields and advance in turtle formation to the main gates. Try to stay in one piece. Draw their fire. Second line—" Gwen turned to Frank's row without much enthusiasm. "You seventeen, from Bobby over, take charge of the elephant and the scaling ladders. Try a flanking attack on the western wall. Maybe we can spread the defenders too thin. Frank, Hazel, Percy... well, just do whatever. Show Percy the ropes. Try to keep him alive." She turned back to the whole cohort. "If anybody gets over the wall first, I'll make sure you get the Mural Crown. Victory for the Fifth!"

The cohort cheered halfheartedly and broke ranks.

Percy frowned. "'Do whatever?'"

"Yeah," Hazel sighed. "Big vote of confidence."

"What's the Mural Crown?" he asked.

"Military medal," Frank said. He'd been forced to memorize all the possible awards. "Big honor for the first soldier to breach an enemy fort. You'll notice nobody in the Fifth is wearing one. Usually we don't even get into the fort because we're burning or drowning or..."

He faltered, and looked at Percy. "Water cannons."

"What?" Percy asked.

"The cannons on the walls," Frank said, "they draw water from the aqueduct. There's a pump system—heck, I don't know how they work, but they're under a lot of pressure. If you could control them, like you controlled the river—"

"Frank!" Hazel beamed. "That's brilliant!"

Percy didn't look so sure. "I don't know how I did that at the river. I'm not sure I can control the cannons from this far away."

"We'll get you closer." Frank pointed to the eastern wall of the fort, where the Fifth Cohort wouldn't be attacking. "That's where the defense will be weakest. They'll never take three kids seriously. I think we can sneak up pretty close before they see us."

"Sneak up how?" Percy asked.

Frank turned to Hazel. "Can you do that thing again?"

She punched him in the chest. "You said you wouldn't tell anybody!"

Immediately Frank felt terrible. He'd gotten so caught up in the idea...

Hazel muttered under her breath. "Never mind. It's fine.

Percy, he's talking about the trenches. The Field of Mars is riddled with tunnels from over the years. Some are collapsed, or buried deep, but a lot of them are still passable. I'm pretty good at finding them and using them. I can even collapse them if I have to."

"Like you did with the gorgons," Percy said, "to slow them down."

Frank nodded approvingly. "I told you Pluto was cool. He's the god of everything under the earth. Hazel can find caves, tunnels, trapdoors—"

"And it was *our* secret," she grumbled.

Frank felt himself blushing. "Yeah, sorry. But if we can get close—"

"And if I can knock out the water cannons . . ." Percy nodded, like he was warming to the idea. "What do we do then?"

Frank checked his quiver. He always stocked up on special arrows. He'd never gotten to use them before, but maybe tonight was the night. Maybe he could finally do something good enough to get Apollo's attention.

"The rest is up to me," he said. "Let's go."

XI

FRANK

FRANK HAD NEVER FELT SO SURE of anything, which made him nervous. Nothing he planned ever went right. He always managed to break, ruin, burn, sit on, or knock over something important. Yet he *knew* this strategy would work.

Hazel found them a tunnel with no problem. In fact, Frank had a sneaking suspicion she didn't just *find* tunnels. It was as though tunnels manufactured themselves to suit her needs. Passages that had been filled in years ago suddenly un-filled, changing direction to lead Hazel where she wanted to go.

They crept along by the light of Percy's glowing sword, Riptide. Above, they heard the sounds of battle—kids shouting, Hannibal the elephant bellowing with glee, scorpion bolts exploding, and water cannons firing. The tunnel shook. Dirt rained down on them.

Frank slipped his hand inside his armor. The piece of wood was still safe and secure in his coat pocket, though one good shot from a scorpion might set his lifeline on fire. . . .

Bad Frank, he chided himself. *Fire* is the "F-word." Don't think about it.

"There's an opening just ahead," Hazel announced. "We'll come up ten feet from the east wall."

"How can you tell?" Percy asked.

"I don't know," she said. "But I'm sure."

"Could we tunnel straight under the wall?" Frank wondered.

"No," Hazel said. "The engineers were smart. They built the walls on old foundations that go down to bedrock. And don't ask how I know. I just do."

Frank stumbled over something and cursed. Percy brought his sword around for more light. The thing Frank had tripped on was gleaming silver.

He crouched down.

"Don't touch it!" Hazel said.

Frank's hand stopped a few inches from the chunk of metal. It looked like a giant Hershey's Kiss, about the size of his fist.

"It's massive," he said. "Silver?"

"Platinum." Hazel sounded scared out of her wits. "It'll go away in a second. Please don't touch it. It's dangerous."

Frank didn't understand how a lump of metal could be dangerous, but he took Hazel seriously. As they watched, the chunk of platinum sank into the ground.

He stared at Hazel. "How did you know?"

In the light of Percy's sword, Hazel looked as ghostly as a Lar. "I'll explain later," she promised.

Another explosion rocked the tunnel, and they forged ahead.

They popped out of a hole just where Hazel had predicted. In front of them, the fort's east wall loomed. Off to their left, Frank could see the main line of the Fifth Cohort advancing in turtle formation, shields forming a shell over their heads and sides. They were trying to reach the main gates, but the defenders above pelted them with rocks and shot flaming bolts from the scorpions, blasting craters around their feet. A water cannon discharged with a jaw-rattling *THRUM,* and a jet of liquid carved a trench in the dirt right in front of the cohort.

Percy whistled. "That's a lot of pressure, all right."

The Third and Fourth Cohorts weren't even advancing. They stood back and laughed, watching their "allies" get beat up. The defenders clustered on the wall above the gates, yelling insults at the tortoise formation as it staggered back and forth. War games had deteriorated into "beat up the Fifth."

Frank's vision went red with anger.

"Let's shake things up." He reached in his quiver and pulled out an arrow heavier than the rest. The iron tip was shaped like the nose cone of a rocket. An ultrathin gold rope trailed from the fletching. Shooting it accurately up the wall would take more force and skill than most archers could manage, but Frank had strong arms and good aim.

Maybe Apollo is watching, he thought hopefully.

"What does that do?" Percy asked. "Grappling hook?"

"It's called a hydra arrow," Frank said. "Can you knock out the water cannons?"

A defender appeared on the wall above them. "Hey!" he shouted to his buddies. "Check it out! More victims!"

"Percy," Frank said, "now would be good."

More kids came across the battlements to laugh at them. A few ran to the nearest water cannon and swung the barrel toward Frank.

Percy closed his eyes. He raised his hand.

Up on the wall, somebody yelled, "Open wide, losers!"

KA-BOOM!

The cannon exploded in a starburst of blue, green, and white. Defenders screamed as a watery shockwave flattened them against the battlements. Kids toppled over the walls but were snatched by giant eagles and carried to safety. Then the entire eastern wall shuddered as the explosion backed up through the pipelines. One after another, the water cannons on the battlements exploded. The scorpions' fires were doused. Defenders scattered in confusion or were tossed through the air, giving the rescue eagles quite a workout. At the main gates, the Fifth Cohort forgot about their formation. Mystified, they lowered their shields and stared at the chaos.

Frank shot his arrow. It streaked upward, carrying its glittering rope. When it reached the top, the metal point fractured into a dozen lines that lashed out and wrapped around anything they could find—parts of the wall, a scorpion, a broken water cannon, and a couple of defending campers, who yelped and found themselves slammed against the battlements as anchors. From the main rope, handholds extended at two-foot intervals, making a ladder.

"Go!" Frank said.

Percy grinned. "You first, Frank. This is your party."

Frank hesitated. Then he slung his bow on his back and began to climb. He was halfway up before the defenders recovered their senses enough to sound the alarm.

Frank glanced back at Fifth Cohort's main group. They were staring up at him, dumbfounded.

"Well?" Frank screamed. "Attack!"

Gwen was the first to unfreeze. She grinned and repeated the order. A cheer went up from the battlefield. Hannibal the elephant trumpeted with happiness, but Frank couldn't afford to watch. He clambered to the top of the wall, where three defenders were trying to hack down his rope ladder.

One good thing about being big, clumsy, and clad in metal: Frank was like a heavily armored bowling ball. He launched himself at the defenders, and they toppled like pins. Frank got to his feet. He took command of the battlements, sweeping his *pilum* back and forth and knocking down defenders. Some shot arrows. Some tried to get under his guard with their swords, but Frank felt unstoppable. Then Hazel appeared next to him, swinging her big cavalry sword like she was born for battle.

Percy leaped onto the wall and raised Riptide.

"Fun," he said.

Together they cleared the defenders off the walls. Below them the gates broke. Hannibal barreled into the fort, arrows and rocks bouncing harmlessly off his Kevlar armor.

The Fifth Cohort charged in behind the elephant, and the battle went hand-to-hand.

Finally, from the edge of the Field of Mars, a battle cry went up. The Third and Fourth Cohorts ran to join the fight.

"A little late," Hazel grumbled.

"We can't let them get the banners," Frank said.

"No," Percy agreed. "Those are ours."

No more talk was necessary. They moved like a team, as if the three of them had been working together for years. They rushed down the interior steps and into the enemy base.

XII

FRANK

AFTER THAT, THE BATTLE WAS MAYHEM.

Frank, Percy, and Hazel waded through the enemy, plowing down anyone who stood in their way. The First and Second Cohorts—pride of Camp Jupiter, a well-oiled, highly disciplined war machine—fell apart under the assault and the sheer novelty of being on the losing side.

Part of their problem was Percy. He fought like a demon, whirling through the defenders' ranks in a completely unorthodox style, rolling under their feet, slashing with his sword instead of stabbing like a Roman would, whacking campers with the flat of his blade, and generally causing mass panic. Octavian screamed in a shrill voice—maybe ordering the First Cohort to stand their ground, maybe trying to sing soprano —but Percy put a stop to it. He somersaulted over a line of shields and slammed the butt of his sword into Octavian's helmet. The centurion collapsed like a sock puppet.

Frank shot arrows until his quiver was empty, using blunt-tipped missiles that wouldn't kill but left some nasty bruises. He broke his *pilum* over a defender's head, then reluctantly drew his *gladius*.

Meanwhile, Hazel climbed onto Hannibal's back. She charged toward the center of the fort, grinning down at her friends. "Let's go, slowpokes!"

Gods of Olympus, she's beautiful, Frank thought.

They ran to the center of the base. The inner keep was virtually unguarded. Obviously the defenders never dreamed an assault would get this far. Hannibal busted down the huge doors. Inside, the First and Second Cohort standard-bearers were sitting around a table playing Mythomagic with cards and figurines. The cohort's emblems were propped carelessly against one wall.

Hazel and Hannibal rode straight into the room, and the standard-bearers fell backward out of their chairs. Hannibal stepped on the table, and game pieces scattered.

By the time the rest of the cohort caught up with them, Percy and Frank had disarmed the enemies, grabbed the banners, and climbed onto Hannibal's back with Hazel. They marched out of the keep triumphantly with the enemy colors.

The Fifth Cohort formed ranks around them. Together they paraded out of the fort, past stunned enemies and lines of equally mystified allies.

Reyna circled low overhead on her pegasus. "The game is won!" She sounded as if she were trying not to laugh. "Assemble for honors!"

Slowly the campers regrouped on the Field of Mars. Frank

saw plenty of minor injuries—some burns, broken bones, black eyes, cuts and gashes, plus a lot of very interesting hairdos from fires and exploding water cannons—but nothing that couldn't be fixed.

He slid off the elephant. His comrades swarmed him, pounding him on the back and complimenting him. Frank wondered if he was dreaming. It was the best night of his life—until he saw Gwen.

"Help!" somebody yelled. A couple of campers rushed out of the fortress, carrying a girl on a stretcher. They set her down, and other kids started running over. Even from a distance, Frank could tell it was Gwen. She was in bad shape. She lay on her side on the stretcher with a *pilum* sticking out of her armor—almost like she was holding it between her chest and her arm, but there was too much blood.

Frank shook his head in disbelief. "No, no, no . . ." he muttered as he ran to her side.

The medics barked at everyone to stand back and give her air. The whole legion fell silent as the healers worked—trying to get gauze and powdered unicorn horn under Gwen's armor to stop the bleeding, trying to force some nectar into her mouth. Gwen didn't move. Her face was ashen gray.

Finally one of the medics looked up at Reyna and shook his head.

For a moment, there was no sound except water from the ruined cannons trickling down the walls of the fort. Hannibal nuzzled Gwen's hair with his trunk.

Reyna surveyed the campers from her pegasus. Her expression was as hard and dark as iron. "There will be an investigation. Whoever did this, you cost the legion a good officer. Honorable death is one thing, but *this...*"

Frank wasn't sure what she meant. Then he noticed the marks engraved in the wooden shaft of the *pilum*: CHT I LEGIO XII F. The weapon belonged to the First Cohort, and the point was sticking out the front of her armor. Gwen had been speared from behind—possibly *after* the game had ended.

Frank scanned the crowd for Octavian. The centurion was watching with more interest than concern, as if he were examining one of his stupid gutted teddy bears. He didn't have a *pilum*.

Blood roared in Frank's ears. He wanted to strangle Octavian with his bare hands, but at that moment, Gwen gasped.

Everyone stepped back. Gwen opened her eyes. The color came back to her face.

"Wh-what is it?" She blinked. "What's everyone staring at?"

She didn't seem to notice the seven-foot harpoon sticking out through her chest.

Behind Frank, a medic whispered, "There's no way. She was dead. She *has* to be dead."

Gwen tried to sit up, but couldn't. "There was a river, and a man asking... for a coin? I turned around and the exit door was open. So I just... I just left. I don't understand. What's happened?"

Everyone stared at her in horror. Nobody tried to help.

"Gwen." Frank knelt next to her. "Don't try to get up. Just close your eyes for a second, okay?"

"Why? What—"

"Just trust me."

Gwen did what he asked.

Frank grabbed the shaft of the *pilum* below its tip, but his hands were shaking. The wood was slick. "Percy, Hazel —help me."

One of the medics realized what he was planning. "Don't!" he said. "You might—"

"What?" Hazel snapped. "Make it worse?"

Frank took a deep breath. "Hold her steady. One, two, three!"

He pulled the *pilum* out from the front. Gwen didn't even wince. The blood stopped quickly.

Hazel bent down to examine the wound. "It's closing on its own," she said. "I don't know how, but—"

"I feel fine," Gwen protested. "What's everyone worried about?"

With Frank and Percy's help, she got to her feet. Frank glowered at Octavian, but the centurion's face was a mask of polite concern.

Later, Frank thought. *Deal with him later.*

"Gwen," Hazel said gently, "there's no easy way to say this. You were dead. Somehow you came back."

"I . . . what?" She stumbled against Frank. Her hand pressed against the ragged hole in her armor. "How—how?"

"Good question." Reyna turned to Nico, who was watching grimly from the edge of the crowd. "Is this some power of Pluto?"

Nico shook his head. "Pluto never lets people return from the dead."

He glanced at Hazel as if warning her to stay quiet. Frank wondered what that was about, but he didn't have time to think about it.

A thunderous voice rolled across the field: *Death loses its hold. This is only the beginning.*

Campers drew weapons. Hannibal trumpeted nervously. Scipio reared, almost throwing Reyna.

"I know that voice," Percy said. He didn't sound pleased.

In the midst of the legion, a column of fire blasted into the air. Heat seared Frank's eyelashes. Campers who had been soaked by the cannons found their clothes instantly steam-dried. Everyone scrambled backward as a huge soldier stepped out of the explosion.

Frank didn't have much hair, but what he *did* have stood straight up. The soldier was ten feet tall, dressed in Canadian Forces desert camouflage. He radiated confidence and power. His black hair was cut in a flat-topped wedge like Frank's. His face was angular and brutal, marked with old knife scars. His eyes were covered with infrared goggles that glowed from inside. He wore a utility belt with a sidearm, a knife holster, and several grenades. In his hands was an oversized M16 rifle.

The worst thing was that Frank felt *drawn* to him. As everyone else stepped back, Frank stepped forward. He realized the soldier was silently willing him to approach.

Frank desperately wanted to run away and hide, but he couldn't. He took three more steps. Then he sank to one knee.

The other campers followed his example and knelt. Even Reyna dismounted.

"That's good," the soldier said. "Kneeling is good. It's been a long time since I've visited Camp Jupiter."

Frank noticed that one person wasn't kneeling. Percy Jackson, his sword still in hand, was glaring at the giant soldier.

"You're Ares," Percy said. "What do you want?"

A collective gasp went up from two hundred campers and an elephant. Frank wanted to say something to excuse Percy and placate the god, but he didn't know what. He was afraid the war god would blast his new friend with that extra-large M16.

Instead, the god bared his brilliant white teeth.

"You've got spunk, demigod," he said. "Ares is my Greek form. But to these followers, to the children of Rome, I am Mars—patron of the empire, divine father of Romulus and Remus."

"We've met," Percy said. "We . . . we had a fight. . . ."

The god scratched his chin, as if trying to recall. "I fight a lot of people. But I assure you—you've never fought me as Mars. If you had, you'd be dead. Now, kneel, as befits a child of Rome, before you try my patience."

Around Mars's feet, the ground boiled in a circle of flame.

"Percy," Frank said, "please."

Percy clearly didn't like it, but he knelt.

Mars scanned the crowd. "Romans, lend me your ears!"

He laughed—a good, hearty bellow, so infectious it almost made Frank smile, though he was still shivering with fear. "I've always wanted to say that. I come from Olympus with a message. Jupiter doesn't like us communicating directly with mortals, especially nowadays, but he has allowed this exception, as you Romans have always been my special people. I'm only permitted to speak for a few minutes, so listen up."

He pointed at Gwen. "This one should be dead, yet she's not. The monsters you fight no longer return to Tartarus when they are slain. Some mortals who died long ago are now walking the earth again."

Was it Frank's imagination, or did the god glare at Nico di Angelo?

"Thanatos has been chained," Mars announced. "The Doors of Death have been forced open, and no one is policing them—at least, not *impartially*. Gaea allows our enemies to pour forth into the world of mortals. Her sons the giants are mustering armies against you—armies that you will not be able to kill. Unless Death is unleashed to return to his duties, you will be overrun. You must find Thanatos and free him from the giants. Only *he* can reverse the tide."

Mars looked around, and noticed that everyone was still silently kneeling. "Oh, you can get up now. Any questions?"

Reyna rose uneasily. She approached the god, followed by Octavian, who was bowing and scraping like a champion groveler.

"Lord Mars," Reyna said, "we are honored."

"*Beyond* honored," said Octavian. "So far beyond honored—"

"Well?" Mars snapped.

"Well," Reyna said, "Thanatos is the god of death, the lieutenant of Pluto?"

"Right," the god said.

"And you're saying that he's been captured by giants."

"Right."

"And therefore people will stop dying?"

"Not all at once," Mars said. "But the barriers between life and death will continue to weaken. Those who know how to take advantage of this will exploit it. Monsters are already harder to dispatch. Soon they will be completely impossible to kill. Some demigods will also be able to find their way back from the Underworld—like your friend Centurion Shish kebab."

Gwen winced. "Centurion Shish kebab?"

"If left unchecked," Mars continued, "even mortals will eventually find it impossible to die. Can you imagine a world in which no one dies—*ever*?"

Octavian raised his hand. "But, ah, mighty all-powerful Lord Mars, if we can't die, isn't that a good thing? If we can stay alive indefinitely—"

"Don't be foolish, boy!" Mars bellowed. "Endless slaughter with no conclusion? Carnage without any point? Enemies that rise again and again and can never be killed? Is that what you want?"

"You're the god of war," Percy spoke up. "Don't you want endless carnage?"

Mars's infrared goggles glowed brighter. "Insolent, aren't you? Perhaps I *have* fought you before. I can understand why I'd want to kill you. I'm the god of Rome, child. I am the god of military might used for a righteous cause. I protect the legions. I am happy to crush my enemies underfoot, but I don't fight without reason. I don't want war without end. You will discover this. You will serve me."

"Not likely," Percy said.

Again, Frank waited for the god to strike him down, but Mars just grinned like they were two old buddies talking trash.

"I order a quest!" the god announced. "You will go north and find Thanatos in the land beyond the gods. You will free him and thwart the plans of the giants. Beware Gaea! Beware her son, the eldest giant!"

Next to Frank, Hazel made a squeaking sound. "The land beyond the gods?"

Mars stared down at her, his grip tightening on his M16. "That's right, Hazel Levesque. You know what I mean. Everyone here remembers the land where the legion lost its honor! Perhaps if the quest succeeds, and you return by the Feast of Fortuna...perhaps then your honor will be restored. If you don't succeed, there won't be any camp left to return to. Rome will be overrun, its legacy lost forever. So my advice is: Don't fail."

Octavian somehow managed to bow even lower. "Um, Lord Mars, just one tiny thing. A quest requires a prophecy, a mystical poem to guide us! We used to get them from the Sibylline books, but now it's up to the augur to glean the will of gods. So if I could just run and get about seventy stuffed animals and possibly a knife—"

"You're the augur?" the god interrupted.

"Y-yes, my lord."

Mars pulled a scroll from his utility belt. "Anyone got a pen?"

The legionnaires stared at him.

Mars sighed. "Two hundred Romans, and *no one's* got a pen? Never mind!"

He slung his M16 onto his back and pulled out a hand grenade. There were many screaming Romans. Then the grenade morphed into a ballpoint pen, and Mars began to write.

Frank looked at Percy with wide eyes. He mouthed: *Can your sword do grenade form?*

Percy mouthed back, *No. Shut up.*

"There!" Mars finished writing and threw the scroll at Octavian. "A prophecy. You can add it to your books, engrave it on your floor, whatever."

Octavian read the scroll. "This says, 'Go to Alaska. Find Thanatos and free him. Come back by sundown on June twenty-fourth or die.'"

"Yes," Mars said. "Is that not clear?"

"Well, my lord...usually prophecies are *unclear*. They're wrapped in riddles. They rhyme, and..."

Mars casually popped another grenade off his belt. "Yes?"

"The prophecy is clear!" Octavian announced. "A quest!"

"Good answer." Mars tapped the grenade to his chin. "Now, what else? There was something else....Oh, yes."

He turned to Frank. "C'mere, kid."

No, Frank thought. The burned stick in his coat pocket felt heavier. His legs turned wobbly. A sense of dread settled over him, worse than the day the military officer had come to the door.

He knew what was coming, but he couldn't stop it. He stepped forward against his will.

Mars grinned. "Nice job taking the wall, kid. Who's the ref for this game?"

Reyna raised her hand.

"You see that play, ref?" Mars demanded. "That was *my* kid. First over the wall, won the game for his team. Unless you're blind, that was an MVP play. You're not blind, are you?"

Reyna looked like she was trying to swallow a mouse. "No, Lord Mars."

"Then make sure he gets the Mural Crown," Mars demanded. "My kid, here!" he yelled at the legion, in case anyone hadn't heard. Frank wanted to melt into the dirt.

"Emily Zhang's son," Mars continued. "She was a good soldier. Good woman. This kid Frank proved his stuff tonight. Happy late birthday, kid. Time you stepped up to a *real* man's weapon."

He tossed Frank his M16. For a split second Frank thought he'd be crushed under the weight of the massive assault rifle, but the gun changed in midair, becoming smaller and thinner. When Frank caught it, the weapon was a spear. It had a shaft of Imperial gold and a strange point like a white bone, flickering with ghostly light.

"The tip is a dragon's tooth," Mars said. "You haven't learned to use your mom's talents yet, have you? Well—that spear will give you some breathing room until you do. You get three charges out of it, so use it wisely."

Frank didn't understand, but Mars acted like the matter was closed. "Now, my kid Frank Zhang is gonna lead the quest to free Thanatos, unless there are any objections?"

Of course, no one said a word. But many of the campers glared at Frank with envy, jealousy, anger, bitterness.

"You can take two companions," Mars said. "Those are the rules. One of them needs to be this kid."

He pointed at Percy. "He's gonna learn some respect for Mars on this trip, or die trying. As for the second, I don't care. Pick whomever you want. Have one of your senate debates. You all are good at those."

The god's image flickered. Lightning crackled across the sky.

"That's my cue," Mars said. "Until next time, Romans. Do not disappoint me!"

The god erupted in flames, and then he was gone.

Reyna turned toward Frank. Her expression was part amazement, part nausea, like she'd finally managed to swallow that mouse. She raised her arm in a Roman salute. *"Ave,* Frank Zhang, son of Mars."

The whole legion followed her lead, but Frank didn't want their attention anymore. His perfect night had been ruined.

Mars was his father. The god of war was sending him to Alaska. Frank had been handed more than a spear for his birthday. He'd been handed a death sentence.

XIII

PERCY

PERCY SLEPT LIKE A MEDUSA VICTIM—which is to say, like a rock.

He hadn't crashed in a safe, comfortable bed since...well, he couldn't even remember. Despite his insane day and the million thoughts running through his head, his body took over and said: *You will sleep now.*

He had dreams, of course. He always had dreams, but they passed like blurred images from the window of a train. He saw a curly-haired faun in ragged clothes running to catch up with him.

"I don't have any spare change," Percy called.

"What?" the faun said. "No, Percy. It's me, Grover! Stay put! We're on our way to find you. Tyson is close—at least we *think* he's the closest. We're trying to get a lock on your position."

"What?" Percy called, but the faun disappeared in the fog.

Then Annabeth was running along beside him, reaching out her hand. "Thank the gods!" she called. "For months and months we couldn't see you! Are you all right?"

Percy remembered what Juno had said—*for months he has been slumbering, but now he is awake.* The goddess had intentionally kept him hidden, but why?

"Are you real?" he asked Annabeth.

He wanted so much to believe it he felt like Hannibal the elephant was standing on his chest. But her face began to dissolve. She cried, "Stay put! It'll be easier for Tyson to find you! Stay where you are!"

Then she was gone. The images accelerated. He saw a huge ship in a dry dock, workers scrambling to finish the hull, a guy with a blowtorch welding a bronze dragon figurehead to the prow. He saw the war god stalking toward him in the surf, a sword in his hands.

The scene shifted. Percy stood on the Field of Mars, looking up at the Berkeley Hills. Golden grass rippled, and a face appeared in the landscape—a sleeping woman, her features formed from shadows and folds in the terrain. Her eyes remained closed, but her voice spoke in Percy's mind:

So this is the demigod who destroyed my son Kronos. You don't look like much, Percy Jackson, but you're valuable to me. Come north. Meet Alcyoneus. Juno can play her little games with Greeks and Romans, but in the end, you will be my pawn. You will be the key to the gods' defeat.

Percy's vision turned dark. He stood in a theater-sized version of the camp's headquarters—a *principia* with walls of ice and freezing mist hanging in the air. The floor was littered with skeletons in Roman armor and Imperial gold weapons encrusted with frost. In the back of the room sat an enormous shadowy figure. His skin glinted of gold and silver, as if he were an automaton like Reyna's dogs. Behind him stood a collection of ruined emblems, tattered banners, and a large golden eagle on a staff of iron.

The giant's voice boomed in the vast chamber. "This will be fun, son of Neptune. It's been eons since I broke a demigod of your caliber. I await you atop the ice."

Percy woke, shivering. For a moment he didn't know where he was. Then he remembered: Camp Jupiter, the Fifth Cohort barracks. He lay in his bunk, staring at the ceiling and trying to control his racing heartbeat.

A golden giant was waiting to break him. Wonderful. But what unnerved him more was that sleeping woman's face in the hills. *You will be my pawn.* Percy didn't play chess, but he was pretty sure that being a pawn was bad. They died a lot.

Even the friendlier parts of his dream were disturbing. A faun named Grover was looking for him. Maybe that's why Don had detected a—what had he called it?—an empathy link. Somebody named Tyson was searching for him, too, and Annabeth had warned Percy to stay where he was.

He sat up in his bunk. His roommates were rushing around, getting dressed and brushing their teeth. Dakota was wrapping himself in a long piece of red-speckled cloth —a toga. One of the Lares was giving him pointers on where to tuck and fold.

"Breakfast time?" Percy asked hopefully.

Frank's head popped up from the bunk below. He had bags under his eyes like he hadn't slept well. "A quick breakfast. Then we've got the senate meeting."

Dakota's head was stuck in his toga. He staggered around like a Kool-Aid-stained ghost.

"Um," Percy said, "should I wear my bedsheets?"

Frank snorted. "That's just for the senators. There're ten of them, elected yearly. You've got to be at camp five years to qualify."

"So how come we're invited to the meeting?"

"Because...you know, the quest." Frank sounded worried, like he was afraid Percy would back out. "We have to be in on the discussion. You, me, Hazel. I mean, if you're willing..."

Frank probably didn't mean to guilt him, but Percy's heart felt pulled like taffy. He had sympathy for Frank. Getting claimed by the war god in front of the whole camp —what a nightmare. Plus, how could Percy say no to that big pouty baby face? Frank had been given a huge task that would most likely get him killed. He was scared. He needed Percy's help.

And the three of them *had* made a good team last night. Hazel and Frank were solid, dependable people. They'd accepted Percy like family. Still, he didn't like the idea of this quest, especially since it came from Mars, and especially after his dreams.

"I, um...I'd better get ready...." He climbed out of bed and got dressed. The whole time, he thought about Annabeth. Help was on the way. He could have his old life back. All he had to do was stay put.

At breakfast, Percy was conscious of everyone looking at him. They were whispering about the previous night:

"Two gods in one day..."

"Un-Roman fighting..."

"Water cannon up my nose..."

He was too hungry to care. He filled up on pancakes, eggs, bacon, waffles, apples, and several glasses of orange juice. He probably would have eaten more, but Reyna announced that the senate would now convene in the city, and all the folks in togas got up to leave.

"Here we go." Hazel fidgeted with a stone that looked like a two-carat ruby.

The ghost Vitellius appeared next to them in a purple shimmer. *"Bona fortuna,* you three! Ah, senate meetings. I remember the one when Caesar was assassinated. Why, the amount of blood on his toga—"

"Thanks, Vitellius," Frank interrupted. "We should get going."

Reyna and Octavian led the procession of senators out of camp, with Reyna's metal greyhounds dashing back and forth along the road. Hazel, Frank, and Percy trailed behind. Percy noticed Nico di Angelo in the group, wearing a black toga and talking with Gwen, who looked a little pale but surprisingly good considering she'd been dead the night before. Nico waved at Percy, then went back to his conversation, leaving Percy more sure than ever that Hazel's brother was trying to avoid him.

Dakota stumbled along in his red-speckled robe. A lot of other senators seemed to be having trouble with their togas, too—hiking up their hems, trying to keep the cloth from slipping off their shoulders. Percy was glad he was wearing a regular purple T-shirt and jeans.

"How could Romans move, in those things?" he wondered.

"They were just for formal occasions," Hazel said. "Like tuxedos. I bet the ancient Romans hated togas as much as we do. By the way, you didn't bring any weapons, did you?"

Percy's hand went to his pocket, where his pen always stayed. "Why? Are we not supposed to?"

"No weapons allowed inside the Pomerian Line," she said.

"The *what* line?"

"Pomerian," Frank said. "The city limits. Inside is a sacred 'safe zone.' Legions can't march through. No weapons allowed. That's so senate meetings don't get bloody."

"Like Julius Caesar getting assassinated?" Percy asked.

Frank nodded. "Don't worry. Nothing like that has happened in months."

Percy hoped he was kidding.

As they got closer to the city, Percy could appreciate how beautiful it was. The tiled roofs and gold domes gleamed in the sun. Gardens bloomed with honeysuckle and roses. The central plaza was paved in white and gray stone, decorated with statues, fountains, and gilded columns. In the surrounding neighborhoods, cobblestone streets were lined with freshly painted town houses, shops, cafés, and parks. In the distance rose the coliseum and the horse racing arena.

Percy didn't notice they'd reached the city limits until the senators in front of him started slowing down.

On the side of the road stood a white marble statue—a

life-size muscular man with curly hair, no arms, and an irritated expression. Maybe he looked mad because he'd been carved only from the waist up. Below that, he was just a big block of marble.

"Single file, please!" the statue said. "Have your IDs ready."

Percy looked to his left and right. He hadn't noticed before, but a line of identical statues ringed the city at intervals of about a hundred yards.

The senators passed through easily. The statue checked the tattoos on their forearms and called each senator by name. "Gwendolyn, senator, Fifth Cohort, yes. Nico di Angelo, ambassador of Pluto—very well. Reyna, praetor, of course. Hank, senator, Third Cohort—oh, nice shoes, Hank! Ah, who have we here?"

Hazel, Frank, and Percy were the last ones.

"Terminus," Hazel said, "this is Percy Jackson. Percy, this is Terminus, the god of boundaries."

"New, eh?" said the god. "Yes, *probatio* tablet. Fine. Ah, weapon in your pocket? Take it out! Take it out!"

Percy didn't know how Terminus could tell, but he took out his pen.

"Quite dangerous," Terminus said. "Leave it in the tray. Wait, where's my assistant? Julia!"

A little girl about six years old peeked out from behind the base of the statue. She had pigtails, a pink dress, and an impish grin with two missing teeth.

"Julia?" Terminus glanced behind him, and Julia scurried in the other direction. "Where did that girl go?"

Terminus looked the other way and caught sight of Julia before she could hide. The little girl squealed with delight.

"Oh, there you are," said the statue. "Front and center. Bring the tray."

Julia scrambled out and brushed off her dress. She picked up a tray and presented it to Percy. On it were several paring knives, a corkscrew, an oversized container of sun lotion, and a water bottle.

"You can pick up your weapon on the way out," Terminus said. "Julia will take good care of it. She's a trained professional."

The little girl nodded. "Pro-fess-ion-al." She said each syllable carefully, like she'd been practicing.

Percy glanced at Hazel and Frank, who didn't seem to find anything odd about this. Still, he wasn't wild about handing over a deadly weapon to a kid.

"The thing is," he said, "the pen returns to my pocket automatically, so even if I give it up—"

"Not to worry," Terminus assured him. "We'll make sure it doesn't wander off. Won't we, Julia?"

"Yes, Mr. Terminus."

Reluctantly, Percy put his pen on the tray.

"Now, a few rules, since you're new," Terminus said. "You are entering the boundaries of the city proper. Keep the peace inside the line. Yield to chariot traffic while walking on public roads. When you get to the Senate House, sit on the left-hand side. And, down there—do you see where I'm pointing?"

"Um," Percy said, "you don't have any hands."

Apparently this was a sore point for Terminus. His marble

face turned a dark shade of gray. "A smart aleck, eh? Well, Mr. Rule Flouter, right down there in the forum—Julia, point for me, please—"

Julia dutifully set down the security tray and pointed toward the main plaza.

"The shop with the blue awning," Terminus continued, "that's the general store. They sell tape measures. Buy one! I want those pants exactly one inch above the ankles and that hair regulation cut. And tuck your shirt in."

Hazel said, "Thank you, Terminus. We need to get going."

"Fine, fine, you may pass," the god said testily. "But stay on the right side of the road! And that rock right there—No, Hazel, look where I'm pointing. That rock is entirely too close to that tree. Move it two inches to the left."

Hazel did what she was told, and they continued down the path, Terminus still shouting orders at them while Julia did cartwheels across the grass.

"Is he always like that?" Percy asked.

"No," Hazel admitted. "Today he was laid back. Usually he's more obsessive/compulsive."

"He inhabits every boundary stone around the city," Frank said. "Kind of our last line of defense if the city's attacked."

"Terminus isn't so bad," Hazel added. "Just don't make him angry, or he'll force you to measure every blade of grass in the valley."

Percy filed that information. "And the kid? Julia?"

Hazel grinned. "Yeah, she's a cutie. Her parents live in the city. Come on. We'd better catch up to the senators."

As they approached the forum, Percy was struck by the sheer number of people. College-age kids were hanging out at the fountain. Several of them waved at the senators as they passed. One guy in his late twenties stood at a bakery counter, flirting with a young woman who was buying coffee. An older couple was watching a little boy in diapers and a miniature Camp Jupiter shirt toddle after seagulls. Merchants were opening their shops for the day, putting out signs in Latin that advertised pottery, jewelry, and half-price tickets for the Hippodrome.

"*All* these people are demigods?" Percy asked.

"Or descended from demigods," Hazel said. "Like I told you, it's a good place to go to college or raise a family without worrying about monster attacks every day. Maybe two, three hundred people live here? The veterans act as, like, advisers and reserve forces as needed, but mostly they're just citizens living their lives."

Percy imagined what that would be like: getting an apartment in this tiny replica of Rome, protected by the legion and Terminus the OCD border god. He imagined holding hands with Annabeth at a café. Maybe when they were older, watching their own kid chase seagulls across the forum...

He shook the idea out of his head. He couldn't afford to indulge in that kind of thinking. Most of his memories were gone, but he knew this place wasn't his home. He belonged somewhere else, with his other friends.

Besides, Camp Jupiter was in danger. If Juno was right, an attack was coming in less than five days. Percy imagined that sleeping woman's face—the face of Gaea—forming in the hills above camp. He imagined hordes of monsters descending into this valley.

If you don't succeed, Mars had warned, *there won't be any camp left to return to. Rome will be overrun, its legacy lost forever.*

He thought about the little girl Julia, the families with kids, his new friends in the Fifth Cohort, even those silly fauns. He didn't want to picture what might happen to them if this place was destroyed.

The senators made their way to a big white-domed building on the west end of the forum. Percy paused at the doorway, trying not to think about Julius Caesar getting slashed to death at a senate meeting. Then he took a deep breath and followed Hazel and Frank inside.

XIV

PERCY

THE SENATE HOUSE INTERIOR looked like a high school lecture hall. A semicircle of tiered seats faced a dais with a podium and two chairs. The chairs were empty, but one had a small velvet package on the seat.

Percy, Hazel, and Frank sat on the left side of the semicircle. The ten senators and Nico di Angelo occupied the rest of the front row. The upper rows were filled with several dozen ghosts and a few older veterans from the city, all in formal togas. Octavian stood in front with a knife and a Beanie Baby lion, just in case anyone needed to consult the god of cutesy collectibles. Reyna walked to the podium and raised her hand for attention.

"Right, this is an emergency meeting," she said. "We won't stand on formalities."

"I love formalities!" a ghost complained.

Reyna shot him a cross look.

"First of all," she said, "we're not here to vote on the quest itself. The quest has been issued by Mars Ultor, patron of Rome. We will obey his wishes. Nor are we here to debate the choice of Frank Zhang's companions."

"All three from the Fifth Cohort?" called out Hank from the Third. "That's not fair."

"And not smart," said the boy next to him. "We *know* the Fifth will mess up. They should take somebody *good*."

Dakota got up so fast, he spilled Kool-Aid from his flask. "We were plenty good last night when we whipped your *podex*, Larry!"

"Enough, Dakota," Reyna said. "Let's leave Larry's *podex* out of this. As quest leader, Frank has the right to choose his companions. He has chosen Percy Jackson and Hazel Levesque."

A ghost from the second row yelled, *"Absurdus!* Frank Zhang isn't even a full member of the legion! He's on *probatio.* A quest must be led by someone of centurion rank or higher. This is completely—"

"Cato," Reyna snapped. "We must obey the wishes of Mars Ultor. That means certain . . . adjustments."

Reyna clapped her hands, and Octavian came forward. He set down his knife and Beanie Baby and took the velvet package from the chair.

"Frank Zhang," he said, "come forward."

Frank glanced nervously at Percy. Then he got to his feet and approached the augur.

"It is my . . . pleasure," Octavian said, forcing out the last word, "to bestow upon you the Mural Crown for being first over the walls in siege warfare." Octavian handed him a bronze badge shaped like a laurel wreath. "Also, by order of Praetor Reyna, to promote you to the rank of centurion."

He handed Frank another badge, a bronze crescent, and the senate exploded in protest.

"He's still a probie!" one yelled.

"Impossible!" said another.

"Water cannon up my nose!" yelled a third.

"Silence!" Octavian's voice sounded a lot more commanding than it had the previous night on the battlefield. "Our praetor recognizes that no one below the rank of centurion may lead a quest. For good or ill, Frank must lead this quest —so our praetor has decreed that Frank Zhang must be made centurion."

Suddenly Percy understood what an effective speaker Octavian was. He sounded reasonable and supportive, but his expression was pained. He carefully crafted his words to put all the responsibility on Reyna. *This was her idea,* he seemed to say.

If it went wrong, Reyna was to blame. If only Octavian had been the one in charge, things would have been done more sensibly. But alas, he had no choice but to support Reyna, because Octavian was a loyal Roman soldier.

Octavian managed to convey all that without saying it, simultaneously calming the senate and sympathizing with them. For the first time, Percy realized this scrawny, funny looking scarecrow of a kid might be a dangerous enemy.

Reyna must have recognized this too. A look of irritation flashed across her face. "There is an opening for centurion," she said. "One of our officers, also a senator, has decided to step down. After ten years in the legion, she will retire to the city and attend college. Gwen of the Fifth Cohort, we thank you for your service."

Everyone turned to Gwen, who managed a brave smile. She looked tired from the previous night's ordeal, but also relieved. Percy couldn't blame her. Compared to getting skewered with a *pilum*, college sounded pretty good.

"As praetor," Reyna continued, "I have the right to replace officers. I admit it's unusual for a camper on *probatio* to rise directly to the rank of centurion, but I think we can agree... last night was unusual. Frank Zhang, your ID, please."

Frank removed the lead tablet from around his neck and handed it to Octavian.

"Your arm," Octavian said.

Frank held up his forearm. Octavian raised his hands to the heavens. "We accept Frank Zhang, Son of Mars, to the Twelfth Legion Fulminata for his first year of service. Do you pledge your life to the senate and people of Rome?"

Frank muttered something like "Ud-dud." Then he cleared his throat and managed: "I do."

The senators shouted, *"Senatus Populusque Romanus!"*

Fire blazed on Frank's arm. For a moment his eyes filled with terror, and Percy was afraid his friend might pass out. Then the smoke and flame died, and new marks were seared onto Frank's skin: SPQR, an image of crossed spears, and a single stripe, representing the first year of service.

"You may sit down." Octavian glanced at the audience as if to say: *This wasn't my idea, folks.*

"Now," Reyna said, "we must discuss the quest."

The senators shifted and muttered as Frank returned to his seat.

"Did it hurt?" Percy whispered.

Frank looked at his forearm, which was still steaming. "Yeah. A lot." He seemed mystified by the badges in his hand —the centurion's mark and the Mural Crown—like he wasn't sure what to do with them.

"Here." Hazel's eyes shone with pride. "Let me."

She pinned the medals to Frank's shirt.

Percy smiled. He'd only known Frank for a day, but he felt proud of him too. "You deserve it, man," he said. "What you did last night? Natural leadership."

Frank scowled. "But *centurion*—"

"Centurion Zhang," called Octavian. "Did you hear the question?"

Frank blinked. "Um . . . sorry. What?"

Octavian turned to the senate and smirked, like *What did I tell you?*

"I was *asking*," Octavian said like he was talking to a three-year-old, "if you have a plan for the quest. Do you even know where you are going?"

"Um . . ."

Hazel put her hand on Frank's shoulder and stood. "Weren't *you* listening last night, Octavian? Mars was pretty clear. We're going to the land beyond the gods—Alaska."

The senators squirmed in their togas. Some of the ghosts shimmered and disappeared. Even Reyna's metal dogs rolled over on their backs and whimpered.

Finally Senator Larry stood. "I know what Mars said, but

that's crazy. Alaska is cursed! They call it the land beyond the gods for a reason. It's so far north, the Roman gods have no power there. The place is swarming with monsters. No demigod has come back from there alive since—"

"Since you lost your eagle," Percy said.

Larry was so startled, he fell back on his *podex*.

"Look," Percy continued, "I know I'm new here. I know you guys don't like to mention that massacre in the nineteen-eighties—"

"He mentioned it!" one of the ghosts whimpered.

"—But don't you get it?" Percy continued. "The Fifth Cohort led that expedition. We failed, and we have to be responsible for making things right. That's why Mars is sending us. This giant, the son of Gaea—he's the one who defeated your forces thirty years ago. I'm sure of it. Now he's sitting up there in Alaska with a chained death god, and all your old equipment. He's mustering his armies and sending them south to attack this camp."

"Really?" Octavian said. "You seem to know a lot about our enemy's plans, Percy Jackson."

Most insults Percy could shrug off—being called weak or stupid or whatever. But it dawned on him that Octavian was calling him a spy—a traitor. That was such a foreign concept to Percy, so *not* who he was, he almost couldn't process the slur. When he did, his shoulders tensed. He was tempted to smack Octavian on the head again, but he realized Octavian was baiting him, trying to make him look unstable.

Percy took a deep breath.

"We're going to confront this son of Gaea," he said,

managing to keep his composure. "We'll get back your eagle and unchain this god..." He glanced at Hazel. "Thanatos, right?"

She nodded. "Letus, in Roman. But his old Greek name is Thanatos. When it comes to Death...we're happy to let him stay Greek."

Octavian sighed in exasperation. "Well, *whatever* you call him...how do you expect to do all this and get back by the Feast of Fortuna? That's the evening of the twenty-fourth. It's the twentieth now. Do you even know where to look? Do you even know who this son of Gaea is?"

"Yes." Hazel spoke with such certainty that even Percy was surprised. "I don't know *exactly* where to look, but I have a pretty good idea. The giant's name is Alcyoneus."

That name seemed to lower the temperature in the room by fifty degrees. The senators shivered.

Reyna gripped her podium. "How do you know this, Hazel? Because you're a child of Pluto?"

Nico di Angelo had been so quiet, Percy had almost forgotten he was there. Now he stood in his black toga.

"Praetor, if I may," he said. "Hazel and I...we learned a little about the giants from our father. Each giant was bred specifically to oppose one of the twelve Olympian gods—to usurp that god's domain. The king of giants was Porphyrion, the anti-Jupiter. But the *eldest* giant was Alcyoneus. He was born to oppose Pluto. That's why we know of him in particular."

Reyna frowned. "Indeed? You sound *quite* familiar with him."

Nico picked at the edge of his toga. "Anyway...the giants

were hard to kill. According to prophecy, they could only be defeated by gods and demigods working together."

Dakota belched. "Sorry, did you say gods and demigods . . . like fighting side by side? That could never happen!"

"It *has* happened," Nico said. "In the first giant war, the gods called on heroes to join them, and they were victorious. Whether it could happen again, I don't know. But with Alcyoneus . . . *he* was different. He was completely immortal, impossible to kill by god or demigod, as long as he remained in his home territory—the place where he was born."

Nico paused to let that sink in. "And if Alcyoneus has been reborn in Alaska—"

"Then he can't be defeated there," Hazel finished. "Ever. By any means. Which is why our nineteen-eighties expedition was doomed to fail."

Another round of arguing and shouting broke out.

"The quest is impossible!" shouted a senator.

"We're doomed!" cried a ghost.

"More Kool-Aid!" yelled Dakota.

"Silence!" Reyna called. "Senators, we must act like Romans. Mars has given us this quest, and we have to believe it *is* possible. These three demigods must travel to Alaska. They must free Thanatos and return before the Feast of Fortuna. If they can retrieve the lost eagle in the process, so much the better. All we can do is advise them and make sure they have a plan."

Reyna looked at Percy without much hope. "You *do* have a plan?"

Percy wanted to step forward bravely and say, *No, I don't!*

That was the truth, but looking around at all the nervous faces, Percy knew he couldn't say it.

"First, I need to understand something." He turned toward Nico. "I thought Pluto was the god of the dead. Now I hear about this other guy, Thanatos, and the Doors of Death from that prophecy—the Prophecy of Seven. What does all that mean?"

Nico took a deep breath. "Okay. Pluto is the god of the Underworld, but the actual god of death, the one who's responsible for making sure souls go to the afterlife and stay there—that's Pluto's lieutenant, Thanatos. He's like . . . well, imagine Life and Death are two different countries. Everybody would like to be in Life, right? So there's a guarded border to keep people from crossing back over without permission. But it's a *big* border, with lots of holes in the fence. Pluto tries to seal up the breaches, but new ones keep popping up all the time. That's why he depends on Thanatos, who's like the border patrol, the police."

"Thanatos catches souls," Percy said, "and deports them back to the Underworld."

"Exactly," Nico said. "But now Thanatos has been captured, chained up."

Frank raised his hand. "Uh . . . how do you chain Death?"

"It's been done before," Nico said. "In the old days, a guy named Sisyphus tricked Death and tied him up. Another time, Hercules wrestled him to the ground."

"And now a giant has captured him," Percy said. "So if we could free Thanatos, then the dead would stay dead?" He glanced at Gwen. "Um . . . no offense."

"It's more complicated than that," Nico said.

Octavian rolled his eyes. "Why does *that* not surprise me?"

"You mean the Doors of Death," Reyna said, ignoring Octavian. "They are mentioned in the Prophecy of Seven, which sent the first expedition to Alaska—"

Cato the ghost snorted. "We all know how that turned out! We Lares remember!"

The other ghosts grumbled in agreement.

Nico put his finger to his lips. Suddenly all the Lares went silent. Some looked alarmed, like their mouths had been glued together. Percy wished he had that power over certain living people...like Octavian, for instance.

"Thanatos is only part of the solution," Nico explained. "The Doors of Death...well, that's a concept even I don't completely understand. There are many ways into the Underworld—the River Styx, the Door of Orpheus—plus smaller escape routes that open up from time to time. With Thanatos imprisoned, all those exits will be easier to use. Sometimes it might work to our advantage and let a friendly soul come back—like Gwen here. More often, it will benefit evil souls and monsters, the sneaky ones who are looking to escape. Now, the Doors of Death—those are the personal doors of Thanatos, his fast lane between Life and Death. Only Thanatos is supposed to know where they are, and the location shifts over the ages. If I understand correctly, the Doors of Death have been forced open. Gaea's minions have seized control of them—"

"Which means Gaea controls who can come back from the dead," Percy guessed.

Nico nodded. "She can pick and choose who to let out—the worst monsters, the most evil souls. If we rescue Thanatos, that means at least he can catch souls again and send them below. Monsters will die when we kill them, like they used to, and we'll get a little breathing room. But unless we're able to retake the Doors of Death, our enemies won't stay down for long. They'll have an easy way back to the world of the living."

"So we can catch them and deport them," Percy summed up, "but they'll just keep coming back across."

"In a depressing nutshell, yes," Nico said.

Frank scratched his head. "But Thanatos knows where the doors are, right? If we free him, he can retake them."

"I don't think so," Nico said. "Not alone. He's no match for Gaea. That would take a massive quest . . . an army of the best demigods."

"Foes bear arms to the Doors of Death," Reyna said. "That's the Prophecy of Seven . . ." She looked at Percy, and for just a moment he could see how scared she was. She did a good job of hiding it, but Percy wondered if she'd had nightmares about Gaea too—if she'd seen visions of what would happen when the camp was invaded by monsters that couldn't be killed. "If this begins the ancient prophecy, we don't have resources to send an army to these Doors of Death *and* protect the camp. I can't imagine even sparing seven demigods—"

"First things first." Percy tried to sound confident, though he could feel the level of panic rising in the room. "I don't know who the seven are, or what that old prophecy means, exactly. But first we have to free Thanatos. Mars told us we only needed three people for the quest to Alaska. Let's concentrate on succeeding with that and getting back before the Feast of Fortuna. Then we can worry about the Doors of Death."

"Yeah," Frank said in a small voice. "That's probably enough for one week."

"So you *do* have a plan?" Octavian asked skeptically.

Percy looked at his teammates. "We go to Alaska as fast as possible..."

"And we improvise," Hazel said.

"A lot," Frank added.

Reyna studied them. She looked like she was mentally writing her own obituary.

"Very well," she said. "Nothing remains except for us to vote what support we can give the quest—transportation, money, magic, weapons."

"Praetor, if I may," Octavian said.

"Oh, great," Percy muttered. "Here it comes."

"The camp is in grave danger," Octavian said. "*Two* gods have warned us we will be attacked four days from now. We must not spread our resources too thin, especially by funding projects that have a slim chance of success."

Octavian looked at the three of them with pity, as if to say, *Poor little things.* "Mars has clearly chosen the least likely candidates for this quest. Perhaps that is because he considers them the most expendable. Perhaps Mars is playing the long odds. Whatever the case, he wisely *didn't* order a massive expedition, nor did he ask us to fund their adventure. I say we keep our resources here and defend the camp. This is where the battle will be lost or won. If these three succeed, wonderful! But they should do so by their own ingenuity."

An uneasy murmur passed through the crowd. Frank jumped to his feet. Before he could start a fight, Percy said, "Fine! No problem. But at least give us transportation. Gaea is the earth goddess, right? Going overland, across the earth— I'm guessing we should avoid that. Plus, it'll be too slow."

Octavian laughed. "Would you like us to charter you an airplane?"

The idea made Percy nauseous. "No. Air travel...I have a feeling that would be bad, too. But a boat. Can you at least give us a boat?"

Hazel made a grunting sound. Percy glanced over. She shook her head and mouthed, *Fine. I'm fine.*

"A boat!" Octavian turned to the senators. "The son of Neptune wants a boat. Sea travel has never been the Roman way, but he isn't much of a Roman!"

"Octavian," Reyna said sternly, "a boat is little enough to ask. And providing no other aid seems very—"

"Traditional!" Octavian exclaimed. "It is very traditional. Let us see if these questers have the strength to survive without help, like true Romans!"

More muttering filled the chamber. The senators' eyes moved back and forth between Octavian and Reyna, watching the test of wills.

Reyna straightened in her chair. "Very well," she said tightly. "We'll put it to a vote. Senators, the motion is as follows: The quest shall go to Alaska. The senate shall provide full access to the Roman navy docked at Alameda. No other aid will be forthcoming. The three adventurers will survive or fail on their own merits. All in favor?"

Every senator's hand went up.

"The motion is passed." Reyna turned to Frank. "Centurion, your party is excused. The senate has other matters to discuss. And, Octavian, if I may confer with you for a moment."

Percy was incredibly glad to see the sunlight. In that dark hall, with all those eyes on him, he'd felt like the world was riding on his shoulders—and he was fairly sure he'd had that experience before.

He filled his lungs with fresh air.

Hazel picked up a large emerald from the path and slipped it in her pocket. "So . . . we're pretty much toast?"

Frank nodded miserably. "If either of you wants to back out, I wouldn't blame you."

"Are you kidding?" Hazel said. "And pull sentry duty for the rest of the week?"

Frank managed a smile. He turned to Percy.

Percy gazed across the forum. *Stay put,* Annabeth had said in his dream. But if he stayed put, this camp would be destroyed. He looked up at the hills, and imagined Gaea's face smiling in the shadows and ridges. *You can't win, little demigod,* she seemed to say. *Serve me by staying, or serve me by going.*

Percy made a silent vow: After the Feast of Fortuna, he would find Annabeth. But for now, he had to act. He couldn't let Gaea win.

"I'm with you," he told Frank. "Besides, I want to check out the Roman navy."

They were only halfway across the forum when some called, "Jackson!" Percy turned and saw Octavian jogging toward them.

"What do you want?" Percy asked.

Octavian smiled. "Already decided I'm your enemy? That's a rash choice, Percy. I'm a loyal Roman."

Frank snarled. "You backstabbing, slimy—" Both Percy and Hazel had to restrain him.

"Oh, dear," Octavian said. "Hardly the right behavior for a new centurion. Jackson, I only followed you because Reyna charged me with a message. She wants you to report to the *principia* without your—ah—two lackeys, here. Reyna will meet you there after the senate adjourns. She'd like a private word with you before you leave on your quest."

"What about?" Percy said.

"I'm sure I don't know." Octavian smiled wickedly. "The last person she had a private talk with was Jason Grace. And that was the last time I ever saw him. Good luck and good-bye, Percy Jackson."

XV

PERCY

PERCY WAS GLAD RIPTIDE HAD RETURNED to his pocket. Judging from Reyna's expression, he thought he might need to defend himself.

She stormed into the *principia* with her purple cloak billowing, and her greyhounds at her feet. Percy was sitting in one of the praetor chairs that he'd pulled to the visitor's side, which maybe wasn't the proper thing to do. He started to get up.

"Stay seated," Reyna growled. "You leave after lunch. We have a lot to discuss."

She plunked down her dagger so hard, the jelly-bean bowl rattled. Aurum and Argentum took their posts on her left and right and fixed their ruby eyes on Percy.

"What'd I do wrong?" Percy asked. "If it's about the chair—"

"It's not you." Reyna scowled. "I *hate* senate meetings. When Octavian gets talking..."

Percy nodded. "You're a warrior. Octavian is a talker. Put him in front of the senate, and suddenly *he* becomes the powerful one."

She narrowed her eyes. "You're smarter than you look."

"Gee, thanks. I hear Octavian might get elected praetor, assuming the camp survives that long."

"Which brings us to the subject of doomsday," Reyna said, "and how you might help prevent it. But before I place the fate of Camp Jupiter in your hands, we need to get a few things straight."

She sat down and put a ring on the table—a band of silver etched with a sword-and-torch design, like Reyna's tattoo. "Do you know what this is?"

"The sign of your mom," Percy said. "The...uh, war goddess." He tried to remember the name but he didn't want to get it wrong—something like bologna. Or salami?

"Bellona, yes." Reyna scrutinized him carefully. "You don't remember where you saw this ring before? You really don't remember me or my sister, Hylla?"

Percy shook his head. "I'm sorry."

"It would've been four years ago."

"Just before you came to camp."

Reyna frowned. "How did you—?"

"You've got four stripes on your tattoo. Four years."

Reyna looked at her forearm. "Of course. It seems so long ago. I suppose you wouldn't recall me even if you *had* your memory. I was just a little girl—one attendant among so many at the spa. But you spoke with my sister, just before you and that other one, Annabeth, destroyed our home."

Percy tried to remember. He really did. For some reason, Annabeth and he had visited a spa and decided to destroy it. He couldn't imagine why. Maybe they hadn't liked the deep-tissue massage? Maybe they'd gotten bad manicures?

"It's a blank," he said. "Since your dogs aren't attacking me, I hope you'll believe me. I'm telling the truth."

Aurum and Argentum snarled. Percy got the feeling they were thinking, *Please lie. Please lie.*

Reyna tapped the silver ring.

"I believe you're sincere," she said. "But not everyone at camp does. Octavian thinks you're a spy. He thinks you were sent here by Gaea to find our weaknesses and distract us. He believes the old legends about the Greeks."

"Old legends?"

Reyna's hand rested halfway between her dagger and the jelly beans. Percy had a feeling that if she made a sudden move, she wouldn't be grabbing for the candy.

"Some believe Greek demigods still exist," she said, "heroes who follow the older forms of the gods. There are legends of battles between Roman and Greek heroes in relatively modern times—the American Civil War, for instance. I have no proof of this, and if our Lares know anything, they refuse to say. But Octavian believes the Greeks are still around, plotting our downfall, working with the forces of Gaea. He thinks you are one of them."

"Is that what you believe?"

"I believe you came from *somewhere*," she said. "You're important, and dangerous. Two gods have taken a special interest in you since you arrived, so I can't believe you'd work against Olympus...or Rome." She shrugged. "Of course, I could be wrong. Perhaps the gods sent you here to test my judgment. But I think...I think you were sent here to make up for the loss of Jason."

Jason... Percy couldn't go very far in this camp without hearing that name.

"The way you talk about him..." Percy said. "Were you two a couple?"

Reyna's eyes bored into him—like the eyes of a hungry wolf. Percy had seen enough hungry wolves to know.

"We might have been," Reyna said, "given time. Praetors work closely together. It's common for them to become romantically involved. But Jason was only praetor for a few months before he disappeared. Ever since then, Octavian has been pestering me, agitating for new elections. I've resisted. I need a partner in power—but I'd prefer someone like Jason. A warrior, not a schemer."

She waited. Percy realized she was sending him a silent invitation.

His throat went dry. "Oh...you mean...oh."

"I believe the gods sent you to help me," Reyna said. "I don't understand where you come from, any more than I understood it four years ago. But I think your arrival is some sort of repayment. You destroyed my home once. Now you've been sent to save my home. I don't hold a grudge against you for the past, Percy. My sister hates you still, it's true, but Fate brought me here to Camp Jupiter. I've done well. All I ask is that you work with me for the future. I intend to save this camp."

The metal dogs glared at him, their mouths frozen in snarl mode. Percy found Reyna's eyes a lot harder to meet.

"Look, I'll help," he promised. "But I'm new here. You've got a lot of good people who know this camp better than I do. If we succeed on this quest, Hazel and Frank will be heroes. You could ask one of them—"

"Please," Reyna said. "No one will follow a child of Pluto. There's something about that girl ... rumors about where she came from. ... No, she won't do. As for Frank Zhang, he has a good heart, but he's hopelessly naïve and inexperienced. Besides, if the others found out about his family history at this camp—"

"Family history?"

"The point is, Percy, *you* are the real power on this quest. *You* are a seasoned veteran. I've seen what you can do. A son of Neptune wouldn't be my first choice, but if you return successfully from this mission, the legion might be saved. The praetorship will be yours for the taking. Together, you and I could expand the power of Rome. We could raise an army and find the Doors of Death, crush Gaea's forces once and for all. You would find me a very helpful ... friend."

She said that word like it could have several meanings, and he could pick which one.

Percy's feet started tapping on the floor, anxious to run. "Reyna ... . I'm honored, and all. Seriously. But I've got a girlfriend. And I don't want power, or a praetorship."

Percy was afraid he'd make her mad. Instead she just raised her eyebrows.

"A man who turns down power?" she said. "That's not very Roman of you. Just think about it. In four days, I have to make a choice. If we are to fight off an invasion, we *must* have two strong praetors. I'd prefer you, but if you fail on your quest, or don't come back, or refuse my offer...Well, I'll work with Octavian. I mean to save this camp, Percy Jackson. Things are worse than you realize."

Percy remembered what Frank said about the monster attacks getting more frequent. "How bad?"

Reyna's nails dug into the table. "Even the senate doesn't know the whole truth. I've asked Octavian not to share his auguries, or we'd have mass panic. He's seen a great army marching south, more than we can possibly defeat. They're led by a giant—"

"Alcyoneus?"

"I don't think so. If he is truly invulnerable in Alaska, he'd be foolish to come here himself. It must be one of his brothers."

"Great," Percy said. "So we've got two giants to worry about."

The praetor nodded. "Lupa and her wolves are trying to slow them down, but this force is too strong even for them. The enemy will be here soon—by the Feast of Fortuna at the very latest."

Percy shuddered. He'd seen Lupa in action. He knew all about the wolf goddess and her pack. If this enemy was too powerful for Lupa, Camp Jupiter didn't stand a chance.

Reyna read his expression. "Yes, it's bad, but not hopeless.

If you succeed in bringing back our eagle, if you release Death so we can actually *kill* our enemies, then we stand a chance. And there's one more possibility. . . ."

Reyna slid the silver ring across the table. "I can't give you much help, but your journey will take you close to Seattle. I'm asking you for a favor, which may also help you. Find my sister Hylla."

"Your sister . . . the one who hates me?"

"Oh, yes," Reyna agreed. "She would love to kill you. But show her that ring as a token from me, and she may help you instead."

"*May?*"

"I can't speak for her. In fact . . ." Reyna frowned. "In fact I haven't spoken to her in weeks. She's gone silent. With these armies passing through—"

"You want me to check on her," Percy guessed. "Make sure she's okay."

"Partially, yes. I can't imagine she's been overcome. My sister has a powerful force. Her territory is well defended. But if you can find her, she could offer you valuable help. It could mean the difference between success and failure on your quest. And if you tell her what's happening here—"

"She might send help?" Percy asked.

Reyna didn't answer, but Percy could see the desperation in her eyes. She was terrified, grasping for *anything* that could save her camp. No wonder she wanted Percy's help. She was the only praetor. The defense of the camp rested on her shoulders alone.

Percy took the ring. "I'll find her. Where do I look? What kind force does she have?"

"Don't worry. Just go to Seattle. They'll find you."

That didn't sound encouraging, but Percy slipped the ring onto his leather necklace with his beads and his *probatio* tablet. "Wish me luck."

"Fight well, Percy Jackson," Reyna said. "And thank you."

He could tell the audience was over. Reyna was having trouble holding herself together, keeping up the image of the confident commander. She needed some time by herself.

But at the door of the *principia,* Percy couldn't resist turning. "How did we destroy your home—that spa where you lived?"

The metal greyhounds growled. Reyna snapped her fingers to silence them.

"You destroyed the power of our mistress," she said. "You freed some prisoners who took revenge on all of us who lived on the island. My sister and I . . . well, we survived. It was difficult. But in the long run, I think we are better off away from that place."

"Still, I'm sorry," Percy said. "If I hurt you, I'm sorry."

Reyna gazed at him for a long time, as if trying to translate his words. "An apology? Not very Roman at all, Percy Jackson. You'd make an interesting praetor. I hope you'll think about my offer."

XVI

PERCY

LUNCH FELT LIKE A FUNERAL PARTY. Everybody ate. People talked in hushed tones. Nobody seemed particularly happy. The other campers kept glancing over at Percy like he was the corpse of honor.

Reyna made a brief speech wishing them luck. Octavian ripped open a Beanie Baby and pronounced grave omens and hard times ahead, but predicted the camp would be saved by an unexpected hero (whose initials were probably OCTAVIAN). Then the other campers went off to their afternoon classes— gladiator fighting, Latin lessons, paintball with ghosts, eagle training, and a dozen other activities that sounded better than a suicide quest. Percy followed Hazel and Frank to the barracks to pack.

Percy didn't have much. He'd cleaned up his backpack from his trip south and had kept most of his Bargain Mart supplies. He had a fresh pair of jeans and an extra purple T-shirt from the camp quartermaster, plus some nectar, ambrosia, snacks, a little mortal money, and camping supplies. At lunch, Reyna had handed him a scroll of introduction from the praetor and camp senate. Supposedly, any retired legionnaires they met on the trip would help them if shown the letter. He also kept his leather necklace with the beads, the silver ring, and the *probatio* tablet, and of course he had Riptide in his pocket. He folded his tattered orange T-shirt and left it on his bunk.

"I'll be back," he said. He felt pretty stupid talking to a T-shirt, but he was really thinking of Annabeth, and his old life. "I'm not leaving for good. But I have to help these guys. They took me in. They deserve to survive."

The T-shirt didn't answer, thankfully.

One of their roommates, Bobby, gave them a ride to the border of the valley on Hannibal the elephant. From the hilltops, Percy could see everything below. The Little Tiber snaked across golden pastures where the unicorns were grazing. The temples and forums of New Rome gleamed in the sunlight. On the Field of Mars, engineers were hard at work, pulling down the remains of last night's fort and setting up barricades for a game of deathball. A normal day for Camp Jupiter—but on the northern horizon, storm clouds were gathering. Shadows moved across the hills, and Percy imagined the face of Gaea getting closer and closer.

Work with me for the future, Reyna had said. *I intend to save this camp.*

Looking down at the valley, Percy understood why she cared so much. Even though he was new to Camp Jupiter, he felt a fierce desire to protect this place. A safe haven where demigods could build their lives—he wanted that to be part of his future. Maybe not the way Reyna imagined, but if he could share this place with Annabeth...

They got off the elephant. Bobby wished them a safe journey. Hannibal wrapped the three questers with his trunk. Then the elephant taxi service headed back into the valley.

Percy sighed. He turned to Hazel and Frank and tried to think of something upbeat to say.

A familiar voice said, "IDs, please."

A statue of Terminus appeared at the summit of the hill. The god's marble face frowned irritably. "Well? Come along!"

"You again?" Percy asked. "I thought you just guarded the city."

Terminus huffed. "Glad to see you, too, Mr. Rule Flouter. Normally, yes, I guard the city, but for international departures, I like to provide extra security at the camp borders. You really should've allowed two hours before your planned departure time, you know. But we'll have to make do. Now, come over here so I can pat you down."

"But you don't have—" Percy stopped himself. "Uh, sure."

He stood next to the armless statue. Terminus conducted a rigorous mental pat down.

"You seem to be clean," Terminus decided. "Do you have anything to declare?"

"Yes," Percy said. "I declare this is stupid."

"Hmph! *Probatio* tablet: Percy Jackson, Fifth Cohort, son of Neptune. Fine, go. Hazel Levesque, daughter of Pluto. Fine. Any foreign currency or, ahem, precious metals to declare?"

"No," she muttered.

"Are you sure?" Terminus asked. "Because last time—"

"No!"

"Well, this is a grumpy bunch," said the god. "Quest travelers! Always in a rush. Now, let's see—Frank Zhang. Ah! Centurion? Well done, Frank. And that haircut is regulation perfect. I approve! Off you go, then, Centurion Zhang. Do you need any directions today?"

"No. No, I guess not."

"Just down to the BART station," Terminus said anyway. "Change trains at Twelfth Street in Oakland. You want Fruitvale Station. From there, you can walk or take the bus to Alameda."

"You guys don't have a magical BART train or something?" Percy asked.

"Magic trains!" Terminus scoffed. "You'll be wanting your own security lane and a pass to the executive lounge next. Just travel safely, and watch out for Polybotes. Talk about scofflaws —bah! I wish I could throttle him with my bare hands."

"Wait—who?" Percy asked.

Terminus made a straining expression, like he was flexing his nonexistent biceps. "Ah, well. Just be careful of him. I imagine he can smell a son of Neptune a mile away. Out you go, now. Good luck!"

An invisible force kicked them across the boundary. When Percy looked back, Terminus was gone. In fact, the entire valley was gone. The Berkeley Hills seemed to be free of any Roman camp.

Percy looked at his friends. "Any idea what Terminus was talking about? Watch out for ... Political something or other?"

"Poh-LIB-uh-tease?" Hazel sounded out the name carefully. "Never heard of him."

"Sounds Greek," Frank said.

"That narrows it down." Percy sighed. "Well, we probably just appeared on the smell radar for every monster within five miles. We'd better get moving."

It took them two hours to reach the docks in Alameda. Compared to Percy's last few months, the trip was easy. No monsters attacked. Nobody looked at Percy like he was a homeless wild child.

Frank had stored his spear, bow, and quiver in a long bag made for skis. Hazel's cavalry sword was wrapped in a bedroll slung on her back. Together the three of them looked like normal high schoolers on their way to an overnight trip. They walked to Rockridge Station, bought their tickets with mortal money, and hopped on the BART train.

They got off in Oakland. They had to walk through some rough neighborhoods, but nobody bothered them. Whenever the local gang members came close enough to look in Percy's eyes, they quickly veered away. He'd perfected his wolf stare over the last few months—a look that said: *However bad you think you are, I'm worse.* After strangling sea monsters and running over gorgons in a police car, Percy wasn't scared of gangs. Pretty much nothing in the mortal world scared him anymore.

In the late afternoon, they made it to the Alameda docks. Percy looked out over San Francisco Bay and breathed in the salty sea air. Immediately he felt better. This was his father's domain. Whatever they faced, he'd have the upper hand as long as they were at sea.

Dozens of boats were moored at the docks—everything from fifty-foot yachts to ten-foot fishing boats. He scanned the slips for some sort of magic vessel—a trireme, maybe, or a dragon-headed warship like he'd seen in his dreams.

"Um...you guys know what we're looking for?"

Hazel and Frank shook their heads.

"I didn't even know we *had* a navy." Hazel sounded as if she wished there wasn't one.

"Oh..." Frank pointed. "You don't think...?"

At the end of the dock was a tiny boat, like a dinghy, covered in a purple tarp. Embroidered in faded gold along the canvas was *S.P.Q.R.*

Percy's confidence wavered. "No way."

He uncovered the boat, his hands working the knots like he'd been doing it his whole life. Under the tarp was an old steel rowboat with no oars. The boat had been painted dark blue at one point, but the hull was so crusted with tar and salt it looked like one massive nautical bruise.

On the bow, the name *Pax* was still readable, lettered in gold. Painted eyes drooped sadly at the water level, as if the boat were about to fall asleep. On board were two benches, some steel wool, an old cooler, and a mound of frayed rope with one end tied to the mooring. At the bottom of the boat, a plastic bag and two empty Coke cans floated in several inches of scummy water.

"Behold," Frank said. "The mighty Roman navy."

"There's got to be a mistake," Hazel said. "This is a piece of junk."

Percy imagined Octavian laughing at them, but he decided not to let it get him down. The *Pax* was still a boat. He jumped aboard, and the hull hummed under his feet, responding to his presence. He gathered up the garbage in the cooler and put it on the dock. He willed the scummy water to flow over the sides and out of the boat. Then he pointed at the steel wool and it flew across the floor, scrubbing and polishing so fast, the steel began to smoke. When it was done, the boat was clean. Percy pointed at the rope, and it untied itself from the dock.

No oars, but that didn't matter. Percy could tell that the boat was ready to move, just awaiting his command.

"This'll do," he said. "Hop in."

Hazel and Frank looked a little stunned, but they climbed aboard. Hazel seemed especially nervous. When they had settled on the seats, Percy concentrated, and the boat slipped away from the dock.

Juno was right, you know. The sleepy voice of Gaea whispered in Percy's mind, startling him so badly the boat rocked. *You could have chosen a new life in the sea. You would have been safe from me there. Now it's too late. You chose pain and misery. You're part of my plan, now—my important little pawn.*

"Get off my ship," Percy growled.

"Uh, what?" Frank asked.

Percy waited, but the voice of Gaea was silent.

"Nothing," he said. "Let's see what this rowboat can do."

He turned the boat to the north, and in no time they were speeding along at fifteen knots, heading for the Golden Gate Bridge.

XVII

HAZEL

HAZEL HATED BOATS.

She got seasick so easily, it was more like sea plague. She hadn't mentioned this to Percy. She didn't want to mess up the quest, but she remembered how horrible her life had been when she and her mother had moved to Alaska—no roads. Everywhere they went, they'd had to take the train or a boat.

She hoped her condition might have improved since she'd come back from the dead. Obviously not. And this little boat, the *Pax*, looked so much like that other boat they'd had in Alaska. It brought back bad memories. . . .

As soon as they left the dock, Hazel's stomach started to churn. By the time they passed the piers along the San Francisco Embarcadero, she felt so woozy she thought she was hallucinating. They sped by a pack of sea lions lounging on the docks, and she swore she saw an old homeless guy sitting among them. From across the water, the old man pointed a bony finger at Percy and mouthed something like *Don't even think about it*.

"Did you see that?" Hazel asked.

Percy's face was red in the sunset. "Yeah. I've been here before. I...I don't know. I think I was looking for my girlfriend."

"Annabeth," Frank said. "You mean, on your way to Camp Jupiter?"

Percy frowned. "No. Before that." He scanned the city like he was still looking for Annabeth until they passed under the Golden Gate Bridge and turned north.

Hazel tried to settle her stomach by thinking of pleasant things—the euphoria she'd felt last night when they'd won the war games, riding Hannibal into the enemy keep, Frank's sudden transformation into a leader. He'd looked like a different person when he'd scaled the walls, calling on the Fifth Cohort to attack. The way he'd swept the defenders off the battlements...Hazel had never seen him like that before. She'd been so proud to pin the centurion's badge to his shirt.

Then her thoughts turned to Nico. Before they had left, her brother had pulled her aside to wish her luck. Hazel hoped he'd stay at Camp Jupiter to help defend it, but he said he'd be leaving today—heading back to the Underworld.

"Dad needs all the help he can get," he said. "The Fields of Punishment look like a prison riot. The Furies can barely keep order. Besides...I'm going to try to track some of the escaping souls. Maybe I can find the Doors of Death from the other side."

"Be careful," Hazel said. "If Gaea is guarding those doors—"

"Don't worry." Nico smiled. "I know how to stay hidden. Just take care of yourself. The closer you get to Alaska...I'm not sure if it'll make the blackouts better or worse."

Take care of myself, Hazel thought bitterly. As if there was any way the quest would end well for her.

"If we free Thanatos," Hazel told Nico, "I may never see you again. Thanatos will send me back to the Underworld...."

Nico took her hand. His fingers were so pale, it was hard to believe Hazel and he shared the same godly father.

"I wanted to give you a chance at Elysium," he said. "That was the best I could do for you. But now, I wish there was another way. I don't want to lose my sister."

He didn't say the word *again*, but Hazel knew that's what he was thinking. For once, she didn't feel jealous of Bianca di Angelo. She just wished that she had more time with Nico and her friends at camp. She didn't want to die a second time.

"Good luck, Hazel," he said. Then he melted into the shadows—just like her father had seventy years before.

The boat shuddered, jolting Hazel back to the present. They entered the Pacific currents and skirted the rocky coastline of Marin County.

Frank held his ski bag across his lap. It passed over Hazel's knees like the safety bar on an amusement ride, which made her think of the time Sammy had taken her to the carnival during Mardi Gras.... She quickly pushed that memory aside. She couldn't risk a blackout.

"You okay?" Frank asked. "You look queasy."

"Seasickness," she confessed. "I didn't think it would be this bad."

Frank pouted like it was somehow his fault. He started digging in his pack. "I've got some nectar. And some crackers. Um, my grandmother says ginger helps...I don't have any of that, but—"

"It's okay." Hazel mustered a smile. "That's sweet of you, though."

Frank pulled out a saltine. It snapped in his big fingers. Cracker exploded everywhere.

Hazel laughed. "Gods, Frank.... Sorry. I shouldn't laugh."

"Uh, no problem," he said sheepishly. "Guess you don't want that one."

Percy wasn't paying much attention. He kept his eyes fixed on the shoreline. As they passed Stinson Beach, he pointed inland, where a single mountain rose above the green hills.

"That looks familiar," he said.

"Mount Tam," Frank said. "Kids at camp are always talking about it. Big battle happened on the summit, at the old Titan base."

Percy frowned. "Were either of you there?"

"No," Hazel said. "That was back in August, before I—um, before I got to camp. Jason told me about it. The legion destroyed the enemy's palace and about a million monsters. Jason had to battle Krios—hand-to hand combat with a Titan, if you can imagine."

"I can imagine," Percy muttered.

Hazel wasn't sure what he meant, but Percy *did* remind her of Jason, even though they looked nothing alike. They had the same aura of quiet power, plus a kind of sadness, like they'd seen their destiny and knew it was only a matter of time before they met a monster they couldn't beat.

Hazel understood the feeling. She watched the sun set in the ocean, and she knew she had less than a week to live. Whether or not their quest succeeded, her journey would be over by the Feast of Fortuna.

She thought about her first death, and the months leading up to it—her house in Seward, the six months she'd spent in Alaska, taking that little boat into Resurrection Bay at night, visiting that cursed island.

She realized her mistake too late. Her vision went black, and she slipped back in time.

Their rental house was a clapboard box suspended on pilings over the bay. When the train from Anchorage rolled by, the furniture shook and the pictures rattled on the walls. At night, Hazel fell asleep to the sound of icy water lapping against the rocks under the floorboards. The wind made the building creak and groan.

They had one room, with a hot plate and an icebox for a kitchen. One corner was curtained off for Hazel, where she kept her mattress and storage chest. She'd pinned her drawings and old photos of New Orleans on the walls, but that only made her homesickness worse.

Her mother was rarely home. She didn't go by Queen Marie anymore. She was just Marie, the hired help. She'd cook and clean all day at the diner on Third Avenue for fishermen, railroad workers, and the occasional crew of navy men. She'd come home smelling like Pine-Sol and fried fish.

At night, Marie Levesque would transform. The Voice took over, giving Hazel orders, putting her to work on their horrible project.

Winter was the worst. The Voice stayed longer because of the constant darkness. The cold was so intense, Hazel thought she would never be warm again.

When summer came, Hazel couldn't get enough sun. Every day of summer vacation, she stayed away from home as long as she could, but she couldn't walk around town. It was a small community. The other kids spread rumors about her—the witch's child who lived in the old shack by the docks. If she came too close, the kids jeered at her or threw bottles and rocks. The adults weren't much better.

Hazel could've made their lives miserable. She could've given them diamonds, pearls, or gold. Up here in Alaska, gold was easy. There was so much in the hills, Hazel could've buried the town without half trying. But she didn't really hate the locals for pushing her away. She couldn't blame them.

She spent the day walking the hills. She attracted ravens. They'd caw at her from the trees and wait for the shiny things that always appeared in her footsteps. The curse never seemed to bother them. She saw brown bears, too, but they kept their distance. When Hazel got thirsty, she'd find a snowmelt waterfall and drink cold, clean water until her throat hurt. She'd climb as high as she could and let the sunshine warm her face.

It wasn't a bad way to pass the time, but she knew eventually she'd have to go home.

Sometimes she thought about her father—that strange pale man in the silver-and-black suit. Hazel wished he'd come back and protect her from her mother, maybe use his powers to get rid of that awful Voice. If he was a god, he should be able to do that.

She looked up at the ravens and imagined they were his emissaries. Their eyes were dark and maniacal, like his. She wondered if they reported her movements to her father.

But Pluto had warned her mother about Alaska. It was a land beyond the gods. He couldn't protect them here. If he was watching Hazel, he didn't speak to her. She often wondered if she had imagined him. Her old life seemed as distant as the radio programs she listened to, or President Roosevelt talking about the war. Occasionally the locals would discuss the Japanese and some fighting on the outer islands of Alaska, but even that seemed far away—not nearly as scary as Hazel's problem.

One day in midsummer, she stayed out later than usual, chasing a horse.

She'd seen it first when she had heard a crunching sound behind her. She turned and saw a gorgeous tan roan stallion with a black mane—just like the one she'd ridden her last day in New Orleans, when Sammy had taken her to the stables. It could've been the same horse, though that was impossible. It was eating something off the path, and for a second, Hazel had the crazy impression it was munching one of the gold nuggets that always appeared in her wake.

"Hey, fella," she called.

The horse looked at her warily.

Hazel figured it must belong to someone. It was too well groomed, its coat too sleek for a wild horse. If she could get close enough...What? She could find its owner? Return it?

No, she thought. I just want to ride again.

She got within ten feet, and the horse bolted. She spent the rest of the afternoon trying to catch it—getting maddeningly close before it ran away again.

She lost track of time, which was easy to do with the summer sun staying up so long. Finally she stopped at a creek for a drink and looked at the sky, thinking it must be around three in the afternoon. Then she heard a train whistle from down in the valley. She realized it had to be the evening run to Anchorage, which meant it was ten at night.

She glared at the horse, grazing peacefully across the creek. "Are you trying to get me in trouble?"

The horse whinnied. Then...Hazel must've imagined it. The horse sped away in a blur of black and tan, faster than forked lightning—almost too quick for her eyes to register. Hazel didn't understand how, but the horse was *definitely* gone.

She stared at the spot where the horse had stood. A wisp of steam curled from the ground.

The train whistle echoed through the hills again, and she realized how much trouble she was in. She ran for home.

Her mother wasn't there. For a second Hazel felt relieved. Maybe her mom had had to work late. Maybe tonight they wouldn't have to make the journey.

Then she saw the wreckage. Hazel's curtain was pulled down. Her storage chest was open and her few clothes strewn across the floor. Her mattress had been shredded as if a lion had attacked it. Worst of all, her drawing pad was ripped to pieces. Her colored pencils were all broken. Pluto's birthday gift, Hazel's only luxury, had been destroyed. Pinned to the wall was a note in red on the last piece of drawing paper, in writing that was not her mother's: *Wicked girl. I'm waiting at the island. Don't disappoint me.* Hazel sobbed in despair. She wanted to ignore the summons. She wanted to run away, but there was nowhere to go. Besides, her mother was trapped. The Voice had promised that they were almost done with their task. If Hazel kept helping, her mother would be freed. Hazel didn't trust the Voice, but she didn't see any other option.

She took the rowboat—a little skiff her mother had bought with a few gold nuggets from a fisherman, who had a tragic accident with his nets the next day. They had only one boat, but Hazel's mother seemed capable on occasion of reaching the island without any transportation. Hazel had learned not to ask about that.

Even in midsummer, chunks of ice swirled in Resurrection Bay. Seals glided by her boat, looking at Hazel hopefully, sniffing for fish scraps. In the middle of the bay, the glistening back of a whale raked the surface.

As always, the rocking of the boat made her stomach queasy. She stopped once to be sick over the side. The sun was finally going down over the mountains, turning the sky blood red.

She rowed toward the bay's mouth. After several minutes,

she turned and looked ahead. Right in front of her, out of the fog, the island materialized—an acre of pine trees, boulders, and snow with a black sand beach.

If the island had a name, she didn't know it. Once Hazel had made the mistake of asking the townsfolk, but they had stared at her like she was crazy.

"Ain't no island there," said one old fisherman, "or my boat would've run into it a thousand times."

Hazel was about fifty yards from the shore when a raven landed on the boat's stern. It was a greasy black bird almost as large as an eagle, with a jagged beak like an obsidian knife.

Its eyes glittered with intelligence, so Hazel wasn't much surprised when it talked.

"Tonight," it croaked. "The last night."

Hazel let the oars rest. She tried to decide if the raven was warning her, or advising her, or making a promise.

"Are you from my father?" she asked.

The raven tilted its head. "The last night. Tonight."

It pecked at the boat's prow and flew toward the island.

The last night, Hazel told herself. She decided to take it as a promise. *No matter what she tells me, I will* make *this the last night.*

That gave her enough strength to row on. The boat slid ashore, cracking through a fine layer of ice and black silt.

Over the months, Hazel and her mother had worn a path from the beach into the woods. She hiked inland, careful to stick to the trail. The island was full of dangers, both natural and magical. Bears rustled in the undergrowth. Glowing white spirits, vaguely human, drifted through the trees. Hazel didn't know what they were, but she knew they were watching her, hoping she'd stray into their clutches.

At the center of the island, two massive black boulders formed the entrance to a tunnel. Hazel made her way into the cavern she called the Heart of the Earth.

It was the only truly warm place Hazel had found since moving to Alaska. The air smelled of freshly turned soil. The sweet, moist heat made Hazel feel drowsy, but she fought to stay awake. She imagined that if she fell asleep here, her body would sink into the earthen floor and turn to mulch.

The cave was as large as a church sanctuary, like the St. Louis Cathedral back home on Jackson Square. The walls glowed with luminescent mosses—green, red, and purple. The whole chamber thrummed with energy, an echoing *boom, boom, boom* that reminded Hazel of a heartbeat. Perhaps it was just the sea's waves battering the island, but Hazel didn't think so. This place was alive. The earth was asleep, but it pulsated with power. Its dreams were so malicious, so fitful, that Hazel felt herself losing her grip on reality.

Gaea wanted to consume her identity, just as she'd over-whelmed Hazel's mother. She wanted to consume every human, god, and demigod that dared to walk across her surface.

You all belong to me, Gaea murmured like a lullaby. *Surrender. Return to the earth.*

No, Hazel thought. *I'm Hazel Levesque. You can't have me.*

Marie Levesque stood over the pit. In six months, her hair had turned as gray as lint. She'd lost weight. Her hands were gnarled from hard work. She wore snow boots and waders and a stained white shirt from the diner. She never would have been mistaken for a queen.

"It's too late." Her mother's frail voice echoed through the cavern. Hazel realized with a shock that it was *her* voice—not Gaea's.

"Mother?"

Marie turned. Her eyes were open. She was awake and conscious. This should have made Hazel feel relieved, but it made her nervous. The Voice had never relinquished control while they were on the island.

"What have I done?" her mother asked helplessly. "Oh, Hazel, what did I do to you?"

She stared in horror at the thing in the pit.

For months they'd been coming here, four or five nights a week as the Voice required. Hazel had cried, she'd collapsed with exhaustion, she'd pleaded, she'd given in to despair. But the Voice that controlled her mother had urged her on relentlessly. *Bring valuables from the earth. Use your powers, child. Bring my most valuable possession to me.*

At first, her efforts had brought only scorn. The fissure in the earth had filled with gold and precious stones, bubbling in a thick soup of petroleum. It looked like a dragon's treasure dumped in a tar pit. Then, slowly, a rock spire began to grow like a massive tulip bulb. It emerged so gradually, night after night, that Hazel had trouble judging its progress. Often she concentrated all night on raising it, until her mind and soul were exhausted, but she didn't notice any difference. Yet the spire *did* grow.

Now Hazel could see how much she'd accomplished. The

thing was two stories high, a swirl of rocky tendrils jutting like a spear tip from the oily morass. Inside, something glowed with heat. Hazel couldn't see it clearly, but she knew what was happening. A body was forming out of silver and gold, with oil for blood and raw diamonds for a heart. Hazel was resurrecting the son of Gaea. He was almost ready to wake.

Her mother fell to her knees and wept. "I'm sorry, Hazel. I'm so sorry." She looked helpless and alone, horribly sad. Hazel should have been furious. *Sorry?* She'd lived in fear of her mother for years. She'd been scolded and blamed for her mother's unfortunate life. She'd been treated like a freak, dragged away from her home in New Orleans to this cold wilderness, and worked like a slave by a merciless evil goddess. *Sorry* didn't cut it. She should have despised her mother.

But she couldn't make herself feel angry.

Hazel knelt and put her arm around her mother. There was hardly anything left of her—just skin and bones and stained work clothes. Even in the warm cave, she was trembling.

"What can we do?" Hazel said. "Tell me how to stop it."

Her mother shook her head. "She let me go. She knows it's too late. There's nothing we can do."

"She . . . the Voice?" Hazel was afraid to get her hopes up, but if her mother was really freed, then nothing else mattered. They could get out of here. They could run away, back to New Orleans. "Is she gone?"

Her mother glanced fearfully around the cave. "No, she's here. There's only one more thing she needs from me. For that, she needs my free will."

Hazel didn't like the sound of that.

"Let's get out of here," she urged. "That thing in the rock ... it's going to hatch."

"Soon," her mother agreed. She looked at Hazel so tenderly. ... Hazel couldn't remember the last time she'd seen that kind of affection in her mother's eyes. She felt a sob building in her chest.

"Pluto warned me," her mother said. "He told me my wish was too dangerous."

"Your—your wish?"

"All the wealth under the earth," she said. "He controlled it. I wanted it. I was so tired of being poor, Hazel. So tired. First I summoned him ... just to see if I could. I never thought the old *gris-gris* spell would work on a god. But he courted me, told me I was brave and beautiful. ..." She stared at her bent, calloused hands. "When you were born, he was so pleased and proud. He promised me anything. He swore on the River Styx. I asked for all the riches he had. He warned me the greediest wishes cause the greatest sorrows. But I insisted. I imagined living like a queen—the wife of a god! And you ... you received the curse."

Hazel felt as if she were expanding to the breaking point, just like that spire in the pit. Her misery would soon become too great to hold inside, and her skin would shatter. "That's why I can find things under the earth?"

"And why they bring only sorrow." Her mother gestured listlessly around the cavern. "That's how *she* found me, how she was able to control me. I was angry with your father. I blamed him for my problems. I blamed you. I was so bitter, I listened to Gaea's voice. I was a fool."

"There's got to be something we can do," Hazel said. "Tell me how to stop her."

The ground trembled. Gaea's disembodied voice echoed through the cave.

My eldest rises, she said, *the most precious thing in the earth —and you have brought him from the depths, Hazel Levesque. You have made him anew. His awakening cannot be stopped. Only one thing remains.*

Hazel clenched her fists. She was terrified, but now that her mother was free, she felt like she could confront her enemy at last. This creature, this evil goddess, had ruined their lives. Hazel wasn't going to let her win.

"I won't help you anymore!" she yelled.

But I am done with your help, girl. I brought you here for one reason only. Your mother required . . . incentive.

Hazel's throat constricted. "Mother?"

"I'm sorry, Hazel. If you can forgive me, please—know that it was only because I loved you. She promised to let you live if—"

"If *you* sacrifice yourself," Hazel said, realizing the truth. "She needs you to give your life willingly to raise that—that *thing.*"

Alcyoneus, Gaea said. *Eldest of the giants. He must rise first, and this will be his new homeland—far from the gods. He will walk these icy mountains and forests. He will raise an army of monsters. While the gods are divided, fighting each other in this mortal World War, he will send forth his armies to destroy Olympus.*

The earth goddess's dreams were so powerful, they cast shadows across the cave walls—ghastly shifting images of

Nazi armies raging across Europe, Japanese planes destroying American cities. Hazel finally understood. The gods of Olympus would take sides in the battle as they always did in human wars. While the gods fought each other to a bloody standstill, an army of monsters would rise in the north. Alcyoneus would revive his brother giants and send them forth to conquer the world. The weakened gods would fall. The mortal conflict would rage for decades until all civilization was swept away, and the earth goddess awakened fully. Gaea would rule forever.

All this, the goddess purred, *because your mother was greedy and cursed you with the gift of finding riches. In my sleeping state, I would have needed decades more, perhaps even centuries, before I found the power to resurrect Alcyoneus myself. But now he will wake, and soon, so shall I!*

With terrible certainty, Hazel knew what would happen next. The only thing Gaea needed was a willing sacrifice—a soul to be consumed for Alcyoneus to awaken. Her mother would step into the fissure and touch that horrible spire—and she would be absorbed.

"Hazel, go." Her mother rose unsteadily. "She'll let you live, but you must hurry."

Hazel believed it. That was the most horrible thing. Gaea would honor the bargain and let Hazel live. Hazel would survive to see the end of the world, knowing that she'd caused it.

"No." Hazel made her decision. "I won't live. Not for that."

She reached deep into her soul. She called on her father, the Lord of the Underworld, and summoned all the riches that lay in his vast realm. The cavern shook.

Around the spire of Alcyoneus, oil bubbled, then churned and erupted like a boiling cauldron.

Don't be foolish, Gaea said, but Hazel detected concern in her tone, maybe even fear. *You will destroy yourself for nothing! Your mother will still die!*

Hazel almost wavered. She remembered her father's promise: someday her curse would be washed away; a descendant of Neptune would bring her peace. He'd even said she might find a horse of her own. Maybe that strange stallion in the hills was meant for her. But none of that would happen if she died now. She'd never see Sammy again, or return to New Orleans. Her life would be thirteen short, bitter years with an unhappy ending.

She met her mother's eyes. For once, her mother didn't look sad or angry. Her eyes shone with pride.

"You were my gift, Hazel," she said. "My most precious gift. I was foolish to think I needed anything else."

She kissed Hazel's forehead and held her close. Her warmth gave Hazel the courage to continue. They would die, but not as sacrifices to Gaea. Instinctively Hazel knew that their final act would reject Gaea's power. Their souls would go to the Underworld, and Alcyoneus would not rise—at least not yet.

Hazel summoned the last of her willpower. The air turned searing hot. The spire began to sink. Jewels and chunks of gold shot from the fissure with such force, they cracked the cavern walls and sent shrapnel flying, stinging Hazel's skin through her jacket.

Stop this! Gaea demanded. *You cannot prevent his rise. At best, you will delay him—a few decades. Half a century. Would you trade your lives for that?*

Hazel gave her an answer.

The last night, the raven had said.

The fissure exploded. The roof crumbled. Hazel sank into her mother's arms, into the darkness, as oil filled her lungs and the island collapsed into the bay.

XVIII

HAZEL

"HAZEL!" FRANK SHOOK HER ARMS, sounding panicked. "Come on, please! Wake up!"

She opened her eyes. The night sky blazed with stars. The rocking of the boat was gone. She was lying on solid ground, her bundled sword and pack beside her.

She sat up groggily, her head spinning. They were on a cliff overlooking a beach. About a hundred feet away, the ocean glinted in the moonlight. The surf washed gently against the stern of their beached boat. To her right, hugging the edge of the cliff, was a building like a small church with a searchlight in the steeple. A lighthouse, Hazel guessed. Behind them, fields of tall grass rustled in the wind.

"Where are we?" she asked.

Frank exhaled. "Thank the gods you're awake! We're in Mendocino, about a hundred and fifty miles north of the Golden Gate."

"A hundred and fifty miles?" Hazel groaned. "I've been out *that* long?"

Percy knelt beside her, the sea wind sweeping his hair. He put his hand on her forehead as if checking for a fever. "We couldn't wake you. Finally we decided to bring you ashore. We thought maybe the seasickness—"

"It wasn't seasickness." She took a deep breath. She couldn't hide the truth from them anymore. She remembered what Nico had said: *If a flashback like that happens when you're in combat...*

"I—I haven't been honest with you," she said. "What happened was a blackout. I have them once in a while."

"A blackout?" Frank took Hazel's hand, which startled her... though pleasantly so. "Is it medical? Why haven't I noticed before?"

"I try to hide it," she admitted. "I've been lucky so far, but it's getting worse. It's not medical... not really. Nico says it's a side effect from my past, from where he found me."

Percy's intense green eyes were hard to read. She couldn't tell whether he was concerned or wary.

"Where exactly did Nico find you?" he asked.

Hazel's tongue felt like cotton. She was afraid if she started talking, she'd slip back into the past, but they deserved to know. If she failed them on this quest, zonked out when they needed her most... she couldn't bear that idea.

"I'll explain," she promised. She clawed through her pack. Stupidly, she'd forgotten to bring a water bottle. "Is... is there anything to drink?"

"Yeah." Percy muttered a curse in Greek. "That was dumb. I left my supplies down at the boat."

Hazel felt bad asking them to take care of her, but she'd woken up parched and exhausted, as if she'd lived the last few hours in both the past and the present. She shouldered her pack and sword. "Never mind. I can walk...."

"Don't even think about it," Frank said. "Not until you've had some food and water. I'll get the supplies."

"No, I'll go." Percy glanced at Frank's hand on Hazel's. Then he scanned the horizon as if he sensed trouble, but there was nothing to see—just the lighthouse and the field of grass stretching inland. "You two stay here. I'll be right back."

"You sure?" Hazel said feebly. "I don't want you to—"

"It's fine," said Percy. "Frank, just keep your eyes open. Something about this place...I don't know."

"I'll keep her safe," Frank promised.

Percy dashed off.

Once they were alone, Frank seemed to realize he was still holding Hazel's hand. He cleared his throat and let go.

"I, um...I think I understand your blackouts," he said. "And where you come from."

Her heartbeat stumbled. "You do?"

"You seem so different from other girls I've met." He blinked, then rushed on. "Not like...*bad* different. Just the way you talk. The things that surprise you—like songs, or TV shows, or slang people use. You talk about your life like it happened a long time ago. You were born in a different time, weren't you? You came from the Underworld."

Hazel wanted to cry—not because she was sad, but because it was such a relief to hear someone say the truth. Frank didn't act revolted or scared. He didn't look at her as if she were a ghost or some awful undead zombie.

"Frank, I—"

"We'll figure it out," he promised. "You're alive now. We're going to keep you that way."

The grass rustled behind them. Hazel's eyes stung in the cold wind.

"I don't deserve a friend like you," she said. "You don't know what I am . . . what I've done."

"Stop that." Frank scowled. "You're great! Besides, you're not the only one with secrets."

Hazel stared at him. "I'm not?"

Frank started to say something. Then he tensed.

"What?" Hazel asked.

"The wind's stopped."

She looked around and noticed he was right. The air had become perfectly still.

"So?" she asked.

Frank swallowed. "So why is the grass still moving?"

Out of the corner of her eye, Hazel saw dark shapes ripple through the field.

"Hazel!" Frank tried to grab her arms, but it was too late.

Something knocked him backward. Then a force like a grassy hurricane wrapped around Hazel and dragged her into the fields.

XIX

HAZEL

HAZEL WAS AN EXPERT ON *WEIRD*. She'd seen her mother possessed by an earth goddess. She'd created a giant out of gold. She'd destroyed an island, died, and come back from the Underworld.

But getting kidnapped by a field of grass? That was new.

She felt as if she were trapped in a funnel cloud of plants. She'd heard of modern-day singers jumping into crowds of fans and getting passed overhead by thousands of hands. She imagined this was similar—only she was moving a thousand times faster, and the grass blades weren't adoring fans.

She couldn't sit up. She couldn't touch the ground. Her sword was still in her bedroll, strapped to her back, but she couldn't reach it. The plants kept her off balance, tossing her around, slicing her face and arms. She could barely make out the stars through the tumble of green, yellow, and black.

Frank's shouting faded into the distance.

It was hard to think clearly, but Hazel knew one thing: She was moving fast. Wherever she was being taken, she'd soon be too far away for her friends to find her.

She closed her eyes and tried to ignore the tumbling and tossing. She sent her thoughts into the earth below her. Gold, silver—she'd settle for anything that might disrupt her kidnappers.

She felt nothing. Riches under the earth—zero.

She was about to despair when she felt a huge cold spot pass beneath her. She locked onto it with all her concentration, dropping a mental anchor. Suddenly the ground rumbled. The swirl of plants released her and she was thrown upward like a catapult projectile.

Momentarily weightless, she opened her eyes. She twisted her body in midair. The ground was about twenty feet below her. Then she was falling. Her combat training kicked in. She'd practiced dropping from giant eagles before. She tucked into a roll, turned the impact into a somersault, and came up standing.

She unslung her bedroll and drew her sword. A few yards to her left, an outcropping of rock the size of a garage jutted from the sea of grass. Hazel realized it was her anchor. She'd *caused* the rock to appear.

The grass rippled around it. Angry voices hissed in dismay at the massive clump of stone that had broken their progress. Before they could regroup, Hazel ran to the rock and clambered to the top.

The grass swayed and rustled around her like the tentacles

of a gigantic undersea anemone. Hazel could sense her kidnappers' frustration.

"Can't grow on this, can you?" she yelled. "Go away, you bunch of weeds! Leave me alone!"

"Schist," said an angry voice from the grass.

Hazel raised her eyebrows. "Excuse me?"

"Schist! Big pile of schist!"

A nun at St. Agnes Academy had once washed Hazel's mouth with lye soap for saying something very similar, so she wasn't sure how to respond. Then, all around her rock island, the kidnappers materialized from the grass. At first glance they looked like Valentine angels—a dozen chubby little Cupid babies. As they stepped closer, Hazel realized they were neither cute nor angelic.

They were the size of toddlers, with rolls of baby fat, but their skin had a strange greenish hue, as if chlorophyll ran through their veins. They had dry, brittle wings like cornhusks, and tufts of white hair like corn silk. Their faces were haggard, pitted with kernels of grain. Their eyes were solid green, and their teeth were canine fangs.

The largest creature stepped forward. He wore a yellow loincloth, and his hair was spiky, like the bristles on a stalk of wheat. He hissed at Hazel and waddled back and forth so quickly, she was afraid his loincloth might fall off.

"Hate this schist!" the creature complained. "Wheat cannot grow!"

"Sorghum cannot grow!" another piped up.

"Barley!" yelled a third. "Barley cannot grow. Curse this schist!"

Hazel's knees wobbled. The little creatures might have been funny if they weren't surrounding her, staring up at her with those pointed teeth and hungry green eyes. They were like Cupid piranhas.

"Y-you mean the rock?" she managed. "This rock is called schist?"

"Yes, greenstone! Schist!" the first creature yelled. "Nasty rock."

Hazel began to understand how she'd summoned it. "It's a precious stone. It's valuable?"

"Bah!" said the one in the yellow loincloth. "Foolish native people made jewelry from it, yes. Valuable? Maybe. Not as good as wheat."

"Or sorghum!"

"Or barley!"

The others chimed in, calling out different types of grain. They circled the rock, making no effort to climb it—at least not yet. If they decided to swarm her, there was no way she could fend off all of them.

"You're Gaea's servants," she guessed, just to keep them talking. Maybe Percy and Frank weren't too far away. Maybe they'd be able to see her, standing so tall above the fields. She wished that her sword glowed like Percy's.

The yellow-diapered Cupid snarled. "We are the *karpoi*, spirits of the grain. Children of the Earth Mother, yes! We have been her attendants since forever. Before nasty humans cultivated us, we were wild. We will be again. Wheat will destroy all!"

"No, sorghum will rule!"

"Barley shall dominate!"

The others joined in, each *karpos* cheering for his own variety.

"Right." Hazel swallowed her revulsion. "So you're Wheat, then—you in the yellow, um, britches."

"Hmmmm," said Wheat. "Come down from your schist, demigod. We must take you to our mistress's army. They will reward us. They will kill you slowly!"

"Tempting," Hazel said, "but no thanks."

"I will give you wheat!" said Wheat, as if this were a very fine offer in exchange for her life. "So much wheat!"

Hazel tried to think. How far had she been carried? How long would it take her friends to find her? The *karpoi* were getting bolder, approaching the rock in twos and threes, scratching at the schist to see if it would hurt them.

"Before I get down..." She raised her voice, hoping it would carry over the fields. "Um, explain something to me, would you? If you're grain spirits, shouldn't you be on the gods' side? Isn't the goddess of agriculture Ceres—"

"Evil name!" Barley wailed.

"Cultivates us!" Sorghum spat. "Makes us grow in disgusting rows. Lets humans harvest us. Pah! When Gaea is mistress of the world again, we will grow wild, yes!"

"Well, naturally," Hazel said. "So this army of hers, where you're taking me in exchange for wheat—"

"Or barley," Barley offered.

"Yeah," Hazel agreed. "This army is where, now?"

"Just over the ridge!" Sorghum clapped his hands excitedly. "The Earth Mother—oh, yes!—she told us: 'Look for the daughter of Pluto who lives again. Find her! Bring her alive! I have many tortures planned for her.' The giant Polybotes will reward us for your life! Then we will march south to destroy the Romans. We can't be killed, you know. But you can, yes."

"That's wonderful." Hazel tried to sound enthusiastic. It wasn't easy, knowing Gaea had special revenge planned for her. "So you—you can't be killed because Alcyoneus has captured Death, is that it?"

"Exactly!" Barley said.

"And he's keeping him chained in Alaska," Hazel said, "at ...let's see, what's the name of that place?"

Sorghum started to answer, but Wheat flew at him and knocked him down. The *karpoi* began to fight, dissolving into funnel clouds of grain. Hazel considered making a run for it. Then Wheat re-formed, holding Sorghum in a headlock. "Stop!" he yelled at the others. "Multigrain fighting is not allowed!"

The *karpoi* solidified into chubby Cupid piranhas again.

Wheat pushed Sorghum away.

"Oh, clever demigod," he said. "Trying to trick us into giving secrets. No, you'll never find the lair of Alcyoneus."

"I already know where it is," she said with false confidence. "He's on the island in Resurrection Bay."

"Ha!" Wheat sneered. "That place sank beneath the waves long ago. You should know that! Gaea hates you for it. When you thwarted her plans, she was forced to sleep again. Decades and decades! Alcyoneus—not until the dark times was he able to rise."

"The nineteen-eighties," Barley agreed. "Horrible! Horrible!"

"Yes," Wheat said. "And our mistress *still* sleeps. Alcyoneus was forced to bide his time in the north, waiting, planning. Only now does Gaea begin to stir. Oh, but she remembers you, and so does her son!"

Sorghum cackled with glee. "You will never find the prison of Thanatos. All of Alaska is the giant's home. He could be keeping Death anywhere! Years it would take you to find him, and your poor camp has only days. Better you surrender. We will give you grain. So much grain."

Hazel's sword felt heavy. She'd dreaded returning to Alaska, but at least she'd had an idea where to start looking for Thanatos. She'd assumed that the island where she had died hadn't been completely destroyed, or possibly had risen again when Alcyoneus woke. She had hoped that his base would be there. But if the island was really gone, she had no idea how to find the giant. Alaska was huge. They could search for decades and never find him.

"Yes," Wheat said, sensing her anguish. "Give up."

Hazel gripped her *spatha*. "Never!" She raised her voice again, hoping it would somehow reach her friends. "If I have to destroy you all, I will. I am the daughter of Pluto!"

The *karpoi* advanced. They gripped the rock, hissing as if it were scalding hot, but they began to climb.

"Now you will die," Wheat promised, gnashing his teeth. "You will feel the wrath of grain!"

Suddenly there was a whistling sound. Wheat's snarl froze. He looked down at the golden arrow that had just pierced his chest. Then he dissolved into pieces of Chex Mix.

X X

HAZEL

FOR A HEARTBEAT, HAZEL WAS just as stunned as the *karpoi*. Then Frank and Percy burst into the open and began to massacre every source of fiber they could find. Frank shot an arrow through Barley, who crumbled into seeds. Percy slashed Riptide through Sorghum and charged toward Millet and Oats. Hazel jumped down and joined the fight.

Within minutes, the *karpoi* had been reduced to piles of seeds and various breakfast cereals. Wheat started to re-form, but Percy pulled a lighter from his pack and sparked a flame.

"Try it," he warned, "and I'll set this whole field on fire. Stay dead. Stay away from us, or the grass gets it!"

Frank winced like the flame terrified him. Hazel didn't understand why, but she shouted at the grain piles anyway: "He'll do it! He's crazy!"

The remnants of the *karpoi* scattered in the wind. Frank climbed the rock and watched them go.

Percy extinguished his lighter and grinned at Hazel.

"Thanks for yelling. We wouldn't have found you otherwise. How'd you hold them off so long?"

She pointed to the rock. "A big pile of schist."

"Excuse me?"

"Guys," Frank called from the top of the rock. "You need to see this."

Percy and Hazel climbed up to join him. As soon as Hazel saw what he was looking at, she inhaled sharply. "Percy, no light! Put up your sword!"

"Schist!" He touched the sword tip, and Riptide shrank back into a pen.

Down below them, an army was on the move.

The field dropped into a shallow ravine, where a country road wound north and south. On the opposite side of the road, grassy hills stretched to the horizon, empty of civilization except for one darkened convenience store at the top of the nearest rise.

The whole ravine was full of monsters—column after column marching south, so many and so close, Hazel was amazed they hadn't heard her shouting.

She, Frank, and Percy crouched against the rock. They watched in disbelief as several dozen large, hairy humanoids passed by, dressed in tattered bits of armor and animal fur. The creatures had six arms each, three sprouting on either side, so they looked like cavemen evolved from insects.

"Gegenes," Hazel whispered. "The Earthborn."

"You've fought them before?" Percy asked.

She shook her head. "Just heard about them in monster

class at camp." She'd never liked monster class—reading Pliny the Elder and those other musty authors who described legendary monsters from the edges of the Roman Empire. Hazel believed in monsters, but some of the descriptions were so wild, she had thought they must be just ridiculous rumors.

Only now, a whole army of those rumors was marching by.

"The Earthborn fought the Argonauts," she murmured. "And those things behind them—"

"Centaurs," Percy said. "But...that's not right. Centaurs are *good* guys."

Frank made a choking sound. "That's not what *we* were taught at camp. Centaurs are crazy, always getting drunk and killing heroes."

Hazel watched as the horse-men cantered past. They were human from the waist up, palomino from the waist down. They were dressed in barbarian armor of hide and bronze, armed with spears and slings. At first, Hazel thought they were wearing Viking helmets. Then she realized they had actual horns jutting from their shaggy hair.

"Are they supposed to have bull's horns?" she asked.

"Maybe they're a special breed," Frank said. "Let's not ask them, okay?"

Percy gazed farther down the road and his face went slack. "My gods...Cyclopes."

Sure enough, lumbering after the centaurs was a battalion of one-eyed ogres, both male and female, each about ten feet tall, wearing armor cobbled out of junkyard metal. Six of the monsters were yoked like oxen, pulling a two-story-tall siege tower fitted with a giant scorpion ballista.

Percy pressed the sides of his head. "Cyclopes. Centaurs. This is wrong. All wrong."

The monster army was enough to make anyone despair, but Hazel realized that something else was going on with Percy. He looked pale and sickly in the moonlight, as if his memories were trying to come back, scrambling his mind in the process.

She glanced at Frank. "We need to get him back to the boat. The sea will make him feel better."

"No argument," Frank said. "There are too many of them. The camp . . . we have to warn the camp."

"They know," Percy groaned. "Reyna knows."

A lump formed in Hazel's throat. There was no way the legion could fight so many. If they were only a few hundred miles north of Camp Jupiter, their quest was already doomed. They could never make it to Alaska and back in time.

"Come on," she urged. "Let's . . ."

Then she saw the giant.

When he appeared over the ridge, Hazel couldn't quite believe her eyes. He was taller than the siege tower—thirty feet, at least—with scaly reptilian legs like a Komodo dragon from the waist down and green-blue armor from the waist up. His breastplate was shaped like rows of hungry monstrous faces, their mouths open as if demanding food. His face was human, but his hair was wild and green, like a mop of seaweed. As he turned his head from side to side, snakes dropped from his dreadlocks. Viper dandruff—gross.

He was armed with a massive trident and a weighted net.

Just the sight of those weapons made Hazel's stomach clench. She'd faced that type of fighter in gladiator training many times. It was the trickiest, sneakiest, most evil combat style she knew. This giant was a supersize *retiarius*.

"Who is he?" Frank's voice quivered. "That's not—"

"Not Alcyoneus," Hazel said weakly. "One of his brothers, I think. The one Terminus mentioned. The grain spirit mentioned him, too. That's Polybotes."

She wasn't sure how she knew, but she could feel the giant's aura of power even from here. She remembered that feeling from the Heart of the Earth as she had raised Alcyoneus— as if she were standing near a powerful magnet, and all the iron in her blood was being drawn toward it. This giant was another child of Gaea—a creature of the earth so malevolent and powerful, he radiated his own gravitational field.

Hazel knew they should leave. Their hiding place on top of the rock would be in plain sight to a creature that tall if he chose to look in their direction. But she sensed something important was about to happen. She and her friends crept a little farther down the schist and kept watching.

As the giant got close, a Cyclops woman broke ranks and ran back to speak with him. She was enormous, fat, and horribly ugly, wearing a chain-mail dress like a muumuu—but next to the giant she looked like a child.

She pointed to the closed-up convenience store on top of the nearest hill and muttered something about food. The giant snapped back an answer, as if he was annoyed. The female Cyclopes barked an order to her kindred, and three of them followed her up the hill.

When they were halfway to the store, a searing light turned night into day. Hazel was blinded. Below her, the enemy army dissolved into chaos, monsters screaming in pain and outrage. Hazel squinted. She felt like she'd just stepped out of a dark theater into a sunny afternoon.

"Too pretty!" the Cyclopes shrieked. "Burns our eye!"

The store on the hill was encased in a rainbow, closer and brighter than any Hazel had ever seen. The light was anchored at the store, shooting up into the heavens, bathing the countryside in a weird kaleidoscopic glow.

The lady Cyclops hefted her club and charged at the store. As she hit the rainbow, her whole body began to steam. She wailed in agony and dropped her club, retreating with multicolored blisters all over her arms and face.

"Horrible goddess!" she bellowed at the store. "Give us snacks!"

The other monsters went crazy, charging the convenience store, then running away as the rainbow light burned them. Some threw rocks, spears, swords, and even pieces of their armor, all of which burned up in flames of pretty colors.

Finally the giant leader seemed to realize that his troops were throwing away perfectly good equipment.

"Stop!" he roared.

With some difficulty, he managed to shout and push and pummel his troops into submission. When they'd quieted down, he approached the rainbow-shielded store himself and stalked around the borders of the light.

"Goddess!" he shouted. "Come out and surrender!"

No answer from the store. The rainbow continued to shimmer.

The giant raised his trident and net. "I am Polybotes! Kneel before me so I may destroy you quickly."

Apparently, no one in the store was impressed. A tiny dark object came sailing out the window and landed at the giant's feet. Polybotes yelled, "Grenade!"

He covered his face. His troops hit the ground.

When the thing did not explode, Polybotes bent down cautiously and picked it up.

He roared in outrage. "A Ding Dong? You dare insult me with a Ding Dong?" He threw the cake back at the shop, and it vaporized in the light.

The monsters got to their feet. Several muttered hungrily, "Ding Dongs? Where Ding Dongs?"

"Let's attack," said the lady Cyclops. "I am hungry. My boys want snacks!"

"No!" Polybotes said. "We're already late. Alcyoneus wants us at the camp in four days' time. You Cyclopes move inexcusably slowly. We have no time for *minor* goddesses!"

He aimed that last comment at the store, but got no response.

The lady Cyclops growled. "The camp, yes. Vengeance! The orange and purple ones destroyed my home. Now Ma Gasket will destroy theirs! Do you hear me, Leo? Jason? Piper? I come to annihilate you!"

The other Cyclopes bellowed in approval. The rest of the monsters joined in.

Hazel's whole body tingled. She glanced at her friends. "Jason," she whispered. "She fought Jason. He might still be alive."

Frank nodded. "Do those other names mean anything to you?"

Hazel shook her head. She didn't know any Leo or Piper at camp. Percy still looked sickly and dazed. If the names meant anything to him, he didn't show it.

Hazel pondered what the Cyclops had said: *Orange and purple ones.* Purple—obviously the color of Camp Jupiter. But orange...Percy had shown up in a tattered orange shirt. That couldn't be a coincidence.

Below them, the army began to march south again, but the giant Polybotes stood to one side, frowning and sniffing the air.

"Sea god," he muttered. To Hazel's horror, he turned in their direction. "I smell sea god."

Percy was shaking. Hazel put her hand on his shoulder and tried to press him flat against the rock.

The lady Cyclops Ma Gasket snarled. "Of course you smell sea god! The sea is right over there!"

"More than that," Polybotes insisted. "I was born to destroy Neptune. I can sense..." He frowned, turning his head and shaking out a few more snakes.

"Do we march or sniff the air?" Ma Gasket scolded. "I don't get Ding Dongs, you don't get sea god!"

Polybotes growled. "Very well. March! March!" He took one last look at the rainbow-encased store, then raked his fingers through his hair. He brought out three snakes that seemed larger than the rest, with white markings around their necks. "A gift, goddess! My name, Polybotes, means 'Many-to-Feed!' Here are some hungry mouths for you. See if your store gets many customers with these sentries outside."

He laughed wickedly and threw the snakes into the tall grass on the hillside.

Then he marched south, his massive Komodo legs shaking the earth. Gradually, the last column of monsters passed over the hills and disappeared into the night.

Once they were gone, the blinding rainbow shut off like a spotlight.

Hazel, Frank, and Percy were left alone in the dark, staring across the road at a closed up convenience store.

"That was different," Frank muttered.

Percy shuddered violently. Hazel knew he needed help, or rest, or something. Seeing that army seemed to have triggered some kind of memory, leaving him shell-shocked. They should get him back to the boat.

On the other hand, a huge stretch of grassland lay between them and the beach. Hazel got the feeling the *karpoi* wouldn't stay away forever. She didn't like the idea of the three of them making their way back to the boat in the middle of the night. And she couldn't shake the dreadful feeling that if she hadn't summoned that schist, she'd be a captive of the giant right now.

"Let's go to the store," she said. "If there's a goddess inside, maybe she can help us."

"Except a bunch of snake things are guarding the hill now," Frank said. "And that burning rainbow might come back."

They both looked at Percy, who was shaking like he had hypothermia.

"We've got to try," Hazel said.

Frank nodded grimly. "Well . . . any goddess who throws a Ding Dong at a giant can't be all bad. Let's go."

FRANK

FRANK HATED DING DONGS. He hated snakes. And he hated his life. Not necessarily in that order.

As he trudged up the hill, he wished that he could pass out like Hazel—just go into a trance and experience some other time, like before he got drafted for this insane quest, before he found out his dad was a godly drill sergeant with an ego problem.

His bow and spear slapped against his back. He hated the spear, too. The moment he got it, he silently swore he'd never use it. *A real man's weapon*—Mars was a moron.

Maybe there had been a mix-up. Wasn't there some sort of DNA test for gods' kids? Perhaps the godly nursery had accidentally switched Frank with one of Mars's buff little bully babies. No way would Frank's mother have gotten involved with that blustering war god.

She was a natural warrior, Grandmother's voice argued.

It is no surprise a god would fall in love with her, given our family.
Ancient blood. The blood of princes and heroes.

Frank shook the thought out of his head. He was no prince or hero. He was a lactose-intolerant klutz, who couldn't even protect his friend from getting kidnapped by wheat.

His new medals felt cold against his chest: the centurion's crescent, the Mural Crown. He should've been proud of them, but he felt like he'd only gotten them because his dad had bullied Reyna.

Frank didn't know how his friends could stand to be around him. Percy had made it clear that he hated Mars, and Frank couldn't blame him. Hazel kept watching Frank out of the corner of her eye, like she was afraid he might turn into a muscle-bound freak.

Frank looked down at his body and sighed. Correction: even *more* of a muscle-bound freak. If Alaska really was a land beyond the gods, Frank might stay there. He wasn't sure he had anything to return to.

Don't whine, his grandmother would say. *Zhang men do not whine.*

She was right. Frank had a job to do. He had to complete this impossible quest, which at the moment meant reaching the convenience store alive.

As they got closer, Frank worried that the store might burst into rainbow light and vaporize them, but the building stayed dark. The snakes Polybotes had dropped seemed to have vanished.

They were twenty yards from the porch when something hissed in the grass behind them.

"Go!" Frank yelled.

Percy stumbled. While Hazel helped him up, Frank turned and nocked an arrow.

He shot blindly. He thought he'd grabbed an exploding arrow, but it was only a signal flare. It skidded through the grass, bursting into orange flame and whistling: *WOO!*

At least it illuminated the monster. Sitting in a patch of withered yellow grass was a lime-colored snake as short and thick as Frank's arm. Its head was ringed with a mane of spiky white fins. The creature stared at the arrow zipping by as if wondering, *What the heck is that?*

Then it fixed its large, yellow eyes on Frank. It advanced like an inchworm, hunching up in the middle. Wherever it touched, the grass withered and died.

Frank heard his friends climbing the steps of the store. He didn't dare turn and run. He and the snake studied each other. The snake hissed, flames billowing from its mouth.

"Nice creepy reptile," Frank said, very aware of the driftwood in his coat pocket. "Nice poisonous, fire-breathing reptile."

"Frank!" Hazel yelled behind him. "Come on!"

The snake sprang at him. It sailed through the air so fast, there wasn't time to nock an arrow. Frank swung his bow and smacked the monster down the hill. It spun out of sight, wailing, *"Screeeee!"*

Frank felt proud of himself until he looked at his bow, which was steaming where it had touched the snake. He watched in disbelief as the wood crumbled to dust.

He heard an outraged hiss, answered by two more hisses farther downhill.

Frank dropped his disintegrating bow and ran for the porch. Percy and Hazel pulled him up the steps. When Frank turned, he saw all three monsters circling in the grass, breathing fire and turning the hillside brown with their poisonous touch. They didn't seem able or willing to come closer to the store, but that wasn't much comfort to Frank. He'd lost his bow.

"We'll never get out of here," he said miserably.

"Then we'd better go in." Hazel pointed to the hand-painted sign over the door: RAINBOW ORGANIC FOODS & LIFESTYLES.

Frank had no idea what that meant, but it sounded better than flaming poisonous snakes. He followed his friends inside.

As they stepped through the door, lights came on. Flute music started up like they'd walked onto a stage. The wide aisles were lined with bins of nuts and dried fruit, baskets of apples, and clothing racks with tie-dyed shirts and gauzy Tinker Bell–type dresses. The ceiling was covered in wind chimes. Along the walls, glass cases displayed crystal balls, geodes, macramé dream catchers, and a bunch of other strange stuff. Incense must have been burning somewhere. It smelled like a bouquet of flowers was on fire.

"Fortune-teller's shop?" Frank wondered.

"Hope not," Hazel muttered.

Percy leaned against her. He looked worse than ever, like he'd been hit with a sudden flu. His face glistened with sweat. "Sit down..." he muttered. "Maybe water."

"Yeah," Frank said. "Let's find you a place to rest."

The floorboards creaked under their feet. Frank navigated between two Neptune statue fountains.

A girl popped up from behind the granola bins. "Help you?"

Frank lurched backward, knocking over one of the fountains. A stone Neptune crashed to the floor. The sea god's head rolled off and water spewed out of his neck, spraying a rack of tie-dyed man satchels.

"Sorry!" Frank bent down to clean up the mess. He almost goosed the girl with his spear.

"Eep!" she said. "Hold it! It's okay!"

Frank straightened slowly, trying not to cause any more damage. Hazel looked mortified. Percy turned a sickly shade of green as he stared at the decapitated statue of his dad.

The girl clapped her hands. The fountain dissolved into mist. The water evaporated. She turned to Frank. "Really, it's no problem. Those Neptune fountains are so grumpy-looking, they bum me out."

She reminded Frank of the college-age hikers he sometimes saw in Lynn Canyon Park behind his grandmother's house. She was short and muscular, with lace-up boots, cargo shorts, and a bright yellow T-shirt that read *R.O.F.L. Rainbow Organic Foods & Lifestyles*. She looked young, but her hair was frizzy white, sticking out on either side of her head like the white of a giant fried egg.

Frank tried to remember how to speak. The girl's eyes were really distracting. The irises changed color from gray to black to white.

"Uh ... sorry about the fountain," he managed. "We were just—"

"Oh, I know!" the girl said. "You want to browse. It's all right. Demigods are welcome. Take your time. You're not like those awful monsters. They just want to use the restroom and never buy anything!"

She snorted. Her eyes flashed with lightning. Frank glanced at Hazel to see if he'd imagined it, but Hazel looked just as surprised.

From the back of the store, a woman's voice called: "Fleecy? Don't scare the customers, now. Bring them here, will you?"

"Your name is Fleecy?" Hazel asked.

Fleecy giggled. "Well, in the language of the *nebulae* it's actually—" She made a series of crackling and blowing noises that reminded Frank of a thunderstorm giving way to a nice cold front. "But you can call me Fleecy."

"*Nebulae...*" Percy muttered in a daze. "Cloud nymphs."

Fleecy beamed. "Oh, I like this one! Usually *no one* knows about cloud nymphs. But dear me, he doesn't look so good. Come to the back. My boss wants to meet you. We'll get your friend fixed up."

Fleecy led them through the produce aisle, between rows of eggplants, kiwis, lotus fruit, and pomegranates. At the back of the store, behind a counter with an old-fashioned cash register, stood a middle-aged woman with olive skin, long black hair, rimless glasses, and a T-shirt that read: *The Goddess Is Alive!* She wore amber necklaces and turquoise rings. She smelled like rose petals.

She looked friendly enough, but something about her made

Frank feel shaky, like he wanted to cry. It took him a second, then he realized what it was—the way she smiled with just one corner of her mouth, the warm brown color of her eyes, the tilt of her head, like she was considering a question. She reminded Frank of his mother.

"Hello!" She leaned over the counter, which was lined with dozens of little statues—waving Chinese cats, meditating Buddhas, Saint Francis bobble heads, and novelty dippy drinking birds with top hats. "So glad you're here. I'm Iris!"

Hazel's eyes widened. "Not *the* Iris—the rainbow goddess?"

Iris made a face. "Well, that's my *official* job, yes. But I don't define myself by my corporate identity. In my spare time, I run this!" She gestured around her proudly. "The R.O.F.L. Co-op—an employee-run cooperative promoting healthy alternative lifestyles and organic foods."

Frank stared at her. "But you throw Ding Dongs at monsters."

Iris looked horrified. "Oh, they're not Ding Dongs." She rummaged under the counter and brought out a package of chocolate-covered cakes that looked exactly like Ding Dongs. "These are gluten-free, no-sugar-added, vitamin-enriched, soy-free, goat-milk-and-seaweed-based cupcake simulations."

"All natural!" Fleecy chimed in.

"I stand corrected." Frank suddenly felt as queasy as Percy.

Iris smiled. "You should try one, Frank. You're lactose intolerant, aren't you?"

"How did you—"

"I know these things. Being the messenger goddess . . . well, I do learn a lot, hearing all the communications from the gods and so on." She tossed the cakes on the counter. "Besides, those monsters should be glad to have some healthy snacks. Always eating junk food and heroes. They're so *unenlightened*. I couldn't have them tromping through my store, tearing up things and disturbing our *feng shui*."

Percy leaned against the counter. He looked like he was going to throw up all over the goddess's *feng shui*. "Monsters marching south," he said with difficulty. "Going to destroy our camp. Couldn't you stop them?"

"Oh, I'm strictly nonviolent," Iris said. "I can act in self-defense, but I won't be drawn into any more Olympian aggression, thank you very much. I've been reading about Buddhism. And Taoism. I haven't decided between them."

"But..." Hazel looked mystified. "Aren't you a Greek goddess?"

Iris crossed her arms. "Don't try to put me in a box, demi-god! I'm not defined by my past."

"Um, okay," Hazel said. "Could you at least help our friend here? I think he's sick."

Percy reached across the counter. For a second Frank was afraid he wanted the cupcakes. "Iris-message," he said. "Can you send one?"

Frank wasn't sure he'd heard right. "Iris-message?"

"It's..." Percy faltered. "Isn't that something you do?"

Iris studied Percy more closely. "Interesting. You're from Camp Jupiter, and yet... Oh, I see. Juno is up to her tricks."

"What?" Hazel asked.

Iris glanced at her assistant, Fleecy. They seemed to have a silent conversation. Then the goddess pulled a vial from behind the counter and sprayed some honeysuckle-smelling oil around Percy's face. "There, that should balance your *chakra*. As for Iris-messages—that's an ancient way of communication. The Greeks used it. The Romans never took to it—always relying on their road systems and giant eagles and whatnot. But yes, I imagine... Fleecy, could you give it a try?"

"Sure, boss!"

Iris winked at Frank. "Don't tell the other gods, but Fleecy handles most of my messages these days. She's wonderful at it, really, and I don't have time to answer all those requests personally. It messes up my *wa*."

"Your *wa*?" Frank asked.

"Mmm. Fleecy, why don't you take Percy and Hazel into the back? You can get them something to eat while you arrange their messages. And for Percy... yes, memory sickness. I imagine that old Polybotes... well, meeting him in a state of amnesia *can't* be good for a child of P—that is to say, Neptune. Fleecy, give him a cup of green tea with organic honey and wheat germ and some of my medicinal powder number five. That should fix him up."

Hazel frowned. "What about Frank?"

Iris turned to him. She tilted her head quizzically, just the way his mother used to—as if Frank were the biggest question in the room.

"Oh, don't worry," Iris said. "Frank and I have a lot to talk about."

XXII

FRANK

FRANK WOULD'VE PREFERRED TO go with his friends, even
if it meant he had to endure green tea with wheat germ. But
Iris roped her arm through his and led him to a café table at
a bay window. Frank set his spear on the floor. He sat across
from Iris. Outside in the dark, the snake monsters restlessly
patrolled the hillside, spewing fire and poisoning the grass.

"Frank, I know how you feel," Iris said. "I imagine that
half-burned stick in your pocket gets heavier every day."

Frank couldn't breathe. His hand went instinctively to his
coat. "How do you—?"

"I told you. I know things. I was Juno's messenger for ages.
I know why she gave you a reprieve."

"A reprieve?" Frank brought out the piece of firewood and
unwrapped it from its cloth. As unwieldy as Mars's spear was,
the piece of tinder was worse. Iris was right. It weighed him
down.

"Juno saved you for a reason," the goddess said. "She wants
you to serve her plan. If she hadn't appeared that day when

you were a baby and warned your mother about the firewood, you would've died. You were born with too many gifts. That sort of power tends to burn out a mortal life."

"Too many gifts?" Frank felt his ears getting warm with anger. "I don't have *any* gifts!"

"That's not true, Frank." Iris swiped her hand in front of her like she was cleaning a windshield. A miniature rainbow appeared. "Think about it."

An image shimmered in the rainbow. Frank saw himself when he was four years old, running across Grandmother's backyard. His mother leaned out the window of the attic, high above, waving and calling to get his attention. Frank wasn't supposed to be in the backyard by himself. He didn't know why his mother was up in the attic, but she told him to stay by the house, not to go too far. Frank did exactly the opposite. He squealed with delight and ran to the edge of the woods, where he came face to face with a grizzly bear.

Until Frank saw that scene in the rainbow, the memory had been so hazy, he thought he'd dreamed it. Now he could appreciate just how surreal the experience had been. The bear regarded the little boy, and it was difficult to tell who was more startled. Then Frank's mother appeared at his side. There was no way she should have been able to get down from the attic so fast. She put herself between the bear and Frank and told him to run to the house. This time, Frank obeyed. When he turned at the back porch, he saw his mother coming out of the woods. The bear was gone. Frank asked what had happened. His mother smiled. *Mama Bear just needed directions*, she said.

The scene in the rainbow changed. Frank saw himself as

a six-year-old, curling up in his mother's lap even though he was much too big for that. His mother's long black hair was pulled back. Her arms were around him. She wore her rimless glasses that Frank always liked to steal, and her fuzzy gray fleece pullover that smelled like cinnamon. She was telling him stories about heroes, pretending they were all related to Frank: one was Xu Fu, who sailed in search of the elixir of life. The rainbow image had no sound, but Frank remembered his mother's words: *He was your great-great-great-*... She would poke Frank's stomach every time she said *great-*, dozens of times, until he was giggling uncontrollably.

Then there was Sung Guo, also called Seneca Gracchus, who fought twelve Roman dragons and sixteen Chinese dragons in the western deserts of China. *He was the strongest dragon of all, you see,* his mother said. *That's how he could beat them!* Frank didn't know what that meant, but it sounded exciting.

Then she poked his belly with so many *greats*, Frank rolled onto the floor to escape the tickling. *And your very oldest ancestor that we know of: he was the Prince of Pylos! Hercules fought him once. It was a hard fight!*

Did we win? Frank asked.

His mother laughed, but there was sadness in her voice. *No, our ancestor lost. But it wasn't easy for Hercules. Imagine trying to fight a swarm of bees. That's how it was. Even Hercules had trouble!*

The comment made no sense to Frank, then or now. His ancestor had been a beekeeper?

Frank hadn't thought about these stories in years, but now they came back to him as clearly as his mother's face. It hurt to see her again. Frank wanted to go back to that time. He wanted to be a little kid and curl up on her lap.

In the rainbow image, little Frank asked where their family was from. So many heroes! Were they from Pylos, or Rome, or China, or Canada?

His mother smiled, tilting her head as if considering how to answer.

Li-Jien, she said at last. *Our family is from many places, but our home is Li-Jien. Always remember, Frank: you have a special gift. You can be anything.*

The rainbow dissolved, leaving just Iris and Frank.

"I don't understand." His voice was hoarse.

"Your mother explained it," Iris said. "You can be anything."

It sounded like one of those stupid things parents say to boost your self-esteem—a worn-out slogan that could be printed on Iris's T-shirts, right along with *The Goddess Is Alive!* and *My Other Car Is a Magic Carpet!* But the way Iris said it, it sounded like a challenge.

Frank pressed his hand against his pants pocket, where he kept his mother's sacrifice medal. The silver medallion was cold as ice.

"I *can't* be anything," Frank insisted. "I've got zero skills."

"What have you tried?" Iris asked. "You wanted to be an archer. You managed that pretty well. You've only scratched the surface. Your friends Hazel and Percy—they're both stretched between worlds: Greek and Roman, the past and the present. But you are stretched more than either of them. Your family is ancient—the blood of Pylos on your mother's side, and your father is Mars. No wonder Juno wants you to be one of her seven heroes. She wants you to fight the giants and Gaea. But think about this: What do *you* want?"

"I don't have any choice," Frank said. "I'm the son of the stupid war god. I have to go on this quest and—"

"Have to," Iris said. "Not *want* to. I used to think like that. Then I got tired of being everyone's servant. Fetch goblets of wine for Jupiter. Deliver letters for Juno. Send messages back and forth across the rainbow for anyone with a golden *drachma.*"

"A golden what?"

"Not important. But I learned to let go. I started R.O.F.L., and now I'm free of that baggage. You can let go, too. Maybe you can't escape fate. Someday that piece of wood *will* burn. I foresee that you'll be holding it when it happens, and your life will end—"

"Thanks," Frank muttered.

"—but that just makes your life more precious! You don't have to be what your parents and your grandmother expect. You don't have to follow the war god's orders, or Juno's. Do your own thing, Frank! Find a new path!"

Frank thought about that. The idea was thrilling: reject the gods, his destiny, his dad. He didn't want to be a war god's son. His mother had *died* in a war. Frank had lost everything thanks to a war. Mars clearly didn't know the first thing about him. Frank didn't want to be a hero.

"Why are you telling me this?" he asked. "You want me to abandon the quest, let Camp Jupiter be destroyed? My friends are counting on me."

Iris spread her hands. "I can't tell you what to do, Frank.

But do what you *want*, not what they tell you to do. Where did conforming ever get me? I spent five millennia serving everyone else, and I never discovered my own identity. What's my sacred animal? No one bothered to give me one. Where are my temples? They never made any. Well, fine! I've found peace here at the co-op. You could stay with us, if you want. Become a ROFLcopter."

"A what, now?"

"The point is you have options. If you continue this quest . . . what happens when you free Thanatos? Will it be good for your family? Your friends?"

Frank remembered what his grandmother had said: she had an appointment with Death. Grandmother infuriated him sometimes; but still, she was his only living family, the only person alive who loved him. If Thanatos stayed chained up, Frank might not lose her. And Hazel—somehow she had come back from the Underworld. If Death took her again, Frank wouldn't be able to stand it. Not to mention Frank's own problem: according to Iris, he should have died when he was a baby. All that stood between him and Death was a half-burned stick. Would Thanatos take him away, too?

Frank tried to imagine staying here with Iris, putting on a R.O.F.L. shirt, selling crystals and dream catchers to demigod travelers and lobbing gluten-free cupcake simulations at passing monsters. Meanwhile, an undying army would overrun Camp Jupiter.

You can be anything, his mother had said.

No, he thought. *I can't be that selfish.*

"I have to go," he said. "It's my job."

Iris sighed. "I expected as much, but I had to try. The task ahead of you...Well, I wouldn't wish it on anyone, especially a nice boy like you. If you must go, at least I can offer some advice. You'll need help finding Thanatos."

"You know where the giants are hiding him?" Frank asked.

Iris gazed thoughtfully at the wind chimes swaying on the ceiling. "No...Alaska is beyond the gods' sphere of control. The location is shielded from my sight. But there *is* someone who would know. Seek out the seer Phineas. He's blind, but he can see the past, present, and future. He knows many things. He can tell you where Thanatos is being held."

"Phineas..." Frank said. "Wasn't there a story about him?"

Iris nodded reluctantly. "In the old days, he committed horrible crimes. He used his gift of sight for evil. Jupiter sent the harpies to plague him. The Argonauts—including your ancestor, by the way—"

"The prince of Pylos?"

Iris hesitated. "Yes, Frank. Though his gift, his story... *that* you must discover on your own. Suffice it to say, the Argonauts drove away the harpies in exchange for Phineas's help. That was eons ago, but I understand Phineas has returned to the mortal world. You'll find him in Portland, Oregon, which is on your way north. But you must promise me one thing. If he's still plagued by harpies, do *not* kill them, no matter what Phineas promises you. Win his help some other way. The harpies are not evil. They're my sisters."

"Your sisters?"

"I know. I don't look old enough to be the harpies' sister, but it's true. And Frank...there's another problem. If you're determined to leave, you'll have to clear those basilisks off the hill."

"You mean the snakes?"

"Yes," Iris said. "Basilisk means 'little crown,' which is a cute name for something that's not very cute. I'd prefer not to have them killed. They're living creatures, after all. But you won't be able to leave until they're gone. If your friends try to battle them . . . well, I foresee see bad things happening. Only *you* have the ability to kill the monsters."

"But how?"

She glanced down at the floor. Frank realized that she was looking at his spear.

"I wish there was another way," she said. "If you had some weasels, for instance. Weasels are deadly to basilisks."

"Fresh out of weasels," Frank admitted.

"Then you will have to use your father's gift. Are you sure you wouldn't like to live here instead? We make excellent lactose-free rice milk."

Frank rose. "How do I use the spear?"

"You'll have to handle that on your own. I can't advocate violence. While you're doing battle, I'll check on your friends. I hope Fleecy found the right medicinal herbs. The last time, we had a mix-up. . . . Well, I don't think those heroes *wanted* to be daisies."

The goddess stood. Her glasses flashed, and Frank saw his own reflection in the lenses. He looked serious and grim, nothing like the little boy he'd seen in those rainbow images.

"One last bit of advice, Frank," she said. "You're destined to die holding that piece of firewood, watching it burn. But perhaps if you didn't keep it yourself. Perhaps if you trusted someone enough to hold it for you..."

Frank's fingers curled around the tinder. "Are you offering?"

Iris laughed gently. "Oh, dear, no. I'd lose it in this collection. It would get mixed up with my crystals, or I'd sell it as a driftwood paperweight by accident. No, I meant a demigod friend. Someone close to your heart."

Hazel, Frank thought immediately. There was no one he trusted more. But how could he confess his secret? If he admitted how weak he was, that his whole life depended on a half-burned stick... Hazel would never see him as a hero. He'd never be her knight in armor. And how could he expect her to take that kind of burden from him?

He wrapped up the tinder and slipped it back into his coat. "Thanks...thanks, Iris."

She squeezed his hand. "Don't lose hope, Frank. Rainbows always stand for hope."

She made her way toward the back of the store, leaving Frank alone.

"Hope," Frank grumbled. "I'd rather have a few good weasels."

He picked up his father's spear and marched out to face the basilisks.

XXIII

FRANK

FRANK MISSED HIS BOW.

He wanted to stand on the porch and shoot the snakes from a distance. A few well-placed exploding arrows, a few craters in the hillside—problem solved.

Unfortunately, a quiver full of arrows wouldn't do Frank much good if he couldn't shoot them. Besides, he had no idea where the basilisks were. They'd stopped blowing fire as soon as he came outside.

He stepped off the porch and leveled his golden spear. He didn't like fighting up close. He was too slow and bulky. He'd done okay during the war games, but this was real. There were no giant eagles ready to snatch him up and take him to the medics if he made a mistake.

You can be anything. His mother's voice echoed in his mind.

Great, he thought. *I want to be good with a spear. And immune to poison—and fire.*

Something told Frank his wish had not been granted. The spear felt just as awkward in his hands.

Patches of flame still smoldered on the hillside. The acrid smoke burned in Frank's nose. The withered grass crunched under his feet.

He thought about those stories his mother used to tell—generations of heroes who had battled Hercules, fought dragons, and sailed monster-infested seas. Frank didn't understand how he could have evolved from a line like that, or how his family had migrated from Greece through the Roman Empire all the way to China, but some unsettling ideas were starting to form. For the first time, he started to wonder about this Prince of Pylos, and his great-grandfather Shen Lun's disgrace at Camp Jupiter, and what the family powers might be.

The gift has never kept our family safe, Grandmother had warned.

A reassuring thought as Frank hunted poisonous fire-breathing devil snakes.

The night was quiet except for the crackle of brush fires. Every time a breeze made the grass rustle, Frank thought about the grain spirits who'd captured Hazel. Hopefully they'd gone south with the giant Polybotes. Frank didn't need any more problems right now.

He crept downhill, his eyes stinging from the smoke. Then, about twenty feet ahead, he saw a burst of flame.

He considered throwing his spear. Stupid idea. Then he'd be without a weapon. Instead he advanced toward the fire.

He wished he had the gorgon's blood vials, but they were back at the boat. He wondered if gorgon blood could cure basilisk poison.... But even if he had the vials and managed to choose the right one, he doubted he'd have time to take it before he crumbled to dust like his bow.

He emerged in a clearing of burned grass and found himself face-to-face with a basilisk.

The snake rose up on its tail. It hissed, and expanded the collar of white spikes around its neck. *Little crown*, Frank remembered. That's what "basilisk" meant. He had thought basilisks were huge dragonlike monsters that could petrify you with their eyes. Somehow the real basilisk was even more terrible. As tiny as it was, this extra-small package of fire, poison, and evil would be much harder to kill than a large, bulky lizard. Frank had seen how fast it could move.

The monster fixed its pale yellow eyes on Frank.

Why wasn't it attacking?

Frank's golden spear felt cold and heavy. The dragon-tooth point dipped toward the ground all on its own—like a dowsing rod searching for water.

"Stop that." Frank struggled to the lift the spear. He'd have enough trouble jabbing the monster without his spear fighting against him. Then he heard the grass rustle on either side of him. The other two basilisks slithered into the clearing.

Frank had walked straight into an ambush.

XXIV

FRANK

FRANK SWEPT HIS SPEAR BACK AND FORTH. "Stay back!" His voice sounded squeaky. "I've got...um...amazing powers —and stuff."

The basilisks hissed in three-part harmony. Maybe they were laughing.

The spear tip was almost too heavy to lift now, as if the jagged white triangle of bone was trying to touch the earth. Then something clicked in the back of Frank's mind: Mars had said the tip was a dragon's tooth. Hadn't there been some story about dragon's teeth planted in the ground? Something he'd read in monster class at camp...?

The basilisks circled him, taking their time. Maybe they were hesitating because of the spear. Maybe they just couldn't believe how stupid Frank was.

It seemed like madness, but Frank let the spear tip drop. He drove it into the ground. *Crack.*

When he lifted it out, the tip was gone—broken off in the dirt.

Wonderful. Now he had a golden stick.

Some crazy part of him wanted to bring out his piece of firewood. If he was going to die anyway, maybe he could set off a massive blaze—incinerate the basilisks, so at least his friends could get away.

Before he could get up the courage, the ground rumbled at his feet. Dirt spewed everywhere, and a skeletal hand clawed the air. The basilisks hissed and backed up.

Frank couldn't blame them. He watched in horror as a human skeleton crawled out of the ground. It took on flesh as if someone were pouring gelatin over its bones, covering them in glowing, transparent gray skin. Then ghostly clothes enveloped it—a muscle shirt, camo pants, and army boots. Everything about the creature was gray: gray clothes on gray flesh on gray bones.

It turned toward Frank. Its skull grinned beneath an expressionless gray face. Frank whimpered like a puppy. His legs shook so badly he had to support himself with the spear shaft. The skeleton warrior was waiting, Frank realized—waiting for orders.

"Kill the basilisks!" he yelped. "Not me!"

The skeletal warrior leaped into action. He grabbed the nearest snake, and though his gray flesh began to smoke on contact, he strangled the basilisk with one hand and flung down its limp body. The other two basilisks hissed with rage. One sprang at Frank, but he knocked it aside with the butt of his spear.

The other snake belched fire directly in the skeleton's face. The warrior marched forward and stomped the basilisk's head under his boot.

Frank turned toward the last basilisk, which was curled at the edge of the clearing studying them. Frank's Imperial gold spear shaft was steaming, but unlike his bow, it didn't seem to be crumbling from the basilisk's touch. The skeleton warrior's right foot and hand were slowly dissolving from poison. His head was on fire, but otherwise he looked pretty good.

The basilisk did the smart thing. It turned to flee. In a blur of motion, the skeleton pulled something from his shirt and flung it across the clearing, impaling the basilisk in the dirt. Frank thought it was a knife. Then he realized it was one of the skeleton's own ribs.

Frank was glad his stomach was empty. "That . . . that was *gross.*"

The skeleton stumbled over to the basilisk. It pulled out its rib and used it to cut off the creature's head. The basilisk dissolved into ashes. Then the skeleton decapitated the other two monster carcasses and kicked all the ashes to disperse them. Frank remembered the two gorgons in the Tiber—the way the river had pulled apart their remains to keep them from re-forming.

"You're making sure they don't come back," Frank realized. "Or slowing them down, anyway."

The skeleton warrior stood at attention in front of Frank. Its poisoned foot and hand were mostly gone. Its head was still burning.

"What—what are you?" Frank asked. He wanted to add, *Please don't hurt me.*

The skeleton saluted with its stump of a hand. Then it began to crumble, sinking back into the ground.

"Wait!" Frank said. "I don't even know what to call you! Tooth Man? Bones? Gray?"

As its face disappeared beneath the dirt, the warrior seemed to grin at the last name—or maybe that was just its skeletal teeth showing. Then it was gone, leaving Frank alone with his pointless spear.

"Gray," he muttered. "Okay...but..."

He examined the tip of his spear. Already, a new dragon tooth was starting to grow out of the golden shaft.

You get three charges out of it, Mars had said, *so use it wisely.*

Frank heard footsteps behind him. Percy and Hazel ran into the clearing. Percy looked better, except he was carrying a tie-dyed man satchel from R.O.F.L.—definitely *not* his style. Riptide was in his hand. Hazel had drawn her *spatha.*

"Are you okay?" she asked.

Percy turned in a circle, looking for enemies. "Iris told us you were out here battling the basilisks by yourself, and we were like, *What?* We came as fast as we could. What happened?"

"I'm not sure," Frank admitted.

Hazel crouched next to the dirt where Gray disappeared. "I sense death. Either my brother has been here or...the basilisks are dead?"

Percy stared at him in awe. "You killed them *all?*"

Frank swallowed. He already felt like enough of a misfit without trying to explain his new undead minion.

Three charges. Frank could call on Gray twice more. But he'd sensed malevolence in the skeleton. It was no pet. It was a vicious, undead killing force, barely controlled by the power of

Mars. Frank got the feeling it would do what he said—but if his friends happened to be in the line of fire, oh well. And if Frank was a little slow giving it directions, it might start killing whatever was in its path, including its master.

Mars had told him the spear would give him breathing room until he learned to use his mother's talents. Which meant Frank needed to learn those talents—*fast*.

"Thanks a lot, Dad," he grumbled.

"What?" Hazel asked. "Frank, are you okay?"

"I'll explain later," he said. "Right now, there's a blind man in Portland we've got to see."

XXV

PERCY

PERCY ALREADY FELT LIKE THE lamest demigod in the history of lame. The purse was the final insult.

They'd left R.O.F.L. in a hurry, so maybe Iris hadn't meant the bag as a criticism. She'd quickly stuffed it with vitamin-enriched pastries, dried fruit leather, macrobiotic beef jerky, and a few crystals for good luck. Then she'd shoved it at Percy: *Here, you'll need this. Oh, that looks good.*

The purse—sorry, *masculine accessory bag*—was rainbow tie-dyed with a peace symbol stitched in wooden beads and the slogan *Hug the Whole World.* Percy wished it said *Hug the Commode.* He felt like the bag was a comment on his massive, incredible uselessness. As they sailed north, he put the man satchel as far away from him as he could, but the boat was small.

He couldn't believe how he'd broken down when his friends had needed him. First, he'd been dumb enough to leave them alone when he had run back to the boat, and Hazel had gotten kidnapped. Then he'd watched that army marching south and had some kind of nervous breakdown. Embarrassing? Yeah. But he couldn't help it. When he'd seen those evil centaurs and Cyclopes, it had seemed so wrong, so backward, that he thought his head would explode. And the giant Polybotes...that giant had given him a feeling the opposite of what he felt when he stood in the ocean. Percy's energy had drained out of him, leaving him weak and feverish, like his insides were eroding.

Iris's medicinal tea had helped his body feel better, but his mind still hurt. He'd heard stories about amputees who had phantom pains where their missing legs and arms used to be. That's how his mind felt—like his missing memories were aching.

Worst of all, the farther north Percy went, the more those memories faded. He had started to feel better at Camp Jupiter, remembering random names and faces. But now even Annabeth's face was getting dimmer. At R.O.F.L., when he'd tried to send an Iris-message to Annabeth, Fleecy had just shaken her head sadly.

It's like you're dialing somebody, she said, *but you've forgotten the number. Or someone is jamming the signal. Sorry, dear. I just can't connect you.*

He was terrified that he'd lose Annabeth's face completely when he got to Alaska. Maybe he'd wake up one day and not remember her name.

Still, he had to concentrate on the quest. The sight of that enemy army had shown him what they were up against. It was early in the morning of June 21, now. They had to get to Alaska, find Thanatos, locate the legion's standard, and make it back to Camp Jupiter by the evening of June 24. Four days. Meanwhile, the enemy had only a few hundred miles to march.

Percy guided the boat through the strong currents off the northern California coast. The wind was cold, but it felt good, clearing some of the confusion from his head. He bent his will to push the boat as hard as he could. The hull rattled as the *Pax* plowed its way north.

Meanwhile, Hazel and Frank traded stories about the events at Rainbow Organic Foods. Frank explained about the blind seer Phineas in Portland, and how Iris had said that he might be able to tell them where to find Thanatos. Frank wouldn't say how he had managed to kill the basilisks, but Percy got the feeling it had something to do with the broken point of his spear. Whatever had happened, Frank sounded more scared of the spear than the basilisks.

When he was done, Hazel told Frank about their time with Fleecy.

"So this Iris message worked?" Frank asked.

Hazel gave Percy a sympathetic look. She didn't mention his failure to contact Annabeth.

"I got in touch with Reyna," she said. "You're supposed to throw a coin into a rainbow and say this incantation, like *O Iris, goddess of the rainbow, accept my offering.* Except Fleecy kind of changed it. She gave us her—what did she call it—her direct number? So I had to say, *O Fleecy, do me a solid. Show Reyna at Camp Jupiter.* I felt kind of stupid, but it worked. Reyna's image appeared in the rainbow, like in a two-way video call. She was in the baths. Scared her out of her mind."

"That I would've paid to see," Frank said. "I mean—her expression. Not, you know, the baths."

"Frank!" Hazel fanned her face like she needed air. It was an old-fashioned gesture, but cute, somehow. "Anyway, we told Reyna about the army, but like Percy said, she pretty much already knew. It doesn't change anything. She's doing what she can to shore up the defenses. Unless we unleash Death, and get back with the eagle—"

"The camp can't stand against that army," Frank finished. "Not without help."

After that, they sailed in silence.

Percy kept thinking about Cyclopes and centaurs. He thought about Annabeth, the satyr Grover, and his dream of a giant warship under construction.

You came from somewhere, Reyna had said.

Percy wished he could remember. He could call for help. Camp Jupiter shouldn't have to fight alone against the giants. There must be allies out there.

He fingered the beads on his necklace, the lead *probatio* tablet, and the silver ring Reyna had given him. Maybe in Seattle he'd be able to talk to her sister Hylla. She might send help—assuming she didn't kill Percy on sight.

After a few more hours of navigating, Percy's eyes started to droop. He was afraid he'd pass out from exhaustion. Then he caught a break. A killer whale surfaced next to the boat, and Percy struck up a mental conversation with him.

It wasn't exactly like talking, but it went something like this: *Could you give us a ride north,* Percy asked, *like as close to Portland as possible?*

Eat seals, the whale responded. *Are you seals?*

No, Percy admitted. *I've got a man satchel full of macrobiotic beef jerky, though.*

The whale shuddered. *Promise not to feed me this, and I will take you north.*

Deal.

Soon Percy had made a makeshift rope harness and strapped it around the whale's upper body. They sped north under whale-power, and at Hazel and Frank's insistence, Percy settled in for a nap.

His dreams were as disjointed and scary as ever.

He imagined himself on Mount Tamalpais, north of San Francisco, fighting at the old Titan stronghold. That didn't make sense. He hadn't been with the Romans when they had attacked, but he saw it all clearly: a Titan in armor, Annabeth and two other girls fighting at Percy's side. One of the girls died in the battle. Percy knelt over her, watching as she dissolved into stars.

Then he saw the giant warship in its dry dock. The bronze dragon figurehead glinted in the morning light. The riggings and armaments were complete, but something was wrong. A hatch in the deck was open, and smoke poured from some kind of engine. A boy with curly black hair was cursing as he pounded the engine with a wrench. Two other demigods squatted next to him, watching with concern. One was a teenage guy with short blond hair. The other was a girl with long dark hair.

"You realize it's the solstice," the girl said. "We're supposed to leave today."

"I know that!" The curly-haired mechanic whacked the engine a few more times. "Could be the fizzrockets. Could be the samophlange. Could be Gaea messing with us again. I'm not sure!"

"How long?" the blond guy asked.

"Two, three days?"

"They may not have that long," the girl warned.

Something told Percy that she meant Camp Jupiter. Then the scene shifted again.

He saw a boy and his dog roaming over the yellow hills of California. But as the image became clearer, Percy realized it wasn't a boy. It was a Cyclops in ragged jeans and a flannel shirt. The dog was a shambling mountain of black fur, easily as big as a rhino. The Cyclops carried a massive club over his shoulder, but Percy didn't feel that he was an enemy. He kept yelling Percy's name, calling him... brother?

"He smells farther away," the Cyclops moaned to the dog. "Why does he smell farther?"

"ROOF!" the dog barked, and Percy's dream changed again.

He saw a range of snowy mountains, so tall they broke the clouds. Gaea's sleeping face appeared in the shadows of the rocks.

Such a valuable pawn, she said soothingly. *Do not fear, Percy Jackson. Come north! Your friends will die, yes. But I will preserve you for now. I have great plans for you.*

In a valley between the mountains lay a massive field of ice. The edge plunged into the sea, hundreds of feet below, with sheets of frost constantly crumbling into the water. On top of the ice field stood a legion camp—ramparts, moats, towers, barracks, just like Camp Jupiter except three times as large. At the crossroads outside the *principia,* a figure in dark robes stood shackled to the ice. Percy's vision swept past him, into the headquarters. There, in the gloom, sat a giant even bigger than Polybotes. His skin glinted gold. Displayed behind him were the tattered, frozen banners of a Roman legion, including a large, golden eagle with its wings spread.

We await you, the giant's voice boomed. *While you fumble your way north, trying to find me, my armies will destroy your precious camps—first the Romans, then the others. You cannot win, little demigod.*

Percy lurched awake in cold gray daylight, rain falling on his face.

"I thought *I* slept heavily," Hazel said. "Welcome to Portland."

Percy sat up and blinked. The scene around him was so different from his dream, he wasn't sure which was real. The *Pax* floated on an iron-black river through the middle of a city. Heavy clouds hung low overhead. The cold rain was so light, it seemed suspended in the air. On Percy's left were industrial warehouses and railroad tracks. To his right was a small downtown area—an almost cozy-looking cluster of towers between the banks of the river and a line of misty forested hills.

Percy rubbed the sleep out of his eyes. "How did we get here?"

Frank gave him a look like, *You won't believe this.* "The killer whale took us as far as the Columbia River. Then he passed the harness to a couple of twelve-foot sturgeons."

Percy thought Frank had said *surgeons.* He had this weird image of giant doctors in scrubs and face masks, pulling their boat upstream. Then he realized Frank meant sturgeons, like the fish. He was glad he hadn't said anything. Would have been embarrassing, his being son of the sea god and all.

"Anyway," Frank continued, "the sturgeons pulled us for a long time. Hazel and I took turns sleeping. Then we hit this river—"

"The Willamette," Hazel offered.

"Right," Frank said. "After that, the boat kind of took over and navigated us here all by itself. Sleep okay?"

As the *Pax* glided south, Percy told them about his dreams. He tried to focus on the positive: a warship might be on the way to help Camp Jupiter. A friendly Cyclops and a giant dog were looking for him. He didn't mention what Gaea had said: *Your friends will die.*

When Percy described the Roman fort on the ice, Hazel looked troubled.

"So Alcyoneus is on a glacier," she said. "That doesn't narrow it down much. Alaska has hundreds of those."

Percy nodded. "Maybe this seer dude Phineas can tell us which one."

The boat docked itself at a wharf. The three demigods stared up at the buildings of drizzly downtown Portland.

Frank wiped the rain off his flat-top hair.

"So now we find a blind man in the rain," Frank said. "Yay."

XXVI

PERCY

IT WASN'T AS HARD AS THEY THOUGHT. The screaming and the weed whacker helped.

They'd brought lightweight Polartec jackets with their supplies, so they bundled up against the cold rain and walked for a few blocks through the mostly deserted streets. This time Percy was smart and brought most of his supplies from the boat. He even stuffed the macrobiotic jerky in his coat pocket, in case he needed to threaten any more killer whales.

They saw some bicycle traffic and a few homeless guys huddled in doorways, but the majority of Portlanders seemed to be staying indoors.

As they made their way down Glisan Street, Percy looked longingly at the folks in the cafés enjoying coffee and pastries. He was about to suggest that they stop for breakfast when he heard a voice down the street yelling: "HA! TAKE THAT, STUPID CHICKENS!" followed by the revving of a small engine and a lot of squawking.

Percy glanced at his friends. "You think—?"

"Probably," Frank agreed.

They ran toward the sounds.

The next block over, they found a big open parking lot with tree-lined sidewalks and rows of food trucks facing the streets on all four sides. Percy had seen food trucks before, but never so many in once place. Some were simple white metal boxes on wheels, with awnings and serving counters. Others were painted blue or purple or polka-dotted, with big banners out front and colorful menu boards and tables like do-it-yourself sidewalk cafés. One advertised Korean/Brazilian fusion tacos, which sounded like some kind of top-secret radioactive cuisine. Another offered sushi on a stick. A third was selling deep-fried ice cream sandwiches. The smell was amazing dozens of different kitchens cooking at once.

Percy's stomach rumbled. Most of the food carts were open for business, but there was hardly anyone around. They could get anything they wanted! Deep-fried ice cream sandwiches? Oh, man, that sounded *way* better than wheat germ.

Unfortunately, there was more happening than just cooking. In the center of the lot, behind all the food trucks, an old man in a bathrobe was running around with a weed whacker, screaming at a flock of bird-ladies who were trying to steal food off a picnic table.

"Harpies," said Hazel. "Which means—"

"That's Phineas," Frank guessed.

They ran across the street and squeezed between the Korean/Brazilian truck and a Chinese egg roll burrito vendor. The backs of the food trucks weren't nearly as appetizing as the fronts. They were cluttered with stacks of plastic buckets, overflowing garbage cans, and makeshift clotheslines hung with wet aprons and towels. The parking lot itself was nothing but a square of cracked asphalt, marbled with weeds. In the middle was a picnic table piled high with food from all the different trucks.

The guy in the bathrobe was old and fat. He was mostly bald, with scars across his forehead and a rim of stringy white hair. His bathrobe was spattered with ketchup, and he kept stumbling around in fuzzy pink bunny slippers, swinging his gas-powered weed whacker at the half-dozen harpies who were hovering over his picnic table.

He was clearly blind. His eyes were milky white, and usually he missed the harpies by a lot, but he was still doing a pretty good job fending them off.

"Back, dirty chickens!" he bellowed.

Percy wasn't sure why, but he had a vague sense that harpies were supposed to be plump. These looked like they were starving. Their human faces had sunken eyes and hollow cheeks. Their bodies were covered in molting feathers, and their wings were tipped with tiny, shriveled hands. They wore ragged burlap sacks for dresses. As they dived for the food, they seemed more desperate than angry. Percy felt sorry for them.

WHIRRRR! The old man swung his weed whacker. He grazed one of the harpies' wings. The harpy yelped in pain and fluttered off, dropping yellow feathers as she flew.

Another harpy circled higher than the rest. She looked younger and smaller than the others, with bright-red feathers.

She watched carefully for an opening, and when the old man's back was turned, she made a wild dive for the table. She grabbed a burrito in her clawed feet, but before she could escape, the blind man swung his weed whacker and smacked her in the back so hard, Percy winced. The harpy yelped, dropped the burrito, and flew off.

"Hey, stop it!" Percy yelled.

The harpies took that the wrong way. They glanced over at the three demigods and immediately fled. Most of them fluttered away and perched in the trees around the square, staring dejectedly at the picnic table. The red-feathered one with the hurt back flew unsteadily down Glisan Street and out of sight.

"Ha!" The blind man yelled in triumph and killed the power on his weed whacker. He grinned vacantly in Percy's direction. "Thank you, strangers! Your help is most appreciated."

Percy bit back his anger. He hadn't meant to help the old man, but he remembered that they needed information from him.

"Uh, whatever." He approached the old guy, keeping one eye on the weed whacker. "I'm Percy Jackson. This is—"

"Demigods!" the old man said. "I can always smell demigods."

Hazel frowned. "Do we smell that bad?"

The old man laughed. "Of course not, my dear. But you'd be surprised how sharp my other senses became once I was blinded. I'm Phineas. And you—wait, don't tell me—"

He reached for Percy's face and poked him in the eyes.

"Ow!" Percy complained.

"Son of Neptune!" Phineas exclaimed. "I thought I smelled the ocean on you, Percy Jackson. I'm also a son of Neptune, you know."

"Hey...yeah. Okay." Percy rubbed his eyes. Just his luck he was related to this grubby old dude. He hoped all sons of Neptune didn't share the same fate. First, you start carrying a man satchel. Next thing you know, you're running around in a bathrobe and pink bunny slippers, chasing chickens with a weed whacker.

Phineas turned to Hazel. "And here...Oh my, the smell of gold and deep earth. Hazel Levesque, daughter of Pluto. And next to you—the son of Mars. But there's more to your story, Frank Zhang—"

"Ancient blood," Frank muttered. "Prince of Pylos. Blah, blah, blah."

"Periclymenus, exactly! Oh, he was a nice fellow. I loved the Argonauts!"

Frank's mouth fell open. "W-wait. Perry *who?*"

Phineas grinned. "Don't worry. I know about your family. That story about your great-grandfather? He didn't *really* destroy the camp. Now, what an interesting group. Are you hungry?"

Frank looked like he'd been run over by a truck, but Phineas had already moved on to other matters. He waved his hand at the picnic table. In the nearby trees, the harpies shrieked miserably. As hungry as Percy was, he couldn't stand to think about eating with those poor bird ladies watching him.

"Look, I'm confused," Percy said. "We need some information. We were told—"

"—that the harpies were keeping my food away from me," Phineas finished, "and if you helped me, I'd help you."

"Something like that," Percy admitted.

Phineas laughed. "That's old news. Do I look like I'm missing any meals?"

He patted his belly, which was the size of an overinflated basketball.

"Um . . . no," Percy said.

Phineas waved his weed whacker in an expansive gesture. All three of them ducked.

"Things have changed, my friends!" he said. "When I first got the gift of prophecy, eons ago, it's true Jupiter cursed me. He sent the harpies to steal my food. You see, I had a bit of a big mouth. I gave away too many secrets that the gods wanted kept." He turned to Hazel. "For instance, you're supposed to be dead. And you—" He turned to Frank. "Your life depends on a burned stick."

Percy frowned. "What are you talking about?"

Hazel blinked like she'd been slapped. Frank looked like the truck had backed up and run over him again.

"And you," Phineas turned to Percy, "well now, you don't even know who you are! I could tell you, of course, but . . . ha! What fun would that be? And Brigid O'Shaughnessy shot Miles Archer in *The Maltese Falcon*. And Darth Vader is actually Luke's father. And the winner of the next Super Bowl will be—"

"Got it," Frank muttered.

Hazel gripped her sword like she was tempted to pommel-whip the old man. "So you talked too much, and the gods cursed you. Why did they stop?"

"Oh, they didn't!" The old man arched his bushy eyebrows like, *Can you believe it?* "I had to make a deal with the Argonauts. They wanted information too, you see. I told them to kill the harpies, and I'd cooperate. Well, they drove those nasty creatures away, but Iris wouldn't let them kill the harpies. An outrage! So *this* time, when my patron brought me back to life—"

"Your patron?" Frank asked.

Phineas gave him a wicked grin. "Why, Gaea, of course. Who do you think opened the Doors of Death? Your girlfriend here understands. Isn't Gaea your patron, too?"

Hazel drew her sword. "I'm not his— I don't— Gaea is not my patron!"

Phineas looked amused. If he had heard the sword being drawn, he didn't seem concerned. "Fine, if you want to be *noble* and stick with the losing side, that's your business. But Gaea is waking. She's already rewritten the rules of life and death! I'm alive again, and in exchange for my help—a prophecy here, a prophecy there—I get my fondest wish. The tables have been turned, so to speak. Now I can eat all I want, all day long, and the harpies have to watch and starve."

He revved his weed whacker, and the harpies wailed in the trees.

"They're cursed!" the old man said. "They can eat only

food from my table, and they can't leave Portland. Since the Doors of Death are open, they can't even die. It's beautiful!"

"Beautiful?" Frank protested. "They're living creatures. Why are you so mean to them?"

"They're monsters!" Phineas said. "And *mean*? Those feather-brained demons tormented me for years!"

"But it was their duty," Percy said, trying to control himself. "Jupiter ordered them to."

"Oh, I'm mad at Jupiter, too," Phineas agreed. "In time, Gaea will see that the gods are properly punished. Horrible job they've done, ruling the world. But for now, I'm enjoying Portland. The mortals take no notice of me. They think I'm just a crazy old man shooing away pigeons!"

Hazel advanced on the seer. "You're awful!" she told Phineas. "You belong in the Fields of Punishment!"

Phineas sneered. "One dead person to another, girlie? I wouldn't be talking. You started this whole thing! If it weren't for you, Alcyoneus wouldn't be alive!"

Hazel stumbled back.

"Hazel?" Frank's eyes got as wide as quarters. "What's he talking about?"

"Ha!" Phineas said. "You'll find out soon enough, Frank Zhang. Then we'll see if you're still sweet on your girlfriend. But that's not what you're here about, is it? You want to find Thanatos. He's being kept at Alcyoneus's lair. I can tell you where that is. Of course I can. But you'll have to do me a favor."

"Forget it," Hazel snapped. "You're working for the enemy. We should send you back to the Underworld ourselves."

"You could try." Phineas smiled. "But I doubt I'd stay dead very long. You see, Gaea has shown me the easy way back. And with Thanatos in chains, there's no one to keep me down! Besides, if you kill me, you won't get my secrets."

Percy was tempted to let Hazel use her sword. In fact he wanted to strangle the old man himself.

Camp Jupiter, he told himself. *Saving the camp is more important.* He remembered Alcyoneus taunting him in his dreams. If they wasted time searching through Alaska looking for the giant's lair, Gaea's armies would destroy the Romans...and Percy's other friends, wherever they were.

He gritted his teeth. "What's the favor?"

Phineas licked his lips greedily. "There's one harpy who's quicker than the rest."

"The red one," Percy guessed.

"I'm blind! I don't know colors!" the old man groused. "At any rate, she's the only one I have trouble with. She's wily, that one. Always does her own thing, never roosts with the others. She gave me these."

He pointed at the scars on his forehead.

"Capture that harpy," he said. "Bring her to me. I want her tied up where I can keep an eye on her...ah, so to speak. Harpies hate being tied up. It causes them extreme pain. Yes, I'll enjoy that. Maybe I'll even feed her so that she lasts longer."

Percy looked at his friends. They came to a silent agreement: they would *never* help this creepy old man. On the other hand, they had to get his information. They needed a Plan B.

"Oh, go talk among yourselves," Phineas said breezily. "I don't care. Just remember that without my help, your quest will fail. And everyone you love in the world will die. Now, off with you! Bring me a harpy!"

XXVII

PERCY

"WE'LL NEED SOME OF YOUR FOOD." Percy shouldered his way around the old man and snatched stuff off the picnic table—a covered bowl of Thai noodles in mac-and-cheese sauce, and a tubular pastry that looked like a combination burrito and cinnamon roll.

Before he could lose control and smash the burrito in Phineas's face, Percy said, "Come on, guys." He led his friends out of the parking lot.

They stopped across the street. Percy took a deep breath, trying to calm down. The rain had slowed to a halfhearted drizzle. The cold mist felt good on his face.

"That man..." Hazel smacked the side of a bus-stop bench. "He needs to die. *Again*."

It was hard to tell in the rain, but she seemed to be blinking back tears. Her long curly hair was plastered down the sides of her face. In the gray light, her gold eyes looked more like tin.

Percy remembered how confident she'd acted when they first met—taking control of the situation with the gorgons and ushering him to safety. She'd comforted him at the shrine of Neptune and made him feel welcome at camp.

Now he wanted to return the favor, but he wasn't sure how. She looked lost, bedraggled, and thoroughly depressed.

Percy wasn't surprised that she had come back from the Underworld. He'd suspected that for a while—the way she avoided talking about her past, the way Nico di Angelo had been so secretive and cautious.

But that didn't change how Percy saw her. She seemed ...well, *alive*, like a regular kid with a good heart, who deserved to grow up and have a future. She wasn't a ghoul like Phincas.

"We'll get him," Percy promised. "He's *nothing* like you, Hazel. I don't care what he says."

She shook her head. "You don't know the whole story. I should have been sent to Punishment. I—I'm just as bad—"

"No, you're not!" Frank balled his fists. He looked around like he was searching for anybody who might disagree with him—enemies he could hit for Hazel's sake. "She's a good person!" he yelled across the street. A few harpies squawked in the trees, but no one else paid them any attention.

Hazel stared at Frank. She reached out tentatively, as if she wanted to take his hand but was afraid he might evaporate.

"Frank..." she stammered. "I—I don't..."

Unfortunately, Frank seemed wrapped up in his own thoughts.

He slung his spear off his back and gripped it uneasily.

"I could intimidate that old man," he offered, "maybe scare him—"

"Frank, it's okay," Percy said. "Let's keep that as a backup plan, but I don't think Phineas can be scared into cooperating. Besides, you've only got two more uses out of the spear, right?"

Frank scowled at the dragon's-tooth point, which had grown back completely overnight. "Yeah. I guess. . . ."

Percy wasn't sure what the old seer had meant about Frank's family history—his great-grandfather destroying camp, his Argonaut ancestor, and the bit about a burned stick controlling Frank's life. But it had clearly shaken Frank up. Percy decided not to ask for explanations. He didn't want the big guy reduced to tears, especially in front of Hazel.

"I've got an idea." Percy pointed up the street. "The red-feathered harpy went that way. Let's see if we can get her to talk to us."

Hazel looked at the food in his hands. "You're going to use that as bait?"

"More like a peace offering," Percy said. "Come on. Just try to keep the other harpies from stealing this stuff, okay?"

Percy uncovered the Thai noodles and unwrapped the cinnamon burrito. Fragrant steam wafted into the air. They walked down the street, Hazel and Frank with their weapons out. The harpies fluttered after them, perching on trees, mailboxes, and flagpoles, following the smell of food.

Percy wondered what the mortals saw through the Mist. Maybe they thought the harpies were pigeons and the weapons were lacrosse sticks or something. Maybe they just thought the Thai mac and cheese was so good it needed an armed escort.

Percy kept a tight grip on the food. He'd seen how quickly the harpies could snatch things. He didn't want to lose his peace offering before he found the red-feathered harpy.

Finally he spotted her, circling above a stretch of parkland that ran for several blocks between rows of old stone buildings. Paths stretched through the park under huge maple and elm trees, past sculptures and playgrounds and shady benches. The place reminded Percy of...some other park. Maybe in his hometown? He couldn't remember, but it made him feel homesick.

They crossed the street and found a bench to sit on, next to a big bronze sculpture of an elephant.

"Looks like Hannibal," Hazel said.

"Except it's Chinese," Frank said. "My grandmother has one of those." He flinched. "I mean, hers isn't twelve feet tall. But she imports stuff...from China. We're Chinese." He looked at Hazel and Percy, who were trying hard not to laugh. "Could I just die from embarrassment now?" he asked.

"Don't worry about it, man," Percy said. "Let's see if we can make friends with the harpy."

He raised the Thai noodles and fanned the smell upward —spicy peppers and cheesy goodness. The red harpy circled lower.

"We won't hurt you," Percy called up in a normal voice. "We just want to talk. Thai noodles for a chance to talk, okay?"

The harpy streaked down in a flash of red and landed on the elephant statue.

She was painfully thin. Her feathery legs were like sticks. Her face would have been pretty except for her sunken cheeks. She moved in jerky birdlike twitches, her coffee-brown eyes darting restlessly, her fingers clawing at her plumage, her earlobes, her shaggy red hair.

"Cheese," she muttered, looking sideways. "Ella doesn't like cheese."

Percy hesitated. "Your name is Ella?"

"Ella. Aella. 'Harpy.' In English. In Latin. Ella doesn't like cheese." She said all that without taking a breath or making eye contact. Her hands snatched at her hair, her burlap dress, the raindrops, whatever moved.

Quicker than Percy could blink, she lunged, snatched the cinnamon burrito, and appeared atop the elephant again.

"Gods, she's fast!" Hazel said.

"And *heavily* caffeinated," Frank guessed.

Ella sniffed the burrito. She nibbled at the edge and shuddered from head to foot, cawing like she was dying. "Cinnamon is good," she pronounced. "Good for harpies. Yum."

She started to eat, but the bigger harpies swooped down. Before Percy could react, they began pummeling Ella with their wings, snatching at the burrito.

"Nnnnnnooo." Ella tried to hide under her wings as her sisters ganged up on her, scratching with their claws. "N-no," she stuttered. "N-n-no!"

"Stop it!" Percy yelled. He and his friends ran to help, but it was too late. A big yellow harpy grabbed the burrito and the whole flock scattered, leaving Ella cowering and shivering on top of the elephant.

Hazel touched the harpy's foot. "I'm so sorry. Are you okay?"

Ella poked her head out of her wings. She was still trembling. With her shoulders hunched, Percy could see the bleeding gash on her back where Phineas had hit her with the weed whacker. She picked at her feathers, pulling out tufts of plumage. "S-small Ella," she stuttered angrily. "W-weak Ella. No cinnamon for Ella. Only cheese."

Frank glared across the street, where the other harpies were sitting in a maple tree, tearing the burrito to shreds. "We'll get you something else," he promised.

Percy set down the Thai noodles. He realized that Ella was different, even for a harpy. But after watching her get picked on, he was sure of one thing: whatever else happened, he was going to help her.

"Ella," he said, "we want to be your friends. We can get you more food, but—"

"Friends," Ella said. "'Ten seasons. 1994 to 2004.'" She glanced sideways at Percy, then looked in the air and started reciting to the clouds. "'A half-blood of the eldest gods, shall reach sixteen against all odds.' Sixteen. You're sixteen. Page sixteen, *Mastering the Art of French Cooking.* 'Ingredients: Bacon, Butter.'"

Percy's ears were ringing. He felt dizzy, like he'd just plunged a hundred feet underwater and back up again. "Ella . . . what was that you said?"

"'Bacon.'" She caught a raindrop out of the air. "'Butter.'"

"No, before that. Those lines...I *know* those lines."

Next to him, Hazel shivered. "It does sound familiar, like ...I don't know, like a prophecy. Maybe it's something she heard Phineas say?"

At the name *Phineas*, Ella squawked in terror and flew away.

"Wait!" Hazel called. "I didn't mean— Oh, gods, I'm stupid."

"It's all right." Frank pointed. "Look."

Ella wasn't moving as quickly now. She flapped her way to the top of a three-story red brick building and scuttled out of sight over the roof. A single red feather fluttered down to the street.

"You think that's her nest?" Frank squinted at the sign on the building. "Multnomah County Library?"

Percy nodded. "Let's see if it's open."

They ran across the street and into the lobby.

A library wouldn't have been Percy's first choice for someplace to visit. With his dyslexia, he had enough trouble reading signs. A whole building full of books? That sounded about as much fun as Chinese water torture or getting his teeth extracted.

As they jogged through the lobby, Percy figured Annabeth would like this place. It was spacious and brightly lit, with big vaulted windows. Books and architecture, that was definitely her....

He froze in his tracks.

"Percy?" Frank asked. "What's wrong?"

Percy tried desperately to concentrate. Where had those thoughts come from? Architecture, books . . . Annabeth had taken him to the library once, back home in—in— The memory faded. Percy slammed his fist into the side of a bookshelf.

"Percy?" Hazel asked gently.

He was so angry, so frustrated with his missing memories that he wanted to punch another bookshelf, but his friends' concerned faces brought him back to the present.

"I'm—I'm all right," he lied. "Just got dizzy for a sec. Let's find a way to the roof."

It took them a while, but they finally found a stairwell with roof access. At the top was a door with a handle alarm, but someone had propped it open with a copy of *War and Peace*.

Outside, Ella the harpy huddled in a nest of books under a makeshift cardboard shelter.

Percy and his friends advanced slowly, trying not to scare her. Ella didn't pay them any attention. She picked at her feathers and muttered under her breath, like she was practicing lines for a play.

Percy got within five feet and knelt down. "Hi. Sorry we scared you. Look, I don't have much food, but . . ."

He took some of the macrobiotic jerky out of his pocket. Ella lunged and snatched it immediately. She huddled back in her nest, sniffing the jerky, but sighed and tossed it away. "N-not from his table. Ella cannot eat. Sad. Jerky would be good for harpies."

"Not from . . . Oh, right," Percy said. "That's part of the curse. You can only eat his food."

"There has to be a way," Hazel said.

"'Photosynthesis,'" Ella muttered. "'Noun. Biology. The synthesis of complex organic materials.' 'It was the best of times, it was the worst of times; it was the age of wisdom, it was the age of foolishness...'"

"What is she saying?" Frank whispered.

Percy stared at the mound of books around her. They all looked old and mildewed. Some had prices written in marker on the covers, like the library had gotten rid of them in a clearance sale.

"She's quoting books," Percy guessed.

"Farmer's Almanac 1965," Ella said. "'Start breeding animals, January twenty-sixth.'"

"Ella," he said, "have you read all of these?"

She blinked. "More. More downstairs. Words. Words calm Ella down. Words, words, words."

Percy picked up a book at random—a tattered copy of *A History of Horseracing.* "Ella, do you remember the, um, third paragraph on page sixty-two—"

"'Secretariat,'" Ella said instantly, "'favored three to two-in the 1973 Kentucky Derby, finished at standing track record of one fifty-nine and two fifths.'"

Percy closed the book. His hands were shaking. "Word for word."

"That's amazing," Hazel said.

"She's a genius chicken," Frank agreed.

Percy felt uneasy. He was starting to form a terrible idea about why Phineas wanted to capture Ella, and it wasn't because she'd scratched him. Percy remembered that line she'd recited, *A half-blood of the eldest gods.* He was sure it was about *him.*

"Ella," he said, "we're going to find a way to break the curse. Would you like that?"

"'It's Impossible,'" she said. "'Recorded in English by Perry Como, 1970.'"

"Nothing's impossible," Percy said. "Now, look, I'm going to say his name. You don't have to run away. We're going to save you from the curse. We just need to figure out a way to beat . . . Phineas."

He waited for her to bolt, but she just shook her head vigorously. "N-n-no! No Phineas. Ella is quick. Too quick for him. B-but he wants to ch-chain Ella. He hurts Ella."

She tried to reach the gash on her back.

"Frank," Percy said, "you have first-aid supplies?"

"On it." Frank brought out a thermos full of nectar and explained its healing properties to Ella. When he scooted closer, she recoiled and started to shriek. Then Hazel tried, and Ella let her pour some nectar on her back. The wound began to close.

Hazel smiled. "See? That's better."

"Phineas is bad," Ella insisted. "And weed whackers. And cheese."

"Absolutely," Percy agreed. "We won't let him hurt you again. We need to figure out how to trick him, though. You harpies must know him better than anybody. Is there any way we can trick him?"

"N-no," Ella said. "Tricks are for kids. *50 Tricks to Teach Your Dog,* by Sophie Collins, call number six-three-six—"

"Okay, Ella." Hazel spoke in a soothing voice, like she was trying to calm a horse. "But does Phineas have any weaknesses?"

"Blind. He's blind."

Frank rolled his eyes, but Hazel continued patiently, "Right. Besides that?"

"Chance," she said. "Games of chance. Two to one. Bad odds. Call or fold."

Percy's spirits rose. "You mean he's a gambler?"

"Phineas s-sees big things. Prophecies. Fates. God stuff. Not small stuff. Random. Exciting. And he is blind."

Frank rubbed his chin. "Any idea what she means?"

Percy watched the harpy pick at her burlap dress. He felt incredibly sorry for her, but he was also starting to realize just how smart she was.

"I think I get it," he said. "Phineas sees the future. He knows tons of important events. But he can't see small things —like random occurrences, spontaneous games of chance. That makes gambling exciting for him. If we can tempt him into making a bet..."

Hazel nodded slowly. "You mean if he loses, he has to tell us where Thanatos is. But what do we have to wager? What kind of game do we play?"

"Something simple, with high stakes," Percy said. "Like two choices. One you live, one you die. And the prize has to be something Phineas wants...I mean, besides Ella. That's off the table."

"Sight," Ella muttered. "Sight is good for blind men.

Healing . . . nope, nope. Gaea won't do that for Phineas. Gaea keeps Phineas b-blind, dependent on Gaea. Yep."

Frank and Percy exchanged a meaningful look. "Gorgon's blood," they said simultaneously.

"What?" Hazel asked.

Frank brought out the two ceramic vials he'd retrieved from the Little Tiber. "Ella's a genius," he said. "Unless we die."

"Don't worry about that," Percy said. "I've got a plan."

XXVIII

PERCY

THE OLD MAN WAS RIGHT WHERE they'd left him, in the middle of the food truck parking lot. He sat on his picnic bench with his bunny slippers propped up, eating a plate of greasy shish kebab. His weed whacker was at his side. His bathrobe was smeared with barbecue sauce.

"Welcome back!" he called cheerfully. "I hear the flutter of nervous little wings. You've brought me my harpy?"

"She's here," Percy said. "But she's not yours."

Phineas sucked the grease off his fingers. His milky eyes seemed fixed on a point just above Percy's head. "I see... Well, actually, I'm blind, so I *don't* see. Have you come to kill me, then? If so, good luck completing your quest."

"I've come to gamble."

The old man's mouth twitched. He put down his shish kebab and leaned toward Percy. "A gamble...how interesting. Information in exchange for the harpy? Winner take all?"

"No," Percy said. "The harpy isn't part of the deal."

Phineas laughed. "Really? Perhaps you don't understand her value."

"She's a person," Percy said. "She isn't for sale."

"Oh, please! You're from the Roman camp, aren't you? Rome was *built* on slavery. Don't get all high and mighty with me. Besides, she isn't even human. She's a monster. A wind spirit. A minion of Jupiter."

Ella squawked. Just getting her into the parking lot had been a major challenge, but now she started backing away, muttering, "'Jupiter. Hydrogen and helium. Sixty-three satellites.' No minions. Nope."

Hazel put her arm around Ella's wings. She seemed to be the only one who could touch the harpy without causing lots of screaming and twitching.

Frank stayed at Percy's side. He held his spear ready, as if the old man might charge them.

Percy brought out the ceramic vials. "I have a different wager. We've got two flasks of gorgon's blood. One kills. One heals. They look exactly the same. Even we don't know which is which. If you choose the right one, it could cure your blindness."

Phineas held out his hands eagerly. "Let me feel them. Let me smell them."

"Not so fast," Percy said. "First you agree to the terms."

"Terms..." Phineas was breathing shallowly. Percy could tell he was hungry to take the offer. "Prophecy *and* sight... I'd be unstoppable. I could *own* this city. I'd build my palace here, surrounded by food trucks. I could capture that harpy myself!"

"N-noo," Ella said nervously. "Nope, nope, nope."

A villainous laugh is hard to pull off when you're wearing pink bunny slippers, but Phineas gave it his best shot. "Very well, demigod. What are your terms?"

"You get to choose a vial," Percy said. "No uncorking, no sniffing before you decide."

"That's not fair! I'm blind."

"And I don't have your sense of smell," Percy countered. "You can hold the vials. And I'll swear on the River Styx that they look identical. They're exactly what I told you: gorgon's blood, one vial from the left side of the monster, one from the right. And I swear that none of us knows which is which."

Percy looked back at Hazel. "Uh, you're our Underworld expert. With all this weird stuff going on with Death, is an oath on the River Styx still binding?"

"Yes," she said, without hesitation. "To break such a vow ... Well, just don't do it. There are worse things than death."

Phineas stroked his beard. "So I choose which vial to drink. You have to drink the other one. We swear to drink at the same time."

"Right," Percy said.

"The loser dies, obviously," Phineas said. "That kind of poison would probably keep even *me* from coming back to life ... for a long time, at least. My essence would be scattered and degraded. So I'm risking quite a lot."

"But if you win, you get everything," Percy said. "If I die, my friends will swear to leave you in peace and not take revenge. You'd have your sight back, which even Gaea won't give you."

The old man's expression soured. Percy could tell he'd struck a nerve. Phineas wanted to see. As much as Gaea had given him, he resented being kept in the dark.

"If I lose," the old man said, "I'll be dead, unable to give you information. How does that help you?"

Percy was glad he'd talked this through with his friends ahead of time. Frank had suggested the answer.

"You write down the location of Alcyoneus's lair ahead of time," Percy said. "Keep it to yourself, but swear on the River Styx it's specific and accurate. You also have to swear that if you lose and die, the harpies will be released from their curse."

"Those are high stakes," Phineas grumbled. "You face death, Percy Jackson. Wouldn't it be simpler just to hand over the harpy?"

"Not an option."

Phineas smiled slowly. "So you *are* starting to understand her worth. Once I have my sight, I'll capture her myself, you know. Whoever controls that harpy ... well, I was a king once. This gamble could make me a king again."

"You're getting ahead of yourself," Percy said. "Do we have a deal?"

Phineas tapped his nose thoughtfully. "I can't foresee the outcome. Annoying how that works. A completely unexpected gamble ... it makes the future cloudy. But I can tell you this, Percy Jackson—a bit of free advice. If you survive today, you're not going to like your future. A big sacrifice is coming, and you won't have the courage to make it. That will cost you dearly. It will cost the *world* dearly. It might be easier if you just choose the poison."

Percy's mouth tasted like Iris's sour green tea. He wanted to think the old man was just psyching him out, but something told him the prediction was true. He remembered Juno's warning when he'd chosen to go to Camp Jupiter: *You will feel pain, misery, and loss beyond anything you've ever known. But you might have a chance to save your old friends and family.*

In the trees around the parking lot, the harpies gathered to watch as if they sensed what was at stake. Frank and Hazel studied Percy's face with concern. He'd assured them the odds weren't as bad as fifty-fifty. He *did* have a plan. Of course, the plan could backfire. His chance of survival might be a hundred percent—or zero. He hadn't mentioned that.

"Do we have a deal?" he asked again.

Phineas grinned. "I swear on the River Styx to abide by the terms, just as you have described them. Frank Zhang, you're the descendant of an Argonaut. I trust your word. If I win, do you and your friend Hazel swear to leave me in peace, and not seek revenge?"

Frank's hands were clenched so tight Percy thought he might break his gold spear, but he managed to grumble, "I swear it on the River Styx."

"I also swear," Hazel said.

"Swear," Ella muttered. "'Swear not by the moon, the inconstant moon.'"

Phineas laughed. "In that case, find me something to write with. Let's get started."

Frank borrowed a napkin and a pen from a food truck vendor. Phineas scribbled something on the napkin and put it in his bathrobe pocket. "I swear this is the location of Alcyoneus's lair. Not that you'll live long enough to read it."

Percy drew his sword and swept all the food off the picnic table. Phineas sat on one side. Percy sat on the other.

Phineas held out his hands. "Let me feel the vials."

Percy gazed at the hills in the distance. He imagined the shadowy face of a sleeping woman. He sent his thoughts into the ground beneath him and hoped the goddess was listening.

Okay, Gaea, he said. *I'm calling your bluff. You say I'm a valuable pawn. You say you've got plans for me, and you're going to spare me until I make it north. Who's more valuable to you—me, or this old man? Because one of us is about to die.*

Phineas curled his fingers in a grasping motion. "Losing your nerve, Percy Jackson? Let me have them."

Percy passed him the vials.

The old man compared their weight. He ran his fingers along the ceramic surfaces. Then he set them both on the table and rested one hand lightly on each. A tremor passed through the ground—a mild earthquake, just strong enough to make Percy's teeth chatter. Ella cawed nervously.

The vial on the left seemed to shake slightly more than the one on the right.

Phineas grinned wickedly. He closed his fingers around the left-hand vial. "You were a fool, Percy Jackson. I choose this one. Now we drink."

Percy took the vial on the right. His teeth were chattering.

The old man raised his vial. "A toast to the sons of Neptune."

They both uncorked their vials and drank.

Immediately, Percy doubled over, his throat burning. His mouth tasted like gasoline.

"Oh, gods," Hazel said behind him.

"Nope!" Ella said. "Nope, nope, nope."

Percy's vision blurred. He could see Phineas grinning in triumph, sitting up straighter, blinking his eyes in anticipation.

"Yes!" he cried. "Any moment now, my sight will return!"

Percy had chosen wrong. He'd been stupid to take such a risk. He felt like broken glass was working its way through his stomach, into his intestines.

"Percy!" Frank gripped his shoulders. "Percy, you can't die!"

He gasped for breath . . . and suddenly his vision cleared.

At the same moment, Phineas hunched over like he'd been punched.

"You—you can't!" the old man wailed. "Gaea, you—you—"

He staggered to his feet and stumbled away from the table, clutching his stomach. "I'm too valuable!"

Steam came out of his mouth. A sickly yellow vapor rose from his ears, his beard, his blind eyes.

"Unfair!" he screamed. "You tricked me!"

He tried to claw the piece of paper out of his robe pocket, but his hands crumbled, his fingers turning to sand.

Percy rose unsteadily. He didn't feel *cured* of anything in particular. His memory hadn't magically returned. But the pain had stopped.

"No one tricked you," Percy said. "You made your choice freely, and I hold you to your oath."

The blind king wailed in agony. He turned in a circle,

steaming and slowly disintegrating until there was nothing left but an old, stained bathrobe and a pair of bunny slippers.

"Those," Frank said, "are the most disgusting spoils of war *ever*."

A woman's voice spoke in Percy's mind. *A gamble, Percy Jackson.* It was a sleepy whisper, with just a hint of grudging admiration. *You forced me to choose, and you are more important to my plans than the old seer. But do not press your luck. When your death comes, I promise it will be much more painful than gorgon's blood.*

Hazel prodded the robe with her sword. There was nothing underneath—no sign that Phineas was trying to re-form. She looked at Percy in awe. "That was either the bravest thing I've ever seen, or the stupidest."

Frank shook his head in disbelief. "Percy, how did you know? You were so confident he'd choose the poison."

"Gaea," Percy said. "She *wants* me to make it to Alaska. She thinks...I'm not sure. She thinks she can use me as part of her plan. She influenced Phineas to choose the wrong vial."

Frank stared in horror at the remains of the old man. "Gaea would kill her own servant rather than you? That's what you were betting on?"

"Plans," Ella muttered. "Plans and plots. The lady in the ground. Big plans for Percy. Macrobiotic jerky for Ella."

Percy handed her the whole bag of jerky and she squeaked with joy. "Nope, nope, nope," she muttered, half-singing. "Phineas, nope. Food and words for Ella, yep."

Percy crouched over the bathrobe and pulled the old man's note out of the pocket. It read: *HUBBARD GLACIER.*

All that risk for two words. He handed the note to Hazel.

"I know where that is," she said. "It's pretty famous. But we've got a long, long way to go."

In the trees around the parking lot, the other harpies finally overcame their shock. They squawked with excitement and flew at the nearest food trucks, diving through the service windows and raiding the kitchens. Cooks shouted in many languages. Trucks shook back and forth. Feathers and food boxes flew everywhere.

"We'd better get back to the boat," Percy said. "We're running out of time."

XXIX

HAZEL

EVEN BEFORE SHE GOT ON THE BOAT, Hazel felt queasy.

She kept thinking about Phineas with steam coming out of his eyes, his hands crumbling to dust. Percy had assured her that she wasn't like Phineas. But she *was*. She'd done something even worse than torment harpies.

You started this whole thing! Phineas had said. *If it weren't for you, Alcyoneus wouldn't be alive!*

As the boat sped down the Columbia River, Hazel tried to forget. She helped Ella make a nest out of old books and magazines they'd liberated from the library's recycling bin.

They hadn't really planned on taking the harpy with them, but Ella acted like the matter was decided.

"Friends," she muttered. "'Ten seasons. 1994 to 2004.' Friends melt Phineas and give Ella jerky. Ella will go with her friends."

Now she was roosting comfortably in the stern, nibbling

bits of jerky and reciting random lines from Charles Dickens and *50 Tricks to Teach Your Dog.*

Percy knelt in the bow, steering them toward the ocean with his freaky mind-over-water powers. Hazel sat next to Frank on the center bench, their shoulders touching, which made her feel as jittery as a harpy.

She remembered how Frank stood up for her in Portland, shouting, "She's a good person!" like he was ready to take on anybody who denied it.

She remembered the way he had looked on the hillside in Mendocino, alone in a clearing of poisoned grass with his spear in hand, fires burning all around him and the ashes of three basilisks at his feet.

A week ago, if someone had suggested that Frank was a child of Mars, Hazel would have laughed. Frank was much too sweet and gentle for that. She had always felt protective of him because of his clumsiness and his knack for getting into trouble.

Since they'd left camp, she saw him differently. He had more courage than she'd realized. He was the one looking out for *her.* She had to admit that the change was kind of nice.

The river widened into the ocean. The *Pax* turned north. As they sailed, Frank kept her spirits up by telling her silly jokes— *Why did the Minotaur cross the road? How many fauns does it take to change a lightbulb?* He pointed out buildings along the coastline that reminded him of places in Vancouver.

The sky started to darken, the sea turning the same rusty color as Ella's wings. June 21 was almost over. The Feast of

Fortuna would happen in the evening, exactly seventy-two hours from now.

Finally Frank brought out some food from his pack—sodas and muffins he'd scavenged from Phineas's table. He passed them around.

"It's okay, Hazel," he said quietly. "My mom used to say you shouldn't try to carry a problem alone. But if you don't want to talk about it, that's okay."

Hazel took a shaky breath. She was afraid to talk—not just because she was embarrassed. She didn't want to black out and slip into the past.

"You were right," she said, "when you guessed I came back from the Underworld. I'm...I'm an *escapee*. I shouldn't be alive."

She felt like a dam had broken. The story flooded out. She explained how her mother had summoned Pluto and fallen in love with the god. She explained her mother's wish for all the riches in the earth, and how that had turned into Hazel's curse. She described her life in New Orleans—everything except her boyfriend Sammy. Looking at Frank, she couldn't bring herself to talk about that.

She described the Voice, and how Gaea had slowly taken over her mother's mind. She explained how they had moved to Alaska, how Hazel had helped to raise the giant Alcyoneus, and how she had died, sinking the island into Resurrection Bay.

She knew Percy and Ella were listening, but she spoke mostly to Frank. When she had finished, she was afraid to look at him. She waited for him to move away from her, maybe tell her she *was* a monster after all.

Instead, he took her hand. "You sacrificed yourself to stop the giant from waking. I could never be that brave."

She felt her pulse throbbing in her neck. "It wasn't bravery. I let my mother die. I cooperated with Gaea too long. I almost let her win."

"Hazel," said Percy. "You stood up to a goddess all by yourself. You did the right..." His voice trailed off, as if he'd had an unpleasant thought. "What happened in the Underworld ... I mean, after you died? You should've gone to Elysium. But if Nico brought you back—"

"I didn't go to Elysium." Her mouth felt dry as sand. "Please don't ask..."

But it was too late. She remembered her descent into the darkness, her arrival on the banks of the River Styx, and her consciousness began to slip.

"Hazel?" Frank asked.

"'Slip Sliding Away,'" Ella muttered. "Number five U.S. single. Paul Simon. Frank, go with her. Simon says, Frank, go with her."

Hazel had no idea what Ella was talking about, but her vision darkened as she clung to Frank's hand.

She found herself back in the Underworld, and this time Frank was at her side.

They stood in Charon's boat, crossing the Styx. Debris swirled in the dark waters—a deflated birthday balloon, a child's pacifier, a little plastic bride and groom from the top of a cake—all the remnants of human lives cut short.

"Wh-where are we?" Frank stood at her side, shimmering with a ghostly purple light as if he'd become a Lar.

"It's my past." Hazel felt strangely calm. "It's just an echo. Don't worry."

The boatman turned and grinned. One moment he was a handsome African man in an expensive silk suit. The next moment he was a skeleton in a dark robe. "'Course you chouldn't worry," he said with a British accent. He addressed Hazel, as if he couldn't see Frank at all. "Told you I'd take you across, didn't I? 'Sall right you don't have a coin. Wouldn't be proper, leaving Pluto's daughter on the wrong side of the river."

The boat slid onto a dark beach. Hazel led Frank to the black gates of Erebos. The spirits parted for them, sensing she was a child of Pluto. The giant three-headed dog Cerberus growled in the gloom, but he let them pass. Inside the gates, they walked into a large pavilion and stood before the judges' bench. Three black-robed figures in golden masks stared down at Hazel.

Frank whimpered. "Who—?"

"They'll decide my fate," she said. "Watch."

Just as before, the judges asked her no questions. They simply looked into her mind, pulling thoughts from her head and examining them like a collection of old photos.

"Thwarted Gaea," the first judge said. "Prevented Alcyoneus from waking."

"But she raised the giant in the first place," the second judge argued. "Guilty of cowardice, weakness."

"She is young," said the third judge. "Her mother's life hung in the balance."

"My mother." Hazel found the courage to speak. "Where is she? What is her fate?"

The judges regarded her, their golden masks frozen in creepy smiles. "Your mother..."

The image of Marie Levesque shimmered above the judges. She was frozen in time, hugging Hazel as the cave collapsed, her eyes shut tight.

"An interesting question," the second judge said. "The division of fault."

"Yes," said the first judge. "The child died for a noble cause. She prevented many deaths by delaying the giant's rise. She had courage to stand against the might of Gaea."

"But she acted too late," the third judge said sadly. "She is guilty of aiding and abetting an enemy of the gods."

"The mother influenced her," said the first judge. "The child can have Elysium. Eternal Punishment for Marie Levesque."

"No!" Hazel shouted. "No, please! That's not fair."

The judges tilted their heads in unison. *Gold masks,* Hazel thought. *Gold has always been cursed for me.* She wondered if the gold was poisoning their thoughts somehow, so that they'd never give her a fair trial.

"Beware, Hazel Levesque," the first judge warned. "Would you take full responsibility? You could lay this guilt on your mother's soul. That would be reasonable. You were destined for great things. Your mother diverted your path. See what you might have been...."

Another image appeared above the judges. Hazel saw herself as a little girl, grinning, with her hands covered in finger paint. The image aged. Hazel saw herself growing up—her hair became longer, her eyes sadder. She saw herself on her thirteenth birthday, riding across the fields on her borrowed horse. Sammy laughed as he raced after her: *What are you running from? I'm not that ugly, am I?* She saw herself in Alaska, trudging down Third Street in the snow and darkness on her way home from school.

Then the image aged even more. Hazel saw herself at twenty. She looked so much like her mother, her hair gathered back in braids, her golden eyes flashing with amusement. She wore a white dress—a wedding dress? She was smiling so warmly, Hazel knew instinctively she must be looking at someone special—someone she loved.

The sight didn't make her feel bitter. She didn't even wonder whom she would have married. Instead she thought: *My mother might've looked like this if she'd let go of her anger, if Gaea hadn't twisted her.*

"You lost this life," the first judge said simply. "Special circumstances. Elysium for you. Punishment for your mother."

"No," Hazel said. "No, it wasn't all her fault. She was misled. She *loved* me. At the end, she tried to protect me."

"Hazel," Frank whispered. "What are you doing?"

She squeezed his hand, urging him to be silent. The judges paid him no attention.

Finally the second judge sighed. "No resolution. Not enough good. Not enough evil."

"The blame must be divided," the first judge agreed. "Both souls will be consigned to the Fields of Asphodel. I'm sorry, Hazel Levesque. You could have been a hero."

She passed through the pavilion, into yellow fields that went on forever. She led Frank through a crowd of spirits to a grove of black poplar trees.

"You gave up Elysium," Frank said in amazement, "so your mother wouldn't suffer?"

"She didn't deserve Punishment," Hazel said.

"But... what happens now?"

"Nothing," Hazel said. "Nothing... for all eternity."

They drifted aimlessly. Spirits around them chattered like bats—lost and confused, not remembering their past or even their names.

Hazel remembered everything. Perhaps that was because she was a daughter of Pluto, but she never forgot who she was, or why she was there.

"Remembering made my afterlife harder," she told Frank, who still drifted next to her as a glowing purple Lar. "So many times I tried to walk to my father's palace...." She pointed to a large black castle in the distance. "I could never reach it. I can't leave the Fields of Asphodel."

"Did you ever see your mother again?"

Hazel shook her head. "She wouldn't know me, even if I could find her. These spirits... it's like an eternal dream for them, an endless trance. This is the best I could do for her."

Time was meaningless, but after an eternity, she and Frank

sat together under a black poplar tree, listening to the screams from the Fields of Punishment. In the distance, under the artificial sunlight of Elysium, the Isles of the Blest glittered like emeralds in a sparkling blue lake. White sails cut across water and the souls of great heroes basked on the beaches in perpetual bliss.

"You didn't deserve Asphodel," Frank protested. "You should be with the heroes."

"This is just an echo," Hazel said. "We'll wake up, Frank. It only *seems* like forever."

"That's not the point!" he protested. "Your life was taken from you. You were going to grow up to be a beautiful woman. You..."

His face turned a darker shade of purple. "You were going to marry someone," he said quietly. "You would have had a good life. You lost all that."

Hazel swallowed back a sob. It hadn't been this hard in Asphodel the first time, when she was on her own. Having Frank with her made her feel so much sadder. But she was determined not to get angry about her fate.

Hazel thought about that image of herself as an adult, smiling and in love. She knew it wouldn't take much bitterness to sour her expression and make her look exactly like Queen Marie. *I deserve better,* her mother always said. Hazel couldn't allow herself to feel that way.

"I'm sorry, Frank," she said. "I think your mother was wrong. Sometimes sharing a problem doesn't make it easier to carry."

"But it does." Frank slipped his hand into his coat pocket.

"In fact... since we've got eternity to talk, there's something I want to tell you."

He brought out an object wrapped in cloth, about the same size as a pair of glasses. When he unfolded it, Hazel saw a half-burned piece of driftwood, glowing with purple light.

She frowned. "What is..." Then the truth hit her, as cold and harsh as a blast of winter wind. "Phineas said your life depends on a burned stick—"

"It's true," Frank said. "This is my lifeline, literally."

He told her how the goddess Juno had appeared when he was a baby, how his grandmother had snatched the piece of wood from the fireplace. "Grandmother said I had gifts —some talent we got from our ancestor, the Argonaut. That, and my dad's being Mars..." He shrugged. "I'm supposed to be too powerful or something. That's why my life can burn up so easily. Iris said I would die holding this, watching it burn."

Frank turned the piece of tinder in his fingers. Even in his ghostly purple form, he looked so big and sturdy. Hazel figured he would be huge when he was an adult—as strong and healthy as an ox. She couldn't believe his life depended on something as small as a stick.

"Frank, how can you carry it around with you?" she asked. "Aren't you terrified something will happen to it?"

"That's why I'm telling you." He held out the firewood. "I know it's a lot to ask, but would you keep it for me?"

Hazel's head spun. Until now, she'd accepted Frank's presence in her blackout. She'd led him along, numbly replaying her past, because it seemed only fair to show him the truth.

But now she wondered if Frank was really experiencing this with her, or if she was just imagining his presence. Why would he trust her with his life?

"Frank," she said, "you *know* who I am. I'm Pluto's daughter. Everything I touch goes wrong. Why would you trust me?"

"You're my best friend." He placed the firewood in her hands. "I trust you more than anybody."

She wanted to tell him he was making a mistake. She wanted to give it back. But before she could say anything, a shadow fell over them.

"Our ride is here," Frank guessed.

Hazel had almost forgotten she was reliving her past. Nico di Angelo stood over her in his black overcoat, his Stygian iron sword at his side. He didn't notice Frank, but he locked eyes with Hazel and seemed to read her whole life.

"You're different," he said. "A child of Pluto. You remember your past."

"Yes," Hazel said. "And you're alive."

Nico studied her like he was reading a menu, deciding whether or not to order.

"I'm Nico di Angelo," he said. "I came looking for my sister. Death has gone missing, so I thought...I thought I could bring her back and no one would notice."

"Back to life?" Hazel asked. "Is that possible?"

"It should have been." Nico sighed. "But she's gone. She chose to be reborn into a new life. I'm too late."

"I'm sorry."

He held out his hand. "You're my sister too. You deserve another chance. Come with me."

XXX

HAZEL

"HAZEL." PERCY WAS SHAKING HER SHOULDER. "Wake up. We've reached Seattle."

She sat up groggily, squinting in the morning sunlight. "Frank?"

Frank groaned, rubbing his eyes. "Did we just...was I just—?"

"You both passed out," Percy said. "I don't know why, but Ella told me not to worry about it. She said you were... sharing?"

"Sharing," Ella agreed. She crouched in the stern, preening her wing feathers with her teeth, which didn't look like a very effective form of personal hygiene. She spit out some red fluff. "Sharing is good. No more blackouts. Biggest American blackout, August 14, 2003. Hazel shared. No more blackouts."

Percy scratched his head. "Yeah...we've been having conversations like that all night. I still don't know what she's talking about."

Hazel pressed her hand against her coat pocket. She could feel the piece of firewood, wrapped in cloth.

She looked at Frank. "You *were* there."

He nodded. He didn't say anything, but his expression was clear: He'd meant what he said. He wanted her to keep the piece of tinder safe. She wasn't sure whether she felt honored or scared. No one had ever trusted her with something so important.

"Wait," Percy said. "You mean you guys *shared* a blackout? Are you guys both going to pass out from now on?"

"Nope," Ella said. "Nope, nope, nope. No more blackouts. More books for Ella. Books in Seattle."

Hazel gazed over the water. They were sailing through a large bay, making their way toward a cluster of downtown buildings. Neighborhoods rolled across a series of hills. From the tallest one rose an odd white tower with a saucer on the top, like a spaceship from the old Flash Gordon movies Sammy used to love.

No more blackouts? Hazel thought. After enduring them for so long, the idea seemed too good to be true.

How could Ella be sure they were gone? Yet Hazel *did* feel different...more grounded, as if she wasn't trying to live in two time periods anymore. Every muscle in her body began to relax. She felt as if she'd finally slipped out of a lead jacket she'd been wearing for months. Somehow, having Frank with her during the blackout had helped. She'd relived her entire past, right through to the present. Now all she had to worry about was the future—assuming she *had* one.

Percy steered the boat toward the downtown docks. As they got closer, Ella scratched nervously at her nest of books.

Hazel started to feel edgy, too. She wasn't sure why. It was a bright, sunny day, and Seattle looked like a beautiful place, with inlets and bridges, wooded islands dotting the bay, and snowcapped mountains rising in the distance. Still, she felt as if she were being watched.

"Um...why are we stopping here?" she asked.

Percy showed them the silver ring on his necklace. "Reyna has a sister here. She asked me to find her and show her this."

"Reyna has a *sister*?" Frank asked, like the idea terrified him.

Percy nodded. "Apparently Reyna thinks her sister could send help for the camp."

"Amazons," Ella muttered. "Amazon country. Hmm. Ella will find libraries instead. Doesn't like Amazons. Fierce. Shields. Swords. Pointy. Ouch."

Frank reached for his spear. "Amazons? Like...female warriors?"

"That would make sense," Hazel said. "If Reyna's sister is also a daughter of Bellona, I can see why she'd join the Amazons. But...is it safe for us to be here?"

"Nope, nope, nope," Ella said. "Get books instead. No Amazons."

"We have to try," Percy said. "I promised Reyna. Besides, the *Pax* isn't doing too great. I've been pushing it pretty hard."

Hazel looked down at her feet. Water was leaking between the floorboards. "Oh."

"Yeah," Percy agreed. "We'll either need to fix it or find a new boat. I'm pretty much holding it together with my will-power at this point. Ella, do you have any idea where we can find the Amazons?"

"And, um," Frank said nervously, "they don't, like, kill men on sight, do they?"

Ella glanced at the downtown docks, only a few hundred yards away. "Ella will find friends later. Ella will fly away now."

And she did.

"Well..." Frank picked a single red feather out of the air. "That's encouraging."

They docked at the wharf. They barely had time to unload their supplies before the *Pax* shuddered and broke into pieces. Most of it sank, leaving only a board with a painted eye and another with the letter *P* bobbing in the waves.

"Guess we're not fixing it," Hazel said. "What now?"

Percy stared at the steep hills of downtown Seattle. "We hope the Amazons will help."

They explored for hours. They found some great salty caramel chocolate at a candy store. They bought some coffee so strong, Hazel's head felt like a vibrating gong. They stopped at a side-walk café and had some excellent grilled salmon sandwiches. Once they saw Ella zooming between high-rise towers, a large book clutched in each foot. But they found no Amazons. All the while, Hazel was aware of the time ticking by. June 22 now, and Alaska was still a long way away.

Finally they wandered south of downtown, into a plaza surrounded by smaller glass and brick buildings. Hazel's nerves started tingling. She looked around, sure she was being watched.

"There," she said.

The office building on their left had a single word etched on the glass doors: AMAZON.

"Oh," Frank said. "Uh, no, Hazel. That's a modern thing. They're a company, right? They sell stuff on the Internet. They're not actually Amazons."

"Unless..." Percy walked through the doors. Hazel had a bad feeling about this place, but she and Frank followed.

The lobby was like an empty fish tank—glass walls, a glossy black floor, a few token plants, and pretty much nothing else. Against the back wall, a black stone staircase led up and down. In the middle of the room stood a young woman in a black pantsuit, with long auburn hair and a security guard's earpiece. Her name tag said KINZIE. Her smile was friendly enough, but her eyes reminded Hazel of the policemen in New Orleans who used to patrol the French Quarter at night. They always seemed to look *through* you, as if they were thinking about who might attack them next.

Kinzie nodded at Hazel, ignoring the boys. "May I help you?"

"Um...I hope so," Hazel said. "We're looking for Amazons."

Kinzie glanced at Hazel's sword, then Frank's spear, though neither should have been visible through the Mist.

"This is the main campus for Amazon," she said cautiously. "Did you have an appointment with someone, or—"

"Hylla," Percy interrupted. "We're looking for a girl named—"

Kinzie moved so fast, Hazel's eyes almost couldn't follow. She kicked Frank in the chest and sent him flying backward across the lobby. She pulled a sword out of thin air, swept Percy off his feet with the flat of the blade, and pressed the point under his chin.

Too late, Hazel reached for her sword. A dozen more girls in black flooded up the staircase, swords in hand, and surrounded her.

Kinzie glared down at Percy. "First rule: Males don't speak without permission. Second rule, trespassing on our territory is punishable by death. You'll meet Queen Hylla, all right. She'll be the one deciding your fate."

The Amazons confiscated the trio's weapons and marched them down so many flights of stairs, Hazel lost count.

Finally they emerged in a cavern so big it could have accommodated ten high schools, sports fields and all. Stark fluorescent lights glowed along the rock ceiling. Conveyor belts wound through the room like waterslides, carrying boxes in every direction. Aisles of metal shelves stretched out forever, stacked high with crates of merchandise. Cranes hummed and robotic arms whirred, folding cardboard boxes, packing shipments, and taking things on and off the belts. Some of the shelves were so tall they were only accessible by ladders and catwalks, which ran across the ceiling like theater scaffolding.

Hazel remembered newsreels she'd seen as a child. She'd always been impressed by the scenes of factories building planes and guns for the war effort—hundreds and hundreds of weapons coming off the line every day. But that was nothing compared to *this*, and almost all the work was being done by computers and robots. The only humans Hazel could see were some black-suited security women patrolling the catwalks, and some men in orange jumpsuits, like prison uniforms, driving forklifts through the aisles, delivering more pallets of boxes. The men wore iron collars around their necks.

"You keep *slaves*?" Hazel knew it might be dangerous to speak, but she was so outraged she couldn't stop herself.

"The men?" Kinzie snorted. "They're not slaves. They just know their place. Now, move."

They walked so far, Hazel's feet began to hurt. She thought they must surely be getting to the end of the warehouse when Kinzie opened a large set of double doors and led them into another cavern, just as big as the first.

"The *Underworld* isn't this big," Hazel complained, which probably wasn't true, but it felt that way to her feet.

Kinzie smiled smugly. "You admire our base of operations? Yes, our distribution system is worldwide. It took many years and most of our fortune to build. Now, finally, we're turning a profit. The mortals don't realize they are funding the Amazon kingdom. Soon, we'll be richer than any mortal nation. Then —when the weak mortals depend on us for everything—the revolution will begin!"

"What are you going to do?" Frank grumbled. "Cancel free shipping?"

A guard slammed the hilt of her sword into his gut. Percy tried to help him, but two more guards pushed him back at sword point.

"You'll learn respect," Kinzie said. "It's males like you who have ruined the mortal world. The only harmonious society is one run by women. We are stronger, wiser—"

"More humble," Percy said.

The guards tried to hit him, but Percy ducked.

"Stop it!" Hazel said. Surprisingly, the guards listened.

"Hylla is going to judge us, right?" Hazel asked. "So take us to her. We're wasting time."

Kinzie nodded. "Perhaps you're right. We have more important problems. And time . . . time is definitely an issue."

"What do you mean?" Hazel asked.

A guard grunted. "We could take them straight to Otrera. Might win her favor that way."

"No!" Kinzie snarled. "I'd sooner wear an iron collar and drive a forklift. Hylla is queen."

"Until tonight," another guard muttered.

Kinzie gripped her sword. For a second Hazel thought the Amazons might start fighting one another, but Kinzie seemed to get her anger under control.

"Enough," she said. "Let's go."

They crossed a lane of forklift traffic, navigated a maze of conveyor belts, and ducked under a row of robotic arms that were packing up boxes.

Most of the merchandise looked pretty ordinary: books, electronics, baby diapers. But against one wall sat a war chariot with a big bar code on the side. Hanging from the yoke was a sign that read: ONLY ONE LEFT IN STOCK. ORDER SOON! (MORE ON THE WAY)

Finally they entered a smaller cavern that looked like a combination loading zone and throne room. The walls were lined with metal shelves six stories high, decorated with war banners, painted shields, and the stuffed heads of dragons, hydras, giant lions, and wild boars. Standing guard along either side were dozens of forklifts modified for war. An iron-collared male drove each machine, but an Amazon warrior stood on a platform in back, manning a giant mounted crossbow. The prongs of each forklift had been sharpened into oversized sword blades.

The shelves in this room were stacked with cages containing live animals. Hazel couldn't believe what she was seeing —black mastiffs, giant eagles, a lion-eagle hybrid that must've been a gryphon, and a red ant the size of a compact car.

She watched in horror as a forklift zipped into the room, picked up a cage with a beautiful white pegasus, and sped away while the horse whinnied in protest.

"What are you doing to that poor animal?" Hazel demanded.

Kinzie frowned. "The pegasus? It'll be fine. Someone must've ordered it. The shipping and handling charges are steep, but—"

"You can *buy* a pegasus online?" Percy asked.

Kinzie glared at him. "Obviously *you* can't, male. But Amazons can. We have followers all over the world. They need supplies. This way."

At the end of the warehouse was a dais constructed from

pallets of books: stacks of vampire novels, walls of James Patterson thrillers, and a throne made from about a thousand copies of something called *The Five Habits of Highly Aggressive Women*.

At the base of the steps, several Amazons in camouflage were having a heated argument while a young woman— Queen Hylla, Hazel assumed—watched and listened from her throne.

Hylla was in her twenties, lithe and lean as a tiger. She wore a black leather jumpsuit and black boots. She had no crown, but around her waist was a strange belt made of interlocking gold links, like the pattern of a labyrinth. Hazel couldn't believe how much she looked like Reyna—a little older, perhaps, but with the same long black hair, the same dark eyes, and the same hard expression, like she was trying to decide which of the Amazons before her most deserved death.

Kinzie took one look at the argument and grunted with distaste. "Otrera's agents, spreading their lies."

"What?" Frank asked.

Then Hazel stopped so abruptly, the guards behind her stumbled. A few feet from the queen's throne, two Amazons guarded a cage. Inside was a beautiful horse—not the winged kind, but a majestic and powerful stallion with a honey-colored coat and a black mane. His fierce brown eyes regarded Hazel, and she could swear he looked impatient, as if thinking: *About time you got here.*

"It's him," Hazel murmured.

"Him, who?" Percy asked.

Kinzie scowled in annoyance, but when she saw where

Hazel was looking, her expression softened. "Ah, yes. Beautiful, isn't he?"

Hazel blinked to make sure she wasn't hallucinating. It was the same horse she'd chased in Alaska. She was *sure* of it... but that was impossible. No horse could live that long.

"Is he..." Hazel could hardly control her voice. "Is he for sale?"

The guards all laughed.

"That's Arion," Kinzie said patiently, as if she understood Hazel's fascination. "He's a royal treasure of the Amazons —to be claimed only by our most courageous warrior, if you believe the prophecy."

"Prophecy?" Hazel asked.

Kinzie's expression became pained, almost embarrassed. "Never mind. But no, he's not for sale."

"Then why is he in a cage?"

Kinzie grimaced. "Because... he is difficult."

Right on cue, the horse slammed his head against the cage door. The metal bars shuddered, and the guards retreated nervously.

Hazel wanted to free that horse. She wanted it more than anything she had ever wanted before. But Percy, Frank, and a dozen Amazon guards were staring at her, so she tried to mask her emotions. "Just asking," she managed. "Let's see the queen."

The argument at the front of the room grew louder. Finally the queen noticed Hazel's group approaching, and she snapped, "Enough!"

The arguing Amazons shut up immediately. The queen waved them aside and beckoned Kinzie forward.

Kinzie shoved Hazel and her friends toward the throne. "My queen, these demigods—"

The queen shot to her feet. "You!"

She glared at Percy Jackson with murderous rage.

Percy muttered something in Ancient Greek that Hazel was pretty sure the nuns at St. Agnes wouldn't have liked.

"Clipboard," he said. "Spa. Pirates."

This made no sense to Hazel, but the queen nodded. She stepped down from her dais of best sellers and drew a dagger from her belt.

"You were incredibly foolish to come here," she said. "You destroyed my home. You made my sister and me exiles and prisoners."

"Percy," Frank said uneasily. "What's the scary woman with the dagger talking about?"

"Circe's Island," Percy said. "I just remembered. The gorgon's blood—maybe it's starting to heal my mind. The Sea of Monsters. Hylla . . . she welcomed us at the docks, took us to see her boss. Hylla worked for the sorceress."

Hylla bared her perfect white teeth. "Are you telling me you've had amnesia? You know, I might actually believe you. Why else would you be stupid enough to come here?"

"We've come in peace," Hazel insisted. "What did Percy do?"

"Peace?" The queen raised her eyebrows at Hazel. "What did he *do*? This *male* destroyed Circe's school of magic!"

"Circe turned me into a guinea pig!" Percy protested.

"No excuses!" Hylla said. "Circe was a wise and generous employer. I had room and board, a good health plan, dental, pet leopards, free potions—everything! And *this* demigod with his friend, the blonde—"

"Annabeth." Percy tapped his forehead like he wanted the memories to come back faster. "That's right. I was there with Annabeth."

"You released our captives—Blackbeard and his pirates." She turned to Hazel. "Have you ever been kidnapped by pirates? It isn't fun. They burned our spa to the ground. My sister and I were their prisoners for months. Fortunately we were daughters of Bellona. We learned to fight quickly. If we hadn't..." She shuddered. "Well, the pirates learned to respect us. Eventually we made our way to California where we—" She hesitated as if the memory was painful. "Where my sister and I parted ways."

She stepped toward Percy until they were nose-to-nose. She ran her dagger under his chin. "Of course, I survived and prospered. I have risen to be queen of the Amazons. So perhaps I should thank you."

"You're welcome," Percy said.

The queen dug her knife in a little deeper. "Never mind. I think I'll kill you."

"Wait!" Hazel yelped. "Reyna sent us! Your sister! Look at the ring on his necklace."

Hylla frowned. She lowered her knife to Percy's necklace until the point rested on the silver ring. The color drained from her face.

"Explain this." She glared at Hazel. "Quickly."

Hazel tried. She described Camp Jupiter. She told the Amazons about Reyna being their praetor, and the army of monsters that was marching south. She told them about their quest to free Thanatos in Alaska.

As Hazel talked, another group of Amazons entered the room. One was taller and older than the rest, with plaited silver hair and fine silk robes like a Roman matron. The other Amazons made way for her, treating her with such respect that Hazel wondered if she was Hylla's mother—until she noticed how Hylla and the older woman stared daggers at each other.

"So we need your help," Hazel finished her story. "*Reyna* needs your help."

Hylla gripped Percy's leather cord and yanked it off his neck—beads, ring, *probatio* tablet and all. "Reyna...that foolish girl—"

"Well!" the older woman interrupted. "Romans need our help?" She laughed, and the Amazons around her joined in.

"How many times did we battle the Romans in my day?" the woman asked. "How many times have they killed our sisters in battle? When I was queen—"

"Otrera," Hylla interrupted, "you are here as a guest. You are *not* queen anymore."

The older woman spread her hands and made a mocking bow. "As you say—at least, until tonight. But I speak the truth, *Queen* Hylla." She said the word like a taunt. "I've been brought back by the Earth Mother herself! I bring tidings of a new war. Why should Amazons follow Jupiter, that foolish king of Olympus, when we can follow a *queen*? When I take command—"

"*If* you take command," Hylla said. "But for now, I am queen. My word is law."

"I see." Otrera looked at the assembled Amazons, who were standing very still, as if they'd found themselves in a pit with two wild tigers. "Have we become so weak that we listen to *male* demigods? Will you spare the life of this son of Neptune, even though he once destroyed your home? Perhaps you'll let him destroy your *new* home, too!"

Hazel held her breath. The Amazons looked back and forth between Hylla and Otrera, watching for any sign of weakness.

"I will pass judgment," Hylla said in an icy tone, "once I have all the facts. That is how *I* rule—by reason, not fear. First, I will talk with this one." She jabbed a finger toward Hazel. "It is my duty to hear out a female warrior before I sentence her or her allies to death. That is the Amazon way. Or have your years in the Underworld muddled your memory, Otrera?"

The older woman sneered, but she didn't try to argue.

Hylla turned to Kinzie. "Take these males to the holding cells. The rest of you, leave us."

Otrera raised her hand to the crowd. "As our *queen* commands. But any of you who would like to hear more about Gaea, and our glorious future with her, come with me!"

About half the Amazons followed her out of the room. Kinzie snorted with disgust, then she and her guards hauled Percy and Frank away.

Soon Hylla and Hazel were alone except for the queen's personal guards. At Hylla's signal, even they moved out of earshot.

The queen turned toward Hazel. Her anger dissolved, and Hazel saw desperation in her eyes. The queen looked like one of her caged animals being whisked off on a conveyor belt.

"We must talk," Hylla said. "We don't have much time. By midnight, I will most likely be dead."

XXXI

HAZEL

Hazel considered making a run for it.

She didn't trust Queen Hylla, and she certainly didn't trust that other lady, Otrera. Only three guards were left in the room. All of them kept their distance.

Hylla was armed with just a dagger. This deep underground, Hazel might be able to cause an earthquake in the throne room, or summon a big pile of schist or gold. If she could cause a distraction, she might be able to escape and find her friends.

Unfortunately, she'd seen the Amazons fight. Even though the queen had only a dagger, Hazel suspected she could use it pretty well. And Hazel was unarmed. They hadn't searched her, which meant thankfully they hadn't taken Frank's firewood from her coat pocket, but her sword was gone.

The queen seemed to be reading her thoughts. "Forget about escape. Of course, we'd respect you for trying. But we'd have to kill you."

"Thanks for the warning."

Hylla shrugged. "The least I can do. I believe you come in peace. I believe Reyna sent you."

"But you won't help?"

The queen studied the necklace she'd taken from Percy. "It's complicated," she said. "Amazons have always had a rocky relationship with other demigods—especially *male* demigods. We fought for King Priam in the Trojan War, but Achilles killed our queen, Penthesilea. Years before that, Hercules stole Queen Hippolyta's belt—this belt I'm wearing. It took us centuries to recover it. Long before that, at the very beginning of the Amazon nation, a hero named Bellerophon killed our first queen, Otrera."

"You mean the lady—"

"—who just left, yes. Otrera, our first queen, daughter of Ares."

"Mars?"

Hylla made a sour face. "No, definitely *Ares*. Otrera lived long before Rome, in a time when all demigods were Greek. Unfortunately, some of our warriors still prefer the old ways. Children of Ares... they are always the worst."

"The old ways..." Hazel had heard rumors about Greek demigods. Octavian believed they existed and were secretly plotting against Rome. But she'd never really believed it, even when Percy came to camp. He just didn't strike her as an evil, scheming Greek. "You mean the Amazons are a mix... Greek *and* Roman?"

Hylla continued to examine the necklace—the clay beads, the *probatio* tablet. She slipped Reyna's silver ring off the cord and put it on her own finger. "I suppose they don't teach you about that at Camp Jupiter. The gods have many aspects. Mars, Ares. Pluto, Hades. Being immortal, they tend to accumulate personalities. They are Greek, Roman, American—a combination of all the cultures they've influenced over the eons. Do you understand?"

"I—I'm not sure. Are all Amazons demigods?"

The queen spread her hands. "We all have *some* immortal blood, but many of my warriors are descended from demigods. Some have been Amazons for countless generations. Others are children of minor gods. Kinzie, the one who brought you here, is the daughter of a nymph. Ah—here she is now."

The girl with the auburn hair approached the queen and bowed.

"The prisoners are safely locked away," Kinzie reported. "But..."

"Yes?" the queen asked.

Kinzie swallowed like she had a bad taste in her mouth. "Otrera made sure *her* followers are guarding the cells. I'm sorry, my queen."

Hylla pursed her lips. "No matter. Stay with us, Kinzie. We were just talking about our, ah, situation."

"Otrera," Hazel guessed. "Gaea brought her back from the dead to throw you Amazons into civil war."

The queen exhaled. "If that was her plan, it is working. Otrera is a legend among our people. She plans to take back the throne and lead us to war against the Romans. Many of my sisters will follow her."

"Not all," Kinzie grumbled.

"But Otrera is a spirit!" Hazel said. "She isn't even—"

"Real?" The queen studied Hazel carefully. "I worked with the sorceress Circe for many years. I know a returned soul when I see one. When did *you* die, Hazel—Nineteen twenty? Nineteen thirty?"

"Nineteen forty-two," Hazel said. "But—but I wasn't sent by Gaea. I came back to *stop* her. This is my second chance."

"Your second chance . . ." Hylla gazed at the rows of battle forklifts, now empty. "I know about second chances. That boy, Percy Jackson—he destroyed my old life. You wouldn't have recognized me back then. I wore dresses and makeup. I was a glorified secretary, an accursed Barbie doll."

Kinzie made a three-fingered claw over her heart, like the voodoo gestures Hazel's mom once used for warding off the Evil Eye.

"Circe's island was a safe place for Reyna and me," the queen continued. "We were daughters of the war goddess, Bellona. I wanted to protect Reyna from all that violence. Then Percy Jackson unleashed the pirates. They kidnapped us, and Reyna and I learned to be tough. We found out that we were good with weapons. The past four years, I've wanted to *kill* Percy Jackson for what he made us endure."

"But Reyna became the praetor of Camp Jupiter," Hazel said. "You became the queen of the Amazons. Maybe this was your destiny."

Hylla fingered the necklace in her hand. "I may not be queen for much longer."

"You will prevail!" Kinzie insisted.

"As the Fates decree," Hylla said without enthusiasm.

"You see, Hazel, Otrera has challenged me to a duel. Every Amazon has that right. Tonight at midnight, we'll battle for the throne."

"But . . . you're good, right?" Hazel asked.

Hylla managed a dry smile. "Good, yes, but Otrera is the founder of the Amazons."

"She's a lot older. Maybe she's out of practice, having been dead for so long."

"I hope you're right, Hazel. You see, it's a battle to the death. . . ."

She waited for that to sink in. Hazel remembered what Phineas had said in Portland—how he had had a shortcut back from death, thanks to Gaea. She remembered how the gorgons had tried to re-form in the Tiber.

"Even if you kill her," Hazel said, "she'll just come back. As long as Thanatos is chained, she won't stay dead."

"Exactly," Hylla said. "Otrera has already told us that she *can't* die. So even if I manage to defeat her tonight, she'll simply return and challenge me again tomorrow. There is no law against challenging the queen multiple times. She can insist on fighting me every night, until she finally wears me down. I can't win."

Hazel gazed at the throne. She imagined Otrera sitting there with her fine robes and her silver hair, ordering her warriors to attack Rome. She imagined the voice of Gaea filling this cavern.

"There has to be a way," she said. "Don't Amazons have . . . special powers or something?"

"No more than other demigods," Hylla said. "We can die,

just like any mortal. There *is* a group of archers who follow the goddess Artemis. They are often mistaken for Amazons, but the Hunters forsake the company of men in exchange for almost endless life. We Amazons—we would prefer to live life to the fullest. We love, we fight, we die."

"I thought you hated men."

Hylla and Kinzie both laughed.

"Hate men?" said the queen. "No, no, we like men. We just like to show them who's in charge. But that's beside the point. If I could, I would rally our troops and ride to my sister's aid. Unfortunately, my power is tenuous. When I am killed in combat—and it's only a matter of time—Otrera will be queen. She will march to Camp Jupiter with our forces, but she will not go to help my sister. She'll go to join the giant's army."

"We've got to stop her," Hazel said. "My friends and I killed Phineas, one of Gaea's other servants in Portland. Maybe we can help!"

The queen shook her head. "You can't interfere. As queen, I must fight my own battles. Besides, your friends are imprisoned. If I let them go, I'll look weak. Either *I* execute you three as trespassers, or Otrera will do so when she becomes queen."

Hazel's heart sank. "So I guess we're both dead. Me for the second time."

In the corner cage, the stallion Arion whinnied angrily. He reared and slammed his hooves against the bars.

"The horse seems to feel your despair," the queen said. "Interesting. He's immortal, you know—the son of Neptune and Ceres."

Hazel blinked. "Two gods had a horse for a kid?"

"Long story."

"Oh." Hazel's face felt hot with embarrassment.

"He's the fastest horse in the world," Hylla said. "Pegasus is more famous, with his wings, but Arion runs like the wind over land and sea. No creature is faster. It took us years to capture him—one of our greatest prizes. But it did us no good. The horse will not allow anyone to ride him. I think he hates Amazons. And he is expensive to keep. He will eat anything, but he prefers gold."

The back of Hazel's neck tingled. "He eats gold?"

She remembered the horse following her in Alaska so many years ago. She had thought he was eating nuggets of gold that appeared in her footsteps.

She knelt and pressed her hand against the floor. Immediately, the stone cracked. A chunk of gold ore the size of a plum was pushed out of the earth. Hazel stood, examining her prize.

Hylla and Kinzie stared at her.

"How did you . . . ?" The queen gasped. "Hazel, be careful!"

Hazel approached the stallion's cage. She put her hand between the bars, and Arion gingerly ate the chunk of gold from her palm.

"Unbelievable," Kinzie said. "The last girl who tried that—"

"Now has a metal arm," the queen finished. She studied Hazel with new interest, as if deciding whether or not to say more. "Hazel . . . we spent years hunting for this horse. It was foretold that the most courageous female warrior would someday master Arion and ride him to victory, ushering in a new era of prosperity for the Amazons. Yet *no* Amazon can touch him, much less control him. Even Otrera tried and failed. Two others died attempting to ride him."

That probably should've worried Hazel, but she couldn't imagine this beautiful horse hurting her. She put her hand through the bars again and stroked Arion's nose. He nuzzled her arm, murmuring contentedly, as if asking, *More gold? Yum.*

"I would feed you more, Arion." Hazel glanced pointedly at the queen. "But I think I'm scheduled for an execution."

Queen Hylla looked from Hazel to the horse and back again. "Unbelievable."

"The prophecy," Kinzie said. "Is it possible . . . ?"

Hazel could almost see the gears turning inside the queen's head, formulating a plan. "You have courage, Hazel Levesque. And it seems Arion has chosen you. Kinzie?"

"Yes, my queen?"

"You said Otrera's followers are guarding the cells?"

Kinzie nodded. "I should have foreseen that. I'm sorry—"

"No, it's fine." The queen's eyes gleamed—the way Hannibal the elephant's did whenever he was unleashed to destroy a fortress. "It would be embarrassing for Otrera if her followers failed in their duties—if, for instance, they were overcome by an outsider and a prison break occurred."

Kinzie began to smile. "Yes, my queen. Most embarrassing."

"Of course," Hylla continued, "none of my guards would know a *thing* about this. Kinzie would *not* spread the word to allow an escape."

"Certainly not," Kinzie agreed.

"And we couldn't help you." The queen raised her eyebrows

at Hazel. "But if you somehow overpowered the guards and freed your friends...if, for instance, you took one of the guards' Amazon cards—"

"With one-click purchasing enabled," Kinzie said, "which will open the jail cells with one click."

"If—gods forbid!—something like that were to happen," the queen continued, "you would find your friends' weapons and supplies in the guard station next to the cells. And who knows? If you made your way back to this throne room while I was off preparing for my duel...well, as I mentioned, Arion is a very fast horse. It would be a shame if he were stolen and used for an escape."

Hazel felt like she'd been plugged into a wall socket. Electricity surged through her whole body. Arion...Arion could be hers. All she had to do was rescue her friends and fight her way through an entire nation of highly trained warriors.

"Queen Hylla," she said, "I—I'm not much of a fighter."

"Oh, there are many kinds of fighting, Hazel. I have a feeling you're quite resourceful. And if the prophecy is correct, you will help the Amazon nation achieve prosperity. If you succeed on your quest to free Thanatos, for instance—"

"—then Otrera wouldn't come back if she were killed," Hazel said. "You'd only have to defeat her...um, every night until we succeed."

The queen nodded grimly. "It seems we both have impossible tasks ahead of us."

"But you're trusting me," said Hazel. "And I trust you. You *will* win, as many times as it takes."

Hylla held out Percy's necklace and poured it into Hazel's hands.

"I hope you're right," the queen said. "But the sooner you succeed the better, yes?"

Hazel slipped the necklace into her pocket. She shook the queen's hand, wondering if it was possible to make a friend so fast—especially one who was about to send her to jail.

"This conversation never happened," Hylla told Kinzie. "Take our prisoner to the cells and hand her over to Otrera's guards. And, Kinzie, be sure you leave before anything unfortunate happens. I don't want my loyal followers held accountable for a prison break."

The queen smiled mischievously, and for the first time, Hazel felt jealous of Reyna. She wished that *she* had a sister like this.

"Good-bye, Hazel Levesque," the queen said. "If we both die tonight...well, I'm glad I met you."

XXXII

HAZEL

THE AMAZON JAIL WAS AT THE TOP OF a storage aisle, sixty feet in the air.

Kinzie led her up three different ladders to a metal catwalk, then tied Hazel's hands loosely behind her back and pushed her along past crates of jewelry.

A hundred feet ahead, under the harsh glow of fluorescent lights, a row of chain-link cages hung suspended from cables. Percy and Frank were in two of the cages, talking to each other in hushed tones. Next to them on the catwalk, three bored-looking Amazon guards leaned against their spears and gazed at little black tablets in their hands like they were reading.

Hazel thought the tablets looked too thin for books. Then it occurred to her they might be some sort of tiny—what did modern people call them?—laptop computers. Secret Amazon technology, perhaps. Hazel found the idea almost as unsettling as the battle forklifts downstairs.

"Get moving, girl," Kinzie ordered, loud enough for the guards to hear. She prodded Hazel in the back with her sword.

Hazel walked as slowly as she could, but her mind was racing. She needed to come up with a brilliant rescue plan. So far she had nothing. Kinzie had made sure she could break her bonds easily, but she'd still be empty-handed against three trained warriors, and she had to act before they put her in a cage.

She passed a pallet of crates marked 24-CARAT BLUE TOPAZ RINGS, then another labeled SILVER FRIENDSHIP BRACELETS. An electronic display next to the friendship bracelets read: *People who bought this item also bought GARDEN GNOME SOLAR PATIO LIGHT and FLAMING SPEAR OF DEATH. Buy all three and save 12%!*

Hazel froze. Gods of Olympus, she was stupid.

Silver. Topaz. She sent out her senses, searching for precious metals, and her brain almost exploded from the feedback. She was standing next to a six-story-tall mountain of jewelry. But in front of her, from here to the guards, was nothing but prison cages.

"What is it?" Kinzie hissed. "Keep moving! They'll get suspicious."

"Make them come here," Hazel muttered over her shoulder.

"Why—"

"Please."

The guards frowned in their direction.

"What are you staring at?" Kinzie yelled at them. "Here's the third prisoner. Come get her."

The nearest guard set down her reading tablet. "Why can't you walk another thirty paces, Kinzie?"

"Um, because—"

"Ooof!" Hazel fell to her knees and tried to put on her best seasick face. "I'm feeling nauseous! Can't...walk. Amazons ...too...scary."

"There you go," Kinzie told the guards. "Now, are you going to come take the prisoner, or should I tell Queen Hylla you're not doing your duty?"

The nearest guard rolled her eyes and trudged over. Hazel had hoped the other two guards would come too, but she'd have to worry about that later.

The first guard grabbed Hazel's arm. "Fine. I'll take custody of the prisoner. But if I were you, Kinzie, I wouldn't worry about Hylla. She won't be queen much longer."

"We'll see, Doris." Kinzie turned to leave. Hazel waited until her steps receded down the catwalk.

The guard Doris pulled on Hazel's arm. "Well? Come on."

Hazel concentrated on the wall of jewelry next to her: forty large boxes of silver bracelets. "Not...feeling so good."

"You are *not* throwing up on me," Doris growled. She tried to yank Hazel to her feet, but Hazel went limp, like a kid throwing a fit in a store. Next to her, the boxes began to tremble.

"Lulu!" Doris yelled to one of her comrades. "Help me with this lame little girl."

Amazons named Doris and Lulu? Hazel thought. Okay...

The second guard jogged over. Hazel figured this was her best chance. Before they could haul her to her feet, she yelled, "Ooooh!" and flattened herself against the catwalk.

Doris started to say, "Oh, give me a—"

The entire pallet of jewelry exploded with a sound like a thousand slot machines hitting the jackpot. A tidal wave of silver friendship bracelets poured across the catwalk, washing Doris and Lulu right over the railing.

They would've fallen to their deaths, but Hazel wasn't *that* mean. She summoned a few hundred bracelets, which leaped at the guards and lashed around their ankles, leaving them hanging upside down from the bottom of the catwalk, screaming like lame little girls.

Hazel turned toward the third guard. She broke her bonds, which were about as sturdy as toilet paper. She picked up one of the fallen guards' spears. She was terrible with spears, but she hoped the third Amazon didn't know that.

"Should I kill you from here?" Hazel snarled. "Or are you going to make me come over there?"

The guard turned and ran.

Hazel shouted over the side to Doris and Lulu. "Amazon cards! Pass them up, unless you want me to undo those friendship bracelets and let you drop!"

Four and a half seconds later, Hazel had two Amazon cards. She raced over to the cages and swiped a card. The doors popped open.

Frank stared at her in astonishment. "Hazel, that was... *amazing.*"

Percy nodded. "I will never wear jewelry again."

"Except this." Hazel tossed him his necklace. "Our weapons and supplies are at the end of the catwalk. We should hurry. Pretty soon—"

Alarms began wailing throughout the cavern.

"Yeah," she said, "that'll happen. Let's go!"

The first part of the escape was easy. They retrieved their things with no problem, then started climbing down the ladder. Every time Amazons swarmed beneath them, demanding their surrender, Hazel made a crate of jewelry explode, burying their enemies in a Niagara Falls of gold and silver. When they got to the bottom of the ladder, they found a scene that looked like Mardi Gras Armageddon—Amazons trapped up to their necks in bead necklaces, several more upside down in a mountain of amethyst earrings, and a battle forklift buried in silver charm bracelets.

"You, Hazel Levesque," Frank said, "are entirely *freaking* incredible."

She wanted to kiss him right there, but they had no time. They ran back to the throne room.

They stumbled across one Amazon who must've been loyal to Hylla. As soon as she saw the escapees, she turned away like they were invisible.

Percy started to ask, "What the—"

"Some of them *want* us to escape," Hazel said. "I'll explain later."

The second Amazon they met wasn't so friendly. She was dressed in full armor, blocking the throne-room entrance. She spun her spear with lightning speed, but this time Percy was ready. He drew Riptide and stepped into battle. As the Amazon jabbed at him, he sidestepped, cut her spear shaft in half, and slammed the hilt of his sword against her helmet.

The guard crumpled.

"Mars Almighty," Frank said. "How did you—that wasn't any Roman technique!"

Percy grinned. "The *graecus* has some moves, my friend. After you."

They ran into the throne room. As promised, Hylla and her guards had cleared out. Hazel dashed over to Arion's cage and swiped an Amazon card across the lock. Instantly the stallion burst forth, rearing in triumph.

Percy and Frank stumbled backward.

"Um...is that thing *tame*?" Frank said.

The horse whinnied angrily.

"I don't think so," Percy guessed. "He just said, *'I will trample you to death, silly Chinese Canadian baby man.'*"

"You speak horse?" Hazel asked.

"'Baby man'?" Frank spluttered.

"Speaking to horses is a Poseidon thing," Percy said. "Uh, I mean a Neptune thing."

"Then you and Arion should get along fine," Hazel said. "He's a son of Neptune too."

Percy turned pale. "Excuse me?"

If they hadn't been in such a bad situation, Percy's expression might have made her laugh. "The point is, he's fast. He can get us out of here."

Frank did not look thrilled. "Three of us can't fit on one horse, can we? We'll fall off, or slow him down, or—"

Arion whinnied again.

"Ouch," Percy said. "Frank, the horse says you're a—you know, actually, I'm not going to translate that. Anyway, he says there's a chariot in the warehouse, and he's willing to pull it."

"There!" someone yelled from the back of the throne room. A dozen Amazons charged in, followed by males in orange jumpsuits. When they saw Arion, they backed up quickly and headed for the battle forklifts.

Hazel vaulted onto Arion's back.

She grinned down at her friends. "I remember seeing that chariot. Follow me, guys!"

She galloped into the larger cavern and scattered a crowd of males. Percy knocked out an Amazon. Frank swept two more off their feet with his spear. Hazel could feel Arion straining to run. He wanted to go full speed, but he needed more room. They had to make it outside.

Hazel bowled into a patrol of Amazons, who scattered in terror at the sight of the horse. For once, Hazel's *spatha* felt exactly the right length. She swung it at everyone who came within reach. No Amazon dared challenge her.

Percy and Frank ran after her. Finally they reached the chariot. Arion stopped by the yoke, and Percy set to work with the reins and harness.

"You've done this before?" Frank asked.

Percy didn't need to answer. His hands flew. In no time the chariot was ready. He jumped aboard and yelled, "Frank, come on! Hazel, go!"

A battle cry went up behind them. A full army of Amazons stormed into the warehouse. Otrera herself stood astride a battle forklift, her silver hair flowing as she swung her mounted crossbow toward the chariot. "Stop them!" she yelled.

Hazel spurred Arion. They raced across the cavern, weaving around pallets and forklifts. An arrow whizzed past Hazel's head. Something exploded behind her, but she didn't look back.

"The stairs!" Frank yelled. "No way this horse can pull a chariot up that many flights of—OH MY GODS!"

Thankfully the stairs were wide enough for the chariot, because Arion didn't even slow down. He shot up the steps with the chariot rattling and groaning. Hazel glanced back a few times to make sure Frank and Percy hadn't fallen off. Their knuckles were white on the sides of the chariot, their teeth chattering like windup Halloween skulls.

Finally they reached the lobby. Arion crashed through the main doors into the plaza and scattered a bunch of guys in business suits.

Hazel felt the tension in Arion's rib cage. The fresh air was making him crazy to run, but Hazel pulled back on his reins.

"Ella!" Hazel shouted at the sky. "Where are you? We have to leave!"

For a horrible second, she was afraid the harpy might be too far away to hear. She might be lost, or captured by the Amazons.

Behind them a battle forklift clattered up the stairs and roared through the lobby, a mob of Amazons behind it.

"Surrender!" Otrera screamed.

The forklift raised its razor-sharp tines.

"Ella!" Hazel cried desperately.

In a flash of red feathers, Ella landed in the chariot. "Ella is here. Amazons are pointy. Go now."

"Hold on!" Hazel warned. She leaned forward and said, "Arion, run!"

The world seemed to elongate. Sunlight bent around them. Arion shot away from the Amazons and sped through downtown Seattle. Hazel glanced back and saw a line of smoking pavement where Arion's hooves had touched the ground. He thundered toward the docks, leaping over cars, barreling through intersections.

Hazel screamed at the top of her lungs, but it was a scream of delight. For the first time in her life—in her *two* lives—she felt absolutely unstoppable. Arion reached the water and leaped straight off the docks.

Hazel's ears popped. She heard a roar that she later realized was a sonic boom, and Arion tore over Puget Sound, seawater turning to steam in his wake as the skyline of Seattle receded behind them.

XXXIII

FRANK

FRANK WAS RELIEVED WHEN THE WHEELS FELL OFF.

He'd already thrown up twice from the back of the chariot, which was not fun at the speed of sound. The horse seemed to bend time and space as he ran, blurring the landscape and making Frank feel like he'd just drunk a gallon of whole milk without his lactose-intolerance medicine. Ella didn't help matters. She kept muttering: "Seven hundred and fifty miles per hour. Eight hundred. Eight hundred and three. Fast. Very fast."

The horse sped north across Puget Sound, zooming past islands and fishing boats and very surprised pods of whales. The landscape ahead began to look familiar—Crescent Beach, Boundary Bay. Frank had gone sailing here once on a school trip. They'd crossed into Canada.

The horse rocketed onto dry land. He followed Highway 99 north, running so fast, the cars seemed to be standing still.

Finally, just as they were getting into Vancouver, the chariot wheels began to smoke.

"Hazel!" Frank yelled. "We're breaking up!"

She got the message and pulled the reins. The horse didn't seem happy about it, but he slowed to subsonic as they zipped through the city streets. They crossed the Ironworkers bridge into North Vancouver, and the chariot started to rattle dangerously. At last Arion stopped at the top of a wooded hill. He snorted with satisfaction, as if to say, *That's how we run, fools.* The smoking chariot collapsed, spilling Percy, Frank, and Ella onto the wet, mossy ground.

Frank stumbled to his feet. He tried to blink the yellow spots out of his eyes. Percy groaned and started unhitching Arion from the ruined chariot. Ella fluttered around in dizzy circles, bonking into the trees and muttering, "Tree. Tree. Tree."

Only Hazel seemed unaffected by the ride. Grinning with pleasure, she slid off the horse's back. "That was fun!"

"Yeah." Frank swallowed back his nausea. "So much fun."

Arion whinnied.

"He says he needs to eat," Percy translated. "No wonder. He probably burned about six million calories."

Hazel studied the ground at her feet and frowned. "I'm not sensing any gold around here.... Don't worry, Arion. I'll find you some. In the meantime, why don't you go graze? We'll meet you—"

The horse zipped off, leaving a trail of steam in his wake.

Hazel knit her eyebrows. "Do you think he'll come back?"

"I don't know," Percy said. "He seems kind of...spirited."

Frank almost hoped the horse would stay away. He didn't say that, of course. He could tell Hazel was distressed by the idea of losing her new friend. But Arion scared him, and Frank was pretty sure the horse knew it.

Hazel and Percy started salvaging supplies from the chariot wreckage. There had been a few boxes of random Amazon merchandise in the front, and Ella shrieked with delight when she found a shipment of books. She snatched up a copy of *The Birds of North America*, fluttered to the nearest branch, and began scratching through the pages so fast, Frank wasn't sure if she was reading or shredding.

Frank leaned against a tree, trying to control his vertigo. He still hadn't recovered from his Amazon imprisonment—getting kicked across the lobby, disarmed, caged, and insulted as a *baby man* by an egomaniacal horse. That hadn't exactly helped his self-esteem.

Even before that, the vision he had shared with Hazel had left him rattled. He felt closer to her now. He knew he'd done the right thing in giving her the piece of firewood. A huge weight had been taken off his shoulders.

On the other hand, he'd seen the Underworld firsthand. He had felt what it was like to sit forever doing nothing, just regretting your mistakes. He'd looked up at those creepy gold masks on the judges of the dead and realized that *he* would stand before them someday, maybe very soon.

Frank had always dreamed of seeing his mother again when he died. But maybe that wasn't possible for demigods. Hazel had been in Asphodel for something like seventy years and never found her mom. Frank hoped he and his mom would both end up in Elysium. But if Hazel hadn't gotten there—sacrificing her life to stop Gaea, taking responsibility for her actions so that her mother wouldn't end up in Punishment—what chance did Frank have? He'd never done anything that heroic.

He straightened and looked around, trying to get his bearings.

To the south, across Vancouver Harbor, the downtown skyline gleamed red in the sunset. To the north, the hills and rainforests of Lynn Canyon Park snaked between the subdivisions of North Vancouver until they gave way to the wilderness.

Frank had explored this park for years. He spotted a bend in the river that looked familiar. He recognized a dead pine tree that had been split by lightning in a nearby clearing. Frank knew this hill.

"I'm practically home," he said. "My grandmother's house is right over there."

Hazel squinted. "How far?"

"Just over the river and through the woods."

Percy raised an eyebrow. "Seriously? To Grandmother's house we go?"

Frank cleared his throat. "Yeah, anyway."

Hazel clasped her hands in prayer. "Frank, *please* tell me she'll let us spend the night. I know we're on a deadline, but we've got to rest, right? And Arion saved us some time. Maybe we could get an actual cooked meal?"

"And a hot shower?" Percy pleaded. "And a bed with, like, sheets and a pillow?"

Frank tried to imagine Grandmother's face if he showed up with two heavily armed friends and a harpy. Everything had changed since his mother's funeral, since the morning the wolves had taken him south. He'd been so angry about leaving. Now, he couldn't imagine going back.

Still, he and his friends were exhausted. They'd been traveling for more than two days without decent food or sleep. Grandmother could give them supplies. And maybe she could answer some questions that were brewing in the back of Frank's mind—a growing suspicion about his family gift.

"It's worth a try," Frank decided. "To Grandmother's house we go."

Frank was so distracted, he would have walked right into the ogres' camp. Fortunately Percy pulled him back.

They crouched next to Hazel and Ella behind a fallen log and peered into the clearing.

"Bad," Ella murmured. "This is bad for harpies."

It was fully dark now. Around a blazing campfire sat half a dozen shaggy-haired humanoids. Standing up, they probably would've been eight feet tall—tiny compared to the giant Polybotes or even the Cyclopes they'd seen in California, but that didn't make them any less scary. They wore only knee-length surfer shorts. Their skin was sunstroke red —covered with tattoos of dragons, hearts, and bikini-clad women. Hanging from a spit over the fire was a skinned animal, maybe a boar, and the ogres were tearing off chunks of meat with their clawlike fingernails, laughing and talking as they ate, baring pointy teeth. Next to the ogres sat several mesh bags filled with bronze spheres like cannonballs. The spheres must have been hot, because they steamed in the cool evening air.

Two hundred yards beyond the clearing, the lights of the Zhang mansion glowed through the trees. *So close*, Frank thought. He wondered if they could sneak around the monsters, but when he looked left and right, he saw more campfires in either direction, as if the ogres had surrounded the property. Frank's fingers dug into the tree bark. His grandmother might be alone inside the house, trapped.

"What are these guys?" he whispered.

"Canadians," Percy said.

Frank leaned away from him. "*Excuse* me?"

"Uh, no offense," Percy said. "That's what Annabeth called them when I fought them before. She said they live in the north, in Canada."

"Yeah, well," Frank grumbled, "we're *in* Canada. *I'm* Canadian. But I've never seen *those* things before."

Ella plucked a feather from her wings and turned it in her fingers. "Laistrygonians," she said. "Cannibals. Northern giants. Sasquatch legend. Yep, yep. They're not birds. Not birds of North America."

"That's what they're called," Percy agreed. "Laistry—uh, whatever Ella said."

Frank scowled at the dudes in the clearing. "They *could* be mistaken for Bigfoot. Maybe that's where the legend came from. Ella, you're pretty smart."

"Ella is smart," she agreed. She shyly offered Frank her feather.

"Oh . . . thanks." He stuck the feather in his pocket, then noticed Hazel was glaring at him. "What?" he asked.

"Nothing." She turned to Percy. "So your memory is coming back? Do you remember how you beat these guys?"

"Sort of," Percy said. "It's still fuzzy. I think I had help. We killed them with Celestial bronze, but that was before . . . you know."

"Before Death got kidnapped," Hazel said. "So now, they might not die at all."

Percy nodded. "Those bronze cannonballs . . . those are bad news. I think we used some of them against the giants. They catch fire and blow up."

Frank's hand went to his coat pocket. Then he remembered Hazel had his piece of driftwood. "If we cause any explosions," he said, "the ogres at the other camps will come running. I think they've surrounded the house, which means there could be fifty or sixty of these guys in the woods."

"So it's a trap." Hazel looked at Frank with concern. "What about your grandmother? We've got to help her."

Frank felt a lump in his throat. Never in a million years had he thought his grandmother would need rescuing, but now he started running combat scenarios in his mind—the way he had back at camp during the war games.

"We need a distraction," he decided. "If we can draw this group into the woods, we might sneak through without alerting the others."

"I wish Arion was here," Hazel said. "I could get the ogres to chase me."

Frank slipped his spear off his back. "I've got another idea."

Frank didn't want to do this. The idea of summoning Gray scared him even more than Hazel's horse. But he didn't see another way.

"Frank, you can't charge out there!" Hazel said. "That's suicide!"

"I'm not charging," Frank said. "I've got a friend. Just... nobody scream, okay?"

He jabbed the spear into the ground, and the point broke off.

"Oops," Ella said. "No spear point. Nope, nope."

The ground trembled. Gray's skeletal hand broke the surface. Percy fumbled for his sword, and Hazel made a sound like a cat with a hairball. Ella disappeared and rematerialized at the top of the nearest tree.

"It's okay," Frank promised. "He's under control!"

Gray crawled out of the ground. He showed no sign of damage from his previous encounter with the basilisks. He was good as new in his camouflage and combat boots, translucent gray flesh covering his bones like glowing Jell-O. He turned his ghostly eyes toward Frank, waiting for orders.

"Frank, that's a *spartus*," Percy said. "A skeleton warrior. They're evil. They're killers. They're—"

"I know," Frank said bitterly. "But it's a gift from Mars. Right now that's all I've got. Okay, Gray. Your orders: attack that group of ogres. Lead them off to the west, causing a diversion so we can—"

Unfortunately, Gray lost interest after the word "ogres." Maybe he only understood simple sentences. He charged toward the ogres' campfire.

"Wait!" Frank said, but it was too late. Gray pulled two of his own ribs from his shirt and ran around the fire, stabbing the ogres in the back with such blinding speed they didn't even have time to yell. Six extremely surprised-looking Laistrygonians fell sideways like a circle of dominoes and crumbled into dust.

Gray stomped around, kicking their ashes apart as they tried to re-form. When he seemed satisfied that they weren't coming back, Gray stood at attention, saluted smartly in Frank's direction, and sank into the forest floor.

Percy stared at Frank. "How—"

"No Laistrygonians." Ella fluttered down and landed next to them. "Six minus six is zero. Spears are good for subtraction. Yep."

Hazel looked at Frank as if he'd turned into a zombie skeleton himself. Frank thought his heart might shatter, but he couldn't blame her. Children of Mars were all about violence. Mars's symbol was a bloody spear for good reason. Why shouldn't Hazel be appalled?

He glared down at the broken tip of his spear. He wished he had *any* father but Mars. "Let's go," he said. "My grandmother might be in trouble."

XXXIV

FRANK

They stopped at the front porch. As Frank had feared, a loose ring of campfires glowed in the woods, completely surrounding the property, but the house itself seemed untouched.

Grandmother's wind chimes jangled in the night breeze. Her wicker chair sat empty, facing the road. Lights shone through the downstairs windows, but Frank decided against ringing the doorbell. He didn't know how late it was, or if Grandmother was asleep or even home. Instead he checked the stone elephant statue in the corner—a tiny duplicate of the one in Portland. The spare key was still tucked under its foot.

He hesitated at the door.

"What's wrong?" Percy asked.

Frank remembered the morning he'd opened this door for the military officer who had told him about his mother. He remembered walking down these steps to her funeral, holding his piece of firewood in his coat for the first time. He remembered standing here and watching the wolves come out of the woods—Lupa's minions, who would lead him to Camp Jupiter. That seemed so long ago, but it had only been six weeks.

Now he was back. Would Grandmother hug him? Would she say, *Frank, thank the gods you've come! I'm surrounded by monsters!*

More likely she'd scold him, or mistake them for intruders and chase them off with a frying pan.

"Frank?" Hazel asked.

"Ella is nervous," the harpy muttered from her perch on the railing. "The elephant—the elephant is looking at Ella."

"It'll be fine." Frank's hand was shaking so badly he could barely fit the key in the lock. "Just stay together."

Inside, the house smelled closed-up and musty. Usually the air was scented with jasmine incense, but all the burners were empty.

They examined the living room, the dining room, the kitchen. Dirty dishes were stacked in the sink, which wasn't right. Grandmother's maid came every day—unless she'd been scared off by the giants.

Or eaten for lunch, Frank thought. Ella had said the Laistrygonians were cannibals.

He pushed that thought aside. Monsters ignored regular mortals. At least, they *usually* did.

In the parlor, Buddha statues and Taoist immortals grinned at them like psycho clowns. Frank remembered Iris, the rainbow goddess, who'd been dabbling in Buddhism and Taoism. Frank figured one visit to this creepy old house would cure her of that.

Grandmother's large porcelain vases were strung with cobwebs. Again—that wasn't right. She insisted that her collection be dusted regularly. Looking at the porcelain, Frank felt a twinge of guilt for having destroyed so many pieces the day of the funeral. It seemed silly to him now—getting angry at Grandmother when he had so many others to be angry at: Juno, Gaea, the giants, his dad Mars. *Especially* Mars.

The fireplace was dark and cold.

Hazel hugged her chest as if to keep the piece of firewood from jumping into the hearth. "Is that—"

"Yeah," Frank said. "That's it."

"That's what?" Percy asked.

Hazel's expression was sympathetic, but that just made Frank feel worse. He remembered how terrified, how repulsed she had looked when he had summoned Gray.

"It's the fireplace," he told Percy, which sounded stupidly obvious. "Come on. Let's check upstairs."

The steps creaked under their feet. Frank's old room was the same. None of his things had been touched—his extra bow and quiver (he'd have to grab those later), his spelling awards from school (yeah, he probably was the only non-dyslexic spelling champion demigod in the world, as if he weren't enough of a freak already), and his photos of his mom—in her flak jacket and helmet, sitting on a Humvee in Kandahar Province; in her soccer coach uniform, the season she'd coached Frank's team; in her military dress uniform, her hands on Frank's shoulders, the time she'd visited his school for career day.

"Your mother?" Hazel asked gently. "She's beautiful."

Frank couldn't answer. He felt a little embarrassed—a

sixteen-year-old guy with a bunch of pictures of his mom. How hopelessly lame was that? But mostly he felt sad. Six weeks since he'd been here. In some ways it seemed like forever. But when he looked at his mom's smiling face in those photos, the pain of losing her was as fresh as ever.

They checked the other bedrooms. The middle two were empty. A dim light flickered under the last door—Grandmother's room.

Frank knocked quietly. No one answered. He pushed open her door. Grandmother lay in bed, looking gaunt and frail, her white hair spread around her face like a basilisk's crown. A single candle burned on the nightstand. At her bedside sat a large man in beige Canadian Forces fatigues. Despite the gloom, he wore dark sunglasses with blood red light glowing behind the lenses.

"Mars," Frank said.

The god looked up impassively. "Hey, kid. Come on in. Tell your friends to take a hike."

"Frank?" Hazel whispered. "What do mean, *Mars*? Is your grandmother ... is she okay?"

Frank glanced at his friends. "You don't see him?"

"See who?" Percy gripped his sword. "Mars? Where?"

The war god chuckled. "Nah, they can't see me. Figured it was better this time. Just a private conversation—father/son, right?"

Frank clenched his fists. He counted to ten before he trusted himself to speak.

"Guys, it's ... it's nothing. Listen, why don't you take the middle bedrooms?"

"Roof," Ella said. "Roofs are good for harpies."

"Sure," Frank said in a daze. "There's probably food in the kitchen. Would you give me a few minutes alone with my grandmother? I think she—"

His voice broke. He wasn't sure if he wanted to cry or scream or punch Mars in the glasses—maybe all three.

Hazel laid her hand on his arm. "Of course, Frank. Come on, Ella, Percy."

Frank waited until his friends' steps receded. Then he walked into the bedroom and closed the door.

"Is it really you?" he asked Mars. "This isn't a trick or illusion or something?"

The god shook his head. "You'd prefer it if it wasn't me?"

"Yes," Frank confessed.

Mars shrugged. "Can't blame you. Nobody welcomes war—not if they're smart. But war finds everyone sooner or later. It's inevitable."

"That's stupid," Frank said. "War isn't inevitable. It kills people. It—"

"—took your mom," Mars finished.

Frank wanted to smack the calm look off his face, but maybe that was just Mars's aura making him feel aggressive. He looked down at his grandmother, sleeping peacefully. He wished she would wake up. If anyone could take on a war god, his grandmother could.

"She's ready to die," Mars said. "She's been ready for weeks, but she's holding on for you."

"For me?" Frank was so stunned he almost forgot his

anger. "Why? How could she know I was coming back? *I* didn't know!"

"The Laistrygonians outside knew," Mars said. "I imagine a certain goddess told them."

Frank blinked. "Juno?"

The war god laughed so loudly the windows rattled, but Grandmother didn't even stir. "Juno? Boar's whiskers, kid. Not Juno! You're Juno's secret weapon. She wouldn't sell you out. No, I meant Gaea. Obviously she's been keeping track of you. I think you worry her more than Percy or Jason or any of the seven."

Frank felt like the room was tilting. He wished there were another chair to sit in. "The seven . . . you mean in the ancient prophecy, the Doors of Death? I'm one of the seven? And Jason, and—"

"Yes, yes." Mars waved his hand impatiently. "Come on, boy. You're supposed to be a good tactician. Think it through! Obviously your friends are being groomed for that mission too, assuming you make it back from Alaska alive. Juno aims to unite the Greeks and Romans and send them against the giants. She believes it's the only way to stop Gaea."

Mars shrugged, clearly unconvinced of the plan. "Anyway, Gaea doesn't want you to be one of the seven. Percy Jackson . . . she believes she can control him. All of the others have weaknesses she can exploit. But *you*—you worry her. She'd rather kill you right away. That's why she summoned the Laistrygonians. They've been here for days, waiting."

Frank shook his head. Was Mars playing some kind of

trick? No way would a *goddess* be worried about Frank, especially when there was somebody like Percy Jackson to worry about.

"No weaknesses?" he asked. "I'm nothing *but* weaknesses. My life depends on a piece of wood!"

Mars grinned. "You're selling yourself short. Anyway, Gaea has these Laistrygonians convinced that if they eat the last member of your family—that being *you*—they'll inherit your family gift. Whether that's true or not, I don't know. But the Laistrygonians are hungry to try."

Frank's stomach twisted into a knot. Gray had killed six of the ogres, but judging from the campfires around the property, there were dozens more—all waiting to cook Frank for breakfast.

"I'm going to throw up," he said.

"No, you're not." Mars snapped his fingers, and Frank's queasiness disappeared. "Battle jitters. Happens to everybody."

"But my grandmother—"

"Yeah, she's been waiting to talk to you. The ogres have left her alone so far. She's the bait, see? Now that you're here, I imagine they've already smelled your presence. They'll attack in the morning."

"Get us out of here, then!" Frank demanded. "Snap your fingers and blow up the cannibals."

"Ha! That would be fun. But I don't fight my kids' battles for them. The Fates have clear ideas about what jobs belong to gods, and what has to be done by mortals. This is *your* quest, kid. And, uh, in case you haven't figured it out yet, your spear won't be ready to use again for twenty-four hours, so I hope you've learned how to use the family gift. Otherwise, you're gonna be breakfast for cannibals."

The family gift. Frank had wanted to talk with Grandmother about it, but now he had no one to consult but Mars. He stared at the war god, who was smiling with absolutely no sympathy.

"Periclymenus." Frank sounded out the word carefully, like a spelling-bee challenge. "He was my ancestor, a Greek prince, an Argonaut. He died fighting Hercules."

Mars rolled his hand in a *"go on"* gesture.

"He had an ability that helped him in combat," Frank said. "Some sort of gift from the gods. My mom said he fought like a swarm of bees."

Mars laughed. "True enough. What else?"

"Somehow, the family got to China. I think, like in the days of the Roman Empire, one of Periclymenus's descendants served in a legion. My mom used to talk about a guy named Seneca Gracchus, but he also had a Chinese name, Sung Guo. I think—well, this is the part I don't know, but Reyna always said there were many lost legions. The Twelfth founded Camp Jupiter. Maybe there was another legion that disappeared into the east."

Mars clapped silently. "Not bad, kid. Ever heard of the Battle of Carrhae? Huge disaster for the Romans. They fought these guys called the Parthians on the eastern border of the empire. Fifteen thousand Romans died. Ten thousand more were taken prisoner."

"And one of the prisoners was my ancestor Seneca Gracchus?"

"Exactly," Mars agreed. "The Parthians put the captured legionnaires to work, since they were pretty good fighters. Except then Parthia got invaded again from the other direction—"

"By the Chinese," Frank guessed. "And the Roman prisoners got captured again."

"Yeah. Kind of embarrassing. Anyway, that's how a Roman legion got to China. The Romans eventually put down roots and built a new hometown called—"

"Li-Jien," Frank said. "My mother said that was our ancestral home. Li-Jien. *Legion.*"

Mars looked pleased. "Now you're getting it. And old Seneca Gracchus, he had your family's gift."

"My mom said he fought dragons," Frank remembered. "She said he was . . . he was the most powerful dragon of all."

"He was good," Mars admitted. "Not good enough to avoid the bad luck of his legion, but good. He settled in China, passed the family gift to his kids, and so on. Eventually your family emigrated to North America and got involved with Camp Jupiter—"

"Full circle," Frank finished. "Juno said I would bring the family full circle."

"We'll see." Mars nodded at his grandmother. "She wanted to tell you all this herself, but I figured I'd cover some of it since the old bird hasn't got much strength. So do you understand your gift?"

Frank hesitated. He had an idea, but it seemed crazy—even crazier than a family moving from Greece to Rome to China to Canada. He didn't want to say it aloud. He didn't want to be wrong and have Mars laugh at him. "I—I think so. But against an army of those ogres—"

"Yeah, it'll be tough." Mars stood and stretched. "When your grandmother wakes up in the morning, she'll offer you some help. Then I imagine she'll die."

"*What?* But I have to save her! She can't just leave me."

"She's lived a full life," Mars said. "She's ready to move on. Don't be selfish."

"Selfish!"

"The old woman only stuck around this long out of a sense of duty. Your mom was the same way. That's why I loved her. She always put her duty first, ahead of everything. Even her life."

"Even me."

Mars took off his sunglasses. Where his eyes should've been, miniature spheres of fire boiled like nuclear explosions. "Self-pity isn't helpful, kid. It isn't worthy of you. Even without the family gift, your mom gave you your most important traits—bravery, loyalty, brains. Now you've got to decide how to use them. In the morning, listen to your grandmother. Take her advice. You can still free Thanatos and save the camp."

"And leave my grandmother behind to die."

"Life is only precious because it ends, kid. Take it from a god. You mortals don't know how lucky you are."

"Yeah," Frank muttered. "Real lucky."

Mars laughed—a harsh metallic sound. "Your mom used to tell me this Chinese proverb. Eat bitter—"

"*Eat bitter, taste sweet,*" Frank said. "I hate that proverb."

"But it's true. What do they call it these days—no pain,

no gain? Same concept. You do the easy thing, the appealing thing, the *peaceful* thing, mostly it turns out sour in the end. But if you take the hard path—ah, *that's* how you reap the sweet rewards. Duty. Sacrifice. They mean something."

Frank was so disgusted he could hardly speak. *This* was his father?

Sure, Frank understood about his mom being a hero. He understood she'd saved lives and been really brave. But she'd left him alone. That wasn't fair. It wasn't right.

"I'll be going," Mars promised. "But first—you said you were weak. That's not true. You want to know why Juno spared you, Frank? Why that piece of wood didn't burn yet? It's because you've got a role to play. You think you're not as good as the other Romans. You think Percy Jackson is better than you."

"He is," Frank grumbled. "He battled *you* and won."

Mars shrugged. "Maybe. Maybe so. But every hero has a fatal flaw. Percy Jackson? He's too loyal to his friends. He can't give them up, not for anything. He was told that, years ago. And someday soon, he's going to face a sacrifice he can't make. Without you, Frank—without your sense of duty—he's going fail. The whole war will go sideways, and Gaea will destroy our world."

Frank shook his head. He couldn't hear this.

"War is a duty," Mars continued. "The only real choice is whether you accept it, and what you fight for. The legacy of Rome is on the line—five thousand years of law, order, civilization. The gods, the traditions, the cultures that shaped the world you live in: it's all going to crumble, Frank, unless you win this. I think that's worth fighting for. Think about it."

"What's mine?" Frank asked.

Mars raised an eyebrow. "Your what?"

"Fatal flaw. You said all heroes have one."

The god smiled dryly. "You gotta answer that yourself, Frank. But you're finally asking the right questions. Now, get some sleep. You need the rest."

The god waved his hand. Frank's eyes felt heavy. He collapsed, and everything went dark.

"Fai," said a familiar voice, harsh and impatient.

Frank blinked his eyes. Sunlight streamed into the room.

"Fai, get up. As much as I would like to slap that ridiculous face of yours, I am in no condition to get out of bed."

"Grandmother?"

She came into focus, looking down at him from the bed. He lay sprawled on the floor. Someone had put a blanket over him during the night and a pillow under his head, but he had no idea how it had happened.

"Yes, my silly ox." Grandmother still looked horribly weak and pale, but her voice was as steely as ever. "Now, get up. The ogres have surrounded the house. We have much to discuss if you and your friends are to escape here alive."

XXXV

FRANK

ONE LOOK OUT THE WINDOW, and Frank knew he was in trouble.

At the edge of the lawn, the Laistrygonians were stacking bronze cannonballs. Their skin gleamed red. Their shaggy hair, tattoos, and claws didn't look any prettier in the morning light.

Some carried clubs or spears. A few confused ogres carried surfboards, like they'd shown up at the wrong party. All of them were in a festive mood—giving each other high fives, tying plastic bibs around their necks, breaking out the knives and forks. One ogre had fired up a portable barbecue and was dancing in an apron that said KISS THE COOK.

The scene would've been almost funny, except Frank knew *he* was the main course.

"I've sent your friends to the attic," Grandmother said. "You can join them when we're done."

"The attic?" Frank turned. "You told me I could never go in there."

"That's because we keep *weapons* in the attic, silly boy. Do you think this is the first time monsters have attacked our family?"

"Weapons," Frank grumbled. "Right. I've *never* handled weapons before."

Grandmother's nostrils flared. "Was that sarcasm, Fai Zhang?"

"Yes, Grandmother."

"Good. There may be hope for you yet. Now, sit. You must eat."

She waved her hand at the nightstand, where someone had set a glass of orange juice and a plate of poached eggs and bacon on toast—Frank's favorite breakfast.

Despite his troubles, Frank suddenly felt hungry. He looked at Grandmother in astonishment. "Did you—"

"Make you breakfast? By Buddha's monkey, of course not! And it wasn't the house staff. Too dangerous for them here. No, your girlfriend Hazel made that for you. And brought you a blanket and pillow last night. And picked out some clean clothes for you in your bedroom. By the way, you should shower. You smell like burning horse hair."

Frank opened and closed his mouth like a fish. He couldn't make sounds come out. *Hazel* had done all that for him? Frank had been sure he'd destroyed any chance with her last night when he had summoned Gray.

"She's . . . um . . . she's not—"

"Not your girlfriend?" Grandmother guessed. "Well, she *should* be, you dolt! Don't let her get away. You need strong women in your life, if you haven't noticed. Now, to business."

Frank ate while Grandmother gave him a sort of military briefing. In the daylight, her skin was so translucent, her veins seemed to glow. Her breathing sounded like a crackly paper bag inflating and deflating, but she spoke with firmness and clarity.

She explained that the ogres had been surrounding the house for three days, waiting for Frank to show up.

"They want to cook you and eat you," she said distastefully, "which is ridiculous. You'd taste terrible."

"Thank you, Grandmother."

She nodded. "I admit, I was somewhat pleased when they said you were coming back. I am glad to see you one last time, even if your clothes are dirty and you need a haircut. Is this how you represent your family?"

"I've been a little busy, Grandmother."

"No excuse for sloppiness. At any rate, your friends have slept and eaten. They are taking stock of the weapons in the attic. I told them you would be along shortly, but there are too many ogres to fend off for long. We must speak of your escape plan. Look in my nightstand."

Frank opened the drawer and pulled out a sealed envelope.

"You know the airfield at the end of the park?" Grandmother asked. "Could you find it again?"

Frank nodded mutely. It was about three miles to the north, down the main road through the canyon. Grandmother had taken him there sometimes when she would charter planes to bring in special shipments from China.

"There is a pilot standing by to leave at a moment's notice," Grandmother said. "He is an old family friend. I have a letter for him in that envelope, asking him to take you north."

"But—"

"Do not argue, boy," she muttered. "Mars has been visiting me these last few days, keeping me company. He told me of your quest. Find Death in Alaska and release him. Do your duty."

"But if I succeed, you'll die. I'll never see you again."

"That is true," Grandmother agreed. "But I'll die anyway. I'm old. I thought I made that clear. Now, did your praetor give you letters of introduction?"

"Uh, yes, but—"

"Good. Show those to the pilot as well. He's a veteran of the legion. In case he has any doubts, or gets cold feet, those credentials will make him honor-bound to help you in any way possible. All you have to do is reach the airfield."

The house rumbled. Outside a ball of fire exploded in midair, lighting up the entire room.

"The ogres are getting restless," Grandmother said. "We must hurry. Now, about your powers, I hope you've figured them out."

"Uh…"

Grandmother muttered some curses in rapid-fire Mandarin. "Gods of your ancestors, boy! Have you learned nothing?"

"Yes!" He stammered out the details of his discussion with Mars the night before, but he felt much more tongue-tied in front of Grandmother. "The gift of Periclymenus...I think, I think he was a son of Poseidon, I mean Neptune, I mean..." Frank spread his hands. "The sea god."

Grandmother nodded grudgingly. "He was the *grandson* of Poseidon, but good enough. How did your brilliant intellect arrive at this fact?"

"A seer in Portland...he said something about my great-grandfather, Shen Lun. The seer said he was blamed for the 1906 earthquake that destroyed San Francisco and the old location of Camp Jupiter."

"Go on."

"At camp, they said a descendant of Neptune had caused the disaster. Neptune is the god of earthquakes. But...but I don't think great-grandfather actually did it. Causing earthquakes isn't our gift."

"No," Grandmother agreed. "But yes, he was blamed. He was unpopular as a descendant of Neptune. He was unpopular because his real gift was much stranger than causing earthquakes. And he was unpopular because he was Chinese. A Chinese boy had never before claimed Roman blood. An ugly truth—but there is no denying it. He was falsely accused, forced out in shame."

"So...if he didn't do anything wrong, why did you tell me to apologize for him?"

Grandmother's cheeks flushed. "Because apologizing for something you didn't do is better than dying for it! I wasn't sure if the camp would hold you to blame. I did not know if the prejudice of the Romans had eased."

Frank swallowed down his breakfast. He'd been teased in school and on the streets sometimes, but not that much, and never at Camp Jupiter. Nobody at camp, not once, had made fun of him for being Asian. Nobody cared about that. They only made fun of him because he was clumsy and slow. He couldn't imagine what it had been like for his great-grandfather, accused of destroying the entire camp, drummed out of the legion for something he didn't do.

"And our real gift?" Grandmother asked. "Have you at least figured out what it is?"

His mother's old stories swirled in Frank's head. *Fighting like a swarm of bees. He was the greatest dragon of all.* He remembered his mother's appearing next to him in the backyard, as if she'd flown from the attic. He remembered her coming out of the woods, saying that she'd given a mama grizzly bear directions.

"You can be anything," Frank said. "That's what she always told me."

Grandmother huffed. "Finally, a dim light goes on in that head of yours. Yes, Fai Zhang. Your mother was not simply boosting your self-esteem. She was telling you the *literal* truth."

"But . . ." Another explosion shook the house. Ceiling plaster fell like snow. Frank was so bewildered he barely noticed. *"Anything?"*

"Within reason," Grandmother said. "Living things. It

helps if you know the creature well. It also helps if you are in a life-and-death situation, such as combat. Why do you look so surprised, Fai? You have always said you are not comfortable in your own body. We *all* feel that way—all of us with the blood of Pylos. This gift was only given *once* to a mortal family. We are unique among demigods. Poseidon must have been feeling especially generous when he blessed our ancestor —or especially spiteful. The gift has often proven a curse. It did not save your mother. . . ."

Outside, a cheer went up from the ogres. Someone shouted, "Zhang! Zhang!"

"You must go, silly boy," Grandmother said. "Our time is up."

"But—I don't know how to use my power. I've never—I can't—"

"You can," Grandmother said. "Or you will not survive to realize your destiny. I don't like this Prophecy of Seven that Mars told me about. Seven is an unlucky number in Chinese —a ghost number. But there is nothing we can do about that. Now, go! Tomorrow evening is the Feast of Fortuna. You have no time to waste. Don't worry about me. I will die in my own time, in my own way. I have no intention of being devoured by those ridiculous ogres. Go!"

Frank turned at the door. He felt like his heart was being squeezed through a juicer, but he bowed formally. "Thank you, Grandmother," he said. "I will make you proud."

She muttered something under her breath. Frank almost thought she had said, *You have.*

He stared at her, dumbfounded, but her expression imme-diately soured. "Stop gaping, boy! Go shower and dress! Comb your hair! My last image of you, and you show me messy hair?"

He patted down his hair and bowed again.

His last image of Grandmother was of her glaring out the window, as if thinking about the terrible scolding she would give the ogres when they invaded her home.

XXXVI

FRANK

FRANK TOOK THE QUICKEST POSSIBLE SHOWER, put on the clothes Hazel had set out—an olive-green shirt with beige cargo pants, really?—then grabbed his spare bow and quiver and bounded up the attic stairs.

The attic was full of weapons. His family had collected enough ancient armaments to supply an army. Shields, spears, and quivers of arrows hung along one wall—almost as many as in the Camp Jupiter armory. At the back window, a scorpion crossbow was mounted and loaded, ready for action. At the front window stood something that looked like a machine gun with a cluster of barrels.

"Rocket launcher?" he wondered aloud.

"Nope, nope," said a voice from the corner. "Potatoes. Ella doesn't like potatoes."

The harpy had made a nest for herself between two old steamer trunks. She was sitting in a pile of Chinese scrolls, reading seven or eight at once.

"Ella," Frank said, "where are the others?"

"Roof." She glanced upward, then returned to her reading, alternately picking at her feathers and turning pages. "Roof. Ogre-watching. Ella doesn't like ogres. Potatoes."

"Potatoes?" Frank didn't understand until he swiveled the machine gun around. Its eight barrels were loaded with spuds. At the base of the gun, a basket was filled with more edible ammunition.

He looked out the window—the same window his mom had watched him from when he had met the bear. Down in the yard, the ogres were milling around, shoving each other, occasionally yelling at the house, and throwing bronze cannonballs that exploded in midair.

"They have cannonballs," Frank said. "And we have a potato gun."

"Starch," Ella said thoughtfully. "Starch is bad for ogres."

The house shook from another explosion. Frank needed to reach the roof and see how Percy and Hazel were doing, but he felt bad leaving Ella alone.

He knelt next to her, careful not to get too close. "Ella, it's not safe here with the ogres. We're going to be flying to Alaska soon. Will you come with us?"

Ella twitched uncomfortably. "Alaska. Six hundred twenty-six thousand, four hundred twenty-five square miles. State mammal: the moose."

Suddenly she switched to Latin, which Frank could just barely follow thanks to his classes at Camp Jupiter: *"To the north, beyond the gods, lies the legion's crown. Falling from ice, the son of Neptune shall drown—"* She stopped and scratched her disheveled red hair. "Hmm. Burned. The rest is burned."

Frank could hardly breathe. "Ella, was . . . was that a prophecy? Where did you read that?"

"Moose," Ella said, savoring the word. "Moose. Moose. Moose."

The house shook again. Dust rained down from the rafters. Outside, an ogre bellowed, "Frank Zhang! Show yourself!"

"Nope," Ella said. "Frank shouldn't. Nope."

"Just . . . stay here, okay?" Frank said. "I've got to go help Hazel and Percy."

He pulled down the ladder to the roof.

"Morning," Percy said grimly. "Beautiful day, huh?"

He wore the same clothes as the day before—jeans, his purple T-shirt, and Polartec jacket—but they'd obviously been freshly washed. He held his sword in one hand and a garden hose in the other. Why there was a garden hose on the roof, Frank wasn't sure, but every time the giants sent up a cannonball, Percy summoned a high-powered blast of water and detonated the sphere in midair. Then Frank remembered —*his* family was descended from Poseidon, too. Grandmother had said their house had been attacked before. Maybe they had put a hose up here for just that reason.

Hazel patrolled the widow's walk between the two attic gables. She looked so good, it made Frank's chest hurt. She wore jeans, a cream-colored jacket, and a white shirt that made her skin look as warm as cocoa. Her curly hair fell around her shoulders. When she came close, Frank could smell jasmine shampoo.

She gripped her sword. When she glanced at Frank, her eyes flashed with concern. "Are you okay?" she asked. "Why are you smiling?"

"Oh, uh, nothing," he managed. "Thanks for breakfast. And the clothes. And... not hating me."

Hazel looked baffled. "Why would I hate you?"

Frank's face burned. He wished he'd kept his mouth shut, but it was too late now. *Don't let her get away*, his grandmother had said. *You need strong women.*

"It's just... last night," he stammered. "When I summoned the skeleton. I thought... I thought that you thought... I was repulsive... or something."

Hazel raised her eyebrows. She shook her head in dismay. "Frank, maybe I was surprised. Maybe I was scared of that thing. But repulsed? The way you commanded it, so confident and everything—like, *Oh, by the way, guys, I have this all-powerful* spartus *we can use.* I couldn't believe it. I wasn't repulsed, Frank. I was impressed."

Frank wasn't sure he'd heard her right. "You were... impressed... by *me*?"

Percy laughed. "Dude, it *was* pretty amazing."

"Honest?" Frank asked.

"Honest," Hazel promised. "But right now, we have other problems to worry about. Okay?"

She gestured at the army of ogres, who were getting increasingly bold, shuffling closer and closer to the house.

Percy readied the garden hose. "I've got one more trick up my sleeve. Your lawn has a sprinkler system. I can blow it up and cause some confusion down there, but that'll destroy your water pressure. No pressure, no hose, and those cannonballs are going to plow right into the house."

Hazel's praise was still ringing in Frank's ears, making it difficult to think. Dozens of ogres were camped on his lawn, waiting to tear him apart, and Frank could barely control the urge to grin.

Hazel didn't hate him. She was impressed.

He forced himself to concentrate. He remembered what his grandmother had told him about the nature of his gift, and how he had to leave her here to die.

You've got a role to play, Mars had said.

Frank couldn't believe he was Juno's secret weapon, or that this big Prophecy of the Seven depended on him. But Hazel and Percy were counting on him. He had to do his best.

He thought about that weird partial prophecy Ella had recited in the attic, about the son of Neptune drowning.

You don't understand her true value, Phineas had told them in Portland. The old blind man had thought that controlling Ella would make him a king.

All these puzzle pieces swirled around in Frank's mind. He got the feeling that when they finally connected, they would create a picture he didn't like.

"Guys, I've got an escape plan." He told his friends about the plane waiting at the airfield, and his grandmother's note for the pilot. "He's a legion veteran. He'll help us."

"But Arion's not back," Hazel said. "And what about your grandmother? We can't just leave her."

Frank choked back a sob. "Maybe—maybe Arion will find us. As for my grandmother . . . she was pretty clear. She said she'd be okay."

It wasn't exactly the truth, but it was as much as Frank could manage.

"There's another problem," Percy said. "I'm not good with air travel. It's dangerous for a son of Neptune."

"You'll have to risk it. . . . and so will I," Frank said. "By the way, we're related."

Percy almost stumbled off the roof. "What?"

Frank gave them the five-second version: "Periclymenus. Ancestor on my mom's side. Argonaut. Grandson of Poseidon."

Hazel's mouth fell open. "You're a—a descendant of Neptune? Frank, that's—"

"Crazy? Yeah. And there's this ability my family has, supposedly. But I don't know how to use it. If I can't figure it out—"

Another massive cheer went up from the Laistrygonians. Frank realized they were staring up at him, pointing and waving and laughing. They had spotted their breakfast.

"Zhang!" they yelled. "Zhang!"

Hazel stepped closer to him. "They keep doing that. Why are they yelling your name?"

"Never mind," Frank said. "Listen, we've got to protect Ella, take her with us."

"Of course," Hazel said. "The poor thing needs our help."

"No," Frank said. "I mean yes, but it's not just that. She

recited a prophecy downstairs. I think...I think it was about *this* quest."

He didn't want to tell Percy the bad news, about a son of Neptune drowning, but he repeated the lines.

Percy's jaw tightened. "I don't know how a son of Neptune can drown. I can breathe underwater. But the crown of the legion—"

"That's got to be the eagle," Hazel said.

Percy nodded. "And Ella recited something like this once before, in Portland—a line from the old Great Prophecy."

"The what?" Frank asked.

"Tell you later." Percy turned his garden hose and shot another cannonball out of the sky.

It exploded in an orange fireball. The ogres clapped with appreciation and yelled, "Pretty! Pretty!"

"The thing is," Frank said, "Ella remembers everything she reads. She said something about the page being burned, like she'd read a damaged text of prophecies."

Hazel's eyes widened. "Burned books of prophecy? You don't think—but that's impossible!"

"The books Octavian wanted, back at camp?" Percy guessed.

Hazel whistled under her breath. "The lost Sibylline books that outlined the entire destiny of Rome. If Ella actually read a copy somehow, and memorized it—"

"Then she's the most valuable harpy in the world," Frank said. "No wonder Phineas wanted to capture her."

"Frank Zhang!" an ogre shouted from below. He was bigger than the rest, wearing a lion's cape like a Roman standard bearer and a plastic bib with a lobster on it. "Come down, son of Mars! We've been waiting for you. Come, be our honored guest!"

Hazel gripped Frank's arm. "Why do I get the feeling that 'honored guest' means the same thing as 'dinner'?"

Frank wished Mars were still there. He could use somebody to snap his fingers and make his battle jitters go away.

Hazel believes in me, he thought. *I can do this.*

He looked at Percy. "Can you drive?"

"Sure. Why?"

"Grandmother's car is in the garage. It's an old Cadillac. The thing is like a tank. If you can get it started—"

"We'll still have to break through a line of ogres," Hazel said.

"The sprinkler system," Percy said. "Use it as a distraction?"

"Exactly," Frank said. "I'll buy you as much time as I can. Get Ella, and get in the car. I'll try to meet you in the garage, but don't wait for me."

Percy frowned. "Frank—"

"Give us your answer, Frank Zhang!" the ogre yelled up. "Come down, and we will spare the others—your friends, your poor old granny. We only want you!"

"They're lying," Percy muttered.

"Yeah, I got that," Frank agreed. "Go!"

His friends ran for the ladder.

Frank tried to control the beating of his heart. He grinned and yelled, "Hey, down there! Who's hungry?" The ogres cheered as Frank paced along the widow's walk and waved like a rock star.

Frank tried to summon his family power. He imagined himself as a fire-breathing dragon. He strained and clenched his fist and thought about dragons so hard, beads of sweat popped up on his forehead. He wanted to sweep down on the enemy and destroy them. That would be extremely cool. But nothing happened. He had no clue how to change himself. He had never even seen a real dragon. For a panicky moment, he wondered if Grandmother had played some sort of cruel joke on him. Maybe he'd misunderstood the gift. Maybe Frank was the only member of the family who hadn't inherited it. That would be just his luck.

The ogres started to become restless. The cheering turned to catcalls. A few Laistrygonians hefted their cannonballs.

"Hold on!" Frank yelled. "You don't want to char me, do you? I won't taste very good that way."

"Come down!" they yelled. "Hungry!"

Time for Plan B. Frank just wished he had one.

"Do you promise to spare my friends?" Frank asked. "Do you swear on the River Styx?"

The ogres laughed. One threw a cannonball that arced over Frank's head and blew up the chimney. By some miracle, Frank wasn't hit with shrapnel.

"I'll take that as a *no*," he muttered. Then he shouted down: "Okay, fine! You win! I'll be right down. Wait there!"

The ogres cheered, but their leader in the lion's-skin cape scowled suspiciously. Frank wouldn't have much time. He descended the ladder into the attic. Ella was gone. He hoped that was a good sign. Maybe they'd gotten her to the Cadillac. He grabbed an extra quiver of arrows labeled ASSORTED

VARIETIES in his mother's neat printing. Then he ran to the machine gun.

He swiveled the barrel, took aim at the lead ogre, and pressed the trigger. Eight high-powered spuds blasted the giant in the chest, propelling him backward with such force that he crashed into a stack of bronze cannonballs, which promptly exploded, leaving a smoking crater in the yard.

Apparently starch *was* bad for ogres.

While the rest of the monsters ran around in confusion, Frank pulled his bow and rained arrows on them. Some of the missiles detonated on impact. Others splintered like buckshot and left the giants with some painful new tattoos. One hit an ogre and instantly turned him into a potted rosebush.

Unfortunately, the ogres recovered quickly. They began throwing cannonballs—dozens at a time. The whole house groaned under the impact. Frank ran for the stairs. The attic disintegrated behind him. Smoke and fire poured down the second-floor hallway.

"Grandmother!" he cried, but the heat was so intense, he couldn't reach her room. He raced to the ground floor, clinging to the banister as the house shook and huge chunks of the ceiling collapsed.

The base of the staircase was a smoking crater. He leaped over it and stumbled through the kitchen. Choking from the ash and soot, he burst into the garage. The Cadillac's headlights were on. The engine was running and the garage door was opening.

"Get in!" Percy yelled.

Frank dove in the back next to Hazel. Ella was curled up

in the front, her head tucked under her wings, muttering, "Yikes. Yikes. Yikes."

Percy gunned the engine. They shot out of the garage before it was fully open, leaving a Cadillac-shaped hole of splintered wood.

The ogres ran to intercept, but Percy shouted at the top of his lungs, and the irrigation system exploded. A hundred geysers shot into the air along with clods of dirt, pieces of pipe, and very heavy sprinkler heads.

The Cadillac was going about forty when they hit the first ogre, who disintegrated on impact. By the time the other monsters overcame their confusion, the Cadillac was half a mile down the road. Flaming cannonballs burst behind them.

Frank glanced back and saw his family mansion on fire, the walls collapsing inward and smoke billowing into the sky. He saw a large black speck—maybe a buzzard—circling up from the fire. It might've been Frank's imagination, but he thought it had flown out of the second-story window.

"Grandmother?" he murmured.

It seemed impossible, but she had promised she would die in her own way, not at the hands of the ogres. Frank hoped she had been right.

They drove through the woods and headed north.

"About three miles!" Frank said. "You can't miss it!"

Behind them, more explosions ripped through the forest. Smoke boiled into the sky.

"How fast can Laistrygonians run?" Hazel asked.

"Let's not find out," Percy said.

The gates of the airfield appeared before them—only a

few hundred yards away. A private jet idled on the runway. Its stairs were down.

The Cadillac hit a pothole and went airborne. Frank's head slammed into the ceiling. When the wheels touched the ground, Percy floored the brakes, and they swerved to a stop just inside the gates.

Frank climbed out and drew his bow. "Get to the plane! They're coming!"

The Laistrygonians were closing in with alarming speed. The first line of ogres burst out of the woods and barreled toward the airfield—five hundred yards away, four hundred yards...

Percy and Hazel managed to get Ella out of the Cadillac, but as soon as the harpy saw the airplane, she began to shriek.

"N-n-no!" she yelped. "Fly with wings! N-n-no airplanes."

"It's okay," Hazel promised. "We'll protect you!"

Ella made a horrible, painful wail like she was being burned.

Percy held up his hands in exasperation. "What do we do? We can't force her."

"No," Frank agreed. The ogres were three hundred yards out.

"She's too valuable to leave behind," Hazel said. Then she winced at her own words. "Gods, I'm sorry, Ella. I sound as bad as Phineas. You're a living thing, not a treasure."

"No planes. N-n-no planes." Ella was hyperventilating.

The ogres were almost in throwing distance.

Percy's eyes lit up. "I've got an idea. Ella, can you hide in the woods? Will you be safe from the ogres?"

"Hide," she agreed. "Safe. Hiding is good for harpies. Ella is quick. And small. And fast."

"Okay," Percy said. "Just stay around this area. I can send a friend to meet you and take you to Camp Jupiter."

Frank unslung his bow and nocked an arrow. "A friend?"

Percy waved his hand in a *tell you later* gesture. "Ella, would you like that? Would you like my friend to take you to Camp Jupiter and show you our home?"

"Camp," Ella muttered. Then in Latin: "'*Wisdom's daughter walks alone, the Mark of Athena burns through Rome.*'"

"Uh, right," Percy said. "That sounds important, but we can talk about that later. You'll be safe at camp. All the books and food you want."

"No planes," she insisted.

"No planes," Percy agreed.

"Ella will hide now." Just like that, she was gone—a red streak disappearing into the woods.

"I'll miss her," Hazel said sadly.

"We'll see her again," Percy promised, but he frowned uneasily, as if he were really troubled by that last bit of prophecy—the thing about Athena.

An explosion sent the airfield's gate spinning into the air.

Frank tossed his grandmother's letter to Percy. "Show that to the pilot! Show him your letter from Reyna too! We've got to take off *now*."

Percy nodded. He and Hazel ran for the plane.

Frank took cover behind the Cadillac and started firing at the ogres. He targeted the largest clump of enemies and shot a tulip-shaped arrow. Just as he'd hoped, it was a hydra. Ropes lashed out like squid tentacles, and the entire front row of ogres plowed facefirst into the dirt.

Frank heard the plane's engines rev.

He shot three more arrows as fast as he could, blasting enormous craters in the ogres' ranks. The survivors were only a hundred yards away, and some of the brighter ones stumbled to a stop, realizing that they were now within hurling range.

"Frank!" Hazel shrieked. "Come on!"

A fiery cannonball hurtled toward him in a slow arc. Frank knew instantly it was going to hit the plane. He nocked an arrow. *I can do this*, he thought. He let the arrow fly. It intercepted the cannonball midair, detonating a massive fireball.

Another two cannonballs sailed toward him. Frank ran.

Behind him, metal groaned as the Cadillac exploded. He dove into the plane just as the stairs started to rise.

The pilot must've understood the situation just fine. There was no safety announcement, no pre-flight drink, and no waiting for clearance. He pushed the throttle, and the plane shot down the runway. Another blast ripped through the runway behind them, but then they were in the air.

Frank looked down and saw the airstrip riddled with craters like a piece of burning Swiss cheese. Swaths of Lynn Canyon Park were on fire. A few miles to the south, a swirling pyre of flames and black smoke was all that remained of the Zhang family mansion.

So much for Frank being impressive. He'd failed to save his grandmother. He'd failed to use his powers. He hadn't even saved their harpy friend. When Vancouver disappeared in the clouds below, Frank buried his head in his hands and started to cry.

The plane banked to the left.

Over the intercom, the pilot's voice said, *"Senatus Populusque Romanus,* my friends. Welcome aboard. Next stop: Anchorage, Alaska."

XXXVII

PERCY

Airplanes or cannibals? No contest.

Percy would've preferred driving Grandma Zhang's Cadillac all the way to Alaska with fireball-throwing ogres on his tail rather than sitting in a luxury Gulfstream.

He'd flown before. The details were hazy, but he remembered a pegasus named Blackjack. He'd even been in a plane once or twice. But a son of Neptune (Poseidon, whatever) didn't belong in the air. Every time the plane hit a spot of turbulence, Percy's heart raced, and he was sure Jupiter was slapping them around.

He tried to focus as Frank and Hazel talked. Hazel was reassuring Frank that he'd done everything he could for his grandmother. Frank had saved them from the Laistrygonians and gotten them out of Vancouver. He'd been incredibly brave.

Frank kept his head down like he was ashamed to have been crying, but Percy didn't blame him. The poor guy had just lost his grandmother and seen his house go up in flames. As far as Percy was concerned, shedding a few tears about something like that didn't make you any less of a man, especially when you had just fended off an army of ogres that wanted to eat you for breakfast.

Percy still couldn't get over the fact that Frank was a distant relative. Frank would be his...what? Great-times-a-thousand nephew? Too weird for words.

Frank refused to explain exactly what his "family gift" was, but as they flew north, Frank *did* tell them about his conversation with Mars the night before. He explained the prophecy Juno had issued when he was a baby—about his life being tied to a piece of firewood, and how he had asked Hazel to keep it for him.

Some of that, Percy had already figured out. Hazel and Frank had obviously shared some crazy experiences when they had blacked out together, and they'd made some sort of deal. It also explained why even now, out of habit, Frank kept checking his coat pocket, and why he was so nervous around fire. Still, Percy couldn't imagine what kind of courage it had taken for Frank to embark on a quest, knowing that one small flame could snuff out his life.

"Frank," he said, "I'm proud to be related to you."

Frank's ears turned red. With his head lowered, his military haircut made a sharp black arrow pointing down. "Juno has some sort of plan for us, about the Prophecy of Seven."

"Yeah," Percy grumbled. "I didn't like her as Hera. I don't like her any better as Juno."

Hazel tucked her feet underneath her. She studied Percy

with her luminescent golden eyes, and he wondered how she could be so calm. She was the youngest one on the quest, but she was always holding them together and comforting them. Now they were flying to Alaska, where she had died once before. They would try to free Thanatos, who might take her back to the Underworld. Yet she didn't show any fear. It made Percy feel silly for being scared of airplane turbulence.

"You're a son of Poseidon, aren't you?" she asked. "You *are* a Greek demigod."

Percy gripped his leather necklace. "I started to remember in Portland, after the gorgon's blood. It's been coming back to me slowly since then. There's another camp—Camp Half-Blood."

Just saying the name made Percy feel warm inside. Good memories washed over him: the smell of strawberry fields in the warm summer sun, fireworks lighting up the beach on the Fourth of July, satyrs playing panpipes at the nightly campfire, and a kiss at the bottom of the canoe lake.

Hazel and Frank stared at him as though he'd slipped into another language.

"Another camp," Hazel repeated. "A *Greek* camp? Gods, if Octavian found out—"

"He'd declare war," Frank said. "He's always been sure the Greeks were out there, plotting against us. He thought Percy was a spy."

"That's why Juno sent me," Percy said. "Uh, I mean, not to spy. I think it was some kind of exchange. Your friend Jason—I think he was sent to *my* camp. In my dreams, I saw a demigod that might have been him. He was working with some other demigods on this flying warship. I think they're coming to Camp Jupiter to help."

Frank tapped nervously on the back of his seat. "Mars said Juno wants to unite the Greeks and Romans to fight Gaea. But, jeez—Greeks and Romans have a long history of bad blood."

Hazel took a deep breath. "That's probably why the gods have kept us apart this long. If a Greek warship appeared in the sky above Camp Jupiter, and Reyna didn't know it was friendly—"

"Yeah," Percy agreed. "We've got to be careful how we explain this when we get back."

"*If* we get back," Frank said.

Percy nodded reluctantly. "I mean, I trust you guys. I hope you trust me. I feel... well, I feel as close to you two as to any of my old friends at Camp Half-Blood. But with the other demigods, at both camps—there's going to be a lot of suspicion."

Hazel did something he wasn't expecting. She leaned over and kissed him on the cheek. It was totally a sisterly kiss. But she smiled with such affection, it warmed Percy right down to his feet.

"Of course we trust you," she said. "We're a family now. Aren't we, Frank?"

"Sure," he said. "Do I get a kiss?"

Hazel laughed, but there was nervous tension in it. "Anyway, what do we do now?"

Percy took a deep breath. Time was slipping away. They were almost halfway through June twenty-third, and tomorrow was the Feast of Fortuna. "I've got to contact a friend—to keep my promise to Ella."

"How?" Frank said. "One of those Iris-messages?"

"Still not working," Percy said sadly. "I tried it last night at your grandmother's house. No luck. Maybe it's because my memories are still jumbled. Or the gods aren't allowing a connection. I'm hoping I can contact my friend in my dreams."

Another bump of turbulence made him grab his seat. Below them, snowcapped mountains broke through a blanket of clouds.

"I'm not sure I can sleep," Percy said. "But I need to try. We can't leave Ella by herself with those ogres around."

"Yeah," Frank said. "We've still got hours to fly. Take the couch, man."

Percy nodded. He felt lucky to have Hazel and Frank watching out for him. What he'd said to them was true—he trusted them. In the weird, terrifying, horrible experience of losing his memory and getting ripped out of his old life —Hazel and Frank were the bright spots.

He stretched out, closed his eyes, and dreamed he was falling from a mountain of ice toward a cold sea.

The dream shifted. He was back in Vancouver, standing in front of the ruins of the Zhang mansion. The Laistrygonians were gone. The mansion was reduced to a burned-out shell. A crew of firefighters was packing up their equipment, getting ready to move out. The lawn looked like a war zone, with smoking craters and trenches from the blown-out irrigation pipes.

At the edge of the forest, a giant shaggy black dog was bounding around, sniffing the trees. The firefighters completely ignored him.

Beside one of the craters knelt a Cyclops in oversized jeans, boots, and a massive flannel shirt. His messy brown hair was spattered with rain and mud. When he raised his head, his big brown eye was red from crying.

"Close!" he moaned. "So close, but gone!"

It broke Percy's heart to hear the pain and worry in the big guy's voice, but he knew they only had a few seconds to talk. The edges of the vision were already dissolving. If Alaska was the land beyond the gods, Percy figured the farther north he went, the harder it would be to communicate with his friends, even in his dreams.

"Tyson!" he called.

The Cyclops looked around frantically. "Percy? Brother?"

"Tyson, I'm okay. I'm here—well, not really."

Tyson grabbed the air like he was trying to catch butterflies. "Can't see you! Where is my brother?"

"Tyson, I'm flying to Alaska. I'm okay. I'll be back. Just find Ella. She's a harpy with red feathers. She's hiding in the woods around the house."

"Find a harpy? A red harpy?"

"Yes! Protect her, okay? She's my friend. Get her back to California. There's a demigod camp in the Oakland Hills— Camp Jupiter. Meet me above the Caldecott Tunnel."

"Oakland Hills…California…Caldecott Tunnel." He shouted to the dog: "Mrs. O'Leary! We must find a harpy!"

"WOOF!" said the dog.

Tyson's face started to dissolve. "My brother is okay? My brother is coming back? I miss you!"

"I miss you, too." Percy tried to keep his voice from cracking. "I'll see you soon. Just be careful! There's a giant's army marching south. Tell Annabeth—"

The dream shifted.

Percy found himself standing in the hills north of Camp Jupiter, looking down at the Field of Mars and New Rome. At the legion's fort, horns were blowing. Campers scrambled to muster.

The giant's army was arrayed to Percy's left and right—centaurs with bull's horns, the six-armed Earthborn, and evil Cyclopes in scrap-metal armor. The Cyclopes' siege tower cast a shadow across the feet of the giant Polybotes, who grinned down at the Roman camp. He paced eagerly across the hill, snakes dropping from his green dreadlocks, his dragon legs stomping down small trees. On his green-blue armor, the decorative faces of hungry monsters seemed to blink in the shadows.

"Yes," he chuckled, planting his trident in the ground. "Blow your little horns, Romans. I've come to destroy you! Stheno!"

The gorgon scrambled out of the bushes. Her lime green viper hair and Bargain Mart vest clashed horribly with the giant's color scheme.

"Yes, master!" she said. "Would you like a Puppy-in-a-Blanket?"

She held up a tray of free samples.

"Hmm," Polybotes said. "What sort of puppy?"

"Ah, they're not actually puppies. They're tiny hot dogs in crescent rolls, but they're on sale this week—"

"Bah! Never mind, then! Are our forces ready to attack?"

"Oh—" Stheno stepped back quickly to avoid getting flattened by the giant's foot. "Almost, great one. Ma Gasket and half her Cyclopes stopped in Napa. Something about a winery tour? They promised to be here by tomorrow evening."

"What?" The giant looked around, as if just noticing that a big portion of his army was missing. "Gah! That Cyclops woman will give me an ulcer. *Winery tour?*"

"I think there was cheese and crackers, too," Stheno said helpfully. "Though Bargain Mart has a much better deal."

Polybotes ripped an oak tree out of the ground and threw it into the valley. "Cyclopes! I tell you, Stheno, when I destroy Neptune and take over the oceans, we will renegotiate the Cyclopes' labor contract. Ma Gasket will learn her place! Now, what news from the north?"

"The demigods have left for Alaska," Stheno said. "They fly straight to their death. Ah, small 'd' *death*, I mean. Not our prisoner Death. Although, I suppose they're flying to him too."

Polybotes growled. "Alcyoneus had better spare the son of Neptune as he promised. I want that one chained at my feet, so I can kill him when the time is ripe. His blood shall water the stones of Mount Olympus and wake the Earth Mother! What word from the Amazons?"

"Only silence," Stheno said. "We do not yet know the winner of last night's duel, but it is only a matter of time before Otrera prevails and comes to our aid."

"Hmm." Polybotes absently scratched some vipers out of his hair. "Perhaps it's just as well we wait, then. Tomorrow at sundown is Fortuna's Feast. By then, we must invade— Amazons or no. In the meantime, dig in! We set up camp here, on high ground."

"Yes, great one!" Stheno announced to the troops: "Puppies-in-Blankets for everyone!"

The monsters cheered.

Polybotes spread his hands in front of him, taking in the valley like a panoramic picture. "Yes, blow your little horns, demigods. Soon, the legacy of Rome will be destroyed for the last time!"

The dream faded.

Percy woke with a jolt as the plane started its descent.

Hazel laid her hand on his shoulder. "Sleep okay?"

Percy sat up groggily. "How long was I out?"

Frank stood in the aisle, wrapping his spear and new bow in his ski bag. "A few hours," he said. "We're almost there."

Percy looked out the window. A glittering inlet of the sea snaked between snowy mountains. In the distance, a city was carved out of the wilderness, surrounded by lush green forests on one side and icy black beaches on the other.

"Welcome to Alaska," Hazel said. "We're beyond the help of the gods."

XXXVIII

PERCY

THE PILOT SAID THE PLANE COULDN'T WAIT for them, but that was okay with Percy. If they survived till the next day, he hoped they could find a different way back—*anything* but a plane.

He should've been depressed. He was stuck in Alaska, the giant's home territory, out of contact with his old friends just as his memories were coming back. He had seen an image of Polybotes's army about to invade Camp Jupiter. He'd learned that the giants planned to use him as some kind of blood sacrifice to awaken Gaea. Plus, tomorrow evening was the Feast of Fortuna. He, Frank, and Hazel had an impossible task to complete before then. At best, they would unleash Death, who might take Percy's two friends to the Underworld. Not much to look forward to.

Still, Percy felt strangely invigorated. His dream of Tyson had lifted his spirits. He *remembered* Tyson, his brother. They'd fought together, celebrated victories, shared good times at Camp Half-Blood. He remembered his home, and that gave him a new determination to succeed. He was fighting for two camps now—two families.

Juno had stolen his memory and sent him to Camp Jupiter for a reason. He understood that now. He still wanted to punch her in her godly face, but at least he got her reasoning. If the two camps could work together, they stood a chance of stopping their mutual enemies. Separately, both camps were doomed.

There were other reasons Percy wanted to save Camp Jupiter. Reasons he didn't dare put into words—not yet, anyway. Suddenly he saw a future for himself and for Annabeth that he'd never imagined before.

As they took a taxi into downtown Anchorage, Percy told Frank and Hazel about his dreams. They looked anxious but not surprised when he told them about the giant's army closing in on camp.

Frank choked when he heard about Tyson. "You have a half-brother who's a Cyclops?"

"Sure," Percy said. "Which makes him your great-great-great—"

"Please." Frank covered his ears. "Enough."

"As long as he can get Ella to camp," Hazel said. "I'm worried about her."

Percy nodded. He was still thinking about the lines of prophecy the harpy had recited—about the son of Neptune drowning, and the mark of Athena burning through Rome.

He wasn't sure what the first part meant, but he was starting to have an idea about the second. He tried to set the question aside. He had to survive *this* quest first.

The taxi turned on Highway One, which looked more like a small street to Percy, and took them north toward downtown. It was late afternoon, but the sun was still high in the sky.

"I can't believe how much this place has grown," Hazel muttered.

The taxi driver grinned in the rearview mirror. "Been a long time since you visited, miss?"

"About seventy years," Hazel said.

The driver slid the glass partition closed and drove on in silence.

According to Hazel, almost none of the buildings were the same, but she pointed out features of the landscape: the vast forests ringing the city, the cold, gray waters of Cook Inlet tracing the north edge of town, and the Chugach Mountains rising grayish-blue in the distance, capped with snow even in June.

Percy had never smelled air this clean before. The town itself had a weather-beaten look to it, with closed stores, rusted-out cars, and worn apartment complexes lining the road, but it was still beautiful. Lakes and huge stretches of woods cut through the middle. The arctic sky was an amazing combination of turquoise and gold.

Then there were the giants. Dozens of bright-blue men, each thirty feet tall with gray frosty hair, were wading through the forests, fishing in the bay, and striding across the mountains. The mortals didn't seem to notice them. The taxi passed within a few yards of one who was sitting at the edge of a lake washing his feet, but the driver didn't panic.

"Um . . ." Frank pointed at the blue guy.

"Hyperboreans," Percy said. He was amazed he remembered that name. "Northern giants. I fought some when Kronos invaded Manhattan."

"Wait," Frank said. "When *who* did *what?*"

"Long story. But these guys look . . . I don't know, *peaceful.*"

"They usually are," Hazel agreed. "I remember them. They're everywhere in Alaska, like bears."

"Bears?" Frank said nervously.

"The giants are invisible to mortals," Hazel said. "They never bothered me, though one almost stepped on me by accident once."

That sounded fairly bothersome to Percy, but the taxi kept driving. None of the giants paid them any attention. One stood right at the intersection of Northern Lights Road, straddling the highway, and they drove between his legs. The Hyperborean was cradling a Native American totem pole wrapped in furs, humming to it like a baby. If the guy hadn't been the size of a building, he would've been almost cute.

The taxi drove through downtown, past a bunch of tourists' shops advertising furs, Native American art, and gold. Percy hoped Hazel wouldn't get agitated and make the jewelry shops explode.

As the driver turned and headed toward the seashore, Hazel knocked on the glass partition. "Here is good. Can you let us out?"

They paid the driver and stepped onto Fourth Street. Compared to Vancouver, downtown Anchorage was tiny—more like a college campus than a city, but Hazel looked amazed.

"It's *huge*," she said. "That—that's where the Gitchell Hotel used to be. My mom and I stayed there our first week in Alaska. And they've moved City Hall. It used to be there."

She led them in a daze for a few blocks. They didn't really have a plan beyond finding the fastest way to the Hubbard Glacier, but Percy smelled something cooking nearby—sausage, maybe? He realized he hadn't eaten since that morning at Grandma Zhang's.

"Food," he said. "Come on."

They found a café right by the beach. It was bustling with people, but they scored a table at the window and perused the menus.

Frank whooped with delight. "Twenty-four-hour breakfast!"

"It's, like, dinnertime," Percy said, though he couldn't tell from looking outside. The sun was so high, it could've been noon.

"I love breakfast," Frank said. "I'd eat breakfast, breakfast, and breakfast if I could. Though, um, I'm sure the food here isn't as good as Hazel's."

Hazel elbowed him, but her smile was playful.

Seeing them like that made Percy happy. Those two definitely needed to get together. But it also made him sad. He thought about Annabeth, and wondered if he'd live long enough to see her again.

Think positive, he told himself.

"You know," he said, "breakfast sounds great."

They all ordered massive plates of eggs, pancakes, and reindeer sausage, though Frank looked a little worried about the reindeer. "You think it's okay that we're eating Rudolph?"

"Dude," Percy said, "I could eat Prancer and Blitzen, too. I'm *hungry.*"

The food was excellent. Percy had never seen anyone eat as fast as Frank. The red-nosed reindeer did not stand a chance.

Between bites of blueberry pancake, Hazel drew a squiggly curve and an X on her napkin. "So this is what I'm thinking. We're here." She tapped X. "Anchorage."

"It looks like a seagull's face," Percy said. "And we're the eye."

Hazel glared at him. "It's a *map*, Percy. Anchorage is at the top of this sliver of ocean, Cook Inlet. There's a big peninsula of land below us, and my old home town, Seward, is at the bottom of the peninsula, *here.*" She drew another X at the base of the seagull's throat. "That's the closest town to the Hubbard Glacier. We could go around by sea, I guess, but it would take forever. We don't have that kind of time."

Frank polished off the last of his Rudolph. "But land is dangerous," he said. "Land means *Gaea.*"

Hazel nodded. "I don't see that we've got much choice, though. We could have asked our pilot to fly us down, but I don't know . . . his plane might be too big for the little Seward airport. And if we chartered another plane—"

"No more planes," Percy said. "Please."

Hazel held up her hand in a placating gesture. "It's okay. There's a train that goes from here to Seward. We might be able to catch one tonight. It only takes a couple of hours."

She drew a dotted line between the two X's.

"You just cut off the seagull's head," Percy noted.

Hazel sighed. "It's the train line. Look, from Seward, the Hubbard Glacier is down here somewhere." She tapped the lower right corner of her napkin. "That's where Alcyoneus is."

"But you're not sure how far?" Frank asked.

Hazel frowned and shook her head. "I'm pretty sure it's only accessible by boat or plane."

"Boat," Percy said immediately.

"Fine," Hazel said. "It shouldn't be too far from Seward. *If* we can get to Seward safely."

Percy gazed out the window. So much to do, and only twenty-four hours left. This time tomorrow, the Feast of Fortuna would be starting. Unless they unleashed Death and made it back to camp, the giant's army would flood into the valley. The Romans would be the main course at a monster dinner.

Across the street, a frosty black sand beach led down to the sea, which was as smooth as steel. The ocean here felt different—still powerful, but freezing, slow, and primal. No gods controlled that water, at least no gods Percy knew. Neptune wouldn't be able to protect him. Percy wondered if he could even manipulate water here, or breathe underwater.

A Hyperborean giant lumbered across the street. Nobody in the café noticed. The giant stepped into the bay, cracking the ice under his sandals, and thrust his hands in the water. He brought out a killer whale in one fist. Apparently that wasn't what he wanted, because he threw the whale back and kept wading.

"Good breakfast," Frank said. "Who's ready for a train ride?"

The station wasn't far. They were just in time to buy tickets for the last train south. As his friends climbed on board, Percy said, "Be with you in a sec," and ran back into the station.

He got change from the gift shop and stood in front of the pay phone.

He'd never used a pay phone before. They were strange antiques to him, like his mom's turntable or his teacher Chiron's Frank Sinatra cassette tapes. He wasn't sure how many coins it would take, or if he could even make the call go through, assuming he remembered the number correctly.

Sally Jackson, he thought.

That was his mom's name. And he had a stepdad...Paul.

What did they think had happened to Percy? Maybe they had already held a memorial service. As near as he could figure, he'd lost *seven months* of his life. Sure, most of that had been during the school year, but still...*not* cool.

He picked up the receiver and punched in a New York number—his mom's apartment.

Voice mail. Percy should have figured. It would be like, midnight in New York. They wouldn't recognize this number. Hearing Paul's voice on the recording hit Percy in the gut so hard, he could barely speak at the tone.

"Mom," he said. "Hey, I'm alive. Hera put me to sleep for a while, and then she took my memory, and..." His voice faltered. How he could possibly explain all this? "Anyway, I'm okay. I'm sorry. I'm on a quest—" He winced. He shouldn't have said that. His mom knew all about quests, and now she'd be worried. "I'll make it home. I promise. Love you."

He put down the receiver. He stared at the phone, hoping it would ring back. The train whistle sounded. The conductor shouted, "All aboard."

Percy ran. He made it just as they were pulling up the steps, then climbed to the top of the double-decker car and slid into his seat.

Hazel frowned. "You okay?"

"Yeah," he croaked. "Just…made a call."

She and Frank seemed to get that. They didn't ask for details.

Soon they were heading south along the coast, watching the landscape go by. Percy tried to think about the quest, but for an ADHD kid like him, the train wasn't the easiest place to concentrate.

Cool things kept happening outside. Bald eagles soared overhead. The train raced over bridges and along cliffs where glacial waterfalls tumbled thousands of feet down the rocks. They passed forests buried in snowdrifts, big artillery guns (to set off small avalanches and prevent uncontrolled ones, Hazel explained), and lakes so clear, they reflected the mountains like mirrors, so the world looked upside down.

Brown bears lumbered through the meadows. Hyperborean giants kept appearing in the strangest places. One was lounging in a lake like it was a hot tub. Another was using a pine tree as a toothpick. A third sat in a snowdrift, playing with two live moose like they were action figures. The train was full of tourists ohhing and ahhing and snapping pictures, but

Percy felt sorry they couldn't see the Hyperboreans. They were missing the really good shots.

Meanwhile, Frank studied a map of Alaska that he'd found in the seat pocket. He located Hubbard Glacier, which looked discouragingly far away from Seward. He kept running his finger along the coastline, frowning with concentration.

"What are you thinking?" Percy asked.

"Just . . . possibilities," Frank said.

Percy didn't know what that meant, but he let it go.

After about an hour, Percy started to relax. They bought hot chocolate from the dining car. The seats were warm and comfortable, and he thought about taking a nap.

Then a shadow passed overhead. Tourists murmured in excitement and started taking pictures.

"Eagle!" one yelled.

"Eagle?" said another.

"Huge eagle!" said a third.

"That's no eagle," Frank said.

Percy looked up just in time to see the creature make a second pass. It was definitely larger than an eagle, with a sleek black body the size of a Labrador retriever. Its wingspan was at least ten feet across.

"There's another one!" Frank pointed. "Strike that. Three, four. Okay, we're in trouble."

The creatures circled the train like vultures, delighting the tourists. Percy wasn't delighted. The monsters had glowing red eyes, sharp beaks, and vicious talons.

Percy felt for his pen in his pocket. "Those things look familiar. . . ."

"Seattle," Hazel said. "The Amazons had one in a cage. They're—"

Then several things happened at once. The emergency brake screeched, pitching them forward. Tourists screamed and tumbled through the aisles. The monsters swooped down, shattering the glass roof of the car, and the entire train toppled off the rails.

XXXIX

PERCY

PERCY WENT WEIGHTLESS.

His vision blurred. Claws grabbed his arms and lifted him into the air. Below, train wheels squealed and metal crashed. Glass shattered. Passengers screamed.

When his eyesight cleared, he saw the beast that was carrying him aloft. It had the body of a panther—sleek, black, and feline—with the wings and head of an eagle. Its eyes glowed blood-red.

Percy squirmed. The monster's front talons were wrapped around his arms like steel bands. He couldn't free himself or reach his sword. He rose higher and higher in the cold wind. Percy had no idea where the monster was taking him, but he was pretty sure he wouldn't like it when he got there.

He yelled—mostly out of frustration. Then something whistled by his ear. An arrow sprouted from the monster's neck. The creature shrieked and let go.

Percy fell, crashing through tree branches until he slammed into a snowbank. He groaned, looking up at a massive pine tree he'd just shredded.

He managed to stand. Nothing seemed broken. Frank stood to his left, shooting down the creatures as fast as he could. Hazel was at his back, swinging her sword at any monster that came close, but there were too many swarming around them—at least a dozen.

Percy drew Riptide. He sliced the wing off one monster and sent it spiraling into a tree, then sliced through another that burst into dust. But the defeated ones began to re-form immediately.

"What are these things?" he yelled.

"Gryphons!" Hazel said. "We have to get them away from the train!"

Percy saw what she meant. The train cars had fallen over, and their roofs had shattered. Tourists were stumbling around in shock. Percy didn't see anybody seriously injured, but the gryphons were swooping toward anything that moved. The only thing keeping them away from the mortals was a glowing gray warrior in camouflage—Frank's pet *spartus*.

Percy glanced over and noticed Frank's spear was gone. "Used your last charge?"

"Yeah." Frank shot another gryphon out of the sky. "I had to help the mortals. The spear just dissolved."

Percy nodded. Part of him was relieved. He didn't like the skeleton warrior. Part of him was disappointed, because that was one less weapon they had at their disposal. But he didn't fault Frank. Frank had done the right thing.

"Let's move the fight!" Percy said. "Away from the tracks!"

They stumbled through the snow, smacking and slicing gryphons that re-formed from dust every time they were killed.

Percy had had no experience with gryphons. He'd always imagined them as huge noble animals, like lions with wings, but these things reminded him more of vicious pack hunters —flying hyenas.

About fifty yards from the tracks, the trees gave way to an open marsh. The ground was so spongy and icy, Percy felt like he was racing across Bubble Wrap. Frank was running out of arrows. Hazel was breathing hard. Percy's own sword swings were getting slower. He realized they were alive only because the gryphons weren't *trying* to kill them. The gryphons wanted to pick them up and carry them off somewhere.

Maybe to their nests, Percy thought.

Then he tripped over something in the tall grass—a circle of scrap metal about the size of a tractor tire. It was a massive bird's nest—a *gryphon's* nest—the bottom littered with old pieces of jewelry, an Imperial gold dagger, a dented centurion's badge, and two pumpkin-sized eggs that looked like real gold.

Percy jumped into the nest. He pressed his sword tip against one of the eggs. "Back off, or I break it!"

The gryphons squawked angrily. They buzzed around the nest and snapped their beaks, but they didn't attack. Hazel and Frank stood back to back with Percy, their weapons ready.

"Gryphons collect gold," Hazel said. "They're crazy for it. Look—more nests over there."

Frank nocked his last arrow. "So if these are their nests,

where were they trying to take Percy? That thing was flying away with him."

Percy's arms still throbbed where the gryphon had grabbed him. "Alcyoneus," he guessed. "Maybe they're working for him. Are these things smart enough to take orders?"

"I don't know," Hazel said. "I never fought them when I lived here. I just read about them at camp."

"Weaknesses?" Frank asked. "Please tell me they have weaknesses."

Hazel scowled. "Horses. They hate horses—natural enemies, or something. I wish Arion was here!"

The gryphons shrieked. They swirled around the nest with their red eyes glowing.

"Guys," Frank said nervously, "I see legion relics in this nest."

"I know," Percy said.

"That means other demigods died here, or—"

"Frank, it'll be okay," Percy promised.

One of the gryphons dived in. Percy raised his sword, ready to stab the egg. The monster veered off, but the other gryphons were losing their patience. Percy couldn't keep this standoff going much longer.

He glanced around the fields, desperately trying to formulate a plan. About a quarter mile away, a Hyperborean giant was sitting in the bog, peacefully picking mud from between his toes with a broken tree trunk.

"I've got an idea," Percy said. "Hazel—all the gold in these nests. Do you think you can use it to cause a distraction?"

"I—I guess."

"Just give us enough time for a head start. When I say *go*, run for that giant."

Frank gaped at him. "You want us to run *toward* a giant?"

"Trust me," Percy said. "Ready? Go!"

Hazel thrust her hand upward. From a dozen nests across the marsh, golden objects shot into the air—jewelry, weapons, coins, gold nuggets, and most importantly, gryphon eggs. The monsters shrieked and flew after their eggs, frantic to save them.

Percy and his friends ran. Their feet splashed and crunched through the frozen marsh. Percy poured on speed, but he could hear the gryphons closing behind them, and now the monsters were *really* angry.

The giant hadn't noticed the commotion yet. He was inspecting his toes for mud, his face sleepy and peaceful, his white whiskers glistening with ice crystals. Around his neck was a necklace of found objects—garbage cans, car doors, moose antlers, camping equipment, even a toilet. Apparently he'd been cleaning up the wilderness.

Percy hated to disturb him, especially since it meant taking shelter under the giant's thighs, but they didn't have much choice.

"Under!" he told his friends. "Crawl under!"

They scrambled between the massive blue legs and flattened themselves in the mud, crawling as close as they could to his loincloth. Percy tried to breathe through his mouth, but it wasn't the most pleasant hiding spot.

"What's the plan?" Frank hissed. "Get flattened by a blue rump?"

"Lay low," Percy said. "Only move if you have to."

The gryphons arrived in a wave of angry beaks, talons, and wings, swarming around the giant, trying to get under his legs.

The giant rumbled in surprise. He shifted. Percy had to roll to avoid getting crushed by his large hairy rear. The Hyperborean grunted, a little more irritated. He swatted at the gryphons, but they squawked in outrage and began pecking at his legs and hands.

"Ruh?" the giant bellowed. "Ruh!"

He took a deep breath and blew out a wave of cold air. Even under the protection of the giant's legs, Percy could feel the temperature drop. The gryphons' shrieking stopped abruptly, replaced by the *thunk, thunk, thunk* of heavy objects hitting the mud.

"Come on," Percy told his friends. "Carefully."

They squirmed out from under the giant. All around the marsh, trees were glazed with frost. A huge swath of the bog was covered in fresh snow. Frozen gryphons stuck out of the ground like feathery Popsicle sticks, their wings still spread, beaks open, eyes wide with surprise.

Percy and his friends scrambled away, trying to keep out of the giant's vision, but the big guy was too busy to notice them. He was trying to figure out how to string a frozen gryphon onto his necklace.

"Percy..." Hazel wiped the ice and mud from her face. "How did you know the giant could do that?"

"I almost got hit by Hyperborean breath once," he said. "We'd better move. The gryphons won't stay frozen forever."

PERCY

THEY WALKED OVERLAND FOR ABOUT an hour, keeping the train tracks in sight but staying in the cover of the trees as much as possible. Once they heard a helicopter flying in the direction of the train wreck. Twice they heard the screech of gryphons, but they sounded a long way off.

As near as Percy could figure, it was about midnight when the sun finally set. It got cold in the woods. The stars were so thick, Percy was tempted to stop and gawk at them. Then the northern lights cranked up. They reminded Percy of his mom's gas stovetop back home, when she had the flame on low—waves of ghostly blue flames rippling back and forth.

"That's amazing," Frank said.

"Bears," Hazel pointed. Sure enough, a couple of brown bears were lumbering in the meadow a few hundred feet away, their coats gleaming in the starlight. "They won't bother us," Hazel promised. "Just give them a wide berth."

Percy and Frank didn't argue.

As they trudged on, Percy thought about all the crazy places he'd seen. None of them had left him speechless like Alaska. He could see why it was a land beyond the gods. Everything here was rough and untamed. There were no rules, no prophecies, no destinies—just the harsh wilderness and a bunch of animals and monsters. Mortals and demigods came here at their own risk.

Percy wondered if this was what Gaea wanted—for the whole world to be like this. He wondered if that would be such a bad thing.

Then he put the thought aside. Gaea wasn't a gentle goddess. Percy had heard what she planned to do. She wasn't like the Mother Earth you might read about in a children's fairy tale. She was vengeful and violent. If she ever woke up fully, she'd destroy human civilization.

After another couple of hours, they stumbled across a tiny village between the railroad tracks and a two-lane road. The city limit sign said: MOOSE PASS. Standing next to the sign was an actual moose. For a second, Percy thought it might be some sort of statue for advertising. Then the animal bounded into the woods.

They passed a couple of houses, a post office, and some trailers. Everything was dark and closed up. On the other end of town was a store with a picnic table and an old rusted petrol pump in front.

The store had a hand-painted sign that read: MOOSE PASS GAS.

"That's just wrong," Frank said.

By silent agreement they collapsed around the picnic table.

Percy's feet felt like blocks of ice—very *sore* blocks of ice. Hazel put her head in her hands and passed out, snoring. Frank took out his last sodas and some granola bars from the train ride and shared them with Percy.

They ate in silence, watching the stars, until Frank said, "Did you mean what you said earlier?"

Percy looked across the table. "About what?"

In the starlight, Frank's face might have been alabaster, like an old Roman statue. "About...being proud that we're related."

Percy tapped his granola bar on the table. "Well, let's see. You single-handedly took out three basilisks while I was sipping green tea and wheat germ. You held off an army of Laistrygonians so that our plane could take off in Vancouver. You saved my life by shooting down that gryphon. And you gave up the last charge on your magic spear to help some defenseless mortals. You are, hands down, the nicest child of the war god I've ever met...maybe the *only* nice one. So what do you think?"

Frank stared up at the northern lights, still cooking across the stars on low heat. "It's just...I was supposed to be in charge of this quest, the centurion, and all. I feel like you guys have had to carry me."

"Not true," Percy said.

"I'm supposed to have these powers I haven't figured out how to use," Frank said bitterly. "Now I don't have a spear, and I'm almost out of arrows. And...I'm scared."

"I'd be worried if you weren't scared," Percy said. "We're all scared."

"But the Feast of Fortuna is..." Frank thought about it. "It's after midnight, isn't it? That means it's June twenty-fourth now. The feast starts tonight at sundown. We have to find our way to Hubbard Glacier, defeat a giant who is undefeatable in his home territory, and get back to Camp Jupiter before they're overrun—all in less than eighteen hours."

"And when we free Thanatos," Percy said, "he might claim your life. And Hazel's. Believe me, I've been thinking about it."

Frank gazed at Hazel, still snoring lightly. Her face was buried under a mass of curly brown hair.

"She's my best friend," Frank said. "I lost my mom, my grandmother... I can't lose her, too."

Percy thought about his old life—his mom in New York, Camp Half-Blood, Annabeth. He'd lost all of that for eight months. Even now, with the memories coming back... he'd never been this far away from home before. He'd been to the Underworld and back. He'd faced death dozens of times. But sitting at this picnic table, thousands of miles away, beyond the power of Olympus, he'd never been so alone—except for Hazel and Frank.

"I'm not going to lose either of you," he promised. "I'm not going to let that happen. And, Frank, you *are* a leader. Hazel would say the same thing. We need you."

Frank lowered his head. He seemed lost in thought. Finally he leaned forward until his head bumped the picnic table. He started to snore in harmony with Hazel.

Percy sighed. "Another inspiring speech from Jackson," he said to himself. "Rest up, Frank. Big day ahead."

• • •

At dawn, the store opened up. The owner was a little surprised to find three teenagers crashed out on his picnic table, but when Percy explained that they had stumbled away from last night's train wreck, the guy felt sorry for them and treated them to breakfast. He called a friend of his, an Inuit native who had a cabin close to Seward. Soon they were rumbling along the road in a beat-up Ford pickup that had been new about the time Hazel was born.

Hazel and Frank sat in back. Percy rode up front with the leathery old man, who smelled like smoked salmon. He told Percy stories about Bear and Raven, the Inuit gods, and all Percy could think was that he hoped he didn't meet them. He had enough enemies already.

The truck broke down a few miles outside Seward. The driver didn't seem surprised, as though this happened to him several times a day. He said they could wait for him to fix the engine, but since Seward was only a few miles away, they decided to walk it.

By midmorning, they climbed over a rise in the road and saw a small bay ringed with mountains. The town was a thin crescent on the right-hand shore, with wharves extending into the water and a cruise ship in the harbor.

Percy shuddered. He'd had bad experiences with cruise ships.

"Seward," Hazel said. She didn't sound happy to see her old home.

They'd already lost a lot of time, and Percy didn't like how fast the sun was rising. The road curved around the hillside, but it looked like they could get to town faster going straight across the meadows.

Percy stepped off the road. "Come on."

The ground was squishy, but he didn't think much about it until Hazel shouted, "Percy, no!"

His next step went straight through the ground. He sank like a stone until the earth closed over his head—and the earth swallowed him.

HAZEL

"**Your bow!**" **Hazel shouted.**

Frank didn't ask questions. He dropped his pack and slipped the bow off his shoulder.

Hazel's heart raced. She hadn't thought about this boggy soil—muskeg—since before she had died. Now, too late, she remembered the dire warnings the locals had given her. Marshy silt and decomposed plants made a surface that looked completely solid, but it was even worse than quicksand. It could be twenty feet deep or more, and impossible to escape.

She tried not to think what would happen if it were deeper than the length of the bow.

"Hold one end," she told Frank. "Don't let go."

She grabbed the other end, took a deep breath, and jumped into the bog. The earth closed over her head.

Instantly, she was frozen in a memory.

Not now! she wanted to scream. *Ella said I was done with blackouts!*

Oh, but my dear, said the voice of Gaea, *this is not one of your blackouts. This is a gift from me.*

Hazel was back in New Orleans. She and her mother sat in the park near their apartment, having a picnic breakfast. She remembered this day. She was seven years old. Her mother had just sold Hazel's first precious stone: a small diamond. Neither of them had yet realized Hazel's curse.

Queen Marie was in an excellent mood. She had bought orange juice for Hazel and champagne for herself, and beignets sprinkled with chocolate and powdered sugar. She'd even bought Hazel a new box of crayons and a pad of paper. They sat together, Queen Marie humming cheerfully while Hazel drew pictures.

The French Quarter woke up around them, ready for Mardi Gras. Jazz bands practiced. Floats were being decorated with fresh-cut flowers. Children laughed and chased each other, decked in so many colored necklaces they could barely walk. The sunrise turned the sky to red gold, and the warm steamy air smelled of magnolias and roses.

It had been the happiest morning of Hazel's life.

"You could stay here." Her mother smiled, but her eyes were blank white. The voice was Gaea's.

"This is fake," Hazel said.

She tried to get up, but the soft bed of grass made her lazy and sleepy. The smell of baked bread and melting chocolate was intoxicating. It was the morning of Mardi Gras, and the world seemed full of possibilities. Hazel could almost believe she had a bright future.

"What is real?" asked Gaea, speaking through her mother's face. "Is your second life *real*, Hazel? You're supposed to be dead. Is it *real* that you're sinking into a bog, suffocating?"

"Let me help my friend!" Hazel tried to force herself back to reality. She could imagine her hand clenched on the end of the bow, but even that was starting to feel fuzzy. Her grip was loosening. The smell of magnolias and roses was overpowering.

Her mother offered her a beignet.

No, Hazel thought. This isn't my mother. This is Gaea tricking me.

"You want your old life back," Gaea said. "I can give you that. This moment can last for years. You can grow up in New Orleans, and your mother will adore you. You'll never have to deal with the burden of your curse. You can be with Sammy—"

"It's an illusion!" Hazel said, choking on the sweet scent of flowers.

"*You* are an illusion, Hazel Levesque. You were only brought back to life because the gods have a task for you. I may have used you, but Nico used you *and* lied about it. You should be glad I captured him."

"Captured?" A feeling of panic rose in Hazel's chest. "What do you mean?"

Gaea smiled, sipping her champagne. "The boy should have known better than to search for the Doors. But no matter—it's not really your concern. Once you release Thanatos, you'll be thrown back into the Underworld to rot forever. Frank and

Percy won't stop that from happening. Would *real* friends ask you to give up your life? Tell me who is lying, and who tells you the truth."

Hazel started to cry. Bitterness welled up inside her. She'd lost her life once. She didn't want to die again.

"That's right," Gaea purred. "You were destined to marry Sammy. Do you know what happened to him after you died in Alaska? He grew up and moved to Texas. He married and had a family. But he never forgot you. He always wondered why you disappeared. He's dead now—a heart attack in the nineteen-sixties. The life you could've had together always haunted him."

"Stop it!" Hazel screamed. "*You* took that from me!"

"And you can have it again," Gaea said. "I have you in my embrace, Hazel. You'll die anyway. If you give up, at least I can make it pleasant for you. Forget saving Percy Jackson. He belongs to me. I'll keep him safe in the earth until I'm ready to use him. You can have an entire life in your final moments— you can grow up, marry Sammy. All you have to do is let go."

Hazel tightened her grip on the bow. Below her, some-thing grabbed her ankles, but she didn't panic. She *knew* it was Percy, suffocating, desperately grasping for a chance at life.

Hazel glared at the goddess. "I'll never cooperate with you! LET—US—GO!"

Her mother's face dissolved. The New Orleans morning melted into darkness. Hazel was drowning in mud, one hand on the bow, Percy's hands around her ankles, deep in the darkness. Hazel wiggled the end of the bow frantically. Frank pulled her up with such force it nearly popped her arm out of the socket.

When she opened her eyes, she was lying in the grass, covered in muck. Percy sprawled at her feet, coughing and spitting mud.

Frank hovered over them, yelling, "Oh, gods! Oh, gods! Oh, gods!"

He yanked some extra clothes from his bag and started toweling off Hazel's face, but it didn't do much good. He dragged Percy farther from the muskeg.

"You were down there so long!" Frank cried. "I didn't think —oh, gods, don't *ever* do something like that again!"

He wrapped Hazel in a bear hug.

"Can't—breathe," she choked out.

"Sorry!" Frank went back to toweling and fussing over them. Finally he got them to the side of the road, where they sat and shivered and spit up mud clods.

Hazel couldn't feel her hands. She wasn't sure if she was cold or in shock, but she managed to explain about the muskeg, and the vision she'd seen while she was under. Not the part about Sammy—that was still too painful to say out loud—but she told them about Gaea's offer of a fake life, and the goddess' claim that she'd captured her brother Nico. Hazel didn't want to keep that to herself. She was afraid the despair would overwhelm her.

Percy rubbed his shoulders. His lips were blue. "You—you saved me, Hazel. We'll figure out what happened to Nico, I promise."

Hazel squinted at the sun, which was now high in the sky.

The warmth felt good, but it didn't stop her trembling. "Does it seem like Gaea let us go too easily?"

Percy plucked a mud clod from his hair. "Maybe she still wants us as pawns. Maybe she was just saying things to mess with your mind."

"She knew what to say," Hazel agreed. "She knew how to get to me."

Frank put his jacket around her shoulders. "This *is* a real life. You know that, right? We're not going to let you die again."

He sounded so determined. Hazel didn't want to argue, but she didn't see how Frank could stop Death. She pressed her coat pocket, where Frank's half-burned firewood was still securely wrapped. She wondered what would've happened to him if she'd sunk in the mud forever. Maybe that would have saved him. Fire couldn't have gotten to the wood down there.

She would have made any sacrifice to keep Frank safe. Perhaps she hadn't always felt that strongly, but Frank had trusted her with his life. He believed in her. She couldn't bear the thought of any harm coming to him.

She glanced at the rising sun. . . . Time was running out. She thought about Hylla, the Amazon Queen back in Seattle. Hylla would have dueled Otrera two nights in a row by now, assuming she had survived. She was counting on Hazel to release Death.

She managed to stand. The wind coming off Resurrection Bay was just as cold as she remembered. "We should get going. We're losing time."

Percy gazed down the road. His lips were returning to

their normal color. "Any hotels or something where we could clean off? I mean... hotels that accept mud people?"

"I'm not sure," Hazel admitted.

She looked at the town below and couldn't believe how much it had grown since 1942. The main harbor had moved east as the town had expanded. Most of the buildings were new to her, but the grid of downtown streets seemed familiar. She thought she recognized some warehouses along the shore. "I might know a place we can freshen up."

XLII

HAZEL

WHEN THEY GOT INTO TOWN, Hazel followed the same route she'd used seventy years ago—the last night of her life, when she'd come home from the hills and found her mother missing.

She led her friends along Third Avenue. The railroad station was still there. The big white two-story Seward Hotel was still in business, though it had expanded to twice its old size. They thought about stopping there, but Hazel didn't think it would be a good idea to traipse into the lobby covered in mud, nor was she sure the hotel would give a room to three minors.

Instead, they turned toward the shoreline. Hazel couldn't believe it, but her old home was still there, leaning over the water on barnacle-encrusted piers. The roof sagged. The walls were perforated with holes like buckshot. The door was boarded-up, and a hand-painted sign read: ROOMS——STORAGE ——AVAILABLE.

"Come on," she said.

"Uh, you sure it's safe?" Frank asked.

Hazel found an open window and climbed inside. Her friends followed. The room hadn't been used in a long time. Their feet kicked up dust that swirled in the buckshot beams of sunlight. Mouldering cardboard boxes were stacked along the walls. Their faded labels read: *Greeting Cards, Assorted Seasonal.* Why several hundred boxes of season's greetings had wound up crumbling to dust in a warehouse in Alaska, Hazel had no idea, but it felt like a cruel joke: as if the cards were for all the holidays she'd never gotten to celebrate—decades of Christmases, Easters, birthdays, Valentine's Days.

"It's warmer in here, at least," Frank said. "Guess no running water? Maybe I can go shopping. I'm not as muddy as you guys. I could find us some clothes."

Hazel only half heard him.

She climbed over a stack of boxes in the corner that used to be her sleeping area. An old sign was propped against the wall: GOLD PROSPECTING SUPPLIES. She thought she'd find a bare wall behind it, but when she moved the sign, most of her photos and drawings were still pinned there. The sign must have protected them from sunlight and the elements. They seemed not to have aged. Her crayon drawings of New Orleans looked so childish. Had she really made them? Her mother stared out at her from one photograph, smiling in front of her business sign: QUEEN MARIE'S GRIS-GRIS— CHARMS SOLD, FORTUNES TOLD.

Next to that was a photo of Sammy at the carnival. He was frozen in time with his crazy grin, his curly black hair, and those beautiful eyes. If Gaea was telling the truth, Sammy had been dead for over forty years. Had he really remembered Hazel all that time? Or had he forgotten the peculiar girl he used to go riding with—the girl who shared one kiss and a birthday cupcake with him before disappearing forever?

Frank's fingers hovered over the photo. "Who . . . ?" He saw that she was crying and clamped back his question. "Sorry, Hazel. This must be really hard. Do you want some time—"

"No," she croaked. "No, it's fine."

"Is that your mother?" Percy pointed to the photo of Queen Marie. "She looks like you. She's beautiful."

Then Percy studied the picture of Sammy. "Who is that?"

Hazel didn't understand why he looked so spooked. "That's . . . that's Sammy. He was my—uh—friend from New Orleans." She forced herself not to look at Frank.

"I've seen him before," Percy said.

"You couldn't have," Hazel said. "That was in 1941. He's . . . he's probably dead now."

Percy frowned. "I guess. Still . . ." He shook his head, like the thought was too uncomfortable.

Frank cleared his throat. "Look, we passed a store on the last block. We've got a little money left. Maybe I should go get you guys some food and clothes and—I don't know—a hundred boxes of wet wipes or something?"

Hazel put the gold prospecting sign back over her mementos. She felt guilty even looking at that old picture of Sammy, with Frank trying to be so sweet and supportive. It didn't do her any good to think about her old life.

"That would be great," she said. "You're the best, Frank."

The floorboards creaked under his feet. "Well . . . I'm the

only one not completely covered in mud, anyway. Be back soon."

Once he was gone, Percy and Hazel made temporary camp. They took off their jackets and tried to scrape off the mud. They found some old blankets in a crate and used them to clean up. They discovered that boxes of greeting cards made pretty good places to rest if you arranged them like mattresses.

Percy set his sword on the floor where it glowed with a faint bronze light. Then he stretched out on a bed of *Merry Christmas 1982*.

"Thank you for saving me," he said. "I should've told you that earlier."

Hazel shrugged. "You would have done the same for me."

"Yes," he agreed. "But when I was down in the mud, I remembered that line from Ella's prophecy—about the son of Neptune drowning. I thought. 'This is what it means. I'm drowning in the earth.' I was sure I was dead."

His voice quavered like it had his first day at Camp Jupiter, when Hazel had shown him the shrine of Neptune. Back then she had wondered if Percy was the answer to her problems —the descendant of Neptune that Pluto had promised would take away her curse someday. Percy had seemed so intimidating and powerful, like a real hero.

Only now, she knew that Frank was a descendant of Neptune, too. Frank wasn't the most impressive-looking hero in the world, but he'd trusted her with his life. He tried so hard to protect her. Even his clumsiness was endearing.

She'd never felt more confused—and since she had spent her whole life confused, that was saying a lot.

"Percy," she said, "that prophecy might not have been complete. Frank thought Ella was remembering a burned page. Maybe you'll drown someone else."

He looked at her cautiously. "You think so?"

Hazel felt strange reassuring him. He was so much older, and more in command. But she nodded confidently. "You're going to make it back home. You're going to see your girlfriend Annabeth."

"You'll make it back, too, Hazel," he insisted. "We're not going to let anything happen to you. You're too valuable to me, to the camp, and especially to Frank."

Hazel picked up an old valentine. The lacy white paper fell apart in her hands. "I don't belong in this century. Nico only brought me back so I could correct my mistakes, maybe get into Elysium."

"There's more to your destiny than that," he said. "We're supposed to fight Gaea together. I'm going to need you at my side way longer than just today. And Frank—you can see the guy is crazy about you. This life is worth fighting for, Hazel."

She closed her eyes. "Please, don't get my hopes up. I can't—"

The window creaked open. Frank climbed in, triumphantly holding some shopping bags. "Success!"

He showed off his prizes. From a hunting store, he'd gotten a new quiver of arrows for himself, some rations, and a coil of rope.

"For the next time we run across muskeg," he said.

From a local tourist shop, he had bought three sets of fresh clothes, some towels, some soap, some bottled water, and, yes, a huge box of wet wipes. It wasn't exactly a hot shower, but Hazel ducked behind a wall of greeting card boxes to clean up and change. Soon she was feeling much better.

This is your last day, she reminded herself. *Don't get too comfortable.*

The Feast of Fortuna—all the luck that happened today, good or bad, was supposed to be an omen of the entire year to come. One way or another, their quest would end this evening.

She slipped the piece of driftwood into her new coat pocket. Somehow, she'd have to make sure it stayed safe, no matter what happened to her. She could bear her own death as long as her friends survived.

"So," she said. "Now we find a boat to Hubbard Glacier."

She tried to sound confident, but it wasn't easy. She wished Arion were still with her. She'd much rather ride into battle on that beautiful horse. Ever since they'd left Vancouver, she'd been calling to him in her thoughts, hoping he would hear her and come find her, but that was just wishful thinking.

Frank patted his stomach. "If we're going to battle to the death, I want lunch first. I found the perfect place."

Frank led them to a shopping plaza near the wharf, where an old railway car had been converted to a diner. Hazel had no memory of the place from the 1940s, but the food smelled amazing.

While Frank and Percy ordered, Hazel wandered down to

the docks and asked some questions. When she came back, she needed cheering up. Even the cheeseburger and fries didn't do the trick.

"We're in trouble," she said. "I tried to get a boat. But... I miscalculated."

"No boats?" Frank asked.

"Oh, I can get a boat," Hazel said. "But the glacier is farther than I thought. Even at top speed, we couldn't get there until tomorrow morning."

Percy turned pale. "Maybe I could make the boat go faster?"

"Even if you could," Hazel said, "from what the captains tell me, it's treacherous—icebergs, mazes of channels to navigate. You'd have to know where you were going."

"A plane?" Frank asked.

Hazel shook her head. "I asked the boat captains about that. They said we could try, but it's a tiny airfield. You have to charter a plane two, three weeks in advance."

They ate in silence after that. Hazel's cheeseburger was excellent, but she couldn't concentrate on it. She'd eaten about three bites when a raven settled on the telephone pole above and began to croak at them.

Hazel shivered. She was afraid it would speak to her like the other raven, so many years ago: *The last night. Tonight.* She wondered if ravens always appeared to children of Pluto when they were about to die. She hoped Nico was still alive, and Gaea had just been lying to make her unsettled. Hazel had a bad feeling that the goddess was telling the truth.

Nico had told her that he'd search for the Doors of Death

from the other side. If he'd been captured by Gaea's forces, Hazel might've lost the only family she had.

She stared at her cheeseburger.

Suddenly, the raven's cawing changed to a strangled yelp.

Frank got up so fast that he almost toppled the picnic table. Percy drew his sword.

Hazel followed their eyes. Perched on top of the pole where the raven had been, a fat ugly gryphon glared down at them. It burped, and raven feathers fluttered from its beak.

Hazel stood and unsheathed her *spatha*.

Frank nocked an arrow. He took aim, but the gryphon shrieked so loudly the sound echoed off the mountains. Frank flinched, and his shot went wide.

"I think that's a call for help," Percy warned. "We have to get out of here."

With no clear plan, they ran for the docks. The gryphon dove after them. Percy slashed at it with his sword, but the gryphon veered out of reach.

They took the steps to the nearest pier and raced to the end. The gryphon swooped after them, its front claws extended for the kill. Hazel raised her sword, but an icy wall of water slammed sideways into the gryphon and washed it into the bay. The gryphon squawked and flapped its wings. It managed to scramble onto the pier, where it shook its black fur like a wet dog.

Frank grunted. "Nice one, Percy."

"Yeah," he said. "Didn't know if I could still do that in Alaska. But bad news—look over there."

About a mile away, over the mountains, a black cloud was

swirling—a whole flock of gryphons, dozens at least. There was no way they could fight that many, and no boat could take them away fast enough.

Frank nocked another arrow. "Not going down without a fight."

Percy raised Riptide. "I'm with you."

Then Hazel heard a sound in the distance—like the whinnying of a horse. She must've been imagining it, but she cried out desperately, "Arion! Over here!"

A tan blur came ripping down the street and onto the pier. The stallion materialized right behind the gryphon, brought down his front hooves, and smashed the monster to dust.

Hazel had never been so happy in her life. "Good horse! *Really* good horse!"

Frank backed up and almost fell off the pier. "How—?"

"He followed me!" Hazel beamed. "Because he's the best —horse—EVER! Now, get on!"

"All three of us?" Percy said. "Can he handle it?"

Arion whinnied indignantly.

"All right, no need to be rude," Percy said. "Let's go."

They climbed on, Hazel in front, Frank and Percy balancing precariously behind her. Frank wrapped his arms around her waist, and Hazel thought that if this was going to be her last day on earth—it wasn't a bad way to go out.

"Run, Arion!" she cried. "To Hubbard Glacier!"

The horse shot across the water, his hooves turning the top of the sea to steam.

XLIII

HAZEL

RIDING ARION, HAZEL FELT POWERFUL, unstoppable, absolutely in control—a perfect combination of horse and human. She wondered if this was what it was like to be a centaur.

The boat captains in Seward had warned her it was three hundred nautical miles to the Hubbard Glacier, a hard, dangerous journey, but Arion had no trouble. He raced over the water at the speed of sound, heating the air around them so that Hazel didn't even feel the cold. On foot, she never would have felt so brave. On horseback, she couldn't wait to charge into battle.

Frank and Percy didn't look so happy. When Hazel glanced back, their teeth were clenched and their eyeballs were bouncing around in their heads. Frank's cheeks jiggled from the g-force. Percy sat in back, hanging on tight, desperately trying not to slip off the horse's rear. Hazel hoped that didn't happen. The way Arion was moving, she might not notice he was gone for fifty or sixty miles.

They raced through icy straits, past blue fjords and cliffs with waterfalls spilling into the sea. Arion jumped over a breaching humpback whale and kept galloping, startling a pack of seals off an iceberg.

It seemed like only minutes before they zipped into a narrow bay. The water turned the consistency of shaved ice in blue sticky syrup. Arion came to a halt on a frozen turquoise slab.

A half a mile away stood Hubbard Glacier. Even Hazel, who'd seen glaciers before, couldn't quite process what she was looking at. Purple snowcapped mountains marched off in either direction, with clouds floating around their middles like fluffy belts. In a massive valley between two of the largest peaks, a ragged wall of ice rose out of the sea, filling the entire gorge. The glacier was blue and white with streaks of black, so that it looked like a hedge of dirty snow left behind on a sidewalk after a snowplow had gone by, only four million times as large.

As soon as Arion stopped, Hazel felt the temperature drop. All that ice was sending off waves of cold, turning the bay into the world's largest refrigerator. The eeriest thing was a sound like thunder that rolled across the water.

"What *is* that?" Frank gazed at the clouds above the glacier. "A storm?"

"No," Hazel said. "Ice cracking and shifting. Millions of tons of ice."

"You mean that thing is breaking up?" Frank asked.

As if on cue, a sheet of ice silently calved off the side of the glacier and crashed into the sea, spraying water and frozen shrapnel several stories high. A millisecond later the sound hit them—a *BOOM* almost as jarring as Arion hitting the sound barrier.

"We can't get close to that thing!" Frank said.

"We have to," Percy said. "The giant is at the top."

Arion nickered.

"Jeez, Hazel," Percy said, "tell your horse to watch his language."

Hazel tried not to laugh. "What did he say?"

"With the cussing removed? He said he can get us to the top."

Frank looked incredulous. "I thought the horse couldn't fly!"

This time Arion whinnied so angrily, even Hazel could guess he was cursing.

"Dude," Percy told the horse, "I've gotten suspended for saying less than that. Hazel, he promises you'll see what he can do as soon as you give the word."

"Um, hold on, then, you guys," Hazel said nervously. "Arion, giddyup!"

Arion shot toward the glacier like a runaway rocket, barreling straight across the slush like he wanted to play chicken with the mountain of ice.

The air grew colder. The crackling of the ice grew louder. As Arion closed the distance, the glacier loomed so large, Hazel got vertigo just trying to take it all in. The side was riddled with crevices and caves, spiked with jagged ridges like ax blades. Pieces were constantly crumbling off—some no larger than snowballs, some the size of houses.

When they were about fifty yards from the base, a

thunderclap rattled Hazel's bones, and a curtain of ice that would have covered Camp Jupiter calved away and fell toward them.

"Look out!" Frank shouted, which seemed a little unnecessary to Hazel.

Arion was way ahead of him. In a burst of speed, he zigzagged through the debris, leaping over chunks of ice and clambering up the face of the glacier.

Percy and Frank both cussed like horses and held on desperately while Hazel wrapped her arms around Arion's neck. Somehow, they managed not to fall off as Arion scaled the cliffs, jumping from foothold to foothold with impossible speed and agility. It was like falling down a mountain in reverse.

Then it was over. Arion stood proudly at the top of a ridge of ice that loomed over the void. The sea was now three hundred feet below them.

Arion whinnied a challenge that echoed off the mountains. Percy didn't translate, but Hazel was pretty sure Arion was calling out to any other horses that might be in the bay: *Beat that, ya punks!*

Then he turned and ran inland across the top of the glacier, leaping a chasm fifty feet across.

"There!" Percy pointed.

The horse stopped. Ahead of them stood a frozen Roman camp like a giant-sized ghastly replica of Camp Jupiter. The trenches bristled with ice spikes. The snow-brick ramparts glared blinding white. Hanging from the guard towers, banners of frozen blue cloth shimmered in the arctic sun.

There was no sign of life. The gates stood wide open. No sentries walked the walls. Still, Hazel had an uneasy feeling in her gut. She remembered the cave in Resurrection Bay where she'd worked to raise Alcyoneus—the oppressive sense of malice and the constant *boom, boom, boom*, like Gaea's heartbeat. This place felt similar, as if the earth were trying to wake up and consume everything—as if the mountains on either side wanted to crush them and the entire glacier to pieces.

Arion trotted skittishly.

"Frank," Percy said, "how about we go on foot from here?"

Frank sighed with relief. "Thought you'd never ask."

They dismounted and took some tentative steps. The ice seemed stable, covered with a fine carpet of snow so that it wasn't too slippery.

Hazel urged Arion forward. Percy and Frank walked on either side, sword and bow ready. They approached the gates without being challenged. Hazel was trained to spot pits, snares, trip lines, and all sorts of other traps Roman legions had faced for eons in enemy territory, but she saw nothing—just the yawning icy gates and the frozen banners crackling in the wind.

She could see straight down the Via Praetoria. At the crossroads, in front of the snow-brick *principia*, a tall, dark-robed figure stood, bound in icy chains.

"Thanatos," Hazel murmured.

She felt as if her soul were being pulled forward, drawn toward Death like dust toward a vacuum. Her vision went dark. She almost fell off Arion, but Frank caught her and propped her up.

"We've got you," he promised. "Nobody's taking you away."

Hazel gripped his hand. She didn't want to let go. He was so *solid*, so reassuring, but Frank couldn't protect her from Death. His own life was as fragile as a half-burned piece of wood.

"I'm all right," she lied.

Percy looked around uneasily. "No defenders? No giant? This has to be a trap."

"Obviously," Frank said. "But I don't think we have a choice."

Before Hazel could change her mind, she urged Arion through the gates. The layout was so familiar—cohort barracks, baths, armory. It was an exact replica of Camp Jupiter, except three times as big. Even on horseback, Hazel felt tiny and insignificant, as if they were moving through a model city constructed by the gods.

They stopped ten feet from the robed figure.

Now that she was here, Hazel felt a reckless urge to finish the quest. She knew she was in more danger than when she'd been fighting the Amazons, or fending off the gryphons, or climbing the glacier on Arion's back. Instinctively she knew that Thanatos could simply touch her, and she would die.

But she also had a feeling that if she *didn't* see the quest through, if she didn't face her fate bravely, she would still die —in cowardice and failure. The judges of the dead wouldn't be lenient to her a second time.

Arion cantered back and forth, sensing her disquiet.

"Hello?" Hazel forced out the word. "Mr. Death?"

The hooded figure raised his head.

Instantly, the whole camp stirred to life. Figures in Roman armor emerged from the barracks, the *principia*, the armory, and the canteen, but they weren't human. They were shades —the chattering ghosts Hazel had lived with for decades in the Fields of Asphodel. Their bodies weren't much more than wisps of black vapor, but they managed to hold together sets of scale armor, greaves, and helmets. Frost-covered swords were strapped to their waists. *Pila* and dented shields floated in their smoky hands. The plumes on the centurions' helmets were frozen and ragged. Most of the shades were on foot, but two soldiers burst out of the stables in a golden chariot pulled by ghostly black steeds.

When Arion saw the horses, he stamped the ground in outrage.

Frank gripped his bow. "Yep, *here's* the trap."

XLIV

HAZEL

THE GHOSTS FORMED RANKS AND ENCIRCLED the crossroads. There were about a hundred in all—not an entire legion, but more than a cohort. Some carried the tattered lightning bolt banners of the Twelfth Legion, Fifth Cohort—Michael Varus's doomed expedition from the 1980s. Others carried standards and insignia Hazel didn't recognize, as if they'd died at different times, on different quests—maybe not even from Camp Jupiter.

Most were armed with Imperial gold weapons—more Imperial gold than the entire Twelfth Legion possessed. Hazel could feel the combined power of all that gold humming around her, even scarier than the crackling of the glacier. She wondered if she could use her power to control the weapons, maybe disarm the ghosts, but she was afraid to try. Imperial gold wasn't just a precious metal. It was deadly to demigods and monsters. Trying to control that much at once would be like trying to control plutonium in a reactor. If she failed, she might wipe Hubbard Glacier off the map and kill her friends.

"Thanatos!" Hazel turned to the robed figure. "We're here to rescue you. If you control these shades, tell them—"

Her voice faltered. The god's hood fell away and his robes dropped off as he spread his wings, leaving him in only a sleeveless black tunic belted at the waist. He was the most beautiful man Hazel had ever seen.

His skin was the color of teakwood, dark and glistening like Queen Marie's old séance table. His eyes were as honey gold as Hazel's. He was lean and muscular, with a regal face and black hair flowing down his shoulders. His wings glimmered in shades of blue, black, and purple.

Hazel reminded herself to breathe.

Beautiful was the right word for Thanatos—not handsome, or hot, or anything like that. He was beautiful the way an angel is beautiful—timeless, perfect, remote.

"Oh," she said in a small voice.

The god's wrists were shackled in icy manacles, with chains that ran straight into the glacier floor. His feet were bare, shackled around the ankles and also chained.

"It's Cupid," Frank said.

"A really buff Cupid," Percy agreed.

"You compliment me," Thanatos said. His voice was as gorgeous as he was—deep and melodious. "I am frequently mistaken for the god of love. Death has more in common with Love than you might imagine. But I am Death. I assure you."

Hazel didn't doubt it. She felt as if she were made of ashes. Any second, she might crumble and be sucked into the vacuum. She doubted Thanatos even needed to touch her to kill her. He could simply tell her to die. She would keel over on the spot, her soul obeying that beautiful voice and those kind eyes.

"We're—we're here to save you," she managed. "Where's Alcyoneus?"

"Save me . . . ?" Thanatos narrowed his eyes. "Do you understand what you are saying, Hazel Levesque? Do you understand what that will mean?"

Percy stepped forward. "We're wasting time."

He swung his sword at the god's chains. Celestial bronze rang against the ice, but Riptide stuck to the chain like glue. Frost began creeping up the blade. Percy pulled frantically. Frank ran to help. Together, they just managed to yank Riptide free before the frost reached their hands.

"That won't work," Thanatos said simply. "As for the giant, he is close. These shades are not mine. They are his."

Thanatos's eyes scanned the ghost soldiers. They shifted uncomfortably, as if an arctic wind were rattling through their ranks.

"So how do we get you out?" Hazel demanded.

Thanatos turned his attention back to her. "Daughter of Pluto, child of my master, you of all people should not wish me released."

"Don't you think I *know* that?" Hazel's eyes stung, but she was done being afraid. She'd been a scared little girl seventy years ago. She'd lost her mother because she acted too late. Now she was a soldier of Rome. She wasn't going to fail again. She wasn't going to let down her friends.

"Listen, Death." She drew her cavalry sword, and Arion reared in defiance. "I didn't come back from the Underworld and travel thousands of miles to be told that I'm stupid for setting you free. If I die, I die. I'll fight this whole army if I have to. Just tell us how to break your chains."

Thanatos studied her for a heartbeat. "Interesting. You do understand that these shades were once demigods like you. They fought for Rome. They died without completing their heroic quests. Like you, they were sent to Asphodel. Now Gaea has promised them a second life if they fight for her today. Of course, if you release me and defeat them, they will have to return to the Underworld where they belong. For treason against the gods, they will face eternal punishment. They are not so different from you, Hazel Levesque. Are you sure you want to release me and damn these souls forever?"

Frank clenched his fists. "That's not fair! Do you want to be freed or not?"

"Fair..." Death mused. "You'd be amazed how often I hear that word, Frank Zhang, and how meaningless it is. Is it fair that your life will burn so short and bright? Was it fair when I guided your mother to the Underworld?"

Frank staggered like he'd been punched.

"No," Death said sadly. "Not fair. And yet it was her time. There is no fairness in Death. If you free me, I will do my duty. But of course these shades will try to stop you."

"So if we let you go," Percy summed up, "we get mobbed by a bunch of black vapor dudes with gold swords. Fine. How do we break those chains?"

Thanatos smiled. "Only the fire of life can melt the chains of death."

"Without the riddles, please?" Percy asked.

Frank drew a shaky breath. "It isn't a riddle."

"Frank, no," Hazel said weakly. "There's got to be another way."

Laughter boomed across the glacier. A rumbling voice said: "My friends. I've waited so long!"

Standing at the gates of the camp was Alcyoneus. He was even larger than the giant Polybotes they'd seen in California. He had metallic golden skin, armor made from platinum links, and an iron staff the size of a totem pole. His rust-red dragon legs pounded against the ice as he entered the camp. Precious stones glinted in his red braided hair.

Hazel had never seen him fully formed, but she knew him better than she knew her own parents. She had *made* him. For months, she had raised gold and gems from the earth to create this monster. She knew the diamonds he used for a heart. She knew the oil that ran in his veins instead of blood. More than anything, she wanted to destroy him.

The giant approached, grinning at her with his solid silver teeth.

"Ah, Hazel Levesque," he said, "you cost me dearly! If not for you, I would have risen decades ago, and this world would already be Gaea's. But no matter!"

He spread his hands, showing off the ranks of ghostly soldiers. "Welcome, Percy Jackson! Welcome, Frank Zhang! I am Alcyoneus, the bane of Pluto, the *new* master of Death. And this is your new legion."

XLV

FRANK

NO FAIRNESS IN DEATH. Those words kept ringing in Frank's head.

The golden giant didn't scare him. The army of shades didn't scare him. But the thought of freeing Thanatos made Frank want to curl into the fetal position. This god had taken his mother.

Frank understood what he had to do to break those chains. Mars had warned him. He'd explained why he loved Emily Zhang so much: *She always put her duty first, ahead of everything. Even her life.*

Now it was Frank's turn.

His mother's sacrifice medal felt warm in his pocket. He finally understood his mother's choice, saving her comrades at the cost of her own life. He got what Mars had been trying to tell him—*Duty. Sacrifice. They mean something.*

In Frank's chest, a hard knot of anger and resentment—a

lump of grief he'd been carrying since the funeral—finally began to dissolve. He understood why his mother never came home. Some things *were* worth dying for.

"Hazel." He tried to keep his voice steady. "That package you're keeping for me? I need it."

Hazel glanced at him in dismay. Sitting on Arion, she looked like a queen, powerful and beautiful, her brown hair swept over her shoulders and a wreath of icy mist around her head. "Frank, no. There has to be another way."

"Please. I—I know what I'm doing."

Thanatos smiled and lifted his manacled wrists. "You're right, Frank Zhang. Sacrifices must be made."

Great. If Death approved of his plan, Frank was pretty sure he wasn't going to like the results.

The giant Alcyoneus stepped forward, his reptilian feet shaking the ground. "What package do you speak of, Frank Zhang? Have you brought me a present?"

"Nothing for you, Golden Boy," Frank said. "Except a whole lot of pain."

The giant roared with laughter. "Spoken like a child of Mars! Too bad I have to kill you. And *this* one . . . my, my, I've been waiting to meet the famous Percy Jackson."

The giant grinned. His silver teeth made his mouth look like a car grille.

"I've followed your progress, son of Neptune," said Alcyoneus. "Your fight with Kronos? Well done. Gaea hates you above all others . . . except perhaps for that upstart Jason Grace. I'm sorry I can't kill you right away, but my brother

Polybotes wishes to keep you as a pet. He thinks it will be amusing when he destroys Neptune to have the god's favorite son on a leash. After that, of course, Gaea has plans for you."

"Yeah, flattering." Percy raised Riptide. "But actually I'm the son of Poseidon. I'm from Camp Half-Blood."

The ghosts stirred. Some drew swords and lifted shields. Alcyoneus raised his hand, gesturing for them to wait.

"Greek, Roman, it doesn't matter," the giant said easily. "We will crush both camps underfoot. You see, the Titans didn't think *big* enough. They planned to destroy the gods in their new home of America. We giants know better! To kill a weed, you must pull up its roots. Even now, while my forces destroy your little Roman camp, my brother Porphyrion is preparing for the real battle in the ancient lands! We will destroy the gods at their source."

The ghosts pounded their swords against their shields. The sound echoed across the mountains.

"The source?" Frank asked. "You mean Greece?"

Alcyoneus chuckled. "No need to worry about that, son of Mars. You won't live long enough to see our ultimate victory. I will replace Pluto as lord of the Underworld. I already have Death in my custody. With Hazel Levesque in my service, I will have all the riches under the earth as well!"

Hazel gripped her *spatha*. "I don't do *service*."

"Oh, but you gave me life!" Alcyoneus said. "True, we hoped to awaken Gaea during World War II. That would've been glorious. But really, the world is in almost as bad a shape now. Soon, your civilization will be wiped out. The Doors of

Death will stand open. Those who serve us will never perish. Alive or dead, you three *will* join my army."

Percy shook his head. "Fat chance, Golden Boy. You're going down."

"Wait." Hazel spurred her horse toward the giant. "I raised this monster from the earth. I'm the daughter of Pluto. It's my place to kill him."

"Ah, little Hazel." Alcyoneus planted his staff on the ice. His hair glittered with millions of dollars' worth of gems. "Are you sure you will not join us of your own free will? You could be quite... *precious* to us. Why die again?"

Hazel's eyes flashed with anger. She looked down at Frank and pulled the wrapped-up piece of firewood from her coat. "Are you sure?"

"Yeah," he said.

She pursed her lips. "You're my best friend, too, Frank. I should have told you that." She tossed him the stick. "Do what you have to. And Percy... can you protect him?"

Percy gazed at the ranks of ghostly Romans. "Against a small army? Sure, no problem."

"Then I've got Golden Boy," Hazel said.

She charged the giant.

XLVI

FRANK

FRANK UNWRAPPED THE FIREWOOD and knelt at the feet of Thanatos.

He was aware of Percy standing over him, swinging his sword and yelling in defiance as the ghosts closed in. He heard the giant bellow and Arion whinny angrily, but he didn't dare look.

His hands trembling, he held his piece of tinder next to the chains on Death's right leg. He thought about flames, and instantly the wood blazed.

Horrible warmth spread through Frank's body. The icy metal began to melt, the flame so bright it was more blinding than the ice.

"Good," Thanatos said. "Very good, Frank Zhang."

Frank had heard about people's lives flashing before their eyes, but now he experienced it literally. He saw his mother the day she left for Afghanistan. She smiled and hugged him. He tried to breath in her jasmine scent so he'd never forget it.

I will always be proud of you, Frank, she said. *Someday, you'll travel even farther than I. You'll bring our family full circle. Years from now, our descendants will be telling stories about the hero Frank Zhang, their great-, great-, great-* —She poked him in the belly for old times' sake. It would be the last time Frank smiled for months.

He saw himself at the picnic bench in Moose Pass, watching the stars and the northern lights as Hazel snored softly beside him, Percy saying, *Frank, you* are *a leader. We need you.*

He saw Percy disappearing into the muskeg, then Hazel diving after him. Frank remembered how alone he had felt holding on to the bow, how utterly powerless. He had pleaded with the Olympian gods—even Mars—to help his friends, but he knew they were beyond the gods' reach.

With a clank, the first chain broke. Quickly, Frank stabbed the firewood at the chain on Death's other leg.

He risked a glance over his shoulder.

Percy was fighting like a whirlwind. In fact...he *was* a whirlwind. A miniature hurricane of water and ice vapor churned around him as he waded through the enemy, knocking Roman ghosts away, deflecting arrows and spears. Since when did he have *that* power?

He moved through the enemy lines, and even though he seemed to be leaving Frank undefended, the enemy was completely focused on Percy. Frank wasn't sure why—then he saw Percy's goal. One of the black vapory ghosts was wearing the lion's-skin cape of a standard bearer and holding a pole with a golden eagle, icicles frozen to its wings.

The legion's standard.

Frank watched as Percy plowed through a line of legion-naires, scattering their shields with his personal cyclone. He knocked down the standard bearer and grabbed the eagle.

"You want it back?" he shouted at the ghosts. "Come and get it!"

He drew them away, and Frank couldn't help being awed by his bold strategy. As much as those shades wanted to keep Thanatos chained, they were *Roman* spirits. Their minds were fuzzy at best, like the ghosts Frank had seen in Asphodel, but they remembered one thing clearly: they were supposed to protect their eagle.

Still, Percy couldn't fight off that many enemies forever. Maintaining a storm like that had to be difficult. Despite the cold, his face was already beaded with sweat.

Frank looked for Hazel. He couldn't see her or the giant.

"Watch your fire, boy," Death warned. "You don't have any to waste."

Frank cursed. He'd gotten so distracted, he hadn't noticed the second chain had melted.

He moved his fire to the shackles on the god's right hand. The piece of tinder was almost half gone now. Frank started to shiver. More images flashed through his mind. He saw Mars sitting at his grandmother's bedside, looking at Frank with those nuclear explosion eyes: *You're Juno's secret weapon. Have you figured out your gift yet?*

He heard his mother say: *You can be anything.*

Then he saw Grandmother's stern face, her skin as thin as rice paper, her white hair spread across her pillow. *Yes, Fai*

Zhang. Your mother was not simply boosting your self-esteem. She was telling you the literal truth.

He thought of the grizzly bear his mother had intercepted at the edge of the woods. He thought of the large black bird circling over the flames of their family mansion.

The third chain snapped. Frank thrust the tinder at the last shackle. His body was racked with pain. Yellow splotches danced in his eyes.

He saw Percy at the end of the Via Principalis, holding off the army of ghosts. He'd overturned the chariot and destroyed several buildings, but every time he threw off a wave of attackers in his hurricane, the ghosts simply got up and charged again. Every time Percy slashed one of them down with his sword, the ghost re-formed immediately. Percy had backed up almost as far as he could go. Behind him was the side gate of the camp, and about twenty feet beyond that, the edge of the glacier.

As for Hazel, she and Alcyoneus had managed to destroy most of the barracks in their battle. Now they were fighting in the wreckage at the main gate. Arion was playing a dangerous game of tag, charging around the giant while Alyconeus swiped at them with his staff, knocking over walls and cleaving massive chasms in the ice. Only Arion's speed kept them alive.

Finally, Death's last chain snapped. With a desperate yelp, Frank jabbed his firewood into a pile of snow and extinguished the flame. His pain faded. He was still alive. But when he took out the piece of tinder, it was no more than a stub, smaller than a candy bar.

Thanatos raised his arms.

"Free," he said with satisfaction.

"Great." Frank blinked the spots from his eyes. "Then do something!"

Thanatos gave him a calm smile. "Do something? Of course. I will watch. Those who die in this battle will stay dead."

"Thanks," Frank muttered, slipping his firewood into his coat. "Very helpful."

"You're most welcome," Thanatos said agreeably.

"Percy!" Frank yelled. "They can die now!"

Percy nodded understanding, but he looked worn out. His hurricane was slowing down. His strikes were getting slower. The entire ghostly army had him surrounded, gradually forcing him toward the edge of the glacier.

Frank drew his bow to help. Then he dropped it. Normal arrows from a hunting store in Seward wouldn't do any good. Frank would have to use his gift.

He thought he understood his powers at last. Something about watching the firewood burn, smelling the acrid smoke of his own life, had made him feel strangely confident.

Is it fair your life burns so short and bright? Death had asked.

"No such thing as fair," Frank told himself. "If I'm going to burn, it might as well be bright."

He took one step toward Percy. Then, from across the camp, Hazel yelled in pain. Arion screamed as the giant got a lucky shot. His staff sent horse and rider tumbling over the ice, crashing into the ramparts.

"Hazel!" Frank glanced back at Percy, wishing he had his spear. If he could just summon Gray... but he couldn't be in two places at once.

"Go help her!" Percy yelled, holding the golden eagle aloft. "I've got these guys!"

Percy *didn't* have them. Frank knew that. The son of Poseidon was about to be overwhelmed, but Frank ran to Hazel's aid.

She was half-buried in a collapsed pile of snow-bricks. Arion stood over her, trying to protect her, rearing and swatting at the giant with his front hooves.

The giant laughed. "Hello, little pony. You want to play?"

Alcyoneus raised his icy staff.

Frank was too far away to help... but he imagined himself rushing forward, his feet leaving the ground.

Be anything.

He remembered the bald eagles they'd seen on the train ride. His body became smaller and lighter. His arms stretched into wings, and his sight became a thousand times sharper. He soared upward, then dove at the giant with his talons extended, his razor-sharp claws raking across the giant's eyes.

Alcyoneus bellowed in pain. He staggered backward as Frank landed in front of Hazel and returned to his normal form.

"Frank..." She stared at him in amazement, a cap of snow dripping off her head. "What just... how did—?"

"Fool!" Alcyoneus shouted. His face was slashed, black oil dripping into his eyes instead of blood, but the wounds were already closing. "I am immortal in my homeland, Frank Zhang! And thanks to your friend Hazel, my new homeland is Alaska. You *cannot* kill me here!"

"We'll see," Frank said. Power coursed through his arms and legs. "Hazel, get back on your horse."

The giant charged, and Frank charged to meet him. He remembered the bear he'd met face to face when he was a child. As he ran, his body became heavier, thicker, rippling with muscles. He crashed into the giant as a full-grown grizzly, a thousand pounds of pure force. He was still small compared to Alcyoneus, but he slammed into the giant with such momentum, Alcyoneus toppled into an icy watchtower that collapsed on top of him.

Frank sprang at the giant's head. A swipe of his claw was like a heavyweight fighter swinging a chain saw. Frank bashed the giant's face back and forth until his metallic features began to dent.

"Urgg," the giant mumbled in a stupor.

Frank changed to his regular form. His backpack was still with him. He grabbed the rope he'd bought in Seward, quickly made a noose, and fastened it around the giant's scaly dragon foot.

"Hazel, here!" He tossed her the other end of the rope. "I've got an idea, but we'll have to—"

"Kill—uh—you—uh . . ." Alcyoneus muttered.

Frank ran to the giant's head, picked up the nearest heavy object he could find—a legion shield—and slammed it into the giant's nose.

The giant said, "Urgg."

Frank looked back at Hazel. "How far can Arion pull this guy?"

Hazel just stared at him. "You—you were a bird. Then a bear. And—"

"I'll explain later," Frank said. "We need to drag this guy inland, as fast and far as we can."

"But Percy!" Hazel said.

Frank cursed. How could he have forgotten?

Through the ruins of the camp, he saw Percy with his back to the edge of the cliff. His hurricane was gone. He held Riptide in one hand and the legion's golden eagle in the other. The entire army of shades edged forward, their weapons bristling.

"Percy!" Frank yelled.

Percy glanced over. He saw the fallen giant and seemed to understand what was happening. He yelled something that was lost in the wind, probably: *Go!*

Then he slammed Riptide into the ice at his feet. The entire glacier shuddered. Ghosts fell to their knees. Behind Percy, a wave surged up from the bay—a wall of gray water even taller than the glacier. Water shot from the chasms and crevices in the ice. As the wave hit, the back half of the camp crumbled. The entire edge of the glacier peeled away, cascading into the void—carrying buildings, ghosts, and Percy Jackson over the edge.

FRANK

FRANK WAS SO STUNNED THAT Hazel had to yell his name a dozen times before he realized Alcyoneus was getting up again.

He slammed his shield into the giant's nose until Alcyoneus began to snore. Meanwhile the glacier kept crumbling, the edge getting closer and closer.

Thanatos glided toward them on his black wings, his expression serene.

"Ah, yes," he said with satisfaction. "There go some souls. Drowning, drowning. You'd best hurry, my friends, or you'll drown, too."

"But Percy..." Frank could barely speak his friend's name. "Is he—?"

"Too soon to tell. As for *this* one..." Thanatos looked down at Alcyoneus with distaste. "You'll never kill him here. You know what to do?"

Frank nodded numbly. "I think so."

"Then our business is complete."

Frank and Hazel exchanged nervous looks.

"Um..." Hazel faltered. "You mean you won't...you're not going to—"

"Claim your life?" Thanatos asked. "Well, let's see..."

He pulled a pure-black iPad from thin air. Death tapped the screen a few times, and all Frank could think was: Please don't let there be an app for reaping souls.

"I don't see you on the list," Thanatos said. "Pluto gives me specific orders for escaped souls, you see. For some reason, he has not issued a warrant for yours. Perhaps he feels your life is not finished, or it could be an oversight. If you'd like me to call and ask—"

"No!" Hazel yelped. "That's okay."

"Are you sure?" Death asked helpfully. "I have video-conferencing enabled. I have his Skype address here somewhere..."

"Really, no." Hazel looked as if several thousand pounds of worry had just been lifted from her shoulders. "Thank you."

"Urgg," Alcyoneus mumbled.

Frank hit him over the head again.

Death looked up from his iPad. "As for you, Frank Zhang, it isn't your time, either. You've got a little fuel left to burn. But don't think I'm doing either of you a favor. We will meet again under less pleasant circumstances."

The cliff was still crumbling, the edge only twenty feet away now. Arion whinnied impatiently. Frank knew they had to leave, but there was one more question he had to ask.

"What about the Doors of Death?" he said. "Where are they? How do we close them?"

"Ah, yes." A look of irritation flickered across Thanatos's face. "The Doors of Me. Closing them would be good, but I fear it is beyond my power. How *you* would do it, I haven't the faintest idea. I can't tell you exactly where they are. The location isn't . . . well, it's not entirely a *physical* place. They must be located through questing. I can tell you to start your search in Rome. The *original* Rome. You will need a special guide. Only one sort of demigod can read the signs that will ultimately lead you to the Doors of Me."

Cracks appeared in the ice under their feet. Hazel patted Arion's neck to keep him from bolting.

"What about my brother?" she asked. "Is Nico alive?"

Thanatos gave her a strange look—possibly pity, though that didn't seem like an emotion Death would understand. "You will find the answer in Rome. And now I must fly south to your Camp Jupiter. I have a feeling there will be many souls to reap, very soon. Farewell, demigods, until we meet again."

Thanatos dissipated into black smoke.

The cracks widened in the ice under Frank's feet.

"Hurry!" he told Hazel. "We've got to take Alcyoneus about ten miles due north!"

He climbed onto the giant's chest and Arion took off, racing across the ice, dragging Alcyoneus like the world's ugliest sled.

It was a short trip.

Arion rode the glacier like a highway, zipping across the ice, leaping crevices, and skidding down slopes that would've made a snowboarder's eyes light up.

Frank didn't have to knock out Alcyoneus too many times, because the giant's head kept bouncing and hitting the ice. As they raced along, the half-conscious Golden Boy mumbled a tune that sounded like "Jingle Bells."

Frank felt pretty stunned himself. He'd just turned into an eagle and a bear. He could still feel fluid energy rippling through his body, like he was halfway between a solid and liquid state.

Not only that: Hazel and he had released Death, and both of them had survived. And Percy... Frank swallowed down his fear. Percy had gone over the side of the glacier to save them.

The son of Neptune shall drown.

No. Frank refused to believe Percy was dead. They hadn't come all this way just to lose their friend. Frank would find him—but first they had to deal with Alcyoneus.

He visualized the map he had been studying on the train from Anchorage. He knew roughly where they were going, but there were no signs or markers on top of the glacier. He'd just have to take his best guess.

Finally Arion zoomed between two mountains into a valley of ice and rocks, like a massive bowl of frozen milk with bits of Cocoa Puffs. The giant's golden skin paled as if it were turning to brass. Frank felt a subtle vibration in his own body, like a tuning fork pressed against his sternum. He knew he'd crossed into friendly territory—*home* territory.

"Here!" Frank shouted.

Arion veered to one side. Hazel cut the rope, and Alcyoneus went skidding past. Frank leaped off just before the giant slammed into a boulder.

Immediately Alcyoneus jumped to his feet. "What? Where? Who?"

His nose was bent in an odd direction. His wounds had healed, though his golden skin had lost some of its luster. He looked around for his iron staff, which was still back at Hubbard Glacier. Then he gave up and pounded the nearest boulder to pieces with his fist.

"You *dare* take me for a sleigh ride?" He tensed and sniffed the air. "That smell . . . like snuffed-out souls. Thanatos is free, eh? Bah! It doesn't matter. Gaea still controls the Doors of Death. Now, why have you brought me here, son of Mars?"

"To kill you," Frank said. "Next question?"

The giant's eyes narrowed. "I've never known a child of Mars who can change his form, but that doesn't mean you can defeat me. Do you think your stupid soldier of a father gave you the strength to face me in one-on-one combat?"

Hazel drew her sword. "How about two on one?"

The giant growled and charged at Hazel, but Arion nimbly darted out of the way. Hazel slashed her sword across the back of the giant's calf. Black oil spouted from the wound.

Alcyoneus stumbled. "You can't kill me, Thanatos or no!"

Hazel made a grabbing gesture with her free hand. An invisible force yanked the giant's jewel-encrusted hair backward. Hazel rushed in, slashed his other leg, and raced away before he could regain his balance.

"Stop that!" Alcyoneus shouted. "This is Alaska. I am immortal in my homeland!"

"Actually," Frank said, "I have some bad news about that. See, I got more from my dad than strength."

The giant snarled. "What are you talking about, war brat?"

"Tactics," Frank said. "That's my gift from Mars. A battle can be won before it's ever fought by choosing the right ground." He pointed over his shoulder. "We crossed the border a few hundred yards back. You're not in Alaska anymore. Can't you feel it, Al? You want to get to Alaska, you have to go through me."

Slowly, understanding dawned in the giant's eyes. He looked down incredulously at his wounded legs. Oil still poured from his calves, turning the ice black.

"Impossible!" the giant bellowed. "I'll—I'll—Gah!"

He charged at Frank, determined to reach the international boundary. For a split second, Frank doubted his plan. If he couldn't use his gift again, if he froze, he was dead. Then he remembered his grandmother's instructions:

It helps if you know the creature well. Check.

It also helps if you are in a life-and-death situation, such as combat. Double check.

The giant kept coming. Twenty yards. Ten yards.

"Frank?" Hazel called nervously.

Frank stood his ground. "I got this."

Just before Alcyoneus smashed into him, Frank changed. He'd always felt too big and clumsy. Now he used that feeling. His body swelled to massive size. His skin thickened. His arms changed to stout front legs. His mouth grew tusks and his nose elongated. He became the animal he knew best—the one he'd cared for, fed, bathed, and even given indigestion to at Camp Jupiter.

Alcyoneus slammed into a full grown ten-ton elephant.

The giant staggered sideways. He screamed in frustration and slammed into Frank again, but Alcyoneus was completely out of his weight division. Frank head-butted him so hard Alcyoneus flew backward and landed spread-eagled on the ice.

"You—can't—kill me," Alcyoneus growled. "You can't—"

Frank turned back to his normal form. He walked up to the giant, whose oily wounds were steaming. The gems fell out of his hair and sizzled in the snow. His golden skin began to corrode, breaking into chunks.

Hazel dismounted and stood next to Frank, her sword ready. "May I?"

Frank nodded. He looked into the giant's seething eyes. "Here's a tip, Alcyoneus. Next time you choose the biggest state for your home, don't set up base in the part that's only ten miles wide. Welcome to Canada, idiot."

Hazel's sword came down on the giant's neck. Alcyoneus dissolved into a pile of very expensive rocks.

For a while Hazel and Frank stood together, watching the remains of the giant melt into the ice. Frank picked up his rope.

"An elephant?" Hazel asked.

Frank scratched his neck. "Yeah. It seemed like a good idea."

He couldn't read her expression. He was afraid he'd finally done something so weird that she'd never want to be around him again. Frank Zhang: lumbering klutz, child of Mars, part-time pachyderm.

Then she kissed him—a real kiss on the lips, much better than the kind of kiss she'd given Percy on the airplane.

"You are amazing," she said. "And you make a very handsome elephant."

Frank felt so flustered that he thought his boots might melt through the ice. Before he could say anything, a voice echoed across the valley:

You haven't won.

Frank looked up. Shadows were shifting across the nearest mountain, forming the face of a sleeping woman.

You will never reach home in time, taunted the voice of Gaea. *Even now, Thanatos is attending the death of Camp Jupiter, the final destruction of your Roman friends.*

The mountain rumbled as if the whole earth were laughing. The shadows disappeared.

Hazel and Frank looked at each other. Neither said a word. They climbed onto Arion and sped back toward Glacier Bay.

XLVIII

FRANK

PERCY WAS WAITING FOR THEM. He looked mad.

He stood at the edge of the glacier, leaning on the staff with the golden eagle, gazing down at the wreckage he'd caused: several hundred acres of newly open water dotted with icebergs and flotsam from the ruined camp.

The only remains on the glacier were the main gates, which listed sideways, and a tattered blue banner lying over a pile of snow-bricks.

When they ran up to him, Percy said, "Hey," like they were just meeting for lunch or something.

"You're alive!" Frank marveled.

Percy frowned. "The fall? That was nothing. I fell twice that far from the St. Louis Arch."

"You did *what*?" Hazel asked.

"Never mind. The important thing was I didn't drown."

"So the prophecy *was* incomplete!" Hazel grinned. "It

probably said something like: *The son of Neptune will drown a whole bunch of ghosts.*"

Percy shrugged. He was still looking at Frank like he was miffed. "I got a bone to pick with you, Zhang. You can turn into an eagle? And a bear?"

"And an elephant," Hazel said proudly.

"An elephant." Percy shook his head in disbelief. "That's your family gift? You can change shape?"

Frank shuffled his feet. "Um ... yeah. Periclymenus, my ancestor, the Argonaut—he could do that. He passed down the ability."

"And he got that gift from Poseidon," Percy said. "That's completely unfair. I can't turn into animals."

Frank stared at him. "Unfair? You can breathe underwater and blow up glaciers and summon freaking hurricanes—and it's unfair that I can be an elephant?"

Percy considered. "Okay. I guess you got a point. But next time I say you're totally *beast*—"

"Just shut up," Frank said. "Please."

Percy cracked a smile.

"If you guys are done," Hazel said, "we need to go. Camp Jupiter is under attack. They could use that gold eagle."

Percy nodded. "One thing first, though. Hazel, there's about a ton of Imperial gold weapons and armor at the bottom of the bay now, plus a really nice chariot. I'm betting that stuff could come in handy...."

It took them a long time—too long—but they all knew

those weapons could make the difference between victory and defeat if they got them back to camp in time.

Hazel used her abilities to levitate some items from the bottom of the sea. Percy swam down and brought up more. Even Frank helped by turning into a seal, which was kind of cool, though Percy claimed his breath smelled like fish.

It took all three of them to raise the chariot, but finally they'd managed to haul everything ashore to a black sand beach near the base of the glacier. They couldn't fit everything in the chariot, but they used Frank's rope to strap down most of the gold weapons and the best pieces of armor.

"It looks like Santa's sleigh," Frank said. "Can Arion even pull that much?"

Arion huffed.

"Hazel," Percy said, "I am seriously going to wash your horse's mouth with soap. He says, yes, he can pull it, but he needs food."

Hazel picked up an old Roman dagger, a *pugio*. It was bent and dull, so it wouldn't be much good in a fight, but it looked like solid Imperial gold.

"Here you go, Arion," she said. "High-performance fuel."

The horse took the dagger in his teeth and chewed it like an apple. Frank made a silent oath never to put his hand near that horse's mouth.

"I'm not doubting Arion's strength," he said carefully, "but will the chariot hold up? The last one—"

"This one has Imperial gold wheels and axle," Percy said. "It should hold."

"If not," Hazel said, "this is going to be a short trip. But we're out of time. Come on!"

Frank and Percy climbed into the chariot. Hazel swung up onto Arion's back.

"Giddyup!" she yelled.

The horse's sonic boom echoed across the bay. They sped south, avalanches tumbling down the mountains as they passed.

XLIX

PERCY

FOUR HOURS.

That's how long it took the fastest horse on the planet to get from Alaska to San Francisco Bay, heading straight over the water down the Northwest Coast.

That's also how long it took for Percy's memory to return completely. The process had started in Portland when he had drunk the gorgon's blood, but his past life had still been maddeningly fuzzy. Now, as they headed back into the Olympian gods' territory, Percy remembered everything: the war with Kronos, his sixteenth birthday at Camp Half-Blood, his trainer Chiron the centaur, his best friend Grover, his brother Tyson, and most of all Annabeth—two great months of dating, and then *BOOM*. He'd been abducted by the alien known as Hera. Or Juno...whatever.

Eight months of his life stolen. Next time Percy saw the Queen of Olympus, he was definitely going to give her a goddess-sized slap upside the head.

His friends and family must be going out of their minds. If Camp Jupiter was in such bad trouble, he could only guess what Camp Half-Blood must be facing without him.

Even worse: Saving both camps would be only the beginning. According to Alcyoneus, the *real* war would happen far away, in the homeland of the gods. The giants intended to attack the *original* Mount Olympus and destroy the gods forever.

Percy knew that giants couldn't die unless demigods and gods fought them together. Nico had told him that. Annabeth had mentioned it too, back in August, when she'd speculated that the giants might be part of the new Great Prophecy— what the Romans called the Prophecy of Seven. (That was the downside of dating the smartest girl at camp: You learn stuff.)

He understood Juno's plan: Unite the Roman and Greek demigods to create an elite team of heroes, then somehow convince the gods to fight alongside them. But first, they had to save Camp Jupiter.

The coastline began to look familiar. They raced past the Mendocino lighthouse. Shortly afterward, Mount Tam and the Marin headlands loomed out of the fog. Arion shot straight under the Golden Gate Bridge into San Francisco Bay.

They tore through Berkeley and into the Oakland Hills. When they reached the hilltop above the Caldecott Tunnel, Arion shuddered like a broken car and came to a stop, his chest heaving.

Hazel patted his sides lovingly. "You did great, Arion."

The horse was too tired even to cuss: *Of course I did great. What did you expect?*

Percy and Frank jumped off the chariot. Percy wished there'd been comfortable seats or an in-flight meal. His legs were wobbly. His joints were so stiff, he could barely walk. If he went into battle like this, the enemy would call him Old Man Jackson.

Frank didn't look much better. He hobbled to the top of the hill and peered down at the camp. "Guys...you need to see this."

When Percy and Hazel joined him, Percy's heart sank. The battle had begun, and it wasn't going well. The Twelfth Legion was arrayed on the Field of Mars, trying to protect the city. Scorpions fired into the ranks of the Earthborn. Hannibal the elephant plowed down monsters right and left, but the defenders were badly outnumbered.

On her pegasus Scipio, Reyna flew around the giant Polybotes, trying to keep him occupied. The Lares had formed shimmering purple lines against a mob of black, vaporous shades in ancient armor. Veteran demigods from the city had joined the battle, and were pushing their shield wall against an onslaught of wild centaurs. Giant eagles circled the battle-field, doing aerial combat with two snake-haired ladies in green Bargain Mart vests—Stheno and Euryale.

The legion itself was taking the brunt of the attack, but their formation was breaking. Each cohort was an island in a sea of enemies. The Cyclopes' siege tower shot glowing green cannonballs into the city, blasting craters in the forum, reducing houses to ruins. As Percy watched, a cannonball hit the Senate House and the dome partially collapsed.

"We're too late," Hazel said.

"No," Percy said. "They're still fighting. We can do this."

"Where's Lupa?" Frank asked, desperation creeping into his voice. "She and the wolves... they should be here."

Percy thought about his time with the wolf goddess. He'd come to respect her teachings, but he'd also learned that wolves had limits. They weren't front-line fighters. They only attacked when they had vastly superior numbers, and usually under the cover of darkness. Besides, Lupa's first rule was self-sufficiency. She would help her children as much as she could, train them to fight—but in the end, they were either predator or prey. Romans had to fight for themselves. They had to prove their worth or die. That was Lupa's way.

"She did what she could," Percy said. "She slowed down the army on its way south. Now it's up to us. We've got to get the gold eagle and these weapons to the legion."

"But Arion is out of steam!" Hazel said. "We can't haul this stuff ourselves."

"Maybe we don't have to." Percy scanned the hilltops. If Tyson had gotten his dream message in Vancouver, help might be close.

He whistled as loud as he could—a good New York cab whistle that would've been heard all the way from Times Square to Central Park.

Shadows rippled in the trees. A huge black shape bounded out of nowhere—a mastiff the size of an SUV, with a Cyclops and a harpy on her back.

"Hellhound!" Frank scrambled backward.

"It's okay!" Percy grinned. "These are friends."

"Brother!" Tyson climbed off and ran toward Percy. Percy

tried to brace himself, but it was no good. Tyson slammed into him and smothered him in a hug. For a few seconds, Percy could only see black spots and lots of flannel. Then Tyson let go and laughed with delight, looking Percy over with that massive baby brown eye.

"You are not dead!" he said. "I like it when you are not dead!"

Ella fluttered to the ground and began preening her feathers. "Ella found a dog," she announced. "A large dog. And a Cyclops."

Was she blushing? Before Percy could decide, his black mastiff pounced on him, knocking Percy to the ground and barking so loudly that even Arion backed up.

"Hey, Mrs. O'Leary," Percy said. "Yeah, I love you too, girl. Good dog."

Hazel made a squeaking sound. "You have a hellhound named Mrs. O'Leary?"

"Long story." Percy managed to get to his feet and wipe off the dog slobber. "You can ask your brother..."

His voice wavered when he saw Hazel's expression. He'd almost forgotten that Nico di Angelo was missing.

Hazel had told him what Thanatos had said about searching for the Doors of Death in Rome, and Percy was anxious to find Nico for his own reasons—to wring the kid's neck for having pretended he didn't know Percy when he first came to camp. Still, he was Hazel's brother, and finding him was a conversation for another time.

"Sorry," he said. "But yeah, this is my dog, Mrs. O'Leary. Tyson—these are my friends, Frank and Hazel."

Percy turned to Ella, who was counting all the barbs in one of her feathers.

"Are you okay?" he asked. "We were worried about you."

"Ella is not strong," she said. "Cyclopes are strong. Tyson found Ella. Tyson took care of Ella."

Percy raised his eyebrows. Ella *was* blushing.

"Tyson," he said, "you big charmer, you."

Tyson turned the same color as Ella's plumage. "Um . . . No." He leaned down and whispered nervously, loud enough for all the others to hear: "She is pretty."

Frank tapped his head like he was afraid his brain had short-circuited. "Anyway, there's this battle happening."

"Right," Percy agreed. "Tyson, where's Annabeth? Is any other help coming?"

Tyson pouted. His big brown eye got misty. "The big ship is not ready. Leo says tomorrow, maybe two days. Then they will come."

"We don't have two *minutes*," Percy said. "Okay, here's the plan."

As quickly as possible, he pointed out which were the good guys and the bad guys on the battlefield. Tyson was alarmed to learn that bad Cyclopes and bad centaurs were in the giant's army. "I have to hit pony-men?"

"Just scare them away," Percy promised.

"Um, Percy?" Frank looked at Tyson with trepidation. "I just . . . don't want our friend here getting hurt. Is Tyson a fighter?"

Percy smiled. "Is he a fighter? Frank, you're looking at

General Tyson of the Cyclops army. And by the way, Tyson, Frank is a descendant of Poseidon."

"Brother!" Tyson crushed Frank in a hug.

Percy stifled a laugh. "Actually he's more like a great-great-...Oh, never mind. Yeah, he's your brother."

"Thanks," Frank mumbled through a mouthful of flannel. "But if the legion mistakes Tyson for an enemy—"

"I've got it!" Hazel ran to the chariot and dug out the biggest Roman helmet she could find, plus an old Roman banner embroidered with SPQR.

She handed them to Tyson. "Put those on, big guy. Then our friends will know you're on our team."

"Yay!" Tyson said. "I'm on your team!"

The helmet was ridiculously small, and he put the cape on backward, like a SPQR baby bib.

"It'll do," Percy said. "Ella, just stay here. Stay safe."

"Safe," Ella repeated. "Ella likes being safe. Safety in numbers. Safety deposit boxes. Ella will go with Tyson."

"What?" Percy said. "Oh...fine. Whatever. Just don't get hurt. And Mrs. O'Leary—"

"ROOOF!"

"How do you feel about pulling a chariot?"

L

PERCY

THEY WERE, WITHOUT A DOUBT, the strangest reinforcements in Roman military history. Hazel rode Arion, who had recovered enough to carry one person at normal horse speed, though he cursed about his aching hooves all the way downhill.

Frank transformed into a bald eagle—which Percy still found totally unfair—and soared above them. Tyson ran down the hill, waving his club and yelling, "Bad pony-men! BOO!" while Ella fluttered around him, reciting facts from the *Old Farmer's Almanac*.

As for Percy, he rode Mrs. O'Leary into battle with a chariot full of Imperial gold equipment clanking and clinking behind, the golden eagle standard of the Twelfth Legion raised high above him.

They skirted the perimeter of the camp and took the northernmost bridge over the Little Tiber, charging onto the Field of Mars at the western edge of the battle. A horde of Cyclopes was hammering away at the campers of the Fifth Cohort, who were trying to keep their shields locked just to stay alive.

Seeing them in trouble, Percy felt a surge of protective rage. These were the kids who'd taken him in. This was *his* family.

He shouted, "Fifth Cohort!" and slammed into the nearest Cyclops. The last things the poor monster saw were Mrs. O'Leary's teeth.

After the Cyclops disintegrated—and *stayed* disintegrated, thanks to Death—Percy leaped off his hellhound and slashed wildly through the other monsters.

Tyson charged at the Cyclops leader, Ma Gasket, her chain-mail dress spattered with mud and decorated with broken spears.

She gawked at Tyson and started to say, "Who—?"

Tyson hit her in the head so hard, she spun in a circle and landed on her rump.

"Bad Cyclops Lady!" he bellowed. "General Tyson says GO AWAY!"

He hit her again, and Ma Gasket broke into dust.

Meanwhile Hazel charged around on Arion, slicing her *spatha* through one Cyclops after another, while Frank blinded the enemies with his talons.

Once every Cyclops within fifty yards had been reduced to ashes, Frank landed in front of his troops and transformed into a human. His centurion's badge and Mural Crown gleamed on his winter jacket.

"Fifth Cohort!" he bellowed. "Get your Imperial gold weapons right here!"

The campers recovered from their shock and mobbed the chariot. Percy did his best to hand out equipment quickly.

"Let's go, let's go!" Dakota urged, grinning like a madman as he swigged red Kool-Aid from his flask. "Our comrades need help!"

Soon the Fifth Cohort was equipped with new weapons and shields and helmets. They weren't exactly consistent. In fact they looked like they'd been shopping at a King Midas clearance sale. But they were suddenly the most powerful cohort in the legion.

"Follow the eagle!" Frank ordered. "To battle!"

The campers cheered. As Percy and Mrs. O'Leary charged onward, the entire cohort followed—forty extremely shiny gold-plated warriors screaming for blood.

They slammed into a herd of wild centaurs that were attacking the Third Cohort. When the campers of the Third saw the eagle standard, they shouted insanely and fought with renewed effort.

The centaurs didn't stand a chance. The two cohorts crushed them like a vise. Soon there was nothing left but piles of dust and assorted hooves and horns. Percy hoped Chiron would forgive him, but these centaurs weren't like the Party Ponies he'd met before. They were some other breed. They had to be defeated.

"Form ranks!" the centurions shouted. The two cohorts came together, their military training kicking in. Shields locked, they marched into battle against the Earthborn.

Frank shouted, *"Pila!"*

A hundred spears bristled. When Frank yelled, "Fire!" they

sailed through the air—a wave of death cutting through the six-armed monsters. The campers drew swords and advanced toward the center of the battle.

At the base of the aqueduct, the First and Second Cohorts were trying to encircle Polybotes, but they were taking a pounding. The remaining Earthborn threw barrage after barrage of stone and mud. *Karpoi* grain spirits—those horrible little piranha Cupids—were rushing through the tall grass abducting campers at random, pulling them away from the line. The giant himself kept shaking basilisks out of his hair. Every time one landed, the Romans panicked and ran. Judging from their corroded shields and the smoking plumes on their helmets, they'd already learned about the basilisks' poison and fire.

Reyna soared above the giant, diving in with her javelin whenever he turned his attention to the ground troops. Her purple cloak snapped in the wind. Her golden armor gleamed. Polybotes jabbed his trident and swung his weighted net, but Scipio was almost as nimble as Arion.

Then Reyna noticed the Fifth Cohort marching to their aid with the eagle. She was so stunned, the giant almost swatted her out of the air, but Scipio dodged. Reyna locked eyes with Percy and gave him a huge smile.

"Romans!" Her voice boomed across the fields. "Rally to the eagle!"

Demigods and monsters alike turned and gawked as Percy bounded forward on his hellhound.

"What is this?" Polybotes demanded. *"What is this?"*

Percy felt a rush of power coursing through the standard's

staff. He raised the eagle and shouted, "Twelfth Legion Fulminata!"

Thunder shook the valley. The eagle let loose a blinding flash, and a thousand tendrils of lightning exploded from its golden wings—arcing in front of Percy like the branches of an enormous deadly tree, connecting with the nearest monsters, leaping from one to another, completely ignoring the Roman forces.

When the lightning stopped, the First and Second Cohorts were facing one surprised-looking giant and several hundred smoking piles of ash. The enemy's center line had been charred to oblivion.

The look on Octavian's face was priceless. The centurion stared at Percy with shock, then outrage. Then, when his own troops started to cheer, he had no choice except to join the shouting: "Rome! Rome!"

The giant Polybotes backed up uncertainly, but Percy knew the battle wasn't over.

The Fourth Cohort was still surrounded by Cyclopes. Even Hannibal the elephant was having a hard time wading through so many monsters. His black Kevlar armor was ripped so that his label just said ANT.

The veterans and Lares on the eastern flank were being pushed toward the city. The monsters' siege tower was still hurling explosive green fireballs into the streets. The gorgons had disabled the giant eagles and now flew unchallenged over the giant's remaining centaurs and the Earthborn, trying to rally them.

"Stand your ground!" Stheno yelled. "I've got free samples!"

Polybotes bellowed. A dozen fresh basilisks fell out of his hair, turning the grass to poison yellow. "You think this changes anything, Percy Jackson? I cannot be destroyed! Come forward, son of Neptune. I will break you!"

Percy dismounted. He handed Dakota the standard. "You are the cohort's senior centurion. Take care of this."

Dakota blinked, then he straightened with pride. He dropped his Kool-Aid flask and took the eagle. "I will carry it with honor."

"Frank, Hazel, Tyson," Percy said, "help the Fourth Cohort. I've got a giant to kill."

He raised Riptide, but before he could advance, horns blew in the northern hills. Another army appeared on the ridge —hundreds of warriors in black-and-gray camouflage, armed with spears and shields. Interspersed among their ranks were a dozen battle forklifts, their sharpened tines gleaming in the sunset and flaming bolts nocked in their crossbows.

"Amazons," Frank said. "Great."

Polybotes laughed. "You, see? Our reinforcements have arrived! Rome will fall today!"

The Amazons lowered their spears and charged down the hill. Their forklifts barreled into battle. The giant's army cheered—until the Amazons changed course and headed straight for the monsters' intact eastern flank.

"Amazons, forward!" On the largest forklift stood a girl who looked like an older version of Reyna, in black combat armor with a glittering gold belt around her waist.

"Queen Hylla!" said Hazel. "She survived!"

The Amazon queen shouted: "To my sister's aid! Destroy the monsters!"

"Destroy!" Her troops' cry echoed through the valley.

Reyna wheeled her pegasus toward Percy. Her eyes gleamed. Her expression said: *I could hug you right now.* She shouted, "Romans! Advance!"

The battlefield descended into absolute chaos. Amazon and Roman lines swung toward the enemy like the Doors of Death themselves.

But Percy had only one goal. He pointed at the giant. "You. Me. To the finish."

They met by the aqueduct, which had somehow survived the battle so far. Polybotes fixed that. He swiped his trident and smashed the nearest brick arch, unleashing a waterfall.

"Go on, then, son of Neptune!" Polybotes taunted. "Let me see your power! Does water do your bidding? Does it heal you? But I am born to oppose Neptune."

The giant thrust his hand under the water. As the torrent passed through his fingers it turned dark green. He flung some at Percy, who instinctively deflected it with his will. The liquid splattered the ground in front of him. With a nasty hiss, the grass withered and smoked.

"My touch turns water to poison," Polybotes said. "Let's see what it does to your blood!"

He threw his net at Percy, but Percy rolled out of the way. He diverted the waterfall straight into the giant's face. While Polybotes was blinded, Percy charged. He plunged Riptide into the giant's belly then withdrew it and vaulted away, leaving the giant roaring in pain.

The strike would have dissolved any lesser monster, but Polybotes just staggered and looked down at the golden *ichor* —the blood of immortals—spilling from his wound. The cut was already closing.

"Good try, demigod," he snarled. "But I will break you still."

"Gotta catch me first," Percy said.

He turned and bolted toward the city.

"What?" the giant yelled incredulously. "You run, coward? Stand still and die!"

Percy had no intention of doing that. He knew he couldn't kill Polybotes alone. But he did have a plan.

He passed Mrs. O'Leary, who looked up curiously with a gorgon wriggling in her mouth.

"I'm fine!" Percy yelled as he ran by, followed by a giant screaming bloody murder.

He jumped over a burning scorpion and ducked as Hannibal threw a Cyclops across his path. Out of the corner of his eye, he saw Tyson pounding the Earthborn into the ground like a game of whack-a-mole. Ella was fluttering above him, dodging missiles and calling out advice: "The groin. The Earthborn's groin is sensitive."

SMASH!

"Good. Yes. Tyson found its groin."

"Percy needs help?" Tyson called.

"I'm good!"

"Die!" Polybotes yelled, closing fast. Percy kept running.

In the distance, he saw Hazel and Arion galloping across the battlefield, cutting down centaurs and *karpoi*. One grain spirit yelled, "Wheat! I'll give you wheat!" but Arion stomped him into a pile of breakfast cereal. Queen Hylla and Reyna joined forces, forklift and pegasus riding together, scattering the dark shades of fallen warriors. Frank turned himself into an elephant and stomped through some Cyclopes, and Dakota held the golden eagle high, blasting lightning at any monsters that dared to challenge the Fifth Cohort.

All that was great, but Percy needed a different kind of help. He needed a god.

He glanced back and saw the giant almost within arm's reach. To buy some time, Percy ducked behind one of the aqueduct's columns. The giant swung his trident. When the column crumbled, Percy used the unleashed water to guide the collapse—bringing down several tons of bricks on the giant's head.

Percy bolted for the city limits.

"Terminus!" he yelled.

The nearest statue of the god was about sixty feet ahead. His stone eyes snapped open as Percy ran toward him.

"Completely unacceptable!" he complained. "Buildings on fire! Invaders! Get them out of here, Percy Jackson!"

"I'm trying," he said. "But there's this giant, Polybotes."

"Yes, I know! Wait—Excuse me a moment." Terminus closed his eyes in concentration. A flaming green cannonball sailed overhead and suddenly vaporized. "I can't stop *all* the missiles," Terminus complained. "Why can't they be civilized and attack more slowly? I'm only one god."

"Help me kill the giant," Percy said, "and this will all be over. A god and demigod working together—that's the only way to kill him."

Terminus sniffed. "I guard borders. I don't kill giants. It's not in my job description."

"Terminus, come on!" Percy took another step forward, and the god shrieked indignantly.

"Stop right there, young man! No weapons inside the Pomerian Line!"

"But we're under attack."

"I don't care! Rules are rules. When people don't follow the rules, I get very, very angry."

Percy smiled. "Hold that thought."

He sprinted back toward the giant. "Hey, ugly!"

"Rarrr!" Polybotes burst from the ruins of the aqueduct. The water was still pouring over him, turning to poison and creating a steaming marsh around his feet.

"You . . . you will die slowly," the giant promised. He picked up his trident, now dripping with green venom.

All around them, the battle was winding down. As the last monsters were mopped up, Percy's friends started gathering, forming a ring around the giant.

"I will take you prisoner, Percy Jackson," Polybotes snarled. "I will torture you under the sea. Every day the water will heal you, and every day I will bring you closer to death."

"Great offer," Percy said. "But I think I'll just kill you instead."

Polybotes bellowed in rage. He shook his head, and more basilisks flew from his hair.

"Get back!" Frank warned.

Fresh chaos spread through the ranks. Hazel spurred Arion and put herself between the basilisks and the campers. Frank changed form—shrinking into something lean and furry...a weasel? Percy thought Frank had lost his mind, but when Frank charged the basilisks, they absolutely freaked out. They slithered away with Frank chasing after them in hot weasely pursuit.

Polybotes pointed his trident and ran toward Percy. As the giant reached the Pomerian Line, Percy jumped aside like a bullfighter. Polybotes barreled across the city limits.

"THAT'S IT!" Terminus cried. "That's AGAINST THE RULES!"

Polybotes frowned, obviously confused that he was being told off by a statue. "What are you?" he growled. "Shut up!"

He pushed the statue over and turned back to Percy.

"Now I'm MAD!" Terminus shrieked. "I'm strangling you. Feel that? Those are my hands around your neck, you big bully. Get over here! I'm going to head-butt you so hard—"

"Enough!" The giant stepped on the statue and broke Terminus in three pieces—pedestal, body, and head.

"You DIDN'T!" shouted Terminus. "Percy Jackson, you've got yourself a deal! Let's kill this upstart."

The giant laughed so hard that he didn't realize Percy was charging until it was too late. Percy jumped up, vaulting off the giant's knee, and drove Riptide straight through one of the metal mouths on Polybotes's breastplate, sinking the Celestial bronze hilt-deep in his chest. The giant stumbled backward, tripping over Terminus's pedestal and crashing to the ground.

While he was trying to get up, clawing at the sword in his chest, Percy hefted the head of the statue.

"You'll never win!" the giant groaned. "You cannot defeat me alone."

"I'm not alone." Percy raised the stone head above the giant's face. "I'd like you to meet my friend Terminus. He's a god!"

Too late, awareness and fear dawned in the giant's face. Percy smashed the god's head as hard as he could into the Polybotes's nose, and the giant dissolved, crumbling into a steaming heap of seaweed, reptile skin, and poisonous muck.

Percy staggered away, completely exhausted.

"Ha!" said the head of Terminus. "That will teach *him* to obey the rules of Rome."

For a moment, the battlefield was silent except for a few fires burning, and a few retreating monsters screaming in panic.

A ragged circle of Romans and Amazons stood around Percy. Tyson, Ella, and Mrs. O'Leary were there. Frank and Hazel were grinning at him with pride. Arion was nibbling contentedly on a golden shield.

The Romans began to chant, "Percy! Percy!"

They mobbed him. Before he knew it, they were raising him on a shield. The cry changed to, "Praetor! Praetor!"

Among the chanters was Reyna herself, who held up her hand and grasped Percy's in congratulation. Then the mob of cheering Romans carried him around the Pomerian Line, carefully avoiding Terminus's borders, and escorted him back home to Camp Jupiter.

L I

PERCY

The Feast of Fortuna had nothing to do with tuna, which was fine with Percy.

Campers, Amazons and Lares crowded the mess hall for a lavish dinner. Even the fauns were invited, since they'd helped out by bandaging the wounded after the battle. Wind nymphs zipped around the room, delivering orders of pizza, burgers, steaks, salads, Chinese food, and burritos, all flying at terminal velocity.

Despite the exhausting battle, everyone was in good spirits. Casualties had been light, and the few campers who'd previously died and come back to life, like Gwen, hadn't been taken to the Underworld. Maybe Thanatos had turned a blind eye. Or maybe Pluto had given those folks a pass, like he had for Hazel. Whatever the case, nobody complained.

Colorful Amazon and Roman banners hung side-by-side from the rafters. The restored golden eagle stood proudly behind the praetor's table, and the walls were decorated with cornucopias—magical horns of plenty that spilled out recycling waterfalls of fruit, chocolate, and fresh-baked cookies.

The cohorts mingled freely with the Amazons, jumping from couch to couch as they pleased, and for once the soldiers of the Fifth were welcome everywhere. Percy changed seats so many times, he lost track of his dinner.

There was a lot of flirting and arm-wrestling—which seemed to be the same thing for the Amazons. At one point Percy was cornered by Kinzie, the Amazon who'd disarmed him in Seattle. He had to explain that he already had a girl-friend. Fortunately Kinzie took it well. She told him what had happened after they'd left Seattle—how Hylla had defeated her challenger Otrera in two consecutive duels to the death, so that the Amazons were now calling their queen Hylla Twice-Kill.

"Otrera stayed dead the second time," Kinzie said, batting her eyes. "We have you to thank for that. If you ever need a new girlfriend . . . well, I think you'd look great in an iron collar and an orange jumpsuit."

Percy couldn't tell if she was kidding or not. He politely thanked her and changed seats.

Once everyone had eaten and the plates stopped flying, Reyna made a short speech. She formally welcomed the Amazons, thanking them for their help. Then she hugged her sister and everybody applauded.

Reyna raised her hands for quiet. "My sister and I haven't always seen eye to eye—"

Hylla laughed. "That's an understatement."

"She joined the Amazons," Reyna continued. "I joined

Camp Jupiter. But looking around this room, I think we both made good choices. Strangely, our destinies were made possible by the hero you all just raised to praetor on the battlefield —Percy Jackson."

More cheering. The sisters raised their glasses to Percy and beckoned him forward.

Everybody asked for a speech, but Percy didn't know what to say. He protested that he really wasn't the best person for praetor, but the campers drowned him out with applause. Reyna took away his *probatio* neck plate. Octavian shot him a dirty look, then turned to the crowd and smiled like this was all his idea. He ripped open a teddy bear and pronounced good omens for the coming year—Fortuna would bless them! He passed his hand over Percy's arm and shouted: "Percy Jackson, son of Neptune, first year of service!"

The Roman symbols burned onto Percy's arm: a trident, SPQR, and a single stripe. It felt like someone was pressing a hot iron into his skin, but Percy managed not to scream.

Octavian embraced him and whispered, "I hope it hurt."

Then Reyna gave him an eagle medal and purple cloak, symbols of the praetor. "You earned these, Percy."

Queen Hylla pounded him on the back. "And I've decided not to kill you."

"Um, thanks," Percy said.

He made his way around the mess hall one more time, because all the campers wanted him at their table. Vitellius the Lar followed, stumbling over his shimmering purple toga and readjusting his sword, telling everyone how he'd predicted Percy's rise to greatness.

"I demanded he join the Fifth Cohort!" the ghost said proudly. "Spotted his talent right away!"

Don the faun popped up in a nurse's hat, a stack of cookies in each hand. "Man, congrats and stuff! Awesome! Hey, do you have any spare change?"

All the attention embarrassed Percy, but he was happy to see how well Hazel and Frank were being treated. Everyone called them the saviors of Rome, and they deserved it. There was even talk about reinstating Frank's great-grandfather, Shen Lun, to the legion's roll of honor. Apparently he hadn't caused the 1906 earthquake after all.

Percy sat for a while with Tyson and Ella, who were honored guests at Dakota's table. Tyson kept calling for peanut-butter sandwiches, eating them as fast as the nymphs could deliver. Ella perched at his shoulder on top of the couch and nibbled furiously on cinnamon rolls.

"Cinnamon rolls are good for harpies," she said. "June twenty-fourth is a good day. Roy Disney's birthday, and Fortuna's Feast, and Independence Day for Zanzibar. And Tyson."

She glanced at Tyson, then blushed and looked away.

After dinner, the entire legion got the night off. Percy and his friends drifted down to the city, which wasn't quite recovered from the battle, but the fires were out, most of the debris had been swept up, and the citizens were determined to celebrate.

At the Pomerian Line, the statue of Terminus wore a paper party hat.

"Welcome, praetor!" he said. "You need any giants' faces smashed while you're in town, just let me know."

"Thanks, Terminus," Percy said. "I'll keep that in mind."

"Yes, good. Your praetor's cape is an inch too low on the left. There—that's better. Where is my assistant? Julia!"

The little girl ran out from behind the pedestal. She was wearing a green dress tonight, and her hair was still in pigtails. When she smiled, Percy saw that her front teeth were starting to come in. She held up a box full of party hats.

Percy tried to decline, but Julia gave him the big adoring eyes.

"Ah, sure," he said. "I'll take the blue crown."

She offered Hazel a gold pirate hat. "I'm gonna be Percy Jackson when I grow up," she told Hazel solemnly.

Hazel smiled and ruffled her hair. "That's a good thing to be, Julia."

"Although," Frank said, picking out a hat shaped like a polar bear's head, "Frank Zhang would be good too."

"Frank!" Hazel said.

They put on their hats and continued to the forum, which was lit up with multicolored lanterns. The fountains glowed purple. The coffee shops were doing a brisk business, and street musicians filled the air with the sounds of guitar, lyre, panpipes, and armpit noises. (Percy didn't get that last one. Maybe it was an old Roman musical tradition.)

The goddess Iris must've been in a party mood too. As Percy and his friends strolled past the damaged Senate House, a dazzling rainbow appeared in the night sky. Unfortunately the goddess sent another blessing, too—a gentle rain of gluten-free R.O.F.L. cupcake simulations, which Percy figured would either make cleaning up harder, or rebuilding easier. The cupcakes would make great bricks.

For a while, Percy wandered the streets with Hazel and Frank, who kept brushing shoulders.

Finally he said, "I'm a little tired, guys. You go ahead."

Hazel and Frank protested, but Percy could tell they wanted some time alone.

As he headed back to camp, he saw Mrs. O'Leary playing with Hannibal in the Field of Mars. Finally, she'd found a playmate she could roughhouse with. They frolicked around, slamming into each other, breaking fortifications, and generally having an excellent time.

At the fort gates, Percy stopped and gazed across the valley. It seemed like so long ago that he'd stood here with Hazel, getting his first good view of camp. Now he was more interested in watching the eastern horizon.

Tomorrow, maybe the next day, his friends from Camp Half-Blood would arrive. As much as he cared about Camp Jupiter, he couldn't wait to see Annabeth again. He yearned for his old life—New York and Camp Half-Blood—but something told him it might be a while before he returned home. Gaea and the giants weren't done causing trouble—not by a long shot.

Reyna had given him the second praetor's house on the Via Principalis, but as soon as Percy looked inside, he knew he couldn't stay there. It was nice, but it was also full of Jason Grace's stuff. Percy already felt uneasy taking Jason's title of praetor. He didn't want to take the guy's house, too. Things would be awkward enough when Jason came back—and Percy was sure that he would be on that dragon-headed warship.

Percy headed back to the Fifth Cohort barracks and climbed into his bunk. He passed out instantly.

He dreamed he was carrying Juno across the Little Tiber.

She was disguised as a crazy old bag lady, smiling and singing an Ancient Greek lullaby as her leathery hands gripped Percy's neck.

"Do you still want to slap me, dear?" she asked.

Percy stopped midstream. He let go and dumped the goddess in the river.

The moment she hit the water, she vanished and reappeared on the shore. "Oh, my," she cackled, "that wasn't very heroic, even in a dream!"

"Eight months," Percy said. "You stole eight months of my life for a quest that took a week. Why?"

Juno tutted disapprovingly. "You mortals and your short lives. Eight months is nothing, my dear. I lost eight centuries once, missed most of the Byzantine Empire."

Percy summoned the power of the river. It swirled around him, spinning into a froth of whitewater.

"Now, now," Juno said. "Don't get testy. If we are to defeat Gaea, our plans must be timed perfectly. First, I needed Jason and his friends to free me from my prison—"

"Your prison? You were in prison and they let you out?"

"Don't sound so surprised, dear! I'm a sweet old woman. At any rate, you weren't needed at Camp Jupiter until *now*, to save the Romans at their moment of greatest crisis. The eight months between...well, I do have other plans brewing, my boy. Opposing Gaea, working behind Jupiter's back, protecting your friends—it's a full-time job! If I had to guard you from Gaea's monsters and schemes as well, and keep you hidden from your friends back east all that time—no, much better you take a safe nap. You would have been a distraction —a loose cannon."

"A distraction." Percy felt the water rising with his anger, spinning faster around him. "A loose cannon."

"Exactly. I'm glad you understand."

Percy sent a wave crashing down on the old woman, but Juno simply disappeared and materialized farther down the shore.

"My," she said, "you *are* in a bad mood. But you know I'm right. Your timing here was perfect. They trust you now. You are a hero of Rome. And while you slept, Jason Grace has learned to trust the Greeks. They've had time to build the *Argo II*. Together, you and Jason will unite the camps."

"Why me?" Percy demanded. "You and I never got along. Why would you want a loose cannon on your team?"

"Because I *know* you, Percy Jackson. In many ways, you are impulsive, but when it comes to your friends, you are as constant as a compass needle. You are unswervingly loyal, and you inspire loyalty. You are the glue that will unite the seven."

"Great," Percy said. "I always wanted to be glue."

Juno laced her crooked fingers. "The Heroes of Olympus must unite! After your victory over Kronos in Manhattan... well, I fear that wounded Jupiter's self-esteem."

"Because I was right," Percy said. "And he was wrong."

The old lady shrugged. "He should be used to that, after so many eons married to me, but alas! My proud and obstinate husband refuses to ask mere demigods for help again. He believes the giants can be fought without you, and Gaea can be forced back to her slumbers. I know better. But you must prove yourself. Only by sailing to the ancient lands and closing the Doors of Death will you convince Jupiter that you are worthy of fighting side-by-side with the gods. It will be the greatest quest since Aeneas sailed from Troy!"

"And if we fail?" Percy said. "If Romans and Greeks don't get along?"

"Then Gaea has already won. I'll tell you this, Percy Jackson. The one who will cause you the most trouble is the one closest to you—the one who hates me most."

"Annabeth?" Percy felt his anger rising again. "You never liked her. Now you're calling her a troublemaker? You don't know her at all. She's the person I *most* want watching my back."

The goddess smiled dryly. "We will see, young hero. She has a hard task ahead of her when you arrive in Rome. Whether she is up to it . . . I do not know."

Percy summoned a fist of water and smashed it down at the old lady. When the wave receded, she was gone.

The river swirled out of Percy's control. He sank into the darkness of the whirlpool.

PERCY

THE NEXT MORNING, PERCY, HAZEL, AND FRANK ate breakfast early, then headed into the city before the senate was due to convene. As Percy was a praetor now, he could go pretty much wherever he wanted, whenever he wanted.

On the way, they passed the stables, where Tyson and Mrs. O'Leary were sleeping in. Tyson snored on a bed of hay next to the unicorns, a blissful look on his face like he was dreaming of ponies. Mrs. O'Leary had rolled on her back and covered her ears with her paws. On the stable roof, Ella roosted in a pile of old Roman scrolls, her head tucked under her wings.

When they got to the forum, they sat by the fountains and watched the sun come up. The citizens were already busy sweeping up cupcake simulations, confetti, and party hats from last night's celebration. The engineer corps was working on a new arch that would commemorate the victory over Polybotes.

Hazel said she'd even heard talk of a formal *triumph* for the three of them—a parade around the city followed by a week of games and celebrations—but Percy knew they'd never get the chance. They didn't have time.

Percy told them about his dream of Juno.

Hazel frowned. "The gods were busy last night. Show him, Frank."

Frank reached into his coat pocket. Percy thought he might bring out his piece of firewood, but instead he produced a thin paperback book and a note on red stationery.

"These were on my pillow this morning." He passed them to Percy. "Like the Tooth Fairy visited."

The book was *The Art of War* by Sun Tzu. Percy had never heard of it, but he could guess who sent it. The letter read: *Good job, kid. A real man's best weapon is his mind. This was your mom's favorite book. Give it a read. P.S.—I hope your friend Percy has learned some respect for me.*

"Wow." Percy handed back the book. "Maybe Mars *is* different than Ares. I don't think Ares can read."

Frank flipped through the pages. "There's a lot in here about sacrifice, knowing the cost of war. Back in Vancouver, Mars told me I'd have to put my duty ahead of my life or the entire war would go sideways. I thought he meant freeing Thanatos, but now...I don't know. I'm still alive, so maybe the worst is yet to come."

He glanced nervously at Percy, and Percy got the feeling Frank wasn't telling him everything. He wondered if Mars had said something about *him*, but Percy wasn't sure he wanted to know.

Besides, Frank had already given enough. He had watched his family home burn down. He'd lost his mother and his grandmother.

"You risked your life," Percy said. "You were willing to burn up to save the quest. Mars can't expect more than that."

"Maybe," Frank said doubtfully.

Hazel squeezed Frank's hand.

They seemed more comfortable around each other this morning, not quite as nervous and awkward. Percy wondered if they'd started dating. He hoped so, but he decided it was better not to ask.

"Hazel, how about you?" Percy asked. "Any word from Pluto?"

She looked down. Several diamonds popped out of the ground at her feet. "No," she admitted. "In a way, I think he sent a message through Thanatos. My name wasn't on that list of escaped souls. It should have been."

"You think your dad is giving you a pass?" Percy asked.

Hazel shrugged. "Pluto can't visit me or even talk to me without acknowledging I'm alive. Then he'd have to enforce the laws of death and have Thanatos bring me back to the Underworld. I think my dad is turning a blind eye. I think—I think he wants me to find Nico."

Percy glanced at the sunrise, hoping to see a warship descending from the sky. So far, nothing.

"We'll find your brother," Percy promised. "As soon as the ship gets here, we'll sail for Rome."

Hazel and Frank exchanged uneasy looks, like they'd already talked about this.

"Percy..." Frank said. "If you want us to come along, we're in. But are you sure? I mean...we know you've got tons of friends at the other camp. And you could pick anyone at Camp Jupiter now. If we're not part of the seven, we'd understand—"

"Are you kidding?" Percy said. "You think I'd leave my team behind? After surviving Fleecy's wheat germ, running from cannibals, and hiding under blue giant butts in Alaska? Come on!"

The tension broke. All three of them started cracking up, maybe a little too much, but it was a relief to be alive, with the warm sun shining, and not worrying—at least for the moment—about sinister faces appearing in the shadows of the hills.

Hazel took a deep breath. "The prophecy Ella gave us— about the child of wisdom, and the mark of Athena burning through Rome...do you know what that's about?"

Percy remembered his dream. Juno had warned that Annabeth had a difficult job ahead of her, and that she'd cause trouble for the quest. He couldn't believe that, but still ...it worried him.

"I'm not sure," he admitted. "I think there's more to the prophecy. Maybe Ella can remember the rest of it."

Frank slipped his book into his pocket. "We need to take her with us—I mean, for her own safety. If Octavian finds out Ella has the Sibylline Books memorized..."

Percy shuddered. Octavian used prophecies to keep his power at camp. Now that Percy had taken away his chance at praetor, Octavian would be looking for other ways to exert influence. If he got hold of Ella...

"You're right," Percy said. "We've got to protect her. I just hope we can convince her—"

"Percy!" Tyson came running across the forum, Ella fluttering behind him with a scroll in her talons. When they reached the fountain, Ella dropped the scroll in Percy's lap.

"Special delivery," she said. "From an aura. A wind spirit. Yes, Ella got a special delivery."

"Good morning, brothers!" Tyson had hay in his hair and peanut butter in his teeth. "The scroll is from Leo. He is funny and small."

The scroll looked unremarkable, but when Percy spread it across his lap, a video recording flickered on the parchment. A kid in Greek armor grinned up at them. He had an impish face, curly black hair, and wild eyes, like he'd just had several cups of coffee. He was sitting in a dark room with timber walls like a ship's cabin. Oil lamps swung back and forth on the ceiling.

Hazel stifled a scream.

"What?" Frank asked. "What's wrong?"

Slowly, Percy realized the curly-haired kid looked familiar —and not just from his dreams. He'd seen that face in an old photo.

"Hey!" said the guy in the video. "Greetings from your friends at Camp Half-Blood, et cetera. This is Leo. I'm the..." He looked off screen and yelled: "What's my title? Am I like admiral, or captain, or—"

A girl's voice yelled back, "Repair boy."

"Very funny, Piper," Leo grumbled. He turned back to the parchment screen. "So yeah, I'm...ah...supreme commander of the *Argo II*. Yeah, I like that! Anyway, we're gonna be sailing toward you in about, I dunno, an hour in this big mother warship. We'd appreciate it if you'd not, like, blow us out of the sky or anything. So okay! If you could tell the Romans that. See you soon. Yours in demigodishness, and all that. Peace out."

The parchment turned blank.

"It can't be," Hazel said.

"What?" Frank asked. "You know that guy?"

Hazel looked like she'd seen a ghost. Percy understood why. He remembered the photo in Hazel's abandoned house in Seward. The kid on the warship looked exactly like Hazel's old boyfriend.

"It's Sammy Valdez," she said. "But how . . . how—"

"It can't be," Percy said. "That guy's name is Leo. And it's been seventy-something years. It has to be a . . ."

He wanted to say *a coincidence*, but he couldn't make himself believe that. Over the past few years he'd seen a lot of things: destiny, prophecy, magic, monsters, fate. But he'd never yet run across a coincidence.

They were interrupted by horns blowing in the distance. The senators came marching into the forum with Reyna at the lead.

"It's meeting time," Percy said. "Come on. We've got to warn them about the warship."

"Why should we trust these Greeks?" Octavian was saying.

He'd been pacing the senate floor for five minutes, going on and on, trying to counter what Percy had told them about Juno's plan and the Prophecy of Seven.

The senate shifted restlessly, but most of them were too afraid to interrupt Octavian while he was on a roll. Meanwhile the sun climbed in the sky, shining through the broken senate roof and giving Octavian a natural spotlight.

The Senate House was packed. Queen Hylla, Frank, and Hazel sat in the front row with the senators. Veterans and ghosts filled the back rows. Even Tyson and Ella had been allowed to sit in the back. Tyson kept waving and grinning at Percy.

Percy and Reyna occupied matching praetors' chairs on the dais, which made Percy self-conscious. It wasn't easy looking dignified wearing a bedsheet and a purple cape.

"The camp is safe," Octavian continued. "I'll be the first to congratulate our heroes for bringing back the legion's eagle and so much Imperial gold! Truly we have been blessed with good fortune. But why do more? Why tempt fate?"

"I'm glad you asked." Percy stood, taking the question as an opening.

Octavian stammered, "I wasn't—"

"—part of the quest," Percy said. "Yes, I know. And you're wise to let me explain, since I was."

Some of the senators snickered. Octavian had no choice but to sit down and try not to look embarrassed.

"Gaea is waking," Percy said. "We've defeated two of her giants, but that's only the beginning. The real war will take place in the old land of the gods. The quest will take us to Rome, and eventually to Greece."

An uneasy ripple spread through the senate.

"I know, I know," Percy said. "You've always thought of

the Greeks as your enemies. And there's a good reason for that. I think the gods have kept our two camps apart because whenever we meet, we fight. But that can change. It *has* to change if we're to defeat Gaea. That's what the Prophecy of Seven means. Seven demigods, Greek and Roman, will have to close the Doors of Death together."

"Ha!" shouted a Lar from the back row. "The last time a praetor tried to interpret the Prophecy of Seven, it was Michael Varus, who lost our eagle in Alaska! Why should we believe you now?"

Octavian smiled smugly. Some of his allies in the senate began nodding and grumbling. Even some of the veterans looked uncertain.

"I carried Juno across the Tiber," Percy reminded them, speaking as firmly as he could. "*She* told me that the Prophecy of Seven is coming to pass. Mars also appeared to you in person. Do you think two of your most important gods would appear at camp if the situation wasn't serious?"

"He's right," Gwen said from the second row. "I, for one, trust Percy's word. Greek or not, he restored the honor of the legion. You saw him on the battlefield last night. Would anyone here say he is not a true hero of Rome?"

Nobody argued. A few nodded in agreement.

Reyna stood. Percy watched her anxiously. Her opinion could change everything—for better or worse.

"You claim this is a combined quest," she said. "You claim Juno intends for us to work with this—this other group, Camp Half-Blood. Yet the Greeks have been our enemies for eons. They are known for their deceptions."

"Maybe so," Percy said. "But enemies can become friends. A week ago, would you have thought Romans and Amazons would be fighting side by side?"

Queen Hylla laughed. "He's got a point."

"The demigods of Camp Half-Blood have *already* been working with Camp Jupiter," Percy said. "We just didn't realize it. During the Titan War last summer, while you were attacking Mount Othrys, we were defending Mount Olympus in Manhattan. I fought Kronos myself."

Reyna backed up, almost tripping over her toga. "You... *what?*"

"I know it's hard to believe," Percy said. "But I think I've earned your trust. I'm on your side. Hazel and Frank—I'm sure they're meant to go with me on this quest. The other four are on their way from Camp Half-Blood right now. One of them is Jason Grace, your old praetor."

"Oh, come on!" Octavian shouted. "He's making things up, now."

Reyna frowned. "It is a lot to believe. Jason is coming back with a bunch of Greek demigods? You say they're going to appear in the sky in a heavily armed warship, but we shouldn't be worried."

"Yes." Percy looked over the rows of nervous, doubtful spectators. "Just let them land. Hear them out. Jason will back up everything I'm telling you. I swear it on my life."

"On your life?" Octavian looked meaningfully at the senate. "We will remember that, if this turns out to be a trick."

Right on cue, a messenger rushed into the Senate House, gasping as if he'd run all the way from camp. "Praetors! I'm sorry to interrupt, but our scouts report—"

"Ship!" Tyson said happily, pointing at the hole in the ceiling. "Yay!

Sure enough, a Greek warship appeared out of the clouds, about a half a mile away, descending toward the Senate House. As it got closer, Percy could see bronze shields glinting along the sides, billowing sails, and a familiar-looking figurchcad shaped like a metal dragon. On the tallest mast, a big white flag of truce snapped in the wind.

The *Argo II*. It was the most incredible ship he'd ever seen.

"Praetors!" the messenger cried. "What are your orders?"

Octavian shot to his feet. "You need to ask?" His face was red with rage. He was strangling his teddy bear. "The omens are *horrible*! This is a trick, a deception. Beware Greeks bearing gifts!"

He jabbed a finger at Percy. "His *friends* are attacking in a warship. He has *led* them here. We must attack!"

"No," Percy said firmly. "You all raised me as praetor for a reason. I will fight to defend this camp with my life. But these aren't enemies. I say we stand ready, but do *not* attack. Let them land. Let them speak. If it is a trick, then I will fight with you, as I did last night. But it is *not* a trick."

All eyes turned toward Reyna.

She studied the approaching warship. Her expression hardened. If she vetoed Percy's orders ... well, he didn't know what would happen. Chaos and confusion, at the very least.

Most likely, the Romans would follow her lead. She'd been their leader much longer than Percy.

"Hold your fire," Reyna said. "But have the legion stand ready. Percy Jackson is your duly chosen praetor. We will trust his word—unless we are given clear reason not to. Senators, let us adjourn to the forum and meet our ... new friends."

The senators stampeded out of the auditorium—whether from excitement or panic, Percy wasn't sure. Tyson ran after them, yelling, "Yay! Yay!" with Ella fluttering around his head.

Octavian gave Percy a disgusted look, then threw down his teddy bear and followed the crowd.

Reyna stood at Percy's shoulder.

"I support you, Percy," she said. "I trust your judgment. But for all our sakes, I hope we can keep the peace between our campers and your Greek friends."

"We will," he promised. "You'll see."

She glanced up at the warship. Her expression turned a little wistful. "You say Jason is aboard ... I hope that's true. I've missed him."

She marched outside, leaving Percy alone with Hazel and Frank.

"They're coming down right in the forum," Frank said nervously. "Terminus is going to have a heart attack."

"Percy," Hazel said, "you swore on your life. Romans take that seriously. If anything goes wrong, even by accident, Octavian is going to kill you. You know that, right?"

Percy smiled. He knew the stakes were high. He knew this day could go horribly wrong. But he also knew that Annabeth was on that ship. If things went *right,* this would be the best day of his life.

He threw one arm around Hazel and one arm around Frank.

"Come on," he said. "Let me introduce you to my *other* family."

Glossary

absurdus out of place, discordant

Achilles the mightiest of the Greek demigods who fought in the Trojan War

Aesculapius the Roman god of medicine and healing

Alcyoneus the eldest of the giants born to Gaea, destined to fight Pluto

Amazons a nation of all-female warriors

Anaklusmos Riptide. The name of Percy Jackson's sword.

argentum silver

Argonauts a band of Greek heroes who accompanied Jason on his quest to find the Golden Fleece. Their name comes from their ship, the *Argo*, which was named after its builder, Argus.

augury a sign of something coming, an omen; the practice of divining the future

aurae invisible wind spirits

aurum gold

basilisk snake, literally "little crown"

Bellerophon a Greek demigod, son of Poseidon, who defeated monsters while riding on Pegasus

Bellona the Roman goddess of war

Byzantium the eastern empire that lasted another 1,000 years after Rome fell, under Greek influence

Celestial bronze a rare metal deadly to monsters

Centaur a race of creatures that is half human, half horse

centurion an officer of the Roman army

Cerberus the three-headed dog that guards the gates of the Underworld

Ceres the Roman goddess of agriculture

Charon the ferryman of Hades who carries souls of the newly deceased across the rivers Styx and Acheron, which divide the world of the living from the world of the dead

cognomen third name

cohort a Roman military unit

Cyclops a member of a primordial race of giants (**Cyclopes**, pl.), each with a single eye in the middle of his or her forehead

denarius (**denarii**, pl.) the most common coin in the Roman currency system

drachma the silver coin of ancient Greece

Elysium the final resting place of the souls of the heroic and the virtuous in the Underworld

Erebos a place of darkness between Earth and Hades

faun a Roman forest god, part goat and part man. Greek form: satyr

Fields of Asphodel the section of the Underworld where the souls of people who lived lives of equal good and evil rest

Fields of Punishment the section of the Underworld where evil souls are eternally tortured

Fortuna the Roman goddess of fortune and good luck

Fulminata armed with lightning. A Roman legion under Julius Caesar whose emblem was a lightning bolt (*fulmen*).

Gaea the earth goddess; mother of Titans, giants, Cyclopes, and other monsters. Known to the Romans as Terra

Gegenes earthborn monsters

gladius a short sword

gorgons three monstrous sisters (Stheno, Euryale, and Medusa) who have hair of living, venomous snakes; Medusa's eyes can turn the beholder to stone

graecus Greek; enemy; outsider

greaves shin armor

gris-gris a voodoo amulet that protects from evil or brings luck

harpy a winged female creature that snatches things

Hercules the Roman equivalent of Heracles; the son of Jupiter and Alcmene, who was born with great strength

Hyperboreans peaceful northern giants

ichor the golden blood of immortals

Imperial gold a rare metal deadly to monsters, consecrated at the Pantheon; its existence was a closely guarded secret of the emperors

Iris the rainbow goddess

Juno   Roman goddess of women, marriage, and fertility; sister and wife of Jupiter; mother of Mars. Greek form: Hera

Jupiter   Roman king of the gods; also called Jupiter Optimus Maximus (the best and the greatest). Greek form: Zeus

karpoi   grain spirits

Laistrygonians   tall cannibals from the north, possibly the source of the Sasquatch legend

Lar   house god, ancestral spirit (**Lares**, pl.)

legion   the major unit of the Roman army, consisting of infantry and cavalry troops

legionnaire   a member of a legion

Liberalia   a Roman festival that celebrated a boy's rite of passage into manhood

Lupa   the sacred Roman she-wolf that nursed the foundling twins Romulus and Remus

Mars   the Roman god of war; also called Mars Ultor. Patron of the empire; divine father of Romulus and Remus. Greek form: Ares

Minerva   Roman goddess of wisdom. Greek form: Athena

Mist   magic force that disguises things from mortals

Mount Othrys   the base of the Titans during the ten-year war with the Olympian gods; Saturn's headquarters

muster   formal military inspection

nebulae   cloud nymphs

Neptune   the Roman god of the sea. Greek form: Poseidon

Otrera   first Amazon queen, daughter of Ares

pallium   a cloak or mantle worn by the Romans

Pantheon   a temple to all the gods of Ancient Rome

Penthesilea   a queen of the Amazons; daughter of Ares and Otrera, another Amazon queen

Periclymenus   a Greek prince of Pylos and a son of Poseidon, who granted him the ability to shape-shift. He was renowned for his strength and participated in the voyage of the Argonauts.

Phineas   a son of Poseidon, who had the gift of prophecy. When he revealed too much of the plans of the gods, Zeus punished him by blinding him.

pilum   a Roman spear

Pluto   the Roman god of death and riches. Greek equivalent: Hades

Polybotes   the giant son of Gaea, the Earth Mother

practor   an elected Roman magistrate and commander of the army

Priam   the king of Troy during the Trojan War

principia   the headquarters of a Roman camp

probatio   testing period for a new recruit in a legion

pugio   a Roman dagger

Queen Hippolyta's belt   Hippolyta wore a golden waist belt, a gift from her father, Ares, that signified her Amazonian queenship and also gave her strength.

retiarius   Roman gladiator who fought with a net and trident

River Styx   the river that forms the boundary between Earth and the Underworld

Romulus and Remus   the twin sons of Mars and the priestess Rhea Silvia who were thrown into the River Tiber by their human father, Amulius. They were rescued and raised by a she-wolf and, upon reaching adulthood, founded Rome.

Saturn the Roman god of agriculture, the son of Uranus and Gaea and the father of Jupiter. Greek equivalent: Kronos

scorpion ballista a Roman missile siege weapon that launched a large projectile at a distant target

***Senatus Populusque Romanus* (SPQR)** "The Senate and People of Rome"; refers to the government of the Roman Republic and is used as an official emblem of Rome

shades spirits

Sibylline Books a collection of prophecies in rhyme written in Greek. Tarquinius Superbus, a king of Rome, bought them from a prophetess named Sibyl and consulted them in times of great danger.

spartus a skeleton warrior

spatha a cavalry sword

Stygian iron like Celestial bronze and Imperial gold, a magical metal capable of killing monsters

Tartarus husband of Gaea; spirit of the abyss; father of the giants; also the lowest region of the world

Terminus the Roman god of boundaries and landmarks

Thanatos the Greek god of death. Roman equivalent: Letus

Tiber River the third-longest river in Italy. Rome was founded on its banks. In ancient Rome, executed criminals were thrown into the river.

trireme a type of warship

triumph a ceremonial procession for Roman generals and their troops in celebration of a great military victory

Trojan War   the war that was waged against the city of Troy by the Greeks after Paris of Troy took Helen from her husband, Menelaus, the king of Sparta. It started with a quarrel between the goddesses Athena, Hera, and Aphrodite.

Coming Fall 2013

The Heroes of Olympus, Book Four

THE HOUSE OF HADES

Still craving adventure?
Travel the globe with Carter and Sadie Kane
as they uncover the secrets of ancient
Egypt and their own family in
The Kane Chronicles, Book One

The
RED
Pyramid

WARNING

The following is a transcript of a digital recording. In certain places, the audio quality was poor, so some words and phrases represent the author's best guesses. Where possible, illustrations of important symbols mentioned in the recording have been added. Background noises such as scuffling, hitting, and cursing by the two speakers have not been transcribed. The author makes no claims for the authenticity of the recording. It seems impossible that the two young narrators are telling the truth, but you, the reader, must decide for yourself.

1. A Death at the Needle

WE ONLY HAVE A FEW HOURS, so listen carefully.

If you're hearing this story, you're already in danger. Sadie and I might be your only chance.

Go to the school. Find the locker. I won't tell you which school or which locker, because if you're the right person, you'll find it. The combination is 13/32/33. By the time you finish listening, you'll know what those numbers mean. Just remember the story we're about to tell you isn't complete yet. How it ends will depend on you.

The most important thing: when you open the package and find what's inside, *don't* keep it longer than a week. Sure, it'll be tempting. I mean, it will grant you almost unlimited power. But if you possess it too long, it will consume you. Learn its secrets quickly and pass it on. Hide it for the next person, the way Sadie and I did for you. Then be prepared for your life to get very interesting.

Okay, Sadie is telling me to stop stalling and get on with

the story. Fine. I guess it started in London, the night our dad blew up the British Museum.

My name is Carter Kane. I'm fourteen and my home is a suitcase.

You think I'm kidding? Since I was eight years old, my dad and I have traveled the world. I was born in L.A. but my dad's an archaeologist, so his work takes him all over. Mostly we go to Egypt, since that's his specialty. Go into a bookstore, find a book about Egypt, there's a pretty good chance it was written by Dr. Julius Kane. You want to know how Egyptians pulled the brains out of mummies, or built the pyramids, or cursed King Tut's tomb? My dad is your man. Of course, there are other reasons my dad moved around so much, but I didn't know his secret back then.

I didn't go to school. My dad homeschooled me, if you can call it "home" schooling when you don't have a home. He sort of taught me whatever he thought was important, so I learned a lot about Egypt and basketball stats and my dad's favorite musicians. I read a lot, too—pretty much anything I could get my hands on, from dad's history books to fantasy novels—because I spent a lot of time sitting around in hotels and airports and dig sites in foreign countries where I didn't know anybody. My dad was always telling me to put the book down and play some ball. You ever try to start a game of pick-up basketball in Aswan, Egypt? It's not easy.

Anyway, my dad trained me early to keep all my posses-sions in a single suitcase that fits in an airplane's overhead compartment. My dad packed the same way, except he was allowed an extra workbag for his archaeology tools. Rule number one: I was not allowed to look in his workbag. That's a rule I never broke until the day of the explosion.

It happened on Christmas Eve. We were in London for visitation day with my sister, Sadie.

See, Dad's only allowed two days a year with her—one in the winter, one in the summer—because our grandparents hate him. After our mom died, her parents (our grandparents) had this big court battle with Dad. After six lawyers, two fistfights, and a near fatal attack with a spatula (don't ask), they won the right to keep Sadie with them in England. She was only six, two years younger than me, and they couldn't keep us both—at least that was their excuse for not taking me. So Sadie was raised as a British schoolkid, and I traveled around with my dad. We only saw Sadie twice a year, which was fine with me.

[Shut up, Sadie. Yes—I'm getting to that part.]

So anyway, my dad and I had just flown into Heathrow after a couple of delays. It was a drizzly, cold afternoon. The whole taxi ride into the city, my dad seemed kind of nervous.

Now, my dad is a big guy. You wouldn't think anything could make him nervous. He has dark brown skin like mine, piercing brown eyes, a bald head, and a goatee, so he looks like a buff evil scientist. That afternoon he wore his cashmere winter coat and his best brown suit, the one he used for public lectures. Usually he exudes so much confidence that he dominates any room he walks into, but sometimes—like that afternoon—I saw another side to him that I didn't really understand. He kept looking over his shoulder like we were being hunted.

"Dad?" I said as we were getting off the A-40. "What's wrong?"

"No sign of them," he muttered. Then he must've realized he'd spoken aloud, because he looked at me kind of startled. "Nothing, Carter. Everything's fine."

Which bothered me because my dad's a terrible liar. I always knew when he was hiding something, but I also knew no amount of pestering would get the truth out of him. He was probably trying to protect me, though from what I didn't know. Sometimes I wondered if he had some dark secret in his past, some old enemy following him, maybe; but the idea seemed ridiculous. Dad was just an archaeologist.

The other thing that troubled me: Dad was clutching his workbag. Usually when he does that, it means we're in danger. Like the time gunmen stormed our hotel in Cairo. I heard shots coming from the lobby and ran downstairs to check on my dad. By the time I got there, he was just calmly zipping up his workbag while three unconscious gunmen hung by their feet from the chandelier, their robes falling over their heads so you could see their boxer shorts. Dad claimed not to have witnessed anything, and in the end the police blamed a freak chandelier malfunction.

Another time, we got caught in a riot in Paris. My dad found the nearest parked car, pushed me into the backseat, and told me to stay down. I pressed myself against the floorboards and kept my eyes shut tight. I could hear Dad in the driver's seat, rummaging in his bag, mumbling something to himself while the mob yelled and destroyed things outside. A few minutes later he told me it was safe to get up. Every other car on the block had been overturned and set on fire. Our car had been freshly washed and polished, and several twenty-euro notes had been tucked under the windshield wipers.

Anyway, I'd come to respect the bag. It was our good luck charm. But when my dad kept it close, it meant we were going to need good luck.

We drove through the city center, heading east toward my grandparents' flat. We passed the golden gates of Buckingham Palace, the big stone column in Trafalgar Square. London is a pretty cool place, but after you've traveled for so long, all cities start to blend together. Other kids I meet sometimes say, "Wow, you're so lucky you get to travel so much." But it's not like we spend our time sightseeing or have a lot of money to travel in style. We've stayed in some pretty rough places, and we hardly ever stay anywhere longer than a few days. Most of the time it feels like we're fugitives rather than tourists.

I mean, you wouldn't think my dad's work was dangerous. He does lectures on topics like "Can Egyptian Magic Really Kill You?" and "Favorite Punishments in the Egyptian Underworld" and other stuff most people wouldn't care about. But like I said, there's that other side to him. He's always very cautious, checking every hotel room before he lets me walk into it. He'll dart into a museum to see some artifacts, take a few notes, and rush out again like he's afraid to be caught on the security cameras.

One time when I was younger, we raced across the Charles de Gaulle airport to catch a last-minute flight, and Dad didn't relax until the plane was off the ground. I asked him point blank what he was running from, and he looked at me like I'd just pulled the pin out of a grenade. For a second I was scared he might actually tell me the truth. Then he said, "Carter, it's nothing." As if "nothing" were the most terrible thing in the world.

After that, I decided maybe it was better not to ask questions.

My grandparents, the Fausts, live in a housing development near Canary Wharf, right on the banks of the River Thames. The taxi let us off at the curb, and my dad asked the driver to wait.

We were halfway up the walk when Dad froze. He turned and looked behind us.

"What?" I asked.

Then I saw the man in the trench coat. He was across the street, leaning against a big dead tree. He was barrel shaped, with skin the color of roasted coffee. His coat and black pinstriped suit looked expensive. He had long braided hair and wore a black fedora pulled down low over his dark round glasses. He reminded me of a jazz musician, the kind my dad would always drag me to see in concert. Even though I couldn't see his eyes, I got the impression he was watching us. He might've been an old friend or colleague of Dad's. No matter where we went, Dad was always running into people he knew. But it did seem strange that the guy was waiting here, outside my grandparents'. And he didn't look happy.

"Carter," my dad said, "go on ahead."

"But—"

"Get your sister. I'll meet you back at the taxi."

He crossed the street toward the man in the trench coat, which left me with two choices: follow my dad and see what was going on, or do what I was told.

I decided on the slightly less dangerous path. I went to retrieve my sister.

Before I could even knock, Sadie opened the door.

"Late as usual," she said.

She was holding her cat, Muffin, who'd been a "going away" gift from Dad six years before. Muffin never seemed to get older or bigger. She had fuzzy yellow-and-black fur like a miniature leopard, alert yellow eyes, and pointy ears that were too tall for her head. A silver Egyptian pendant dangled from her collar. She didn't look anything like a muffin, but Sadie had been little when she named her, so I guess you have to cut her some slack.

Sadie hadn't changed much either since last summer.

[As I'm recording this, she's standing next to me, glaring, so I'd better be careful how I describe her.]

You would never guess she's my sister. First of all, she'd been living in England so long, she has a British accent. Second, she takes after our mom, who was white, so Sadie's skin is much lighter than mine. She has straight caramel-colored hair, not exactly blond but not brown, which she usually dyes with streaks of bright colors. That day it had red streaks down the left side. Her eyes are blue. I'm serious. *Blue* eyes, just like our mom's. She's only twelve, but she's exactly as tall as me, which is really annoying. She was chewing gum as usual, dressed for her day out with Dad in battered jeans, a leather jacket, and combat boots, like she was going to a concert and was hoping to stomp on some people. She had headphones dangling around her neck in case we bored her.

[Okay, she didn't hit me, so I guess I did an okay job of describing her.]

"Our plane was late," I told her.

She popped a bubble, rubbed Muffin's head, and tossed the cat inside. "Gran, going out!"

From somewhere in the house, Grandma Faust said something I couldn't make out, probably "Don't let them in!"

Sadie closed the door and regarded me as if I were a dead mouse her cat had just dragged in. "So, here you are again."

"Yep."

"Come on, then." She sighed. "Let's get on with it."

That's the way she was. No "Hi, how you been the last six months? So glad to see you!" or anything. But that was okay with me. When you only see each other twice a year, it's like you're distant cousins rather than siblings. We had absolutely nothing in common except our parents.

We trudged down the steps. I was thinking how she smelled like a combination of old people's house and bubble gum when she stopped so abruptly, I ran into her.

"Who's that?" she asked.

I'd almost forgotten about the dude in the trench coat. He and my dad were standing across the street next to the big tree, having what looked like a serious argument. Dad's back was turned so I couldn't see his face, but he gestured with his hands like he does when he's agitated. The other guy scowled and shook his head.

"Dunno," I said. "He was there when we pulled up."

"He looks familiar." Sadie frowned like she was trying to remember. "Come on."

"Dad wants us to wait in the cab," I said, even though I knew it was no use. Sadie was already on the move.

Instead of going straight across the street, she dashed up the sidewalk for half a block, ducking behind cars, then crossed to the opposite side and crouched under a stone wall. She started sneaking toward our dad. I didn't have much choice but to follow her example, even though it made me feel kind of stupid.

"Six years in England," I muttered, "and she thinks she's James Bond."

Sadie swatted me without looking back and kept creeping forward.

A couple more steps and we were right behind the big dead tree. I could hear my dad on the other side, saying, "—have to, Amos. You know it's the right thing."

"No," said the other man, who must've been Amos. His voice was deep and even—very insistent. His accent was American. "If *I* don't stop you, Julius, *they* will. The Per Ankh is shadowing you."

Sadie turned to me and mouthed the words "Per *what?*"

I shook my head, just as mystified. "Let's get out of here," I whispered, because I figured we'd be spotted any minute and get in serious trouble. Sadie, of course, ignored me.

"They don't know my plan," my father was saying. "By the time they figure it out—"

"And the children?" Amos asked. The hairs stood up on the back of my neck. "What about them?"

"I've made arrangements to protect them," my dad said. "Besides, if I don't do this, we're all in danger. Now, back off."

"I can't, Julius."

"Then it's a duel you want?" Dad's tone turned deadly serious. "You never could beat me, Amos."

I hadn't seen my dad get violent since the Great Spatula Incident, and I wasn't anxious to see a repeat of that, but the two men seemed to be edging toward a fight.

Before I could react, Sadie popped up and shouted, "Dad!"

He looked surprised when she tackle-hugged him, but not nearly as surprised as the other guy, Amos. He backed up so quickly, he tripped over his own trench coat.

He'd taken off his glasses. I couldn't help thinking that Sadie was right. He did look familiar—like a very distant memory.

"I—I must be going," he said. He straightened his fedora and lumbered down the road.

Our dad watched him go. He kept one arm protectively around Sadie and one hand inside the workbag slung over his shoulder. Finally, when Amos disappeared around the corner, Dad relaxed. He took his hand out of the bag and smiled at Sadie. "Hello, sweetheart."

Sadie pushed away from him and crossed her arms. "Oh, now it's sweetheart, is it? You're late. Visitation Day's nearly over! And what was that about? Who's Amos, and what's the Per Ankh?"

Dad stiffened. He glanced at me like he was wondering how much we'd overheard.

"It's nothing," he said, trying to sound upbeat. "I have a wonderful evening planned. Who'd like a private tour of the British Museum?"

Sadie slumped in the back of the taxi between Dad and me.

"I can't believe it," she grumbled. "One evening together, and you want to do research."

Dad tried for a smile. "Sweetheart, it'll be fun. The curator of the Egyptian collection personally invited—"

"Right, big surprise." Sadie blew a strand of red-streaked hair out of her face. "Christmas Eve, and we're going to see some moldy old relics from Egypt. Do you ever think about *anything* else?"

Dad didn't get mad. He never gets mad at Sadie. He just stared out the window at the darkening sky and the rain.

"Yes," he said quietly. "I do."

Whenever Dad got quiet like that and stared off into nowhere, I knew he was thinking about our mom. The last few months, it had been happening a lot. I'd walk into our hotel room and find him with his cell phone in his hands, Mom's picture smiling up at him from the screen—her hair tucked under a headscarf, her blue eyes startlingly bright against the desert backdrop.

Or we'd be at some dig site. I'd see Dad staring at the horizon, and I'd know he was remembering how he'd met her—two young scientists in the Valley of the Kings, on a dig to discover a lost tomb. Dad was an Egyptologist. Mom was an anthropologist looking for ancient DNA. He'd told me the story a thousand times.

Our taxi snaked its way along the banks of the Thames. Just past Waterloo Bridge, my dad tensed.

"Driver," he said. "Stop here a moment."

The cabbie pulled over on the Victoria Embankment.

"What is it, Dad?" I asked.

He got out of the cab like he hadn't heard me. When Sadie and I joined him on the sidewalk, he was staring up at Cleopatra's Needle.

In case you've never seen it: the Needle is an obelisk, not a needle, and it doesn't have anything to do with Cleopatra. I guess the British just thought the name sounded cool when they brought it to London. It's about seventy feet tall, which would've been really impressive back in Ancient Egypt, but on the Thames, with all the tall buildings around, it looks small and sad. You could drive right by it and not even realize you'd just passed something that was a thousand years older than the city of London.

"God." Sadie walked around in a frustrated circle. "Do we have to stop for *every* monument?"

My dad stared at the top of the obelisk. "I had to see it again," he murmured. "Where it happened..."

A freezing wind blew off the river. I wanted to get back in the cab, but my dad was really starting to worry me. I'd never seen him so distracted.

"What, Dad?" I asked. "What happened here?"

"The last place I saw her."

Sadie stopped pacing. She scowled at me uncertainly, then back at Dad. "Hang on. Do you mean Mum?"

Dad brushed Sadie's hair behind her ear, and she was so surprised, she didn't even push him away.

I felt like the rain had frozen me solid. Mom's death had always been a forbidden subject. I knew she'd died in an accident in London. I knew my grandparents blamed my dad. But no one would ever tell us the details. I'd given up asking my dad, partly because it made him so sad, partly because he absolutely refused to tell me anything. "When you're older" was all he would say, which was the most frustrating response ever.

"You're telling us she died here," I said. "At Cleopatra's Needle? What happened?"

He lowered his head.

"Dad!" Sadie protested. "I go past this *every* day, and you mean to say—all this time—and I didn't even *know*?"

"Do you still have your cat?" Dad asked her, which seemed like a really stupid question.

"Of course I've still got the cat!" she said. "What does that have to do with anything?"

"And your amulet?"

Sadie's hand went to her neck. When we were little, right before Sadie went to live with our grandparents, Dad had given us both Egyptian amulets. Mine was an Eye of Horus, which was a popular protection symbol in Ancient Egypt.

In fact my dad says the modern pharmacist's symbol, ℞, is a simplified version of the Eye of Horus, because medicine is supposed to protect you.

Anyway, I always wore my amulet under my shirt, but I figured Sadie would've lost hers or thrown it away.

To my surprise, she nodded. "'Course I have it, Dad, but don't change the subject. Gran's always going on about how you caused Mum's death. That's not true, is it?"

We waited. For once, Sadie and I wanted exactly the same thing—the truth.

"The night your mother died," my father started, "here at the Needle—"

A sudden flash illuminated the embankment. I turned, half blind, and just for a moment I glimpsed two figures: a tall pale man with a forked beard and wearing cream-colored robes, and a coppery-skinned girl in dark blue robes and a headscarf—the kind of clothes I'd seen hundreds of times in Egypt. They were just standing there side by side, not twenty feet away, watching us. Then the light faded. The figures melted into a fuzzy afterimage. When my eyes readjusted to the darkness, they were gone.

"Um…" Sadie said nervously. "Did you just see that?"

"Get in the cab," my dad said, pushing us toward the curb. "We're out of time."

From that point on, Dad clammed up.

"This isn't the place to talk," he said, glancing behind us. He'd promised the cabbie an extra ten pounds if he got us to the museum in under five minutes, and the cabbie was doing his best.

"Dad," I tried, "those people at the river—"

"And the other bloke, Amos," Sadie said. "Are they Egyptian police or something?"

"Look, both of you," Dad said, "I'm going to need your help tonight. I know it's hard, but you have to be patient. I'll explain everything, I promise, after we get to the museum. I'm going to make everything right again."

"What do you mean?" Sadie insisted. "Make *what* right?"

Dad's expression was more than sad. It was almost guilty. With a chill, I thought about what Sadie had said: about our grandparents blaming him for Mom's death. That *couldn't* be what he was talking about, could it?

The cabbie swerved onto Great Russell Street and screeched to a halt in front of the museum's main gates.

"Just follow my lead," Dad told us. "When we meet the curator, act normal."

I was thinking that Sadie never acted *normal*, but I decided not to say anything.

We climbed out of the cab. I got our luggage while Dad paid the driver with a big wad of cash. Then he did something strange. He threw a handful of small objects into the backseat—they looked like stones, but it was too dark for me to be sure. "Keep driving," he told the cabbie. "Take us to Chelsea."

That made no sense since we were already out of the cab, but the driver sped off. I glanced at Dad, then back at the cab, and before it turned the corner and disappeared in the dark, I caught a weird glimpse of three passengers in the backseat: a man and two kids.

I blinked. There was no way the cab could've picked up another fare so fast. "Dad—"

"London cabs don't stay empty very long," he said matter-of-factly. "Come along, kids."

He marched off through the wrought iron gates. For a second, Sadie and I hesitated.

"Carter, *what* is going on?"

I shook my head. "I'm not sure I want to know."

"Well, stay out here in the cold if you want, but *I'm* not leaving without an explanation." She turned and marched after our dad.

Looking back on it, I should've run. I should've dragged Sadie out of there and gotten as far away as possible. Instead I followed her through the gates.

Don't miss any of
Rick Riordan's exciting series . . .

PERCY JACKSON & THE OLYMPIANS

Praise for The Kane Chronicles by Rick Riordan:

The Red Pyramid

★ "The first volume in the Kane Chronicles, this fantasy adventure delivers what fans loved about the Percy Jackson and the Olympians series: young protagonists with previously unsuspected magical powers, a riveting story marked by headlong adventure, a complex background rooted in ancient mythology, and wry, witty twenty-first-century narration."

—*ALA Booklist* (starred review)

The Throne of Fire

★ "... Riordan kickstarts the action, never lets up on the gas, balances laughs and losses with a sure hand, and expertly sets up the coming climactic struggle without (thankfully) ending on a cliff-hanger. It's a grand ride so far, showing nary a sign of slowing down."

—*School Library Journal* (starred review)

The Serpent's Shadow

"Beyond the explosive action and fireworks, Riordan deftly develops the theme of the duality of the universe—order versus chaos, living a normal life versus risking the extraordinary, being protected by parents versus growing up and stepping out of their shadows. A rousing adventure with plenty of magic and food for thought."

—*Kirkus Reviews*

RICK RIORDAN is the author of the *New York Times* #1 best-selling Percy Jackson and the Olympians series: Book One: *The Lightning Thief*; Book Two: *The Sea of Monsters*; Book Three: *The Titan's Curse*; Book Four: *The Battle of the Labyrinth*; and Book Five: *The Last Olympian*. He also penned the *New York Times* #1 best-selling *The Lost Hero*, *The Son of Neptune*, and *The Mark of Athena*, the first three books in his Heroes of Olympus series. The three books in his Kane Chronicles, based on Egyptian mythology, *The Red Pyramid*, *The Throne of Fire*, and *The Serpent's Shadow*, were *New York Times* best sellers as well. To learn more about him, visit his Web site at www.rickriordan.com.